Graham Sutherland

OLD
CAVENDISH

and other supernatural tales

Published by Knowle Villa Books

ISBN 978-1-84396-548-0

Also available as a Kindle ebook
ISBN 978-1-84396-547-3

A catalogue record for this
book is available from the British Library.
and the American Library of Congress

Typesetting and pre-press production
eBook Versions
127 Old Gloucester Street
London WC1N 3AX
www.ebookversions.com

Other books by Graham Sutherland

Dastardly Deeds in Victorian Warwickshire
Leamington Spa, a photographic history of your Town
Leamington Spa, Francis Frith`s Town & City Memories
Around Warwick, Francis Frith`s Photographic Memories
Knights of the Road
Warwick Chronicles 1806-1812
Warwick Chronicles 1813-1820
North to Alaska
A Taste of Ale
Wicked Women
Fakes, Forgers and Frauds
Warwickshire Crimes and Criminals
Midland Murders
English Eccentrics
Edward`s Warwickshire January-March 1901
Edward`s Warwickshire (North) April-June 1901
Edward`s Warwickshire (South) April-June 1901
Edward`s Warwickshire (Old) April-June 1901
Curious Clerics
Dastardly Doctors
Women at Work
A Mixture of Mysteries
Bloody British History – Warwick
Warwick in the Great War
Warwick at War 1939-45 (publication early 2020)

Fiction:
Mayfield
Mayfield`s Law
Mayfield`s Last Case
Conspiracy of Fate
A Villa in Spain (Short Crime Stories)
To Kill The King

In preparation:
Sleepers Awake
Early One Morning

Joint Author:
Policing Warwickshire, a Pictorial History
of the Warwickshire Constabulary

1
2

About the Author

Graham Sutherland is a retired police inspector, married with three adult daughters and two granddaughters. He has lived in Warwick for more than forty years where, until 2014, he was beadle and town crier.

He is a Blue Badge tourist guide for the Heart of England Region, with special interests in Warwick, Royal Leamington Spa, Stratford-upon-Avon, Oxford and the Cotswolds.

A keen historian, he gives numerous talks each year, mainly on social and crime related topics. At one time he was secretary of the Warwickshire Constabulary History Society, where he developed a special interest in policing during Victorian and Edwardian times.

For more information about Graham, please visit his website

www.talksandwalks.co.uk

or visit him on Facebook.

Acknowledgements

This book is dedicated to my long-suffering wife Mo, for her help and understanding, and to daughters Claire, Jo and Ali, their partners Michael and Alan, plus Clara and Seren.

A special mention must be made of Ali`s husband Marcus, who sadly passed away in June 2019.

I must also thank John Fletcher and Samantha Gibbs for posing on the front cover of this book. An even bigger thank you goes to Gill Fletcher, without whose skill the cover would never have been created.

The front cover photo of a 1925 Morris Oxford Red Flash Special is courtesy of britishmotormuseum.co.uk

OLD
CAVENDISH

and other supernatural tales

Graham Sutherland

KNOWLE VILLA BOOKS

Contents

Introduction

Old Cavendish is a collection of stories involving supernatural happenings, ranging from the late 18th century to the modern day.

Ghosts can be seen, heard, smelt, felt and occasionally tasted. They can take the form of living creatures, both human and animal, as well as inanimate objects. Just because we live in modern times, ghosts and supernatural happenings are not confined to the past. Contrary to popular misconception, ghosts do not only appear at night: they are encountered anywhere during the day and night.

Many reported ghostly experiences are called *Time Slips* and occur when people literally seem *to slip* back in time, and witness events which happened many years previously.

Some supernatural appearances are malevolent and intended to upset people. These happenings might be combined with a desire for revenge for past wrongs, or to set the record straight. Whether we believe in ghosts or not, I suspect many of us have visited places and houses, which have an unwelcoming atmosphere about them, whilst others exude a happy feeling. Undoubtedly local superstition and folklore may be influencing factors.

Not all ghosts are malevolent or mischievous: some can be helpful.

Stories 1-12 originally appeared in Cold and Unwelcoming, now no longer available and have been televised.

In the following stories, discover:

1) What was Danny Baker's favourite food?
2) When did Pierre Rideau re-appear?
3) What was the question which unsettled Howard Claybury?
4) What was so special about Lot 351?
5) Where did Tristram Jarvis leave his mobile phone?
6) What did the members of Blue Flight see?

7) Who did Jethro Hamilton arrange to sit in the best seat in the house?

8) What really happened to Joselyn Danvers' grandmother?

9) Why was Vikki Manton-Lodge alone on the sea front?

10) Where did Diana Corbett purchase the serviette rings?

11) Who was the Watcher?

12) Was Marjorie Candlestone a witch?

13) Why would Archie Cameron never forget Christmas 1925?

14) What happened during the week-end reunion?

15) Why did Lionel Norton return to his old school?

16) What happened to the money Gervaise and Emily Troughton left at the inn?

17) Who was Obadiah Turkman?

18) What happened to Walter Tuck?

19) Whose wish came true?

20) Whose face was at the window?

21) Who did Alistair's pipes protect?

22) Why was Leonard Carver Maxstoke hiding?

23) What did Michael Carter inherit?

24) What happened to Police Sergeant Alan Marton?

25) Who protected the Filtonbury snuffbox?

26) What happened to Rebecca Jayne Plummerton née Foxton?

27) Did Tobias Ransome get his hand back?

28) Who was Adriana Doward?

29) What was the secret of Miss Smith's House?

30) How did Old Cavendish take his revenge?

Coming Home

It was a cold Christmas Eve, somewhere in one of the more exposed and lonely parts of the Midlands, and old Danny Baker hesitated at the entrance to the lane.

He had hoped to have reached the nearby town by early evening, and taken advantage of one of its hostels, which offered accommodation to homeless people like himself. But matters had not gone according to plan.

Having spent the previous night in a barn, Danny had been discovered earlier that morning by its irate owner, who clearly was not in a Christmas frame of mind. As the man carried a shotgun and was accompanied by two large ferocious looking dogs, which looked like they were eyeing him up for a meal, Danny did not stop to argue, but left immediately.

After travelling about a mile, Danny realised he had left his bundle behind. As it held his very few possessions, Danny had no alternative but to return and retrieve it. Once back near the barn, he needed to wait for the owner to finish his work and move on to another part of the farm with his dogs. Fortunately, none of them looked back, but the whole episode left Danny well behind on his schedule.

Whenever he passed this way, Danny had always fought shy of going down the lane to where he once lived. But now, as he looked up at the dark sky with his watery blue eyes, it was obvious winter had already closed its icy grip on the land. It had come early this year and Danny's old bones told him it would soon be snowing.

When it came to weather forecasting, they were seldom wrong.

Danny shivered and pulled his ragged, threadbare coat around his equally thin and worn out shoulders. All those years of wandering the roads as a tramp, had finally taken their toll on his health.

Now he needed somewhere to shelter, as going to a hostel for the night was no longer an option. The nearest town was too far away

Over the years Danny had tramped these roads several times but had never gone down the lane. The burning question was: could he do so now? He knew it was at least sixty years ago, and probably even longer since his last visit. Danny had long since given up counting the days and the years as they had no meaning for him.

He studied the lane once more.

At the end of it stood his mother's cottage, or at least it had done so that morning in 1920 when he left home for the last time, never seriously thinking about going back until now. Like so many others of his generation, Danny was unable to settle down on his return from fighting in the trenches: his mental and emotional wounds were far too deep.

His mother died during the Spanish Flu epidemic and her death helped him decide. Having no reason to stay at home, he just left and never gone back.

One Spring morning Danny simply locked the cottage door and took to the roads. He was accompanied at first by Rex, his faithful black and white collie dog. But, after Rex died, he never had another dog and always kept his own company.

It was a long and lonely life, yet it suited him. The peace of the countryside was in complete contrast to all the noise in his mind, caused by the countless shell bombardments and rifle fire he had experienced in the trenches, coupled with the sobbing of wounded, frightened and screaming men. It helped to soothe his troubled thoughts. Whilst he was lucky not to have been gassed, it was a long time before he stopped being frightened by fog, especially the swirling variety.

In the years that followed, he travelled all over mainland Britain, only moving on when he wished, or was forced to do so. During all this time, Danny had never wanted to go back home to the cottage where he had once lived.

Until tonight.

Few, if any people remembered him now, yet he was once a familiar face to most of the local residents and the police. He caused no trouble and sometimes turned his hand to doing the odd job for people.

Recently, Danny felt an overwhelming desire to return home. With it came the realisation he had grown old, and his instinct told him he might never get another chance. Tired, cold and hungry, he shuffled in the gathering gloom through his old home village on the edge of the Cotswolds.

He saw no one and was dismayed to see the local shop was not just closed but had become a house, which meant he would not have a proper meal that night, although he would not exactly starve. The shop still functioned when he was last here, and in his childhood days it rarely closed.

The first snowflakes drifted past his face, soon becoming more persistent as he struggled to make up his mind about going down the lane or not. He knew there was more snow in the air, which meant he must find some sort of shelter for the night. With nothing else to tempt him, the cottage seemed very inviting. His old cottage could be what he needed, assuming it was still standing.

Suddenly and for no apparent reason, other than thinking about the old cottage, Danny was suddenly overwhelmed with wanting a slice of his mother's special cherry cake. Only she knew how to bake a cherry cake exactly as he liked it, not that he would get any tonight.

Unable to delay making a decision any longer, he thrust a hand enclosed in a threadbare fingerless mitten, into a pocket and clutched a coin. Clenching his fist tightly, he took it out and placed the coin on the back of his other hand, carefully keeping it covered.

'Heads I go and tails I don't,' he said aloud, as he slowly took his hand away and peered at the coin in the gloom.

It was heads.

Picking up his bundle, Danny trudged down the once familiar lane with his head bowed against the ever increasing and settling snow.

At the end of the lane, he was pleasantly surprised, and relieved to see the remains of the cottage still stood, alone and set back from the road. The gate had long since rotted away, but the old cracked and now heavily overgrown path was still there. He saw by the reflected whiteness from the settling snow, how the cottage's woodwork had also long since rotted away. Aided by vandals all the windows were broken, and there were more holes in the roof than tiles.

The other cottages which once stood in the lane, had long since gone and were now business units, all of which were closed for the Christmas break.

A large notice, with peeling paint, was just legible as it stood in what had been his mother's well-kept front garden. It instructed:

DANGER – KEEP OUT

Danny could just make out its words in the gloom, but he ignored their instruction and pushed his way inside the ruin. After all, he argued, it was still his property.

Surprisingly he found the kitchen was reasonably intact, although its stone floor added to the overall chill. He wedged some pieces of timber across the flapping, glassless window and decided to spend the night here.

He knew there was no other choice.

His needs were few, and he soon had a small fire going in the hearth. Although very smoky, it was still hot enough to slowly boil his billycan, which he had filled with snow. Danny found a stock cube in his bundle which he crumbled into the heating water. It was all he would have for supper tonight, but it was better than nothing.

And he was used to doing without.

Once the water boiled and the stock cube fully dissolved, Danny sat cradling the billycan in his hands enjoying its warmth and staring into the fire.

After all these years he had finally come home.

How well Danny remembered the last time he had come home, after having been away at the war, and what a different welcome that had been when compared with the lonely one he was experiencing now.

Danny joined the Colours in late September 1914, soon after the outbreak of war, having lied about his age. He was an only child and his father had been dead for several years. The thoughts of having to live with his mother, much as he loved her, and becoming an agricultural labourer did not appeal to him. Going to fight for his country was a much better idea, a great adventure and a way of avoiding all that drudgery. Luckily the cottage was paid for, so there was no risk of his mother being evicted for not paying any rent.

He spent most of the war in France, apart from the occasional home leave.

When Danny was demobilised in late 1918, to all outward appearances he was still a youngster. But it was a different story when you looked into his eyes. They told the truth. Inside, like so many of his contemporaries, he was an old man, worn out long before his time by the horrors of war. When the Armistice came, Danny had no wish to remain in the army for a day longer than he had to. He was lucky in having an agricultural background which made him one of the first soldiers to be sent home, where there was a dire need for food production.

How well he remembered coming home.

Walking down the lane, Danny was impatient to get home, but also apprehensive. After all this time in the trenches, how would he be able to settle down again? What would he do for a living? Work on the land? The future terrified him.

He had no trade except being a soldier: well skilled in the art of survival and killing his fellow men. Not exactly much of a selling point for him. In any case, he would be no different to the tens of thousands of other men in similar situations.

Nearing the cottage, he caught the gentle, warm smell of cooking in the air and knew his mother was baking.

He was not surprised to see all the cottages in the lane were a blaze of light, with their windows showing shining lamps to welcome home the returning soldier. Nevertheless, Danny had no difficulty in recognising his mother's cottage, even if he had not known which one it was.

Its lights shone brighter than all the others.

Danny opened the creaking gate and started to walk up the path. But as he did so, Rex hurtled out of the cottage towards him barking furiously and happily.

The returning soldier dropped what he was carrying and held out his arms to the dog. Without stopping, Rex jumped up into them, whimpering with pleasure and wildly licking his beloved master's face. For several moments man and dog only had eyes for each other: and the world stood still. Danny buried his face in Rex's fur trying, unsuccessfully, to hold back his tears.

He was home.

'Welcome home, Danny,' called his mother.

Looking up, he saw her standing in the doorway with her familiar cottage loaf shaped body silhouetted against the light. Her face was rosy and shining from the heat of the kitchen. He ran towards her, with Rex following still barking happily.

'We knew you were coming and Rex hasn't left the door all day,' she said and held him tightly, ineffectively brushing at the tears which fell down her flour blotched cheeks and mingled with his own. The smell of baking filled his nostrils. 'It's a cherry cake: your favourite,' she explained, as if he needed to be told.

'Oh mam! Oh mam!' was all he could reply, and his tears fell even more freely.

She waited on the step until he returned to the gate and picked up his bundle, before leading him into the cottage. Rex followed them, still whimpering happily. For a while they just stood in the kitchen holding each other and saying nothing. Finally, she crossed to the oven, took out the cherry cake and turned it out of the baking tin and on to a cooling tray. 'It's all for you,' she smiled and patted the seat next to her at the table. 'Happy Christmas.'

'Oh mam! I'd forgotten it was Christmas Eve and I haven't even got you a present.'

'Your safe return from the war is the best Christmas present you could ever give me.'

Later, after a supper of fresh bread and cheese, she cut him a large slice of the cherry cake.

'Oh mam! You'll never know how your cherry cakes used to keep me and me mates going in the trenches.' Danny touched the back of her hand.

'How are your mates? Have they gone home too?' She looked up at Danny, with her face all rosy from baking and pleasure at his safe return.

He looked away from her and stared into the fire. 'Yes. They've all gone home,' he told her. 'At least, the ones who were still living,' he added silently. 'That is if you could call their wrecked bodies and minds living'. But he smiled through the lie hoping to save her from the harsh realities of war.

It would be a long time before he stopped having the regular nightmares of living, fighting and dying in the trenches. He could never talk to her about the deafening crashes of shells firing and landing, with men screaming and urgent calls being made for stretcher bearers. Nobody would understand such tales unless they had shared the experience of living in that hell of mud and destruction. Danny never really got over hearing a bell clanging: it reminded him too much of an imminent gas attack warning.

Sensing his mood, she left him sitting by the fire. For his part, Danny found it hard to believe he was home. Finally, he ate another slice of cherry cake and smiled in appreciation. It was just as good as ever. Unable to face sleeping in a bed after all these years, he lay down in front of the fire where Rex snuggled contentedly up to him.

They both slept.

Old Danny finished his stock cube and threw some more wood on the fire. He heard the wind howling outside and was glad to have found some shelter. This part of the country was very exposed, and the wind could be very wintery. Slowly his eyes began to close, and he lay down in front of the fire, just as he did all those Christmas Eves ago.

But as he did so, Danny became aware of a faint smell which grew stronger. Somewhere, someone was baking: and he recognised the smell.

A freshly baking cherry cake.

'Welcome home, Danny,' said a familiar voice interrupting his thoughts.

It was a voice he knew so well but had not heard for a very long time and never expected to do so again. Danny opened his eyes and he was not surprised to see his mother standing there. She was still as he remembered her that night all those years ago. He smiled happily when he saw the blotches of flour on her face.

'We both knew you were coming,' she smiled. 'And Rex hasn't left the door all day.'

Danny's mother handed him a piece of warm and freshly baked cherry cake, which he took. Moments later he was dimly aware of a black and white collie dog snuggling up against him whimpering with pleasure.

'Hello Rex,' he mumbled, and his eyes closed.

Old Danny had come home.

It was some days after Christmas, before Old Danny's body was discovered Someone reported seeing lights in the old cottage and smoke coming from the chimney. But severe snow storms delayed any immediate investigation. Slowly a police Land Rover made the difficult journey over the snow-packed lanes to the cottage.

It was obvious from the undisturbed snow no one had been near the ruin for several days. Nevertheless, the two police constables checked its cold interior, where they found Danny's body.

'It's Old Danny Baker,' explained the older policeman to his colleague as he recognised the dead man. 'Apparently he used to live round here years ago.'

Moving Old Danny, they were surprised to find the body of a black and white collie dog lying next to him. They examined the animal's collar, which was old, but with a name tag on it, which was just legible.

They read the animal was called Rex.

It was a simple matter to explain away the dog as being a stray animal which had crept into the ruins in search of shelter, warmth and companionship. But it was not so easy to explain what a still smiling Danny was clutching in his hand, freshly baked and still warm.

It was a piece of cherry cake.

AUTHOR'S NOTE

Many underage young men lied about their ages when they enlisted into the army soon after war was declared in 1914. Recruiting sergeants were more concerned with acquiring numbers of recruits and made little or no checks into men's backgrounds.

For the duration of the war, it was a continual battle between the army wanting more men and the government needing more food. Both claimed their needs took priority. Whilst the war effectively ended on 11 November 1918, with the Armistice, it would not end officially until June 1919. However, such was the demand for agricultural workers such as Danny, these men were among the first to be demobbed long before June 1919.

Festival Night

The *Festival Night's* highlight came when darkness fell, and the moon rose. It heralded the burning of a straw figure, known as the *sin man*, and was meant to represent the cleansing of all the villagers' sins, which they had committed since the last *Festival Night*. Custom dictated the villagers had the opportunity of confessing all their sins, and putting them onto the *sin man,* just before it was burnt.

Nobody knew the origins of the *Festival Night*, as they had been lost somewhere in the mists of time. It was generally believed to have started as a pagan rite involving a real human sacrifice. With the growth of Christianity, the custom continued but now used a straw effigy which made it less barbaric. Tradition demanded the lord of the manor always lit the straw effigy, unless someone else could prove they had a better claim to do so. For as long as the oldest villagers could remember, no one had ever made such a challenge.

As the aristocracy established an ever-increasing firm hold on their lands, the villagers were obliged to comply with whatever demands were made upon them. Only a very brave, or foolish individual, ever stood against *les aristos*. No one had ever challenged the lord's right to light the *sin man*.

In common with other communities, the village had been forced to abandon many of its old customs like *Festival Night* as the Revolution spread across France. Old superstitions were brushed aside in the struggle for *Libertié, Egalitié and Fraternitié.*

Following Napoleon's final defeat at Waterloo the previous year, France now struggled to return to normality. This small village on the borders of Languedoc and the Cevennes was no exception.

And it quickly agreed to resurrect *Festival Night.*

Pierre Rideau passed unnoticed through the crowds, as did many other strangers who had come to witness the first revival of this ancient custom. But Pierre was not a stranger to the village: he had lived here twenty-seven years ago.

He left the same time as the last *Festival Night* and no one had seen or heard of him since. Now his haunted, deep set, hooded, dark eyes smouldered with hatred, as he remembered what had happened all those years ago: a night which could never be forgotten by all those who witnessed it, or been told the tale years later.

All the while, his eyes searched expectantly over the assembled crowds. He had every intention of ensuring this *Festival Night* would also be long remembered.

His eyes narrowed as they focussed on the man he sought: the object of his hatred: Comte Charles de Billeagues. Pierre noticed with satisfaction when he saw how the man's exile in England had aged him. Yet Pierre was also glad he had escaped the guillotine, because he had his own plans for him.

Plans which would give Pierre much more satisfaction.

The comte also remembered the last *Festival Night* in the village. But unlike Pierre he wished he could forget it, although he knew there was never any chance of that happening.

That last *Night* began like all the previous ones.

As usual the villagers assembled in the Market Place close to the church. They mingled with the annual influx of many visitors from elsewhere. Yet everyone felt a sense of tension and foreboding in the air. There were numerous rumours of an uprising having happened in Paris. But that was at the other end of the country and there was no positive news.

Nevertheless, deep in rural France, just as in Paris, most of the aristocracy was unpopular. Their autocratic abuse of the local inhabitants fuelled much of the resentment and insolence directed towards them. In this part of France, they all loathed the young aristocrat. He believed the peasants should never be permitted to gather in large numbers, as they were doing for the annual *Festival Night*: even more so if the rumours coming from Paris were true.

De Billeagues was not a man to be deterred by mere rumours and he decided to attend the *Festival* and use it as an excuse to teach these villagers a lesson for their insolence. It would forestall any thoughts they might have about rising above their lowly status and attacking their betters. He would ensure it was a lesson they would not forget in a hurry.

And in his mind, that would be the end of any thoughts of revolution on his lands.

It was his first mistake.

Only too aware of his unpopularity, he brought a motley collection of bodyguards to look after him during the evening. He had also given them certain other instructions which appealed to their general lawlessness.

This was his second and more serious mistake.

During the ritualistic burning of the *sin man*, as instructed his bodyguards seized the opportunity to ransack certain buildings in the village. In the ensuing chaos, several houses were burned down, one of which belonged to the Rideau family.

As Pierre and his father struggled to rescue his crippled mother and young sister, a blazing wall fell on them. His father died instantly, but Pierre was dragged out, hideously burned: more dead than alive. Neither his mother nor his sister survived the blaze.

De Billeagues had instructed his bodyguards not to kill anyone, believing the ransacking would be sufficient for his purpose. But as far as he was concerned, the fires and the deaths of the Rideau family were an unexpected bonus. Pierre's father was a well-known radical villager who took every opportunity to criticise the comte and his family.

Pierre was taken away by his aunt, Marie Gondelait, who lived in a nearby village, where she enjoyed the reputation of being both a witch and a healer. But as Pierre had not been seen in the village again: everyone believed he was dead.

Until tonight.

The comte brought his thoughts back to the present. He knew his unpopularity had not declined during his long exile in England: but now he was back. The Revolution was over, and it was time for the aristocracy to reassert itself once more. Granted his chateau had been destroyed, but it would be rebuilt. This was not a time for him to show any weakness. He was not going to be intimidated by these peasants.

'Will you light the *sin man* once the confessions have been heard?' The voice came from behind him. 'As you know custom demands it, unless there is someone with a better claim.' The speaker was the mayor, who was accompanied by Michel Sancerre, the curé.

Both men were at the last *Festival Night.*

The curé did not approve of the *Festival Night* which he considered bordered on paganism. But since his return from exile, he only had a very small congregation. If the villagers wanted to take part in a mass confession, he considered it a small price to pay for their continued attendance at his services. He raised his arms which was the traditional signal for the villagers and other visitors, to kneel in prayer.

Their mumbled confessions did not take long.

Firstly, they did not want their neighbours to hear what they had been doing. But much more importantly for them, once the *sin man* had been set alight, then the real party could begin. It was the one time in the year when loose morals were officially permitted, and the evening tended to drift into an orgy.

'Have you all confessed?' the curé called when they had finished.

'**YES!**' The whole assembly responded.

The mayor handed the comte the dry wood torch and stood by holding a tinder box which he struck and applied to the torch. Moments later it caught light.

'Is it your wish that your sins should be burned with the *sin man*?' called the curé.

'**YES!**' Again, the mass response was the same.

'Is there anyone here with a better claim to light the *sin man* than the comte?' At first the congregation remained quiet.

Then the silence was broken by a cry… '**Yes! Me!**'

Everybody felt the warm summer night suddenly turn very cold, and they looked towards the voice.

As he spoke, Pierre stepped up to the curé, threw back his hood, and glared at the villagers. The full moon lit up his hideously scarred and ravaged face. The villagers began exclaiming:

'It's Pierre Rideau!'

'It can't be!'

'He's come back from the dead!'

They watched fascinated as a strange light began to glow around Pierre. The comte's flaming torch spluttered and went out. In the shocked silence that followed they all heard an unearthly cackle and a small stooped woman, leaning heavily on a wooden staff, joined Pierre. The curé crossed himself and clutched at his crucifix.

'Charles de Billeagues!' Pierre called, pointing at the comte. 'I have come to call you to account for causing the deaths of my parents and sister.' Pierre stood tall, with hate emanating from his whole body.

De Billeagues stood very still saying nothing. Terrified, and unable to move, he knew every eye was watching him. The silence was broken again by another unearthly cackle from the stooped woman. Still clutching his crucifix, the curé pushed his way towards her.

His face paled when he recognised Marie Gondelait. 'What are you doing here woman?' He demanded with a show of confidence which he did not feel, only too aware of her awesome reputation of being a witch. During his exile, the curé hoped and prayed she had died. But now he saw those prayers had not been answered.

'Just watch! Just watch!' She instructed before breaking off into another fit of cackling.

The curé crossed himself again, and looked at the comte, knowing he was powerless to intervene, even if he wanted to. Like the assembled crowd, he was also fascinated to see what would happen.

'For twenty-seven long years, I have waited for this moment,' cried Pierre. 'And you couldn't keep away, could you?'

'It was an accident,' pleaded the comte, as he desperately looked for some friendly faces in the crowd. But there were none. He had not brought any bodyguards with him, thinking Pierre had also died in the fire, and the previous *Festival Night* was long since forgotten.

'How can you say that after you gave those brigands the pickings of our village?' cried Pierre.

'I never meant them to hurt anyone.' The comte pleaded again and lowered his head into his hands. 'I said they could help themselves to whatever they wanted, but they were not to hurt anyone. I didn't know they would riot and set light to houses.'

He frantically looked through his fingers for an escape route, but there was none. The villagers all had hard faces, and after his brief confession, confirming what they had always suspected. They had no sympathy for him.

Pierre's eyes now gleamed like hot coals, and he pointed his right forefinger at the cowering man in front of him. A shaft of crackly blue flame left his finger, and fastened on the toes of the comte's boots, and set them on fire.

In a few seconds the flames had spread, and soon the man was burning, being unable to move. His screams lingered, and he begged the curé and the mayor to help him, but they were transfixed with horror and watching what was happening. And like the villagers, their feet would not move.

The comte died horribly.

Within minutes his charred body had assumed the appearance of a wax dummy before it crumbled into ashes. Meanwhile Pierre had vanished, although no one could remember having seen him go. All their eyes had been watching the burning man.

'What have you done, woman?' demanded the trembling curé, still clutching his crucifix.

'I breathed that hatred into him,' Marie replied with her eyes aglow. 'There's another man in hell tonight.'

'God help you, woman. This is an evil night's work!' He crossed himself again.

'No!' She shook her head vehemently and her eyes glistened brightly. 'Pierre's spirit will rest in peace now.'

Realisation suddenly showed on his face.

'That's right priest,' she spat. 'I was unable to help him that night. He's been dead for these past twenty-seven years.'

'Are There Any Questions?'

Alexander Curzon watched the long queue of people waiting patiently to get into the town hall. An astute businessman, Alexander, never Alex, knew he had a crowd puller with this particular appearance of crime writer celebrity, Howard Claybury. He was a well-known local character who could be relied upon to bring in the crowds. There was always a big demand for seats at any place where he spoke, and Alexander made a point of signing him up whenever he became available.

But tonight's event was different.

It was Howard's first public engagement since the mysterious disappearance of his wife, Sandra, some months earlier.

As Howard's fans knew, he had been interviewed three times by the police, and was considered their prime suspect for her disappearance. But the police had no concrete evidence and were obliged to release him.

He always stuck to his story about their having an argument whilst walking with their dog on Brindley Moor. They had argued about one of his characters and he had walked off, leaving her with the dog. Neither Sandra nor the dog had ever been seen again.

Claybury revelled in the ongoing press coverage and milked it for all it was worth. He made no secret of his belief there was no such thing as bad publicity: just publicity.

And if tonight's crowds were anything to go by, it was working well for him.

Although he only wrote crime novels, Claybury had a very low opinion of the police, and considered himself to be far and away mentally superior to any of them. He seized every opportunity to criticise them, especially the local ones. His novels always had the criminals coming out on top, making the fictitious

Dymshire Constabulary look stupid.

The failure of the local police to find Sandra did nothing to change his low opinion of them.

Claybury was an entertaining speaker and could expect to sell many of his books, including his latest novel, which were already displayed out in the bar area, once his talk was finished. His audience knew this, and they were looking forward to an interesting and entertaining evening.

Alexander watched the hall quickly fill to capacity and hoped he had enough extra staff to cope in the bars. He knew it would be a busy evening, but the actual bar space limited the amount of staff who could work there. Consequently, he had created a temporary bar elsewhere, but inevitably there would be some complaints if people had to wait for service.

Once everyone was settled with some standing allowed, he went to find Claybury who was waiting in the wings.

'It's a good audience tonight, Howard.'

Claybury nodded smugly. 'Of course! They'll come miles just to see me. Are we ready?' He smoothed his hair and went through the motions of straightening his open shirt collar.

Alexander nodded and walked out onto the stage. 'You smug, egotistical oik,' he thought. But whilst he disliked Claybury, he enjoyed the money the man brought in to his business: and tonight's takings promised to be good. As he appeared on stage, a sudden expectant silence fell on the audience.

'Ladies and Gentlemen!' he announced. 'It gives me great pleasure to welcome you to what promises to be an entertaining and memorable evening. Please give a warm welcome to our special guest tonight…a man who really needs no introduction…Mr Howard Claybury!' As Alexander finished speaking, Claybury trotted on to the stage to a rapturous applause.

He revelled in the applause, acting more like a child than a man in his late fifties.

'Good evening,' he smarmed once the applause finally died down. 'I really wanted to call tonight's talk…***How to get away with Murder***…but the local plod are as bad as the Dymshire Constabulary, and they would be offended!'

He waited for the subsequent applause and laughter to die down, before speaking again. 'As you know, my darling wife Sandra has gone missing. And guess what? Surprise! Surprise! The local plod, who as you know are my role model for the Dymshires, can't find her. I wonder sometimes if they could even find a bar of chocolate in a sweet shop.' He paused and appeared to be sniffing back some tears, whilst the audience waited sympathetically.

For the next hour Claybury held them enthralled whilst he related various anecdotes from his writing career. The audience loved his stories, although they had heard many of them before. But conscious of the time and having his books to sell, Claybury drew the talk to a close. Yet again there was a thunderous applause.

Alexander came back on stage and waited whilst Claybury took several bows. Once the applause died down, he spoke. 'Howard has agreed to answer a few questions then it will be time for his book signing. Are there any questions?'

'Yes. I have one.' The question came almost before Alexander finished speaking. As far as he could see, the speaker was a slender woman of indeterminate age. It was difficult to describe her, and somehow her face was in the shadows. Later, even those people who sat in adjoining seats were unable to remember clearly what she looked like.

'Yes, my dear,' smarmed Claybury in a patronising tone. 'Please go ahead with your question.'

'Would you please tell us where you hid your wife's body after you murdered her?'

A shocked gasp followed by an expectant hush came over the audience. This was not a question any of them had anticipated. How would he answer it?

'Really! I don't think that's a proper question…' Alexander started half-heartedly, although he too wanted to see how Claybury responded.

'It doesn't matter,' smirked Claybury. 'I'm happy to answer it.'

Just off stage in the wings and unseen by Claybury, two men in suits waited.

'I hope this plan of yours works, boss,' said Detective Sergeant Ray Dalton dubiously.

'Not half as much as I do,' replied Detective Inspector Tony Saddler. 'We know he's killed her, but we haven't got any evidence to prove it. If only we could find her body. I just hope Helen can do the job.'

'She's got experience in acting on the stage which is why we chose her,' reassured Ray. 'I've seen her perform, and she's very good and really sinks into the role. And don't forget, she's a good interrogator.'

Helen Brewer was one of Tony's detectives, and it had been arranged for her to be in the audience tonight and start asking awkward questions. Tony knew it was a desperate tactic, but it would be such a help if they could only find Sandra's body.

'As I keep telling the plod, I didn't kill her.' Claybury's voice came from the stage. Yet both policemen, and many people in the audience, felt it did not have quite the same degree of confidence it had earlier.

'Oh, but you did, and then you buried her somewhere, didn't you?' The questioner continued relentlessly and tossed back her head as she spoke.

'That's…that's…just not true.' Claybury faltered. Although he could not see her face that last movement of tossing her head reminded him so much of Sandra: But it couldn't possibly be her, could it? 'That's…that's…just not true.'

The audience noticed his hesitation and the atmosphere became even more charged with expectation. Claybury, along with everybody else in the audience, found himself staring at the questioner. But although he could not see her clearly, Claybury could not take his eyes off her.

How she reminded him of Sandra. She was the same height and build: and even spoke in the same manner. And the way she tossed her head! If only he could see her face properly…but it couldn't really be Sandra: could it? he asked himself again.

His confidence began to fade.

'Good girl,' muttered Tony. 'But don't overdo it.'

Alexander thought briefly about stopping the questions, but like everyone else, he was fascinated by the change in Claybury. Gone was his egotistical and bombastic attitude. Even as he watched, Alexander saw him licking his lips. He thought the man was clearly very nervous about something: as did the rest of the audience.

This was not something any of them had expected. The audience all knew about Sandra's disappearance and they looked toward the questioner. But all they saw was a slender woman who seemed to be in shadow. She had chosen her position well, whoever she was.

'Let me ask you again, Howard. Where did you hide Sandra's body?'

'I…I…' Sweat was now pouring off his face, and Claybury could not finish his answer.

'Come on Howard! Tell us! It was in Daynton Woods, wasn't it?'

'Oh no!' muttered Tony. 'That's wrong. It was on Brindley Moor. Don't muck it up, Helen.'

Claybury had always insisted they had been walking their dog on Brindley Moor.

'Yes,' whispered Claybury. Had the clip-on microphone not been live, no one would have heard his answer…but they all did.

'Where is Sandra's body in Daynton Woods?' continued the questioner, tossing her head again.

'What's she playing at?' Tony asked Ray. 'Brindley Moor is miles away from Daynton Woods.'

His colleague shrugged his shoulders and held out his hands, palms upwards. 'She was properly briefed. We had no reason to search Daynton Woods. He always maintained they were on the Moor when they had that argument over one of his characters and it was where he last saw her.' There was nothing else he could say. Like Tony, he too was worried. They had put a great deal of planning into this scheme. If it failed, then Claybury would have won, and he would have a wonderful time at their expense.

'Come on Howard. Where's my body?

Everybody noticed how the questioner had used the word *my*.

'Underneath the old ranger's hut, with the dog.'

'How did you murder me?'

Claybury fell to his knees, unable to take his eyes off her. 'I strangled you with the dog lead, and then did the same to him. Oh God help me, Sandra! I'm so sorry I strangled you.'

Tony and Ray looked at each other. 'We never thought of looking there,' said Tony.

'We had no cause to,' added Ray.

Moments later they walked on stage to a now sobbing Howard Claybury.

'We've just heard what you've said in front of all these people,' Tony announced, pointing to the audience. 'And we are now arresting you for the murder of your wife.'

After being cautioned, Claybury looked at the two policemen. 'Gentlemen,' he said and gone was his normal arrogant tone. 'I must congratulate you. That was a clever trick to make me think Sandra was in the audience. Who was she? One of your people, I suspect?'

Tony ignored him and beckoned to the wings. Two uniformed policemen appeared and took Claybury away in handcuffs. In the distance. they heard the sound of approaching two-tone horns, as the audience began, albeit unwillingly, to leave the hall.

'Helen did a grand job,' commented Ray. 'Though I'm surprised she hasn't joined us by now. But whatever made her talk about Daynton Woods?'

Neither of them had an answer to that question.

The last of the audience reluctantly left the hall, but there was still no sign of Helen. The two-tones came nearer.

'Someone's in a hurry,' smiled Tony. 'Probably late for tea.' He was in a good mood. Provided they found Sandra's body under the ranger's hut, they would have a good case against Claybury.

Just as he and Ray reached the front of the town hall, a police patrol car, with its blue lights flashing and two-tones blaring, pulled up outside. It had barely stopped before Helen Brewer climbed out of the front passenger door and ran across to Tony.

'I'm so sorry, boss,' she apologised.

'What for? You did a brilliant job in there getting Claybury to confess to the murder and tell us where Sandra's buried in Daynton Woods. Whatever made you talk about Daynton Woods and not Brindley Moor? But whatever it was, it certainly did the trick.'

Helen looked puzzled. 'What are you talking about, boss? I've only just got here. That's what I'm trying to tell you. My car broke down on Brindley Moor and as you know, mobiles won't work up there and it took me ages to find a phone.'

'That's right sir,' added PC Steve Berry, who had just got out of the driver's door and joined the group on the town hall steps. 'Once I got the call from HQ, it took me a good twenty minutes to get there and We've been on the way here ever since.'

'I don't know who you're talking about doing my job in the hall, but it certainly wasn't me,' protested Helen.

Tony looked at Ray. 'If it wasn't Helen in there in the seat we arranged for her, asking those questions, then who was it?'

Lot 351

It was a typical day at Wormell's Auction Rooms in Warwick. The business began in the late nineteenth century, and now nearly 100 years later it was still run by the same family. But as the auction's customers would tell you, the business was slowly dying, and none of the current auctioneer's children had any interest in following in their family's footsteps.

Any chance the business might have had was being steadily eroded by the internet. And the various television programmes, concerning the buying and selling of antiques, did not help. The auctioneer rarely sold many quality items these days. Should he be given any passable or really good items for sale, these were either sent to more up-market auctioneers or put on e-Bay. Most of the lots came from house clearances, interspersed with imported mass-produced items from the Far East.

As the quality of the goods for sale decreased, so did the hopeful bidders. Despite all this, the salerooms still had a few faithful followers, and the odd stranger hoping to find a bargain. But they all knew the saleroom's days were numbered.

So far today, and as anticipated, the auctioneer had struggled with the first 350 lots, but he was more optimistic about the next one.

'And now, ladies and gentlemen, we have a most unusual item…the one you've all been waiting for …Lot 351 in your catalogues.' Geoffrey Wormell, the tired auctioneer paused to see what effect his words had on the people expectantly gathered in the equally tired salerooms.

He was disappointed to see none of them showed any real interest in the item.

There was no sudden buzz of excitement. People, who were reading newspapers or magazines carried on doing so. And it was the same with the coffee drinkers. He once thought, fleetingly, about stopping the sales of coffee and cakes, etc, but it would have been a bad mistake. They were too good an earner.

It was not a hopeful sign, as he had anticipated getting a good price for this item. Their apathy merely confirmed the realisation the time was rapidly coming when he would have to close the business: it barely made a profit these days. Mentally he sighed and began to bolster the lot's description, trying to build up some enthusiasm in the process.

'As you can see,' he began in a hushed, conspiratorial voice and nodded to Fred the porter, who immediately pointed to the item with an old car radio aerial. Fred had been a porter at the salerooms for longer than most people could remember. As everyone who knew him remarked, he had been born old and his appearance had never changed over the years. His face looked like it had been drawn by a cartoonist and resembled a caricature of a real person.

'This is a very real lifelike looking, and life-sized model of a king cobra, albeit in brass: and look at those fierce red stone eyes!' Geoffrey paused for a few moments letting his words sink in.

'It is part of a religious cult…and as I say…is a most unusual item.' He paused again, waving his gavel at the audience, aware that all eyes were now fixed on him. 'But beware,' he cautioned. 'You must treat it with the greatest respect. If you do so, then no harm will come to you. However,…be warned… Do not insult or abuse it…otherwise…' He broke off and drew a finger across his throat.

An excited gasp from the audience greeted his words, which was what he wanted. At last, he had their attention. At the same moment, Fred tapped the snake with the aerial, which they all saw and heard. Then he suddenly gripped his throat and made strange gurgling noises.

There was another gasp from the room.

'When you've quite finished Fred,' smiled Geoffrey. 'Can we get on with the sale, please?' Fred immediately recovered and grinned, confirming it had all been part of an act. Many of the potential bidders only came to the auction to be entertained by Fred with his various tricks such as this one.

'Who will open the bidding?' Geoffrey queried. 'Shall we say £200?'
There was no response.

'Come on, ladies and gentlemen! Surely someone will open the bidding?'

'£5!' A female voice called from the back of the room.

'£10!' came another bid.

Slowly the price rose to £45, where it stuck.

'Very well, ladies and gentlemen,' the auctioneer summed up the item again. 'Make no mistake I will sell this most unusual lot for a mere £45 as there is no reserve. Going for the first time… going for the second time… going for…'

'£75!' It was a fresh male bidder.

The regular patrons did not need to turn and look where this new bid had come from. They all recognised the voice and knew if he really wanted something then money was no object. At other times, if he felt someone, usually a stranger was pushing the price up, he would happily go along with the competition, and then drop out of the bidding, leaving his rival with the lot and a large bill to pay. Not wanting to be caught out, people rarely bid against him.

As they all knew, there were no strangers in the auction room, so no other bids were made. The brass snake was sold to Harold Johnson.

Harold was a well-known local antiques dealer who specialised in quality china and unusual items. He lived in a once quality but now rundown area of a nearby town, from where despite continual advice from his family, refused to move. It had been Harold's marital home, and although he had been a widower for several years, he had no intention of moving from there.

Nevertheless, Harold acknowledged there were risks and installed the very latest, most expensive and sophisticated security systems in his house, which were regularly upgraded. The only weakness in the systems was the time it took for his front gates to open. They were operated electronically from inside his car, so he did not have to leave the vehicle, but there was still a delay.

After paying for his purchases, Harold packed them into his car, left the saleroom and drove home. It was not a long journey. Harold stopped outside his house and pressed the remote control. As the gates started to open, he was attacked by Ricky Walker, who had been one of the coffee drinkers at the auction and followed him home.

Before Harold knew what was happening, his car door window was smashed, and Ricky's knife wielding hand was thrust at him. The knife was jabbed into Harold's face and he felt the warm blood running down his cheek.

Ricky was best described as being *a very unpleasant individual*, who had no scruples when it came to using violence. It was always his first resort, regardless of the age or gender of his victims.

'Get out!' Ricky snarled.

Harold did not know his assailant, because Ricky came from outside the town, but he made no attempt to resist him. As he struggled to undo his seat belt, Ricky opened the car door and pulled him out. He had not expected to have any trouble with the old man, but he was not going to take any chances. Moments later, Harold was lying on the ground alongside his car.

'Stay there!' instructed Ricky as he slid into the driving seat, put the car into reverse and drove backwards onto the road. Once he was off Harold's driveway, Ricky put the car gratingly into first gear and drove off with screeching tyres.

After that, he kept meticulously to the speed limits, and drove to the quiet lane where he had left his van earlier that day. He stopped alongside it.

Only when he was satisfied, he had not been followed, and there were no police around, did Ricky get out of the car. Moments later he opened the van's double rear doors. It did not take him long to take the boxes out of Harold's car, and quickly put them into the other vehicle, alongside all the other items he had stolen that day.

Closing the van's doors, he climbed into the driving seat, started the engine and drove the few miles away to the old rambling house where he rented several ground floor rooms and outbuildings. The landlord was not interested in what his tenants did for a living, and never visited the site. Provided they paid their rent when it was due and caused him no trouble, he left them alone.

Such an arrangement suited Ricky, and he happily used his rooms as a store for all the property he stole. Most of these items were easily disposed of, and he was never short of buyers. Like his landlord, Ricky had no idea, and was even less interested in how his fellow tenants earned a living: and in their turn, they ignored him.

Later that evening, Ricky looked at the items he had stolen from Harold and was disappointed to find they were nearly all pieces of china and similar figures, which he put on one side, uncertain of what to do with them. He knew such figures could command a high price in the collectors' market and would make him good money if he could sell them. But he did not know if these ones were valuable or not. The obvious way to sell them was on e-bay, which was not without its problems such as being paid by cheque and having to use the postal or other delivery services. His was a strictly cash and carry business, with cash being the operative word. All transactions were carried out well away from where he lived.

There was only one item which him, and still bore its auction label…***Lot 351***…a brass ornamental king cobra with glittering red eyes.

Ricky liked its aggressive posture, with fully expanded hood and exposed fangs…poised and ready to strike! He felt the snake was like himself, and he decided to keep it. For a day or two he moved the snake around, trying it in different sites. At last he put it on the sideboard, close to a dish which was overflowing with cigarette ends.

And that gave him an idea.

Taking the lit cigarette out of his mouth, he put it into the snake's jaws, and was pleased to see that it fitted perfectly. But as he watched the cigarette smoke swirling around the ornament, it seemed as if the snake's red eyes glittered angrily. Ricky dismissed it as a trick of the light.

An hour or so later, he went out in his van on another crime spree.

The long, hot summer day was over, and it was dark before Ricky returned after a fairly unsuccessful foray. He had not been home very long before he realised something was missing. After spending several minutes searching, he realised what had gone.

It was the snake.

His first thoughts were, he had been burgled and such irony did not escape him. He was, after all, an accomplished burglar himself, as well as a general thief. And now he had become a victim of crime! But the one thing he could not do was call the police!

Then he stopped to think. With all the quality goods he had all round the room, why should someone just concentrate on the snake? It didn't make sense! Yet the snake was definitely missing, which meant someone had stolen it!

Ricky gave a harsh laugh and planned what he would do to the thief if he ever caught him. Suddenly he heard a sound from behind him.

'Who's there?' he called, turning around.

Several days later, Police Constables Neil Hewer and Martin Templeton arrived at the door to Ricky's flat. Here they were met by a man who was anxiously waiting for them. He explained how he lived above Ricky's rooms and added nobody had seen or heard him for a few days. But that was not what was worrying the other tenants.

'There's something else…' he began. Even as he spoke, the police officers noticed the smell coming from Ricky's flat.

Having more than just a suspicion what was causing it, they were not surprised when there was no reply to their knocking.

After a long struggle, they forced open the door, which was far from easy because Ricky had reinforced it with heavy-duty bolts. Once inside, they found Ricky's body lying on the floor between a table and the sideboard. But what really took their interest was the amount of obviously stolen property stored in the flat. It was a real *Aladdin's Cave* and clearly a job for the C.I.D.

When Detective Inspector Michael Willetts arrived, his first concern was, how had Ricky met his demise? He knew Ricky of old and the criminal was not short of enemies. People like him never were. Police Doctor Balbir Sohal was already at work and Michael waited impatiently for him to finish his examination of the body.

'I don't suppose there's any chance he died from natural causes, is there?' Michael asked forlornly, thinking of his budgetary restraints if he had to run a murder enquiry.

'I'm afraid not,' replied the doctor. 'He was definitely killed as opposed to having just died.'

'Can you say how he was killed?'

'Oh yes: that's easy,' Balbir smiled. 'Although I must say that I never thought to see such a death here in England. Back home in India…yes. But never in England. Look!'

The doctor pointed towards two sets of small puncture wounds, which were clearly visible in Ricky's neck. 'These undoubtedly caused his death.'

'What are they?'

'This is the bite of an *Ophiophagus Hannah*, more commonly known as an Asian king cobra, just like the snake here.'

He pointed to the large brass snake with the glittering red eyes, which was coiled on the sideboard near to an overflowing dish of cigarette ends.

The Mobile Phone

Tristram Jarvis was fully into his afternoon presentation at the annual sales conference, when he felt his mobile phone ring. Fortunately for him it was on vibrate, as he knew the managing director or MD as he was usually called, did not take kindly to such interruptions.

Well used to thinking on his feet, Tristram gave a cough as he re-arranged his thoughts. He really should have switched it off before the meeting began. At last the session ended and he was grateful when the managing director called for a short break.

Making an excuse to go to the gents, he went to see who had phoned him, but was more than a little disconcerted when the MD immediately followed him.

'A good presentation, Tris, and glad to see you quickly recovered from your coughing fit,' he said knowingly. 'I suggest you switch your mobile off next time!'

Tristram nodded, hoping albeit in vain the man would leave him, so he could see who had called. But his boss had no intention of leaving, and he now stood with his back to the door, effectively stopping anyone else from coming in. Tristram wondered what his colleagues would do if any of them tried to enter.

And much more to the point, what would they think? He could just imagine their banter, although probably not in front of the MD who was renowned for not having a sense of humour.

'Tris!' he came straight to the point. 'We're looking for a new director to join us on the Board, and we all believe you should be our first choice. Obviously discuss it with Liz and let me know. And now perhaps it might be a good idea to get back to the meeting, before people start talking about us.'

A question and answer session followed, during which Tristram twice felt his mobile phone vibrate again. Luckily, he was not speaking on either occasion.

When the meeting broke up, they all adjourned to the bar. Seizing the opportunity, Tristram returned to the gents and took out his phone to see who had called him. The calls had come from his wife, and although he tried calling her back, the number was permanently engaged. He hoped there was no problem with her or the children.

Back in the bar, Tristram settled for a small shandy, as he had a drive uphill across the winding country lanes ahead of him to get home, which did not appeal. The atmosphere in the bar was very convivial, and the roaring real log fire all added to the ambience, as the short wintery daylight faded. And the last thing he wanted to do was drive home.

Suddenly the digital strains of Wagner's *Ride of the Valkyries* sounded in an ever-increasing volume.

A series of ribald comments greeted him as he took out his phone and answered it.

'Tris!' called Liz. 'I've been trying to get hold of you for ages. I don't want to worry you, but it's snowing very heavily here, and has been all afternoon. If I were you, I wouldn't delay coming home for much longer. It's likely to be grim up on the wolds.'

Even as she ended the call, a man came into the bar covered in fresh snowflakes. 'It's blowing a right blizzard out there,' he said to no one in particular, brushing the snowflakes off his shoulders, and had difficulty in closing the door against the wind. Even in the bar, they all felt the icy blast from the open door and saw the flames dance in the hearth. 'I think it's time I went chaps,' Tristram announced as he finished his shandy.

'Little woman calling you, is she?'

'Got a date, have we?'

'Got your orders have you?'

'Unlike you lot, I have to drive home tonight. Not for me the luxury of a warm bar and several drinks. I've just got a cold and snowy trip to look forward to, I don't think,' Tristram replied to their banter.

More good-natured banter followed him as he collected his coat, waved goodbye, and stepped towards the door. He hesitated for a moment, knowing it made more sense to stay at the hotel, but they did not have enough rooms owing to a mix up with the bookings. The only other hotel in the village was closed whilst being refurbished. Living the closest, Tristram had agreed to travel.

'Have a good night,' he called, casting a last envious look at the roaring fire and assembled drinkers. 'Think about me driving across the Cotswolds in this.'

Moments later he stepped out into the snowstorm.

Liz had not been joking when she said it was snowing heavily. Leaving the village, he made his way up towards the open countryside, where the snow came down even more thickly. After crawling along for just over a mile, Tristram realised he would never get home at this rate and decided to go back to the hotel. He would quite happily settle for an armchair in a warm room. At least it was downhill back into the village.

The problem was to find somewhere to turn around.

Inching his way round a bend, he came to some crossroads and decided this was where he would turn. But before he could do so, a car suddenly came from his right, skidded in the snow and headed in his direction. He thought for a moment it was going to hit him, but luckily it slewed off the road and toppled sideways into a snow-covered ditch.

Against his better judgement, Tristram stopped his car, got out and slithered across to the other vehicle. Already he had visions of not being able to get his car started again, and what could he do if the other driver was badly hurt? There were no houses nearby. True he had his mobile phone with him, but he knew reception was not brilliant in this part of the Cotswolds. Just as he reached the car, its door opened, and a young woman started to climb out. Tristram helped her.

'What am I going to do?' she despaired. 'I'll never get it out of this ditch.'

Tristram studied her as she spoke. Although well wrapped up against the weather, he saw she was slimly built, about his own age and quite attractive, although her face looked rather haggard. He put it down to her running off the road. It was impossible to see what make of car she was driving, because it was well covered in snow.

'I'm going back into the village, and hopefully find some shelter for the night,' he replied. 'You'd better come with me, as I can't leave you here. Your car will have to take its chances.'

'As it happens, I don't live that far away, and it's closer than the village,' she pointed back the way she had come. 'I run the *Cotswold Shepherd Hotel* with my husband. We've no guests in tonight and you're more than welcome to stay with us.'

Tristram glanced back towards the village, where it was still snowing heavily. Looking to where she had pointed, it seemed as if the snow had eased off, albeit just a little. It really was no contest.

'If you're sure you don't mind?'

'Of course not,' she smiled and climbed gratefully into his car.

During the short drive, he did not find her particularly talkative, but discovered she was Carol Wakeford, and her husband was called Terry. She tensed up as they neared the *Cotswold Shepherd,* but Tristram thought she was worried about the car and telling her husband what had happened to it.

It never occurred to him to ask where she had been going on such a dreadfully snowy night.

After what seemed an eternity, they arrived at the *Cotswold Shepherd*, and he drove into the empty car park. Gratefully he parked his car and followed her into the hotel. Tristram had never heard of this hotel, but then he, Liz and the children had not been in the area very long.

Almost at once Tristram noticed a chilly and unfriendly atmosphere in the building, and Terry was far from welcoming. At any other time, Tristram would have found an excuse not to stay. But the current weather did not make it an option.

He politely refused to have a drink with them, and pleading tiredness asked to be shown to his room. Terry took him to a room on the ground floor, wished him a curt goodnight, and left. Like Terry, the room was cold and unwelcoming. Somehow, he was not surprised the hotel was empty and looking so rundown.

If this was the way Terry treated his guests, it was not surprising no one came here. He felt desperately sorry for Carol being married to such a man. Thinking about her, reminded him he needed to call Liz and let her know he was safe.

Tristram took out his mobile phone and tried dialling home but could not get a signal. After a while he gave up trying, put the phone down on the window sill and looked out into the car park.

He was glad to see the snow had stopped and it was now raining heavily. Already some of the snow had been washed away, so he decided to wait a while longer before going to bed. If the snow went, then so would he. There was a strange, unfriendly atmosphere about the *Cotswold Shepherd*, which made him uneasy and he wanted to get away from it as soon as possible.

Two hours later, he considered the snow had gone sufficiently for him to leave.

Putting on his coat, he quietly opened the bedroom door and made his way into the car park. Momentarily he thought about letting his hosts know what he was doing, but then heard their raised voices in another part of the building. Whilst he could not hear what was being said, it was obvious they were having an argument, and he left them to it. Thankfully he climbed into his own car. It started first time and he was relieved to drive away.

He was surprised to see Carol's car had gone. Shrugging his shoulders, he drove on: it was none of his business.

Much later the next day whilst back at the conference hotel, Tristram remembered he had left his phone at the *Cotswold Shepherd*. Somewhat reluctantly he drove back there after the conference finished and wondered what sort of reception he would receive. For a while he was tempted to leave his phone there. But he knew it was an expensive model which Liz had given him as a birthday present. He had no choice but to return to the *Cotswold Shepherd*.

It was early afternoon when he arrived at the building and could not believe what he saw.

The building was little more than a ruin, with its doors and windows all boarded up. There was very little left of the roof, and much of the security fence had rotted away. Looking at the large clumps of weeds, nettles and straggly undergrowth all around, it was obvious nobody lived here.

And it had clearly been in this state for a considerable time.

How could he possibly have been here last night? Had he dreamt it all?

It was easy to think so, but if he had, where was his mobile phone? And why had he come here to retrieve it?

Getting out of his car, Tristram walked round the security fence and the brambles, until he found a hole large enough to give him access. He quickly climbed through and went to where he remembered his room had been.

Like the rest of the building, it was in ruins, boarded up and overgrown with weeds. Tristram could not understand it. How had the building got into such a state in just a few hours?

'What are you doing here sir?'

The strange voice broke in on his thoughts. Tristram turned and saw two police constables standing behind him.

'I know it sounds strange, officers,' he started to explain. 'But I stayed here last night, and I left my mobile phone behind in that room, and I've come to find it…but…' His voice tailed off as he pointed to the ruins.

'Is that so sir?' PC Michael Townsend replied sarcastically. 'And I'm Queen Victoria. Tell him, John. After all it was your dad's case.'

'It was thirty years ago,' explained PC John Burton. 'In fact, it was thirty years ago last night, when the landlord here murdered his wife. He was convinced she was going off with a lover.'

'Apparently Carol was quite attractive,' Michael added.

'It seems she was leaving her husband because he used to beat her up. Terry Wakeford was a right miserable and violent individual,' John continued. 'It was a night just like last night, and she'd only gone a couple of miles when her car went off the road and into a ditch.'

Tristram shivered as the story unfolded: and it was not just the chilly afternoon which made him feel cold.

'Apparently a passing motorist picked her up and brought her back here. Her husband, Terry, immediately assumed this bloke was her lover,' John continued. 'It was agreed her rescuer should stay the night. A couple of hours later, Terry strangled her and went to do the other bloke as well but there had been a sudden thaw, and he'd scarpered.'

'Was it a sudden thaw like last night?' Tristram asked, although he knew what the answer would be.

'Yes,' replied John. 'It undoubtedly saved this bloke's life. My dad was the superintendent in charge of the case, and he told me the full story.'

'Did he ever find this mystery man or at least learn his name?' Tristram asked.

'No: but dad always believed he would come back here at some time or other. Dad always came up here every anniversary night, but the man never showed up.'

'Is your dad...'

'No, he died some years ago.' John shook his head sadly.

'I'm sorry,' apologised Tristram. 'But what happened to the *Cotswold Shepherd*? How did it get into such a state?'

'Terry topped himself in prison, or at least that was the official version, and nobody wanted to buy it, so it gradually became the ruin you see today.'

'Just a minute,' Michael interrupted. 'How do you know it was called the *Cotswold Shepherd*? The sign vanished soon after the murder and it was never replaced: some ghoul of a souvenir hunter probably. Most people round here today have never even heard of it. But I'll ask you again. How did you know it was called the *Cotswold Shepherd*?'

'Because I really was here last night, and it looked nothing like this: and the sign was up then.'

'I don't know where you were last night,' Michael said. 'But you can't have stayed here. Look sir! Look at those weeds!'

'But I did stay here! It's where I left my mobile phone. It's in there!' Tristram pointed to the room in which he had stayed.

'Look at the state of the building! It's all boarded up. Nobody's been through here in ages, let alone inside the building. I would suggest you tell your wife a more plausible story.'

'Was your mobile switched on?' John asked.

'Yes.'

'We can sort this quite quickly. Give me your number and I'll call it. If your phone's in there...then ...we'll hear it, won't we? What's its ring tone?'

'*The Ride of the Valkyries.*'

'The what?'

'I know it,' Michael smiled. 'These youngsters don't know their classical music.'

Tristram gave his number to John, who dialled it. They waited expectantly, but all remained quiet.

Then softly at first, but with an ever-increasing volume, they all heard the ringing tone of a mobile phone playing *The Ride of the Valkyries.* They turned towards the source of the sound, and there was no mistaking where it was ringing.

It was in the room where Tristram had stayed last night.

A room which was clearly boarded up: a room which had not been entered for many years.

AUTHOR'S NOTE

The *Phantom Hitch hiker* is a well-known type of *time slip* ghost story which comes in various versions and many people maintain the have experienced it in one form or another. The Mobile Phone is a more modern version of this story.

10.43 Hours

The three fighter pilots who made up Blue Flight, were bored as they listened, yet again, to their briefing. It was a word-for-word repetition of their last briefing and the countless ones before that.

Having been conscripted into the RAF in late 1944, none of them had much experience of flying, let alone seen any action. It was easy to appreciate their frustration when they were posted to a remote station in the North African Desert. As the Allies were already in the outskirts of Berlin, they knew the war in Europe had but a few days left to run. And out here they stood no chance of taking part in any fighting.

'Finally,' stressed the briefing officer. 'Let me remind you there is still a war on and urge you to take care.'

Doug Taylor, Rory Hammond and Pete Evans, the three pilots, silently mouthed his last words. They knew them by heart.

'As if,' moaned Doug, as they left the briefing tent and headed towards the airfield. 'As if we're likely to see any enemy aircraft, let alone fight them.'

'I would have liked the chance to shoot one of the bastards down,' added Rory with feeling.

Pete Evans said nothing.

He was not a coward, but his sole aim was to survive the war and return home in one piece. It was a view his elder brother, Bill, had shared with him. Bill was also a pilot, but he had been shot down. How well Pete remembered the day they had received the dreaded telegram, with its brief and formal message:

Missing believed killed in action.

The family could only wait and pray.

It was many months before their prayers were answered…to a degree. Flight Lieutenant William Evans was being held in a prisoner-of-war camp somewhere in Eastern Germany, but news ceased following the Russian advance. It was anybody's guess where he was now. Hopefully he was still alive, but who knew? At least Pete was alive and with luck seemed likely to survive the war.

Doug, the Blue Flight leader, was the oldest of the three who had been late in joining up. His elderly father's business produced war materials, and he ensued Doug was kept at home to help run it. But it was not what Doug had wanted. Every day he was obliged to travel into Birmingham by train and was very conscious of being the only young man on it who was not wearing a uniform. Regardless of the times he protested, his father would not relent and called in all the favours he could, to ensure his son remained at home.

It all changed dramatically when his father suffered a fatal stroke. Leaving his two sisters in charge of the factory, Doug soon obtained a commission in the RAF, but that was only the beginning. Although Doug was now in uniform, he had no medal ribbons, and was envious of those younger men who did.

He desperately wanted to make up for the time he had missed. But being posted to this quiet part of North Africa was not what he had in mind. It did not give him the action he craved. He tried several times, unsuccessfully, to get a transfer to a more active zone. With the end of the war in sight, unless something drastic happened very soon out in the desert, he would not have any war stories to tell his children.

Rory Hammond was a youngster of Anglo-Irish parents, who had a happy-go-lucky approach to life. With a father who had been a pilot in the Royal Flying Corps during the last war, it seemed only natural he was called up into the RAF. He was not unduly worried about his lack of experience, because unlike Doug, he knew the war in the Far East was not yet over. Undoubtedly there would still be a need for pilots out there for some time yet to come.

Until then, Rory was not in any hurry to die. He had too much to live for. And he knew all these extra hours flying time he could accumulate now increased his chances of survival.

With Doug leading, the others followed him out onto the runway. After checking their equipment, they flew up into the clear blue sky. It was another hot, sunny and cloudless day. Once they were fully airborne, they checked their guns and turned into their patrol.

Doug looked at his watch and saw that it had just gone 09.45 hours. Inwardly he moaned about this pointless flight. There was nothing to see, just as there had been on all their previous patrols. Nevertheless, he forced himself to keep checking the sky all around him, being conscious of the warnings the older pilots had given him about not being complacent. But it was not always easy.

At first, they could not wait from the end of one patrol until their next one and had enjoyed being in the desert with its ever-changing colours and moods. But this happy feeling soon palled, and apart from the actual flying, they loathed these patrols. With nothing happening, their minds began to wander.

It was certainly not a recommended way to fly, especially when the country was still at war.

'Leader to Blue Flight!' Doug called over the radio, yet again. 'Keep checking for bandits!' He only called such messages to break up the monotony.

Back at the base, life went on as normal. The duty staff in the operations centre were just as bored as Doug's flight, and like them they had no option. Someone had just gone to make a brew of tea, when Pete's urgent voice broke the silence.

'LEADER! BANDITS AT FIVE O'CLOCK!'

The tea was immediately forgotten as the staff's training and expertise took over.

'What's your position Blue Leader?' one of the operators called.

Doug replied, giving their co-ordinates.

'THEY'RE FIRING AT US!' shouted Pete.

'Keep calm!' instructed Doug. 'How many are there?'

'Two!'

'I see them.'

Rat-tat-tat! Rat-tat-tat! Rory opened fire and cried excitedly: 'I've got him! I've got him…but…but…my bullets are just going straight through him!'

The plane kept coming on, seemingly unaffected by his bullets.

Rat-tat-tat! Rat-tat-tat! Doug started firing at the second plane, but his bullets also just went straight through it without causing any damage.

These enemy planes seemed to be oblivious to Blue Flight's presence.

'Blue Leader!' called one of the base operators. 'What type of aircraft are they?'

'I don't know for sure, but they're tri-planes, just like the ones the Red Baron flew in the last show.'

Back in the operations centre there was a stunned silence.

'Are you sure?' queried the duty officer.

'Oh yes,' replied Doug. 'They're definitely tri-planes, complete with open cockpits.'

'They can't be,' continued the duty officer, incredulously. 'Unless they're relics held over in reserve from the last war. What have they got on their wings?'

'Just crosses: no swastikas.'

'They're definitely German tri-planes,' interrupted Rory. 'My father was something of an expert on aircraft, and he bored us rigid with their pictures. But that's what they are: almost certainly Fokkers, but I can't be sure of the actual model.'

'They can't be,' repeated the duty officer testily, and instructed an operator to fetch the Commanding Officer. 'You're having us on!'

Meanwhile a strange aerial dance developed amongst the five planes. None of Blue Flight had any doubts their bullets were hitting the targets: but there were no signs of them causing any damage. And the tri-planes seemed totally unconcerned about them.

'It's as if they can't see us,' said Rory, summing up all their thoughts. 'And don't even know we're here!'

'BANDIT AT NINE O'CLOCK!' called Pete Evans. Unlike the others, he had not stopped looking around them, very mindful of his brother's advice.

'No, it's one of ours,' corrected Rory.

'But it can't be,' called the duty officer back at base. 'There are no other flights in your sector. What type of plane is it?'

'It's a Bristol of some sorts,' replied Rory. 'But they also haven't flown since the last war.'

'Look!' called Doug, abandoning any attempt at proper radio procedure. 'It's engaging with them!'

As they watched, the Bristol headed straight for the first of the tri-planes. Its pilot, in an uncovered cockpit, commenced firing his machine gun. Clearly the tri-plane had been caught unawares. The bullets hit it and smoke started to appear, followed by flames. In a matter of moments, it was spiralling to earth, with a long plume of smoke trailing behind.

'How come he's shot it down, when our bullets didn't have any effect?' Doug voiced their thoughts. 'It's as if we don't exist.'

The second tri-plane pilot was now aware of the incoming danger and fired back at the Bristol. Some of the bullets hit the Bristol's pilot, and he slumped forwards. Moments later, he seemed to have a sudden burst of renewed energy, sat up and flew straight at the German plane. Their propellers collided, and both planes fell to the earth.

A shocked Doug reported back to base what had happened.

'Your message timed at 10.43 hours,' came a new voice which they all recognised as being the commanding officer. 'Return to base at once and report to me.'

Even as he spoke, the members of Blue Flight watched the two planes hit the desert, but they did not burst into flames.

Forty-five minutes later, Doug and his flight stood in front of their commanding officer. He was obviously in a foul mood.

'Just what the hell were you playing at?' he snapped. 'A Great War dog-fight? Are you drunk or something?'

'It's what we saw,' they insisted.

But he remained unconvinced. 'You're grounded indefinitely.'

Two years later, Doug, Rory and Pete attended a squadron re-union. It was the first one they had been to and they went reluctantly. Following being grounded, they were the butt of many jokes and nicknames from the other squadron members. They never flew again and were glad to be demobbed.

Then out of the blue, they each received their invitations, which were accompanied by hand-written letters, almost begging them to attend. They had no difficulty in recognising their old commanding officer's handwriting and wondered what game he was playing. Reluctantly they agreed to go.

Conscious of the sniggers from their former brothers-in-arms, they arrived at the venue and took their seats.

'Well look who's here!' someone called. 'It's the Red Baron!' A chorus of ribald laughter greeted his remark.

'That will do!' The commanding officer's voice called out with a sharp edge to it and the room quietened. 'I'm very glad to see you all again, especially you three,' he looked pointedly at Doug, Rory and Pete. 'Because gentlemen, I owe you a very sincere apology.'

The room was now so quiet you could have heard a pin drop. The atmosphere was electric with anticipation. Doug looked askance at the other members of Blue Flight, but they shrugged their shoulders in total ignorance of what he meant.

'You see,' he continued. 'Not that long ago, I received a report from the team who went and checked out the location you gave us for that famous dogfight, and where the planes crashed.'

There was a sudden buzz of excitement, which he quelled by raising a hand. 'It may surprise you to know I reported the incident and ultimately it was checked out.' He paused again.

'I have to tell you the wreckage of three planes was found, exactly where you reported them to be. All three came from the Great War and were in one of those strange parts you get sometimes in the desert, where nothing has changed for years. The wreckage consisted of two German Fokker Dr.1 tri-planes and a Bristol M.1C. There was no way they could have been identified as such from the air. It needed a much closer inspection on the ground to confirm what make of aircraft they were. The still unsolved mystery was what they were doing there in the first place as both sets of aircraft didn't fly out here. But…that wasn't all,' his voice faltered.

'Surprisingly the bodies of two of the pilots were in reasonably good shape,' he hesitated once more. 'But the strangest thing of all was the British pilot's watch. It had stopped at 10.43 hours: at exactly the time you reported he had been shot down at the end of the fight.'

The Best Seat in the House

Jethro Hamilton was struggling.

A little-known music composer, he had been awarded a contract to create the musical score for a new film. Initially he was very enthusiastic about the project and the fame it would bring him. The reality of it all struck him once he studied the script and discovered it was a mixture of a Victorian whodunnit and a thriller, set in England and elsewhere in Europe. The music had to contain a hint of mystery, excitement and romance.

With no experience of any previous similar work, Jethro was never quite sure why he had been awarded the contract. Later he learnt all the other composers, who had been approached, declined to be considered. They knew how demanding this particular film producer was and did not even tender for the contract.

Being so much younger and inexperienced, Jethro did not appreciate these difficulties until it was too late. Somehow all his ideas just drifted away, and he now faced a massive attack of *Composer's Block*. No matter how hard he tried, Jethro could not make any of his few ideas work.

He was getting nowhere: and getting there fast.

To make matters worse, time was not on his side. Already the film producer was chasing to see what progress he was making. So far, he had managed to fob her off, but he could not do so for very much longer.

His wife, Denise, was only too aware of the problems her husband faced, but from a different point of view. When he was not composing music, Jethro often conducted small orchestras for a fee, but he could not do both at the same time. A clear mind was necessary for composing music, with a minimum of other distractions. He could not afford to waste time rehearsing an orchestra, and technically speaking he was out of work, with all the financial problems that brought. Luckily, she was working full time, but it was not always easy to make ends meet.

'Why don't you admit defeat?' she nagged him time and time again.

'If I only had more time.'

'But you haven't. Face the facts! You're just not good enough.'

It was not what Jethro wanted to hear.

He needed her support and encouragement: not discouragement. Unfortunately, it was a view shared by both his parents and her side of the family. They could come to terms with him being a musician and a conductor: but never saw him as a composer.

After a while he gave up trying to reply to her nagging. It was no use telling her how he was committed to this contract, which would cost him a considerable amount of money to cancel: money he did not have. Deep down Jethro knew she was probably right, and he should not have aimed so high so quickly. But he had done so, knowing it would either make or break him.

Just now it looked like the latter was happening.

Later, when Jethro looked back, he could never really say where the idea originated. He was stifled at home with his nagging wife, telephone calls, visitors etc. What he needed was somewhere quiet to do his thinking, and hopefully composing. When he suggested it, Denise readily agreed knowing it would get him out from under her feet for a while.

Taking out a road map of the British Isles, she closed her eyes, opened it at random and pointed to a spot. It was in Suffolk, not too far from the coast. Within a few days, Jethro had arrived at his rented cottage, which was ideally situated in a lonely location.

At first, he spent his time simply wandering round the nearby village, enjoying the bright but chilling autumnal air and trying to get some ideas. He was soon very recognisable in his long light- coloured coat, long scarf and broad brimmed hat as he roamed around the area humming to himself. None of his tunes was recognisable, which was not surprising, as they were his attempts to create the music he urgently needed. Most people nodded to him, but remained unwilling to engage him in any conversations, which suited him. Jethro dreaded interruptions when he was working.

The clear days and gold tinged leaves should have done the trick, but they did not, and the *Block* was still there. Would it ever go away?

*   *   *

One afternoon, feeling totally frustrated and despondent, Jethro wandered out into the woods not knowing what to do next. He was concentrating so much on the gentle breeze it was a while before he heard the music.

It came from a piano being played somewhere nearby, and the music was out of this world. Jethro was so entranced by the sounds he unconsciously moved towards them. He felt incredibly amazed how someone had created such wonderful music. Strangely it was not anything he had ever heard before, which surprised him because it was so haunting and beautiful.

'Why can't I compose something like that?' he asked himself enviously.

Several minutes later Jethro found himself in the driveway leading to a large, old, rather rundown Jacobean house. Surprisingly he had not seen any reference to it in the local guidebooks. Crossing the untidy lawn, he found himself in front of an open pair of French windows which were completely out of place in such an old house and obviously not part of the original building.

He stood outside the windows totally entranced by the music. As it moved into a quieter mode, a voice called to him: 'Don't just stand there: come in.'

Jethro obeyed the command and saw the speaker was the pianist. She was a tall, slender, well-dressed woman aged about 65-70 years. Her dark, greying hair was drawn back in a bun, yet it did not make her look stern. It was a friendly face. Her clothes were old fashioned, with a high-necked white blouse, complete with a gold cameo brooch on a black velvet choker.

She turned towards him and stopped playing.

'Please don't stop,' he begged. 'It's the loveliest piece of music I have ever heard. Yet, I've never heard it before. Who composed it?'

'I did.'

'But why have you kept such a beautiful piece to yourself?' He could not keep the surprise out of his voice.

'Because...because I had a father who did not approve of my composing music and did everything in his power to belittle my work and stop me publishing.'

'I know how you feel,' replied Jethro with feeling. 'I have the same problem.'

*   *   *

For the next few minutes Jethro explained his problems to her. She nodded sympathetically. 'I know what it's like to have such a *Block*.' During this period, he learnt her name was Charlotte Bickersleigh.

'What if…what if,' started Charlotte, when he had finished his story. 'What if you were to use my music for your contract?'

'I couldn't possibly do that,' protested Jethro, with his mind in a whirl. 'It's your work. Surely you want to take the credit for it?'

'Not any more. My time for fame has long since gone. But you appreciate my music and I know you will treat it properly. No more arguments! I insist you use it. But, on no account are you to mention me. Everybody must believe it's your own work.'

Jethro really did not need much persuasion. Apart from being the answer to his prayers, he knew it was a very good piece of music.

'There's just one other thing,' she added. 'You'll have to write it down as I play it.'

'Of course. That won't be a problem, but I haven't got much paper on me.'

'There's plenty here, although my father tried to destroy it, just as he did my original score. But, you'll have to fetch it. You see, I'm blind, which is why I've never been able to rewrite it.'

Charlotte explained how one day her father had seized the piece of music she was writing. She tried to retrieve it but during the struggle had fallen downstairs, banging her head on the way, which permanently damaged the optic nerves and made her blind. Charlotte never mentioned a mother or any siblings. It seemed she just lived on her own in this old rambling house.

She received no sympathy from her father, such was his religious fanaticism. He considered it was a judgement on her for conspiring with the Devil to compose music. He destroyed the rest of her music and as far as he was concerned, that was the end of the matter.

Charlotte was left in a dark world, although her father had no objections to her playing hymns and other religious music. Only after he had died, was she able to return to creating her own music. But sadly, she had no means of writing it down.

The next few days and nights passed in a blur, as Charlotte played, and he wrote down the music. At last it was finished, but that was only the beginning for him. He now had to orchestrate all the other instrumental parts.

Before he left, Jethro offered to conduct a recital of the finished score in the nearby town hall. And when he did, Jethro promised to give her the best seat in the house.

The film, and especially Jethro's music, became an overnight box office success. Whilst the critics agreed it was not the best film ever to have been made, they could not praise the music highly enough. Even Jethro's family and his in-laws approved. Although he wrote many more film scores, none of them ever surpassed this one.

Very conscious of his promise to Charlotte, it was many months later before he could arrange a concert in the nearby town hall. It was only when he prepared to post her ticket for the best seat in the house, Jethro realised he did not know her address. He wrote vague directions on the envelope as best as he could remember and hoped it would get there: but was not surprised when the ticket was returned to the town hall and forwarded to him.

Taking time out from rehearsing, Jethro drove out to see Charlotte and deliver her ticket personally, realising he should have done this in the first place. But, like the postman, he too could not find her house. Yet he was adamant he had the right location, although his last visit had been just over three years ago.

What he did find in its place was a small, but very select housing development, which had clearly been well established for several years, yet he could not remember having seen it before. Totally confused, he went into the local sub-post office.

'I'm trying to find an old house', he explained. 'You know, a really old building that's somewhere near here. Do you know where it is?' Jethro went on to describe it.

The middle-aged woman behind the counter shook her head. 'I'm sorry, but it doesn't mean anything to me, although I've lived here all my life. Just a minute, I'll call my mum. **MUM!**'

An elderly woman appeared from the rear of the shop, and Jethro repeated his question.

'An old house, you say? Oh yes, I remember it. We used to play there when we were children. It was an old ruin.'

'But it can't be the same one,' protested Jethro as he explained about his earlier visit three years earlier but did not mention the music.

When he had finished, she told him to wait a minute, and disappeared. She reappeared several minutes later carrying a large sketch book with her. 'I used to draw a lot when I was young,' she explained, and began leafing through the pages. Suddenly she stopped and turned the book to Jethro. 'Is this your house?'

There was no doubt whatsoever in his mind.

It was a picture of the old house, albeit in ruins. He saw the picture was dated 1933. 'That's it,' he said. 'Only it wasn't a ruin when I last saw it!'

'It must have been, because that's the year they knocked it down, only a few weeks after I drew this picture.' She pointed to the date on the picture. 'Then they built all these houses.' She nodded out of the post office window towards the nearby buildings.

'What happened to the owner?'

'You mean the old blind lady who played the piano? My ma used to talk about her. She died in the 1880s, and nobody ever lived in the house again. They all said it was haunted. Sometimes when we played there, we heard a piano playing, but we were too scared to go and see where it was.'

Totally bemused, Jethro returned to the town hall for the concert.

Everyone who heard the concert all agreed they had never heard anything so moving before or ever again. Jethro put his whole heart into this performance and the orchestra responded accordingly. They all received a lengthy standing ovation at the end of it. As Jethro took his final bow, he looked up again into the best seat in the house, which had been empty all night.

Only it was not empty anymore.

Charlotte Bickersleigh was sitting there and smiling down at him. He opened his mouth to speak and give her the credit for the music. But Charlotte shook her head, and he lip read her instructions.

'Keep me out of it.'

Reluctantly he nodded…but by then she had gone.

Cold and Unwelcoming

Jenny Morrison was having a quiet time.

Although she enjoyed the well-deserved reputation of being a talented artist, commissions were short just now: such was the nature of her work. Only twelve months ago, she had been rushed off her feet. But as she knew from experience, what happened one year would not necessarily be repeated the next. It was often a case of feast or famine. Everybody wanted her work at the same time…or nobody did!

Yet it was not all doom and gloom, as her picture gallery was thriving, and it had the added advantage of being in an attractive Worcestershire village, not far from Birmingham. The whole area was becoming a honey pot for tourists. Taking advantage of this, Jenny pitched her prices to suit all pockets, and sold many prints of her more expensive original watercolours. As the main influx of tourists for the year had not yet started, she had the freedom to paint whatever took her fancy and hopefully might sell.

The problem was she had already painted most of the local beauty spots and was trying to find a different angle for some old favourites. Sometimes she changed the period by adding old-fashioned vehicles, people and animals to a well-known and popular location. Each creation was carefully researched and correct in every detail. That was all part of the fun, yet she missed the creative commission work, and the pressures which came with it, plus the guaranteed income.

It was now Spring, and she was keen to get outside and enjoy the glorious weather.

On this particular morning, she was working in the gallery because her assistant would be late, having taken her young son to the doctor. The shop doorbell rang, and she looked up expectantly hoping it was her assistant.

But it was not.

Instead she saw a good looking, well-built man, probably in his mid-fifties: only slightly older than herself. 'Good morning,' she smiled. 'Please feel free to browse around in your own time. If you have any questions, then please don't hesitate to ask.'

'Thank you,' he smiled back. It was a warm and friendly smile. 'Actually I'm looking for Jenny Morrison. Would you be her, by chance?' he continued holding out his right hand.

'At your service, sir,' she smiled. 'How can I help you?' She returned his handshake, which matched his warm and friendly smile.

'I'm Joselyn Danvers and I recently moved into the old *Park House* after my father died.'

Jenny nodded, knowing as did the locals where the house was, although she had never been to it. Not many people had. It was situated at the end of a quiet lane, and uninvited callers were actively discouraged from visiting. Did this visit mean she might get the chance to paint it?

'As you probably know,' he continued. 'My father was something of a recluse who rarely left home. I moved out at an early age and never went back until recently, when I inherited it on his death. And I have to say I'm appalled by the state it's in.' Joselyn went on to explain how he wanted the house up and running again and enlarged on some of his ideas.

'Don't forget, I'm an artist and not an interior decorator,' she commented, disappointed as this was not her field of expertise and possibly not seeing him again.

'I realise that,' he smiled. 'But I would like you to do some paintings for me of both the inside and the outside of the house, showing how it looks now, and how it could look. Then I'll get the designers to work.'

Just as they agreed on a price, Jenny's assistant arrived. Seizing the opportunity, she agreed to go out to the house with him but in her own car.

She followed him up the main drive to the house, passing several signs instructing:

PRIVATE – KEEP OUT
TRESPASSERS WILL BE PROSECUTED

This drive was heavily overgrown, and Jenny could only just get her car through some of the tangles. For a fleeting moment, she wondered whether this really was sensible, coming out to such a property with a complete stranger. But her assistant knew where she was going.

To say the house was a mess, both inside and outside, was an understatement. The inside was on a par with the overgrown gardens. Joselyn showed her the inside before moving back into the garden. Although it was a warm spring day, Jenny found the house was cold and unwelcoming, and she was more than happy to get outside again and into the sunshine.

'You feel it too? Isn't it cold and unwelcoming?' he asked, seeing her shiver on several occasions.

She nodded in reply.

'I'm not surprised. Perhaps I should have warned you, but then you probably wouldn't have come. The house has an unhappy history,' he explained. 'It seems my grandmother disappeared in 1919. Popular rumour had it she was...how can I put it?...not true to her marriage vows during the First World War, whilst her husband was away fighting in the navy. The story goes he came home soon after the Armistice and found her with a small child, who was my father.' He paused. 'The problem was grandfather had not seen her since 1914, so the child was obviously not his. Then she suddenly just disappeared leaving my father behind to be looked after by my grandfather's mother.'

'Did she just run away?'

'Without her child? You're a woman: you tell me?

Jenny shook her head. 'Unlikely.'

'It was always believed grandfather had murdered her, but there was no evidence to prove if he had. Soon after she disappeared, he contracted the Spanish Flu. As he was dying, he sent for the village constable to come and see him. Unfortunately, the bobby also had the 'flu and by the time a policeman came to see my grandfather, it was too late. He was dead.'

'And no one's seen your grandmother since?'

'No. We just know she was here long enough to give her news to my grandfather, and that was it. Nobody saw her go, and nobody has seen her since.'

Joselyn led the way out into the heavily overgrown garden, which was even more untidy than the house, if that was possible! The whole area was a wilderness of brambles, nettles, ivy and various trees, all of which desperately needed clearing.

'I appreciate you can't really start until some of this has been cleared,' he acknowledged seeing the look of horror and total disbelief on her face. 'I've got some contractors starting next week, but I've no idea how long they'll take.'

'What I could do,' Jenny replied. 'Is to take some photos of it as it is now, and then do some basic sketches from them. This way we can do a *before and after* comparison. What do you think?'

She was delighted when he readily agreed to her idea, having already taken a liking to him. And the feeling appeared to be mutual. When he offered to take her to the village pub for lunch, she happily agreed.

During the meal, she discovered like herself he too was divorced with two adult children. They had both been the innocent parties in the subsequent legal proceedings. Neither was in any hurry to finish their lunch.

When they finally parted, Jenny agreed to start on the project the next morning.

Over the course of the next few days she made a photographic record of the property, starting with the interior. Once the contractors started to clear the undergrowth, she began properly on the house's exterior.

During the second week of the contractors working, they were all surprised when a medium sized statue was uncovered standing on a plinth.

Jenny took several photographs of it and the surrounding area, but as she did so there was a sudden chill in the air and the clouds began to thicken. Minutes later the first few spots of rain fell. These were soon followed by more persistent rain. The next day was too wet for working out of doors, so she spent some time in her studio.

Downloading the previous day's photographs onto her computer, she studied their details and suddenly stopped.

For some reason, the pictures she had taken of the statue were different to the ones which had just been downloaded. These showed the statue as being much nearer to the house. Curious as to what had happened, she e-mailed them to Joselyn and drove out to the house.

He was waiting for her with the printouts in his hand.

Together they checked on the statue. But it was there, in the same place where she had originally photographed it and not as it appeared in the downloaded pictures. They both took more photographs of it on different cameras, which they downloaded onto Joselyn's computer.

Just like the ones she had taken the day before and downloaded on to her own computer, both sets showed the statue to be much nearer the house than it was. They took several more photographs both with his and her cameras, but the results were still the same.

The statue was always shown much nearer the house.

Joselyn snapped his fingers. 'Of course!' he cried. 'I'm sure that's where the statue used to be. Come on!'

He led the way into the large study, which was full of books and papers, and crossed to a large desk, where he began thumbing through numerous old photographs, many of them faded and curling at their corners. Jenny saw most of them tended to be of the house, albeit having been taken many years ago.

'Eureka!' He extracted one and handed it to her.

The photograph was of a young woman holding a small child, and standing in front of the statue, which was much nearer to the house than in its present position. In fact, it was in the same position as shown on their photographs. The date 1918 was written across one corner.

'That's my grandmother Adelaide holding my father,' he explained. His words began to confirm her suspicions. Why had the statue been moved?

Leaving Jenny holding the photograph, he started scrabbling through more piles of documents littering another desk. 'Ah, here it is!' He removed what appeared to be a printed booklet, which he opened and handed to her.

This other document was the printed sale catalogue for the house dated Friday 30 January 1920. 'My great-uncle sold the house following grandfather's death,' he explained. 'Although, my father bought it back many years later, and spent the rest of his life here. But look!'

He pointed to a faded photograph in the catalogue. It showed the statue in its current site.

'So, your grandfather moved the statue?'

'It looks like it. But why has it moved in our pictures...' he broke off as a sudden chilly thought struck him.

'What's up?' Jenny asked, although she too was thinking along the same lines and she went cold. 'You don't think…?'

'Yes, I do. We've got to have that statue moved.'

He had it moved the following day, and their fears were confirmed.

As they had suspected, a human skeleton was found underneath it.

In due course, the police arrived, and the skeleton was removed. After forensic examination, it was confirmed to be that of a female aged about 30–40 years. She was thought to have been dead somewhere in the region of 90 years. Further examination revealed a hole in her skull which had undoubtedly been caused by the bullet found in it. Joselyn's DNA confirmed the skeleton almost certainly belonged to his missing grandmother, Adelaide Danvers.

'It certainly seems as if the rumours were true and my grandfather really did kill her,' said Joselyn. 'Then he buried her here after having moved the statue. It certainly explains her disappearance. No doubt that's what he wanted to confess on his death bed, but it was too late.'

Once the police investigation had finished, Adelaide was properly buried in the local churchyard. On their return to the house after the funeral, Jenny was the first to notice the change. 'Can you feel it?'

'Yes, I can.'

No longer cold and unwelcoming, the house had now become a warm and welcoming place.

The following year, Joselyn and Jenny had some of their wedding photographs taken by the statue, which was now fully restored and back in its original position.

Expendable

Commodore Christopher Manton-Lodge was not in the best of moods.

The reason being his shore leave was not going as planned and was soon due to end. For some reason his wife, Vikki, had become very moody and off hand with him. He could not understand why as they had been married for a considerable number of years, all of which he had been serving in the Royal Navy, so that should not have upset her.

His leave had started well, but then Vikki had changed a few days ago. Their conversation dwindled, and she only spoke to him when necessary. Whenever he asked what was wrong, her terse answer was, *'Nothing!'* If he suggested they went somewhere, she replied: *'It's not convenient.'*

He was now counting the days to the end of his shore leave and a much welcome return to sea.

He did not know she had found a text on his phone from Zoe, the wife of his second-in-command, Andrew Partridge. Vikki had heard her husband's mobile ping and knowing he was out, having forgotten to take it with him, she opened the text message to check it was not important. Just because Chris was on leave did not mean he could not be contacted if the Navy wanted to do so.

The text came as a nasty shock as she read how it confirmed the reservation which Zoe had made at a nearby expensive restaurant for dinner in a few days time. Vikki read the message again and again, but it did not change, and still showed the same message.

It was definitely a secret assignation between the two of them. The message included Zoe saying she would find a reason to keep it a secret from Andrew.

Vikki was convinced the pair of them were having an affair and felt very hurt and betrayed.

This was the reason for her indifferent attitude towards him.

Soon after reading the text, Vikki announced she was going to see her sister in London and would be away for the night of the secret dinner. But she had other plans.

On the actual day she went through the motions of packing a suitcase, gave her husband a cursory peck on his cheek and drove off. He did not see the tears in her eyes.

It was a long day and she just drove around the countryside, taking care not to visit certain places in case Chris might be there. Finally, she drove up to the restaurant, where the secret dinner was happening, and parked outside. By now it was dark, and she had no worries about being seen.

Vikki stopped in a secluded part of the car park and was surprised not to see her husband's car anywhere. She panicked for a moment thinking it was the wrong venue. Then she realised they had probably come by taxi, so they could enjoy a drink, and no one had to drive. Carefully looking through all the windows, she finally saw him and Zoe. They were sat at a table, which was larger than she had expected. It was partially hidden by some potted plans, which limited her view, and she could only just see their heads.

She had intended going into the restaurant and challenging them, but then decided against it, returned to her car and drove away. Totally unwilling to believe what was happening, Vikki drove into the town, parked up and walked onto the seafront, still angry but more upset by her husband's betrayal. From here she could see the docks and the silhouette of *HMS Tarquin*, her husband's ship.

It all looked peaceful and quiet.

Sometime later, she found herself sitting in a shelter on the seafront. It was a warm, clear May night and the gentle lapping of the waves was very relaxing. Her temper slowly subsided, although she still felt devastated by her husband's betrayal.

'Excuse me,' the voice broke in on her thoughts. 'But do you have a light please?'

Vikki looked up and saw a young man, wearing a seaman's uniform standing in front of her, with an unlit cigarette in his slightly trembling hand. She carefully moved a hand towards her handbag.

'Please don't be frightened,' he continued. 'I'm not trying to pick you up and I don't mean you any harm.'

Vikki opened the handbag and gripped her personal attack alarm. 'I'm sorry,' she replied. 'But I don't smoke.'

In the light from the street lamps, she saw his face fall and realised he was very close to tears. 'Are you all right?' she asked, as her fear subsided only to be replaced by concern for this young sailor. 'Do you want to tell me what's worrying you?'

At the same time, she forgot, albeit for just a while, about her own problems.

He nodded and sat down beside her. She saw that the name of his ship was missing from his cap band. It just said HMS.

'You see,' he started slowly, taking off his cap as he spoke, and twisting it round in his hands. 'I'm just an ordinary seaman on *HMS Tarquin*, although I shouldn't have told you that.'

Vikki started at the mention of her husband's ship but forbore to mention any connection with the vessel's commanding officer.

'I've just learnt that we're sailing soon after midnight on a special mission,' he paused. 'For which we are considered expendable. Do you know what that means?' He stared out to sea.

She nodded and shivered as the warm night went very cold. Vikki knew only too well being expendable meant just that. You were not expected to return from the mission you were being sent on and would probably be killed in the process.

Suddenly her thoughts came back to Chris. Why hadn't he told her about this mission? Had it only just cropped up? She had to see him before it was too late: all thoughts of his betrayal now out of her mind. Yet she felt unable to leave this obviously distressed young man.

Haltingly he explained his name was Albert Romsley, and he was in his early twenties. His wife, Norah, was due to give birth to their first child any time now and this was the problem. Being classed as expendable and due to leave harbour just after midnight, meant he would never know if he had a son or a daughter.

'Hasn't she had a scan?' Vikki asked.

'A scan? What's one of them?'

'Never mind,' she smiled despite her fears. What a wonderfully naïve couple they must be, she thought, complete with such old-fashioned names. 'Shouldn't you be back on board your ship?' Vikki asked gently, knowing it was close to midnight.

He nodded. 'I suppose so, but I can't go now.'

'Yes, you can. You must!'

'If I go then I'll almost certainly be killed. And if I don't go, then I'll be shot as a deserter, but at least I'll be able to see my child first.'

Vikki was appalled. Shot as a deserter? What sort of ship did her husband command? What nonsense was this man being fed? After all, this was the year 2008 and not the dark ages. Then she had an idea.

'How would you want your child to remember you? As a hero or a deserter?'

He sniffed away his tears.

'It's not yet midnight,' she continued, looking at her watch. 'You can still get back on board if you leave now.'

'Will you walk to the dock gates with me please?'

It was the last thing she really wanted to do, but knew Chris would be on board already, which meant there was no chance of seeing him now. 'Of course, I will.'

She left him at the dockyard gate at five to midnight. The sailor would be late, but at least the ship would not sail without him, and he would not be classified as a deserter. In the moonlight, she could easily make out *HMS Tarquin*, although she was not close enough to see any activity or sense of urgency on or around the ship.

For a fleeting moment Vikki had hoped there might be a chance of getting closer, but she did not know the sentry. He was a hard-faced stranger. When she looked up, there was no sign of Albert Romsley.

With a heavy heart, she made her way home.

Vikki was not really surprised to see her husband's car was still on the drive. Undoubtedly, he would have been collected. For a while she just sat in her car, reluctant to go indoors, but at last she did. On entering the hallway, she heard voices and laughter coming from the lounge and saw a light shining around the door frame. She assumed he had forgotten to switch off the television. Trust Chris to have left it and the light on, she thought.

Vikki opened the door and stopped in amazement.

Inside the lounge, each with a glass in their hands, were Chris, Andrew Partridge, Zoe and Martin Coleman, who was Zoe's father.

'Hello, my love,' said Chris, filling and thrusting a glass into her hand. 'We didn't expect you back tonight. You missed a cracking meal, didn't she?' His last remark was addressed to his guests. They all agreed, and Vikki was completely lost for words.

'It was such a pity you couldn't make it,' said Zoe. 'It was a secret celebration dinner because Andrew,' she smiled and put her arm through his. 'Has just been promoted, and it was a surprise dinner, which we arranged for him. He knew nothing about it. Daddy brought him to the restaurant where I was waiting with Christopher.'

Vikki's mind was in a whirl. She had got this wrong big time.

'We must be going,' said Andrew after a few more minutes, when they heard their taxi draw up outside. 'Thank you once again Chris and Zoe for arranging such a wonderful surprise evening. I just don't know how you managed to keep it a secret from me.'

After they had gone, Vikki suddenly remembered her conversation with the seaman. 'Chris! What are you doing here? I thought you were sailing at midnight…on a special mission for which you are expendable? Shouldn't you be at sea?'

'Sailing? At sea? Special mission? Expendable? What are you talking about?' He was clearly very puzzled.

In a few fleeting sentences she told him about meeting Albert Romsley.

'You met Albert Romsley, did you?' He grinned. 'Well! Well! Well! He normally only appears to sailors.'

'What do you mean appears?'

At his suggestion, they sat down.

'Albert's been dead for many years,' began Chris. 'He served on the old *HMS Tarquin* during the Great War…' Chris held up his hand to stop her from interrupting. 'Basically, what he told you tonight was true. But what he did not know then was the time of sailing had been brought forward by an hour to midnight, not 1 am. *Tarquin* was to have led the flotilla. They were scheduled to carry out a raid on the French coast and for which they were all considered to be expendable. This was 1918, when deserters were shot.'

He poured them both another drink.

'Albert had good mates and everyone, including the skipper, knew about his wife being very close to giving birth. The messenger, who had been tasked with recalling the crew back from leave, claimed he was unable to find Albert and reported back to that effect. Provided he was back on board by midnight, there would be no problem. As I said, he had good mates and they faked a mechanical fault, which meant they could not lead off. Just when they could wait no longer, Albert appeared, and they joined the rear of the flotilla. Apparently, he had thought about deserting, but had met a woman on the front, who persuaded him to return to his ship.'

Chris raised his glass and took a swallow.

'The lead ship, which should have been *Tarquin,* was sunk with a heavy loss of life. And by the time *Tarquin* joined them at the rendez-vous, the raid had been cancelled, and they all returned home, where Albert was soon able to see his son. It seemed the lessons of Zeebrugge had been learnt, albeit too late for many sailors. *Tarquin's* crew never saw any more action during that conflict.'

'You say this all happened in 1918, and not tonight?'

'Yes, it was on 30th May 1918 to be precise: nearly ninety years ago.'

By now Vikki was totally confused and tried to absorb what she had just been told.

'Ever afterwards,' Chris finished his story. 'Albert was always considered to be a good luck charm. People felt safe in his company. When the war ended, he returned to Civvy Street, had another three sons and became a successful businessman. He died in the 1950s, but his descendants still run *Romsleys Stores* in town today.'

'But why did he come to me?' she asked.

'Ever since he died, various sailors have reported seeing him, usually on 30th May, but also at other times. And if they had any problem, he was more than happy to help them. As for coming to you…?' Chris raised an eyebrow.

Shamefacedly Vikki explained what had happened ever since she had found that text on his phone: put two and two together and come up with the totally wrong answer. She told him about going to the restaurant and only seeing him with Zoe. How glad Vikki was she had not gone into the restaurant and challenged them.

'You thought I was having an affair with Zoe?' There was a twinkle in his eye even as he asked the question. 'We had to arrange it secretly without Andrew knowing anything what was being planned. You were going to be invited, but you made it so clear that you were going to stay with your sister, so there was no point in asking you.'

'After leaving the restaurant I was determined to have it out with you, but then I met Albert and he told me about the raid, and I thought I'd never see you again…' Vikki broke off and began to sob. 'Oh, what a bloody fool I've been. So that's why Albert came to me: to stop me being any more stupid.'

Moments later she was in her husband's arms.

Six Silver Serviette Rings

When Alec, her husband, broke the news, Diana Corbett was far from thrilled at the idea, but knew she had to decide. Should she or should she not accompany him on a golfing trip with his club? She hated golf and most of its players. In short, it was fair to say she just about hated everything to do with the sport.

'But you know how I detest the sport…and…as for the attitude of your fellow members and their wives? Just how much enjoyment do you think I am going to get out of the visit? They're such a load of snobs.' Time and time again she made her opinion known. But deep down, she knew how he would appreciate her support.

Alec knew only too well about the snobbish attitudes his wife was complaining about. He enjoyed a low handicap and desperately wanted to be accepted by his fellow club members. Whilst his playing skills worked in his favour, he was still not fully accepted by several of the older members. Money was not a problem to Alec and Diana: and they lived at the right address. Nevertheless, they were still regarded by many of the members as newcomers. And there was another problem.

They both worked.

He and Diana dealt in antiques, albeit very upmarket ones, which did not sit too easily with some of the more influential and snobbish members of the club. Whilst most of them accepted Alec as a member, if not exactly one of *them*, they tended to keep away from Diana, although not necessarily from choice.

She was a very down to earth person who had no qualms about telling the truth, regardless of whom she upset. Many of the other wives envied her figure, expensive clothes and jewellery. Her natural good looks meant she only needed the minimum amount of make-up. And they worked hard to keep their men away from her.

'I'll make a deal with you, if you agree to come,' Alec proposed. 'I won't expect you to follow me round the course. If you did, it would be done with such bad grace as to put me off my stroke!'

Diana grinned.

'You can go off and do your own thing. I believe it's quite an interesting area and who knows, there might even be the odd bargains to be found.'

Faced with such a compromise, Diana felt she had no alternative but to agree, albeit unwillingly with him.

All too soon the dreaded day arrived, and she reluctantly accompanied Alec on his golfing week-end. They travelled on the Thursday, so he could play on Friday, Saturday afternoon and Sunday morning, before coming home.

It was early evening when they arrived, and Diana had to endure a tediously boring buffet reception given by their hosts. She tried to be sociable and made polite conversation with some of them, but Diana was not enjoying herself.

This was hardly surprising when the sole topic of conversation everywhere was golf.

Towards the end of the evening, she found herself talking to a tall well-dressed, middle-aged woman who stood on her own. Diana noticed that the woman's quality clothes were dated. Even her hair style had a 1940s look about it.

'You look as bored as I am,' announced the woman to Diana, who nodded and smiled in agreement.

They spent the remainder of the reception together and Diana learnt the other woman's name was Sheila Driscoll. She used to live in the house which had once been on the site of what was now the golf club. Before they left, the two women agreed to meet the next morning in town for coffee.

They met next day as arranged and enjoyed their coffee in some quaint, old fashioned tea-rooms, complete with staff smartly dressed in black, wearing white aprons, head bands and cuffs. A musical trio played softly in the background. Diana thought their selection of 1930s and 1940s music seemed most appropriate for the genteel ambience of the place. She noticed the other coffee drinkers wore old-fashioned clothes and thought how delightful they were and really suited their surroundings.

Whilst they drank their coffee, out of quality china cups, Diana told Sheila about their antiques business.

'Ah!' replied Sheila. 'An antiques dealer! There are several places in town, nearly all worth a visit, but I don't know what their prices are like.' She suggested some for Diana to visit in a half-hearted way, but added there was only one place to go: Driscoll's. It was her father's business, she added with a smile.

They parted company and Diana began to trawl the antique shops. She lost track of time but was not particularly impressed by them. They were very expensive and not keen on giving trade discounts to a fellow dealer. It was late afternoon before she found Driscoll's.

And what a find!

The shop was situated down a narrow alley which Diana had not noticed before. If Sheila had not given her specific instructions, she would never have found it. When she opened the door, an old-fashioned bell rang, and Diana felt like she had stepped back in time.

The shop did not just sell antiques, but also stocked numerous other quality items, which Diana estimated would have been made in the 1930s-40s if not earlier. Before the sound of the bell died away, an elderly, white haired and stooped man appeared.

Diana was both surprised and impressed to see he was wearing an old-fashioned white shirt with a wing collar, waistcoat and tail coat. A gold watch chain and pince-nez completed his outfit. Yet, he did not look at all out of place in the shop.

'Good afternoon, madam,' he greeted her with a genuine smile. 'How may I be of assistance to you?'

'I was wondering if I might just look round, as I don't really know what I want.'

'Of course. Please feel free to browse. If you have any questions, then don't hesitate to ask.'

Diana felt like a small child who had been let loose in a toy shop, as she looked at all manner of items, almost in disbelief. The prices were all very low and many of them were priced in guineas. How quaint, she thought. Coming on Alec's golfing tour seemed to have been not such a bad idea after all.

Becoming so involved in the items, Diana completely lost all track of time.

'I'm afraid we're closing soon, madam.' The man's voice broke in on her thoughts.

'You've got so much here, I'm spoilt for choice.' Diana quickly checked her handbag, but found only a few coins, her cheque book and cards. 'I do hope you take plastic?'

'Plastic? What do you mean, madam?'

Taken aback, she explained about credit and debit cards.

But he shook his head. 'I'm sorry madam, but we only deal in cash, or cheques up to the value of £10.'

'Never mind, I'll buy something now and come back tomorrow with some more cash.'

'As madam wishes.'

She finally purchased a set of six early Victorian silver serviette rings in very good condition, for the princely sum of £10 and paid for them with a cheque. They were priced at ten guineas, but he gave her a discount when he discovered she was a fellow dealer. Diana watched as he carefully wrapped them in tissue paper and wrote out a receipt in beautiful copperplate handwriting.

After shaking hands, Diana picked up her purchase, put it in her handbag and went back to meet up with Alec.

He was on a high after having enjoyed a very good score and was well in the running for being one of the winners. As per their arrangement, they dined together, and did not go back to the golf club bar afterwards. 'How was your day?' he finally asked, having already noticed her bubbly excitement.

She told him about meeting up with Sheila Driscoll and going to the antique shop. Diana was surprised he had not noticed Sheila at the reception because she was a very striking woman. But now she remembered how strange it was Sheila had been on her own.

As Diana finished the tale, she opened her bag with a flourish. 'DAH! DAH! DAH! What do you think of these?' She produced the serviette rings and Alec was impressed. Having inspected them carefully, he could not believe how little she had paid for them. He agreed they would have to visit the shop again in the morning.

Soon after breakfast and having taken a fair amount of money from a cashpoint, she took Alec back to Driscoll's, as he was not playing again until the afternoon.

The problem was she could not find it. Neither could she find the tea rooms from the previous morning.

After spending time in a fruitless search and asking questions, she still could not find the shop. Yet Diana knew she had not forgotten Sheila's directions. Unwilling to admit defeat, they went into the nearby police station and asked the same question. 'Can you direct me to Driscoll's Antiques, please?'

'I'm sorry, madam, but the name doesn't ring a bell with me. But then I haven't been here very long,' replied the counter clerk. 'Do you have an address for this shop?'

'Oh, stupid me!' sighed Diana. 'Of course, it's on the receipt.' Reaching into her handbag, she found the receipt and handed it over.

The clerk looked at it for a moment. 'Just a moment madam: as I said, I'm new to this area, but I know someone who might be able to help you.' He went back into the front office, lifted a telephone and dialled a number. After a few seconds he spoke quietly into the receiver and then replaced it. A couple of minutes later, an elderly man appeared from another door and approached Diana and Alec.

'Are you the people trying to find Driscoll's Antiques?'

They nodded.

'Will you come this way please?' He led them into a small office.

Totally puzzled they followed him and took the proffered seats.

'Would you mind telling me why you want to know about Driscoll's?'

Briefly Diana told him about buying the serviette rings and wanting to return to the shop to make some more purchases.

'Just a minute,' interrupted Alec. 'Why all the interest in my wife's purchases and who are you?'

'I'm Arthur Driscoll, a former detective sergeant here. I'm also a local historian and police archivist.' He paused, seeing they had made the connection between his name and the antique shop. 'Driscoll's Antiques and the alley in which it stood, were totally destroyed in an air raid on 14

September 1942: Exactly seventy years ago last night. The whole area was never rebuilt as such and today's Shopping Mall was ultimately built on the old site.'

'But I was recommended to go there,' spluttered Diana, totally disbelieving what she had just heard.

'Was it by a good-looking woman called Sheila Driscoll, who you met at the golf club?' queried Arthur. 'I appreciate it's an old photo, but is this her?' Even as he spoke Arthur showed them an old black and white photograph. It was a picture of a good-looking woman.

'Why yes. That's her. How did you know that? Who is she?'

'My grandmother, whom I never knew. She and her father were killed in the same air raid, which also demolished their house which stood where the golf club is today. You're not the first person she's sent to the shop.'

'I still don't understand. I definitely bought these serviette rings yesterday and I've got the receipt to prove it.'

'Can I see it please?'

Diana handed the receipt to Arthur.

He read it carefully before speaking. 'Did you read it properly?' he asked.

'I was there when he wrote it,' Diana replied testily.

'But did you read it, or just pick it up?'

'He wrapped it up with the serviette rings.'

'Have another look at the date.'

Both Diana and Alec looked at the receipt more closely.

The date read 14 September 1942.

Diana was lost for words. 'You don't believe me, do you?' she said at last.

Arthur said nothing but opened the briefcase he had brought with him and took out a large ledger. He put it on the desk and opened it where a book mark showed between the pages. Then he turned it round for Diana and Alec to read. 'Oh, I do believe you. Somehow this sales ledger survived the blast,' he explained. 'Take a look at its very last entry.'

They saw that the last page was dated 14 September 1942. But what intrigued them more, was the final entry for that day. It read:

6 Silver serviette rings ... £10.0s.0d.

The Watcher

Vic Field was more than satisfied with his day's work.

He had just sold a very expensive motor car for a very good profit: all of which was tax free. As far as Her Majesty's Revenue and Customs were concerned, Vic did not exist. Even if they knew about him, he could hardly admit his true occupation and declare all the money he made by selling stolen cars.

In fact, Vic was much more than just a car thief.

He specialised in stealing expensive motors to order. Most of his clients were foreigners and by the time they collected their new motor, it would be totally unrecognisable to its original owner. All its previous unique identifying features had been removed, altered or others added.

A change of colour: number plates: important looking stickers on the windscreen, were only some of the changes he made. With his computer skills, Vic had no problems in creating fake log books and tax discs.

The icing on the cake for Vic was the fact the new purchaser would never realise the car had done many more miles than were showing on the clock, as he was an expert at changing these. The fact they were supposed to be tamperproof was no problem to him. Most of his customers were under no illusions about the motor's true origins, but provided the car and its price were right, they asked no questions.

Having no real overhead expenses to worry about, Vic always ensured the price was right. And he only dealt in cash. Besides, he could hardly set off any expenses against tax! He simply added them to the price.

Now he was on his way home in a non-descript car which he had just stolen from a nearby housing development. And as an unexpected bonus, its owner had left all his driving documents in the car. Vic knew he was taking a risk and would normally have travelled home by train, first class naturally. But it was Sunday with a very limited service aggravated by repairs being undertaken on the track. It had been a long, busy day and he really wanted to get home.

The strange thing about this transaction was it happened in his home town of Warwick: a place which he had not dared to visit for more than thirty years in case someone might have recognised him.

How well he remembered all those years ago, when along with several other youths of a similar age, Vic was bored and always craving for excitement. When he looked back on those times, he could never be sure exactly how their *sport* began: only boredom was the cause.

Sport was probably not the correct word for what they did.

Their *Sport* involved stealing and racing motor cars. Whoever did the agreed circuit in the fastest time became the winner and was awarded a prize: usually alcohol or cigarettes stolen from local off-licences or newsagents. There was an extra bonus if they could complete the course without being stopped by the police or damaging the car.

This latter practice was not out of any consideration for the car's rightful owner, but because the *joy riders* as they were called, looked upon it as being a real test of their driving skills.

Not everything always went to plan, and mishaps sometimes happened along the way. Quite often cars were damaged, and arrests made. But despite these *occupational hazards* for the *joy riders,* the police failed to make much impact on their activities.

Until Vic's fateful night some thirty years ago.

The evening had started just like all the others, and it was Vic's turn to try and beat the existing speed record. Several members of the gang, and other outsiders, had considerable sums of money riding on the outcome.

All started well, and Vic was making very good time until he left the town and sped out into the country, when he became aware of a car quickly coming up behind him. He soon realised it was a police car when it activated its blue light and siren.

As far as Vic was concerned this all added to the fun. He had been chased before, albeit unsuccessfully, by the police and he felt sufficiently confident in his driving ability to out run them on this occasion.

Vic quickly sped away. As he and everyone else knew, the general radio and television reception out here was very poor. And he had little doubt it was the same for the police radio equipment.

The police car stayed with him as he accelerated up the main road and into the countryside. At the very last minute, and without giving any warning and using the handbrake, Vic turned sharply right into the unsigned Monks Lane. It was so named after the old religious house which was once sited nearby.

Local folklore maintained the monks had the task of watching over the safety of all travellers using the lane. Today only a few shapeless chunks of ruined walls were left of the building. The area was reputed to be haunted by the ghosts of those old monks.

The ancient but still current belief was the monks were succeeded by the ghosts belonging to other travellers who died on this stretch of road. The legend stated whenever a traveller was killed here, their spirit remained earthbound until it was relieved by the next victim. Only then could it escape.

Whilst earthbound, the spirit had to prevent any other travellers being killed. The irony being if successful, the spirit was condemned to wait even longer for release.

Vic never believed such tales. Nobody in living memory could remember having seen any ghosts round here, although the stories were used regularly to frighten younger children.

Very much to Vic's chagrin and dismay, the police car had anticipated such a move and still followed him. Vic was forced to slow for the vicious right-handed bend half way down the lane, which enabled the police car to get closer to him. Suddenly he saw a dark figure step out in front of him. Swerving sharply, Vic braked hard and missed hitting it, although his car ran slightly off the road before it regained the carriageway.

The police car was not so lucky.

Its driver also swerved to miss the figure, but in doing so lost control. The car ran off the road and collided with a tree before it overturned.

For a few seconds Vic studied it from his car mirror, but nobody climbed out. He thought for a moment about going to see if he could help, then shrugged his shoulders and drove away.

It was not his problem.

Later it was revealed the police driver had still been alive after the initial impact, and even the most elementary first aid could have saved his life. But Monks Lane was a quiet backwater and he was not found until much later.

By then it was too late, and he had died.

For all his bravado, the experience shook Vic more than he had expected. To make matters worse, he had gone to school with the dead man's brother. Realising it would not be long before his name was given to the police, he quickly left Warwick and never returned.

Until tonight.

Vic was just over seventeen years old when he left home, which his parents agreed was a blessing. Having no time for their wayward, rebellious and lawless son, they were glad to see him get out of their lives. The feeling was entirely mutual. If he had not left of his own accord, it was only a matter of time before they threw him out.

After Vic left home, his parents were grateful they never saw or heard from him again.

Now, after all those years he was back in his old town, but it had changed so much as to be almost unrecognisable with new houses being built all over the place.

A few minutes later, and quite by chance, or so it seemed, he found himself driving out of town in the direction of Monks Lane. Suddenly, he was aware of a police car pulling in behind him with its blue lights flashing. He was tempted, but only for moment, to drive off, but decided to stay and bluff it out. Police cars were much more powerful than they had been in his younger days.

Vic indicated and pulled over into the nearside of the road, stopped his car, wound down the window and waited.

'What's the problem, officer?' he politely asked the policeman who approached him, confident that there would not be any of them left now who had known him thirty years ago.

'Good evening sir: it's just a routine check. There's been a spate of burglaries in the area.'

'Please feel free to check the boot,' Vic replied with a confidence that was rapidly deserting him.

There was something very familiar about the constable who was checking out the boot. The man was clearly coming towards the end of his service, but Vic found his face seemed worryingly familiar.

'Have we met somewhere before?' queried the constable, who was also experiencing similar feelings. 'Only your face seems familiar to me. Weren't we at school together?'

'I don't think so. I'm not from round here. You must have me muddled up with someone else.'

Vic now recognised the policeman only too well. He had been at school with him, although in the year below: and his name was Mathew Davie: the brother of PC Colin Davie who had been killed in Monks Lane whilst chasing him all those years ago.

'I've only just moved into the area,' explained Vic with a confidence which he no longer felt. 'Look, here's my driving licence and insurance. As you can see, I'm Derek Harper.' Vic handed over the documents for the constable to inspect.

Vic silently thanked the real Mr Harper, whoever he was, for leaving them in the car.

'That's fine, Mr Harper. I'm sorry to have bothered you,' replied Mathew Davie as he handed back the documents. 'By the way, I see you're heading out towards Monks Lane. Just a quick word of warning: the whole site has been purchased for a housing development, and the lane ceases to be a public road at midnight tonight and will be blocked off. So, don't get caught up there.'

'Thank you, officer. I won't. Good night.' Vic watched Mathew return to his car. Of all the policemen to have stopped him! Nevertheless, Vic was confident he had got away with it.

Vic did not see the thoughtful look on Mathew's face as he returned to the police car.

'There's something not quite right here,' he confided to his colleague. 'Despite what he says, I do know him.'

'You and your suspicious mind,' chided his crew mate. 'What are you going to do when you retire next year? Still keep chasing ghosts?'

'I really would like to know what happened to Vic Field, who was responsible for my brother's death all those years ago in Monks Lane. We must make a final visit there before it closes tonight.'

His companion remained quiet.

He had been in the police for fourteen years, and in his early days well remembered his older colleagues talking about Colin Davie's death. As far as Mathew Davie was concerned the case was still open. And like many policemen he believed criminals always returned to the scenes of their crimes sooner or later. Perhaps Mathew was right to keep the case open: after all it was his brother who had been killed. But, realistically, even if he found Vic, there would be little chance of taking him to court after such a long time.

'Bear with me a moment,' said Mathew as he picked up the radio transmitter and contacted their control room.

Meanwhile, although he knew he should be miles away by now, for some reason Vic felt himself being drawn to Monks Lane. Whilst it was an unfortunate part of his life, it had also been the making of him. He knew too if he was now identified, there was little chance of the case ever coming to court. The worry was if he was arrested, what else might the police discover about him: his thieving and his contacts? They would certainly not take kindly to having their details going to the police. Whilst Vic knew better than to tell the police about them, there was always the risk about what the police might find. His best bet was to leave the area as quickly as he could and ditch the car.

Turning into the Lane, he put his foot hard down on the accelerator. 'Just for old times sake,' he said aloud to himself.

As he came to the sharp right-handed bend, a dark figure suddenly stepped out in front of him. Vic swerved to miss it, but in doing so lost control of the car, which went off the road and wrapped itself around a tree.

It was the same tree which Colin Davie's car and others had hit, although those scars had long since grown over.

When Vic slowly opened his eyes, he was relieved to see a police car arrive. But on looking closer, he saw it was an old-fashioned model from about thirty years earlier, with a single blue light on its roof, instead of the more modern light clusters. Also, the policeman who climbed out of it was not wearing any fluorescent jacket and his tunic looked old fashioned.

Although the figure of the policeman seemed hazy and indistinct, Vic had no difficulty in recognising him. He had seen enough of his photographs in the newspapers following the crash.

'Hello Vic,' said Colin Davie. 'I always knew you'd come back here sooner or later.'

'I never meant to kill you that night.'

'I know, but if you had only given me a little bit of first aid, then I would have survived. Instead you left me to die. And I left a widow and two small children.' Although quiet, Colin's voice was still accusing.

Even as he spoke, Colin's image seemed to be slightly fading. In the distance Vic gratefully heard approaching two-tone horns, which meant real help was on the way.'

'It's all yours now,' said Colin.

'What do you mean?'

'Don't you remember the legend? Believe me it's all true. It's your job now to look after travellers on this lane until the next one is killed, who will have to take your place. Only then will your spirit be freed. That was why the monks were here in the first place. This lane has been cursed for hundreds of years and it was their job to protect travellers. But they've long since gone and now the dead protect the living. I tried to stop you, just as my predecessor tried to stop me. It's been a long wait for you. But as the lane closes in a few minutes, I fear you'll have a much longer wait than I did… probably for all eternity.' Colin's voice tailed off and both he and his police car faded away.

Vic's eyes closed.

When Vic opened his eyes again, he was aware of several fire fighters and ambulance personnel all trying to free him from the wreckage. He also saw Mathew Davie looking pleased. Mathew's colleague stood nearby and was very quiet as he tried to understand what had happened.

A quick radio call followed by a visit to Derek Harper soon established his car and driving documents had been stolen. This information strengthened Mathew's suspicion the driver was Vic Field who had stolen the car. The police car had driven to Monks Lane where they found him in the wreckage.

Even as he watched what was happening to him, Vic was surprised to see he was hovering above his own body. He saw a paramedic put his stethoscope away and shake his head.

'He's dead,' he announced to the policemen.

'Justice has finally been done,' Mathew said quietly. 'Rest in peace Colin. It's Vic Field's turn to watch the lane now.'

'NO...O...O...!' howled Vic.

Marjorie's Cat

After a busy few days, everything on this Sunday afternoon suddenly seemed very quiet and dull to Jack Hazelwood.

He was the latest addition to 'A' Shift at Warwick police station. Having only just finished his initial training, Jack was now a probationer learning the practical side of the job, under the watchful eye of Don Avery. Although his mentor had only been a policeman for just over four years, he was a steady constable who happily passed on his knowledge and experience, to the younger members of the Shift.

Both men worked well together, although Don was a few years older than the probationer, having been late in joining the police. Because of the way the shift pattern fell, Jack had only started on Wednesday for the 2-10pm shift, usually called *lates*. The first four days were busy, but this Sunday afternoon was different. It was a good time for catching up on paperwork, or just carrying out routine patrols, without too many emergencies happening. And they had just called back to the police station for a mug of tea.

'It's so quiet! Doesn't anything ever happen? On a Sunday afternoon?' moaned Jack. 'Can't we have a murder or something?'

'Even if we did,' Don replied tolerantly. 'We'd never have anything to do with it. It'd be a job for the CID…and don't you go tempting fate by mentioning the **Q** word,' he smiled wagging his finger at Jack. 'When it's quiet, we like to keep it that way.'

Just as he finished speaking, Don's personal radio came to life. 'Control to Echo 4!' It was their call sign.

'Echo 4. Go ahead control,' answered Don, still wagging his finger at Jack.

'Apologies for interrupting your tea break, Echo 4, but can you go to…'

Don made a writing sign to Jack, who took down the details of some shop premises, where an ambulance was attending the scene of a sudden death.

*   *   *

Swallowing the rest of their tea, Don and Jack went to the newsagent and confectionery shop where the ambulance was waiting. They drew up behind it and Paramedic Ted Hammerton came out of the nearby shop and met them. He and Don knew each other, and Jack was introduced to Ted.

'Forgive me for perhaps stating the obvious,' Ted announced without any preamble. 'But she's not one we can take as she's very obviously dead, so you'll need an undertaker…But…I think you'll need a police surgeon first or even a pathologist for this one.'

Don looked expectantly as Ted continued. 'The deceased woman is a Mrs Marjorie Candlestone, who was an alcoholic. And on the face of it, alcohol appears to have caused her death. But…it doesn't feel right. Come and have a look for yourselves and see what you think?'

As they followed him, Don looked at Jack, grimaced, shook his head and wagged a finger at him. 'Remember what you've been taught,' he instructed. 'Don't touch anything. Put your hands in your pockets!'

Ted led the way into the shop, which was a very small and narrow building. It seemed to Jack as if it had been squeezed in between two larger premises. Downstairs consisted of the shop area, stockroom, kitchen and a small living room, complete with a bed. Upstairs was reached by a steep staircase running off the main part of the shop area, with a curtained downstairs entrance, and leading into a small bathroom and bedroom.

Going into the shop, Ted introduced them to Harvey Candlestone, the elderly husband of the dead woman. He ignored them and just sat in the shop area as if in a trance. The policemen assumed he was in shock.

The three men wrinkled their noses as the stale smell of alcohol hit them long before they went into the bedroom.

Ted pushed open the door and the two policemen saw the naked and emaciated body of Marjorie Candlestone lying on the bed. Even the most inexperienced eye could see she was dead.

'What's bothering you, Ted?' asked Don.

'The old man downstairs says she drank herself to death, which may or may not be true, but firstly I'm not happy with these.' Ted indicated some blue and red marks around her mouth 'A post mortem will decide what they are, but I think they're bruises. And if so, they were caused before she died… and if that's the case, then drink could have been forced down her, which resulted in her death.'

Ted paused before he pointed at four empty whisky bottles lying on the floor around her bed. 'Whilst I'm no expert, she could not have drunk the contents of all those bottles in one session. She'd have been unconscious, if not dead, long before she got anywhere near finishing the first one.'

'Could she have kept them on her bed and they just fell off at some stage?' Jack asked.

'Possibly, and a good question,' answered Ted. 'I've been to other similar deaths, but these bottles don't look like they've fallen on the floor. They look more like they've been placed there and made to look as if they've fallen. But they're all empty. And that's what I find strange. Almost certainly the last one she was drinking from would still have had some whisky in it.'

Don nodded his head in agreement.

'Perhaps the old man downstairs polished her off,' Ted added cheerfully. 'But I'm off for my tea now, so I'll leave it with you. Bye!'

Leaving the room, Ted paused at the top of the stairs and turned back to the policemen. 'By the way,' he warned with a mischievous grin. Shaking his hands on either side of his face. 'Take care. Old Marjorie here was reckoned to be a witch, who often turned herself in to a big black cat. You have been warned. Take care.'

Then he was gone.

Jack gazed, fascinated, at the scene. 'Do you think it really is a murder?' There was a quaver in his voice. 'Do we call the CID?'

'I really don't know, but we'll tell the CID to be on the safe side.' Even as he spoke, Don picked up his radio and began to speak.

Control replied it would be at least an hour or more before the CID or anyone else could arrive. In the meantime, they were to make do as best as they could.

'Bloody typical!' moaned Don. 'Just what you'd expect from Esso House workers!'

'What's Esso House?' asked Jack

'Every Saturday and Sunday Off,' explained Don with a grin. 'Let's go and have a word with the old man downstairs: what's his name?'

'Harvey Candlestone.'

'You can take a statement from him.'

*   *   *

Harvey Candlestone was a small, neatly-dressed man with thinning grey hair. A pair of narrow gold-rimmed spectacles gave him the appearance of being a doctor or an academic, and not the small newsagent and confectionery seller he really was. Some of his older customers usually referred to him as *Crippen*. It was unkind of them to call him after Hawley Harvey Crippen, the man who was hanged for murdering his wife in 1910. They all said Candlestone looked like him.

He was very reticent at first when they asked about his wife. Whilst he admitted she was an alcoholic, he was unwilling to volunteer any other information about her. At first Don and Jack thought his reticence was due to the shock of Marjorie's death and accepted it as such.

Gradually he admitted she spent most of the time in bed, emptying one bottle of whisky after another. 'That's why we sleep in separate rooms,' he explained, unnecessarily. Whilst he spoke, Harvey kept pulling his jacket cuff down over his right wrist. Finally, and only after much prompting, he began to tell them about the events leading up to Marjorie's death.

'I heard her shouting upstairs and the sound of falling bottles,' he began hesitantly. 'So, I went upstairs and tried to take another bottle off her: but she wouldn't let it go. There were other empty bottles lying on the floor…it looked like she'd had a right session…'

BUMP!

The noise came from the top of the stairs, and it sounded like someone was coming down them. All three men looked in that direction, but it all went quiet.

'What did you do then?' asked Jack as he continued writing the statement.

'I just left her…'

BUMP!

It was a similar sound to the other one only it sounded slightly closer. The two policemen looked at each other.

'What's that?' Jack asked nervously. 'Are we sure she's really dead? Could that paramedic have made a mistake?'

'If Ted says she's expired, then she has,' replied Don. He turned to Harvey. 'Is there anybody else upstairs?'

Harvey shook his head. Don and Jack saw he was sweating copiously across his brow and temples.

'How did the bottles come to be all over the floor?' Don took up the questioning again.

'I don't know. I just heard the clatter and I went upstairs again to see what had happened…'

BUMP!

The sounds were closer and each of the three men was a little disconcerted, but also very unwilling to go upstairs and investigate. Harvey Candlestone was sweating profusely, and Don now noticed how he was continually pulling his jacket cuff down over his right wrist.

'And then what happened?' Don continued with his questions.

'I think she must just have died and dropped the bottles, or else they fell off the bed.' Harvey licked his dry lips and fiddled with his fingers.

BUMP!

There was no doubt the thump sounds were getting closer.

'Did you try and revive her?' Don asked whilst Harvey just looked ashen faced towards the stairs

'Of course! But it was no use!' Harvey answered woodenly still looking towards the stairs.

BUMP! BUMP!

Jack abandoned his writing of Harvey's statement, stood up, crossed the room to the stairs, and pulled back the curtain. But there was nothing to be seen. He let the curtain fall back into place and turned to Don. They both saw the sweat was pouring off Harvey, and he was trembling violently.

He was also holding his right jacket sleeve cuff down with his fingers, trying to make it look inconspicuous. But, every time he moved his wrist, the cuff slid up. When it did, he pulled it back down again.

'What's wrong, Mr Candlestone?' Jack asked.

'Nothing,' came Harvey's reply. It was so quiet they had difficulty in hearing him. 'It's just the shock of her death.'

BUMP! BUMP!

The sounds were even louder and closer.

Harvey took out a handkerchief and started to mop his brow with his right hand. In doing so his cuff rose up his arm, and both policemen saw several long and freshly blooded scratches on his wrist.

'How did those happen, Mr Candlestone?' Jack asked before Don could and pointed to the scratches.

Harvey swallowed loudly before he replied. 'It was when I was trying to revive her…' He broke off and stared fixedly at the curtain. 'Her bloody cat scratched me.'

BUMP! BUMP!

Even before the sound of the last bump died away, they all saw the curtain begin to shake gently. Don and Jack drew their truncheons whilst Harvey cowered down on the floor with his hands shaking in front of his face.

'**Keep it away from me!**' screamed Harvey and he shrank even further away from the curtain. '**It's her familiar. She's a witch!**' By now he was up against the corner of the wall, cowering in fear. '**Keep it away from me!**' he pleaded. '**I didn't mean to kill her. It was an accident!**'

BUMP! BUMP! BUMP!

All three men stared as the lower part of the curtain wavered and seemed as it was going to be pulled back.

'**All right! All right!**' cried Harvey. '**Yes! I killed her! She bloody well deserved it! She made my life hell for all these years. She had it coming to her. Just keep her bloody cat away from me!**'

As Harvey finished confessing, Jack leapt up, drew back the curtain and recoiled in horror.

Standing on the bottom step was the largest totally black cat he had ever seen. The animal's back was arched: its fur bristled, and a pair of hate-filled green eyes glared at Harvey. Its tail was twitching, and the animal hissed continually through shining white fangs.

Jack let the curtain fall, hiding the cat.

Harvey Candlestone was sobbing uncontrollably as he confessed to having forced excess whisky down his wife, which had killed her. Then he had laid the bottles all around the floor. When Harvey finished his confession, Jack pulled back the curtain once more, but the cat was nowhere to be seen.

Later, and although the evidence never came out in court, the forensic scientists all agreed a cat had caused the scratches on Harvey's wrist. But they were unable to find any trace of a cat, black or otherwise, having been in the house or the shop for a considerable number of years!

AUTHOR'S NOTE

Some readers will say cats do not make that sort of noise, but I can assure you they do.

Many years ago, in my younger policing days, I went to the scene of a sudden death, with a colleague, just like as in this story, but without any suggestions of foul play. Whilst waiting for the undertaker, we were taking a statement from the deceased's husband, when we heard these heavy footsteps coming very slowly down the stairs. It was just as I described above, even the way the curtain in front of the stairs waved before revealing the cat.

Knowing there were only three of us alive in the building, it was most unnerving, and we had our truncheons at the ready, not knowing what to expect. We were very relieved when the steps were identified as belonging to a cat.

The Train Ticket

Archie Cameron would never forget Christmas 1925.

Against all the odds, he was a young man who had survived for two years in the trenches, leaving the army with the rank of captain. Even before he enlisted, Archie had no real idea of how he was going to earn a living. At one time he had considered going into the army as a regular soldier, but his experiences in the Great War put paid to such an idea.

He had seen far too many of his fellow officers and men killed or terribly wounded: and he never really came to terms with ordering his men into battle, in the certain knowledge many of them would never come back alive. To be fair, he never ordered them to do anything he was not prepared to do himself, but it all took its toll on his health. When the Armistice came, Archie was recouping in hospital having been seriously wounded a few weeks before. It had been emphasised how the army would not want him back. He was delighted and could not leave the army soon enough.

Not that he had any idea of what he would do for a living.

As luck had it, whilst Archie was convalescing, his commanding officer, Wilfred Shawbury, a successful solicitor based in Warwick, came to visit him. He respected Archie's abilities but was also conscious of the man's poor health. Wilfred once hoped his son would follow him into the practice, but a well-aimed German U-boat torpedo put paid to that idea.

Archie was a very capable officer, and Wilfred invited him to join his practice as soon as he was fit enough to be discharged from hospital and military service. Unable to think of any excuse for not doing so, Archie accepted the offer, not that he knew anything about law other than enforcing military matters. Wilfred had influence in some quarters, and quickly arranged for Archie to be discharged in late January 1919, well ahead of his anticipated demob date.

Surprisingly, Archie found he had a flair for law and enjoyed the work.

It was in such a quiet contrast when compared to all the noise on the Western Front. After some initial training, he started to follow Wilfred, specialising in property and inheritance law. Wilfred soon made it clear Archie would ultimately take over his clients after he had retired. And Archie had another very good reason for staying in the practice.

Edith Shawbury who was Wilfred's only daughter, although he always found himself tongue-tied in her company.

She was an attractive young woman, slightly less than a year older than Archie, but with a sad lined face, which was understandable. As if losing her only brother was not enough, her fiancé had been killed on the Somme. To make matters worse, her mother died soon after the Armistice.

Initially she resented Archie, feeling he was trying to worm his way into the family practice, completely forgetting it was her father's idea to employ him.

Edith also worked in the practice, and albeit unwillingly, slowly realised Archie was highly competent in his field. He quickly acquired a good reputation and brought several new wealthy clients into the practice. As the months progressed, Edith found her animosity slowly vanishing, although she still kept him at a distance. She found him quite good looking, and the shrapnel scar on his left cheek added to his appeal.

For his part, Archie slowly began to relax as his immediate war nightmares started receding. Gradually his self-confidence began to re-assert itself. He was a glutton for work and did not have much of a social life. His parents had died during the war and he had no siblings. Wilfred asked him around for the occasional meal although Edith would rarely be there, usually finding some excuse to be elsewhere. Obviously, he was aware she worked in a nearby office, but always found her to be unfriendly, aloof, and rarely spoke to him, let alone acknowledging his presence. Being aware of the family losses during and just after the war, plus her general hostility towards him, he made little attempt to get to know her, keeping their few communications to the barest minimum and then only to do with work.

It all changed one evening in 1923 when he found her crying in her office.

Enquiring what was wrong, Edith tearfully explained how she was having problems with a very complicated lease. Taking his jacket off, he spent the rest of the night helping her to get it right. As a *thank you*, she later invited him to accompany her to a ball. He desperately wanted to decline her invitation, but finally accepted it, unable to find a suitable excuse for not going.

The evening was a success and the two of them soon became good friends. In the middle of 1925, they announced their intention of getting married the following year. Wilfred was delighted. And it did not take Edith long to persuade her father to invite her fiancé to spend Christmas with them. Archie needed no second urging to accept the invitation.

On Christmas Eve, Archie intended to finish early as it was snowing, having already sent the other staff home. He was putting on his coat, when the street door opened, and Herbert Wainwright rushed into the office reception area.

'Thank goodness you're still here, Cameron,' he said, undoing his coat and flopping down into a nearby chair. 'I've got the very devil of a problem which just has to be sorted out today. Tomorrow will be too late. And you're just the man to do it.'

Suppressing a sigh, Archie took off his coat and sat down. Picking up his fountain pen, he unscrewed its top, opened a notebook and began to write as Wainwright outlined his problem.

Herbert Wainwright was a very wealthy property developer, and Wilfred's practice handled all of his considerable amount of legal work. In other words, he was a valuable client. He now had the option to acquire several run-down houses which were ripe for re-development. The difficulty was the agreement had to be signed before 9.00pm that night or the deal would be off, and the option passed to one of his rivals.

The vendor would be at Wainwright's house for drinks later that evening, but he could not wait any longer than 9.00pm, hence the urgency. Reluctantly Archie agreed to prepare the contract and bring it to Wainwright's house on his way to join Wilfred. Edith was not very pleased when he rang and told her, but Wilfred understood.

Wainwright was too good a client to lose, and business was business.

Archie put some more coal on his office fire and settled down to work.

It was nearly 7.30pm when he had finished and put the document into his brief case. Putting on his coat he checked the fire was nearly out and safe to leave, switched off the lights and left the office. A bitterly cold wind struck him, and he was surprised to see snow everywhere.

He had forgotten about the weather.

Leaving Warwick, Archie drove his car carefully along the icy and snowy lanes to the large country mansion where Wainwright lived. The house was ablaze with lights and several cars were parked in the large driveway. Wainwright's butler opened the door to him, and Archie stepped inside the house. He had been here several times before, but not at this season of the year.

The hallway was dominated by a large Christmas tree, complete with baubles and lights. Archie recognised many of Wainwright's guests as belonging to the great and the good of local Warwickshire society. Several of them knew Archie and spoke to him as he passed. Wainwright soon appeared with another guest, whom he introduced as the vendor, and led them both into his study. Archie waited whilst they carefully examined the contract. Only one or two very minor alterations were required which were rectified then and there.

The two men signed their respective parts of the contract, with Archie witnessing their signatures and adding the time.

Just as they finished, the grandfather clock in the hall struck nine.

Suddenly Archie felt very warm and tired. Wainwright offered him a drink, but Archie insisted on something non-alcoholic, said his good-byes and left the house.

As he drove away, Archie remembered he had no real idea of the way to Wilfred's house from here. He hesitated for a moment and thought about going back to the house and ask for directions. In the end he decided not to, believing he would soon pick up some signposts.

It was a wrong decision and a lack of signposts soon meant he was totally lost.

After a while he saw some lights in the distance and drove towards them. As they came closer, Archie saw it was a railway station with a train standing at one of the platforms. 'With luck,' he said aloud to himself. 'Someone can give me directions.' But even as he spoke the words, his car engine spluttered and died. Archie let it freewheel up to the station where he stopped and got out.

Archie decided to leave his car here and continue his journey by train, if at all possible. He went into the station and was relieved to see a man in the ticket office. Going up to the counter, Archie enquired if there was any train due which could take him to his destination.

'Why you be in luck, sir,' replied the ticket seller. 'That train on the other platform be leaving for there in five minutes time.'

Archie purchased his ticket and watched as the seller selected a small piece of green coloured cardboard, which he put into a franking machine. This would print the time and date from which it was valid. He saw the wall mounted clock showed the time as 10.10pm and knew the ticket would say the same. It was much later than he had realised. Putting the ticket into a trouser pocket, Archie climbed on to the footbridge which crossed the lines to the other platform where his train waited.

He saw a cosy red glow coming from the roaring fire in the engine of the waiting train illuminating the increasing clouds of steam and smoke as it prepared to depart. It all looked inviting and reminded him of his younger days, when he and his friends sometimes persuaded an engine driver to let them have a ride inside the cab.

About half-way across the bridge he heard an express train approaching at speed. Horrified he saw it was on the same line as his train. As he struggled to understand what was happening, the express hurtled into the rear of the other train: the one he was about to catch. Totally mesmerised Archie watched as debris hurtled towards him and he knew no more.

It was daylight when he awoke in a strange bed and saw Edith sitting alongside it. Her face broke into a smile as he opened his eyes.

'Where am I?' he asked.

'Here in my house.'

'What happened?'

'We were worried when you didn't arrive, so daddy phoned Herbert Wainwright, who said you'd left some time before. Anyway, Herbert organised a search party and they found you. For some reason you weren't in your car.'

'Oh yes, I remember now. It had broken down.'

'That's funny,' commented a puzzled Wilfred who had just joined them. 'It started first time and was perfectly driveable when it was found.'

'What about the train crash?'

'Train crash? What train crash?' queried Wilfred.

Archie told them what had happened.

Edith shook her head. 'I'm not aware of any railway station or even a line being there. Are you daddy?'

Wilfred thought for a moment. 'Actually, there was,' he said slowly. 'It was a big crash at the station when the night express ran into the local train which was waiting to come here. As I recall it was on Christmas Eve in 1875. Why that's fifty years ago.' He paused as he thought back. 'In fact, the station was never rebuilt, and the line was closed soon afterwards. There was always a strange atmosphere about the place, and we shunned it. No, that's not strictly true.' He grinned. 'It was always thought to be haunted, but we used to play *dare* on the old site. But we had always gone before 10.15pm which was moments before the crash happened. Strangely that's where the search party found you.'

They both persuaded Archie it must have been some sort of strange dream to do with the atmosphere of the site. Yet it seemed so real to him: he just could not believe it was only a dream.

Archie enjoyed his Christmas dinner with Wilfred, Edith and their friends, but was quite happy to see them go as he was feeling tired. He helped father and daughter wave good-bye to their guests and returned to the lounge with them. When he entered the warm room from the chill of the night air, Archie had a fit of sneezing. Needing his handkerchief, he retrieved it from a trouser pocket.

As he removed it, a small object fell out of his pocket and onto the floor. Edith bent down and picked it up for him. Her eyes opened wide in amazement when she saw what it was and passed it over to her father. He also looked at it in amazement.

It was a green coloured railway ticket timed at 10.15pm on Friday 24th December 1875.

AUTHOR'S NOTE

As a young boy, I would stay with my nana at in Dorridge near Solihull, then in Warwickshire. I had a schoolfriend who lived there, and in the winter, we would sometimes cadge a ride in a steam engine in the late afternoon as it was driven to the sheds for the night. I can still feel the heat from its fire, and see the flames and sparks dancing in the dark. Somehow diesel and electric trains do not have the same romance. Even if we still had steam trains today, no driver would risk taking youngsters in the cab with him.

Weekend Reunion

'**You've reached the chambers of Adrian Templar,**' announced the automatic voice on the telephone answering machine. 'I'm sorry there's no one here to take your call just now, but please leave your name and telephone number and someone will get back to you just as soon as they can.'

'Well old buddy,' started the message. 'Your voice hasn't changed so I know I've got the right number. Though I must say I'd have thought such an important and prosperous man as yourself, would run to employing a night shift…but obviously not. But just in case you don't recognise the voice, and it's one from your past…It's Trevor Baxter.'

Adrian sat back and replayed the message. He had never expected to hear from Trevor Baxter again, and if he was truly honest with himself, nor had he wanted to do so.

The two men had been old school friends who remained in contact for many years before drifting apart. Adrian became a very successful barrister, whilst Trevor made his money by gambling on the Futures market. Here the profits were significant, but the losses could be devastating and had financially ruined many people over the years.

Against all expectations, Trevor succeeded in this way of life, undoubtedly, as most people suspected, helped by his very wealthy wife Anna.

All had gone well until nearly eight years ago when Anna disappeared.

The police had not been particularly interested as she was an adult and there were no reasons to believe she might be at risk. Trevor had employed Ray Higgins, a private detective to try and find her, but to no avail. He was a local retired detective inspector who came with a good reputation.

His enquiries found a witness who had seen a woman answering Anna's description, getting into a car driven by a man. The witness related how he had seen the car stop and the driver get out. They had then embraced passionately, before the driver put her cases into the boot, whilst she climbed into the car and they drove off together. Ray was disappointed the witness could not describe the man nor his car, let alone remember its registration number.

A few days later he uncovered another witness who had seen a woman answering Anna's description, boarding the Paris train at St Pancras Station.

Neither of these two sightings could be confirmed and there were no others.

It has often been said once a policeman, always a policeman and such was the case with Ray Higgins. Something bothered him about this case and despite being paid off by Trevor, he continued his own enquiries. In due course he arranged a meeting with the local police to discuss the matter, but never kept the appointment.

In fact, he was never seen again and there the matter rested.

Meanwhile Trevor moved to Spain.

Seven years later Anna was officially declared dead or beyond the seas, which left him free to marry again. Not that he had been celibate during the intervening period.

It was around the time of Anna's disappearance when Trevor stopped communicating with Adrian, who was quite happy with this change in their friendship. Adrian had been aware of Trevor's growing dubious reputation about his business activities, and people he now regarded as his friends. These were not people Adrian would wish to know socially. There were also rumours of his being in debt, which was probably why Trevor moved somewhat unexpectedly to Spain.

But now he had come back into Adrian's life. The big question was why?

Adrian's immediate problem on hearing Trevor's message was he was due in court within the hour and was already running late. He had much to think about the forthcoming trial as he sat in the taxi on the way to court. Phoning Trevor would have to wait.

Although the trial was scheduled to last for three weeks, the defendant changed his plea to guilty just as Adrian started his opening speech. Whilst this sped matters up, it was still early afternoon before Adrian returned to his chambers.

Once there he had several letters to sign and telephone calls to make. By then all he wanted to do was to go home and phone Trevor from there, preferably with a large glass of Jameson's Irish Whiskey in his hand. As an added bonus, his wife, Maggie, should be there, provided she had not been called out. She knew Trevor and had been friends with Anna.

Once home, Adrian explained to Maggie what had happened, filled two glasses of Jameson's and phoned his old school friend.

After a few initial pleasantries, Trevor explained why he had rung.

In short, he invited them both to come and stay with him in three weeks' time.

He was back living in the old rambling farmhouse where he and Anna once lived, situated in South Warwickshire on the edge of the Cotswolds. Trevor had let the house whilst he was away and they would be his first guests since returning from Spain.

Maggie was not enamoured by the thoughts of spending a week-end with Trevor and could not understand why he had contacted them after all these years. Whilst she did not exactly like Trevor, she did not actively dislike him. She found a little of him went a long way and could think of many other people she would rather visit for a week-end. He was an overpowering character and a little bit free with his hands. Finally, she agreed to go with Adrian, albeit reluctantly.

Yet in spite of her misgivings, Maggie was interested.

Along with many other people, she never understood what Anna had seen in Trevor: it never appeared to be a love match. And she wanted to hear what Trevor would have to say about Anna's disappearance, and to meet Delia, his new wife.

It could be argued Maggie's interest in Anna's disappearance was not entirely idle curiosity. She was a detective superintendent and second in command of a squad which concentrated on investigating cold cases especially where domestic abuse and murder were suspected. Anna's disappearance intrigued her professionally, and she was keen to hear his version of what had happened.

*　　*　　*

Adrian left his chambers just after lunch on the warm Friday as soon as Maggie joined him. They were clear of the City by mid-afternoon and moving up to the Midlands, avoiding the motorway by mutual consent. But it was a strained, almost icy journey despite having the roof of the car down and passing through pleasant summer countryside.

'What's wrong?' Adrian asked, only too aware of her growing quietness and tension.

'I just wish we weren't going.'

'Any particular reason?'

'You've obviously forgotten it was eight years ago this week-end when Anna disappeared.'

'You mean run off, don't you?'

'Stop being a barrister and trying to make me change my story!' Maggie snapped. 'No. I mean disappeared. I know I'm suspicious, but it comes with being a detective.'

'You'll be telling me next,' Adrian retorted waspishly. 'That Trevor murdered Anna for her money and the insurance pay out. If so, then he's had a long wait.'

'It wouldn't be the first time murderers have had to wait a long time for their money, as you should well know.'

They passed the remainder of the journey in stony silence and it was with some relief when they arrived at their destination.

Trevor was the perfect host and Maggie soon found herself warming to Delia as did Adrian. After a few minutes of stilted conversation and embarrassing silences, they soon settled down in each other's company. It was if they were continuing from where they had last met only a few days ago, instead of several years. A pleasant summer evening as they sat outside on the patio having a few drinks and enjoying the sunshine, all added to the ambience.

They moved inside to eat their dinner as the evening became chilly on the patio. As Trevor and Delia had limited culinary skills, they had hired a cook for the week-end, as was their practice when entertaining guests at home in Spain. It seemed natural to continue the habit back in England. She would also prepare dinner at home for the next night and a traditional roast on Sunday lunchtime, before his guests returned to the City. Breakfast was a do-it-yourself affair which suited Adrian and Maggie as they only ever had toast and coffee. Lunch would be at a local hostelry.

Time passed, and it was 8.30pm before they sat down to dinner and by then Maggie had long since recovered her good humour. A combination of good food, and excellent wine, all added to the general ambience around the table. For a while they talked about old friends, until Delia was the first to leave and Maggie left with her.

'You know what this week-end is, don't you?' Trevor asked quietly and sombrely soon after they had gone.

'Sadly yes,' replied Adrian, silently thanking Maggie for reminding him.

Trevor had left for a business meeting earlier that morning and it was the last time he saw her. He found her missing on returning home and complained about the lack of interest shown by the police. As he spoke, Trevor became more maudlin and Adrian guessed it was mainly the wine talking. Finally, Trevor's head kept falling forwards before he accepted the inevitable, and they both staggered off to bed with mumbled *goodnights*.

Adrian had drunk a fair amount of wine, but not as much as Trevor. Climbing into bed he lay listening to Maggie's gentle snores and mulling over what Trevor had told them about Anna's disappearance.

Not for the first time he began to experience some doubts.

He was well experienced in listening to people's testimonies in court and this was how Trevor had sounded. His friend had not sounded natural, but more as if he was reading from a prepared script and trying to make his listeners believe what he was saying.

Drifting off to sleep, Adrian felt he was missing something, but he could not lay his finger on what it was.

Adrian had no idea how long he had been asleep before a strange noise awoke him. It was a scratching sound at their bedroom door accompanied by the mournful cry of an animal. Instantly he switched on the bedside light and prodded Maggie, but she remained snoring. The scratching continued, and he climbed out of bed and opened the door.

A large nondescript black dog sat outside on the landing and looked up expectantly at Adrian with big pleading eyes. The dog stood up and trotted to the stairs, where he stopped and looked hopefully back at Adrian.

'What's up pooch?' he asked gently. 'Do you want to go out?'

Going back into the bedroom Adrian put on his dressing gown and returned to the landing where the dog waited patiently. When he appeared, the dog led the way down the stairs. Following him, Adrian went through the hall towards the back door by the kitchen, which he opened. But the dog refused to go through it and went to another door instead which Adrian remembered led to the wine cellar.

'You're not going down there,' he instructed. 'It's out the back or not at all.'

The dog still did not move, so Adrian bent down, took his collar and pulled him towards the back door. As he did so, the dog fastened his teeth onto Adrian's arm and pulled him over towards the cellar door.

'Get off!' snapped Adrian as the dog's jaws hurt.

'WHAT'S GOING ON? WHO'S DOWN THERE?' called Trevor's anxious voice from upstairs.

'It's only me, Trevor. Your damned dog woke me up and I thought he wanted to go out, but apparently he doesn't…'

'Dog? Dog? We don't have a dog!'

Even as he spoke, Adrian became aware the animal had disappeared. 'I must have been dreaming,' he muttered.

'Too much wine and cheese,' chuckled Trevor, but Adrian found there was no warmth in his voice.

Trevor made quite a joke about Adrian's adventures at breakfast next morning and they all had a laugh. It was only when they were back in their room when Adrian told Maggie the full story.

'You must have been well away,' she smiled knowingly. 'Meeting up with a phantom dog indeed!'

'Then how do you explain this?' Adrian rolled up his sleeve. 'It's as if he was trying to tell me something.'

Her eyes widened when she saw the double row of fresh and obviously teeth marks on his arm.

'And that's not all,' he added and explained his feeling about Trevor not telling him the truth. 'Of course!' he exclaimed. 'That's what's missing. Anna's dog. She never went anywhere without him and it was just like the one I saw last night…'

'Don't forget,' Maggie interrupted. 'Her dog hasn't been seen since she disappeared. And the mystery witnesses who supposedly saw her getting into the car or waiting for the train, make no mention of any dog.'

'Are you two ever going to get ready?' called Trevor from below.

Adrian and Maggie had no opportunity to discuss the matter again until they were getting ready for bed later that night. By an unspoken agreement, they made a great play of appearing to be drunk whilst consuming very little alcohol. Neither of them got undressed but waited in expectation of another visit from the phantom dog.

They heard the grandfather clock in the hall strike midnight and then 1.00am.

'I think this is a waste of time,' Adrian muttered sleepily. 'I must have dreamt the…'

'Sh!' hissed Maggie. 'Listen!'

There was no doubt.

They both heard the same scratching sounds and the mournful cry of the animal. It was just as he had heard it the previous night. Now completely awake, Adrian crossed to the bedroom door and pulled it open.

Sat outside on the landing was the same black dog he had seen the night before. 'It's just like Anna's dog,' whispered Maggie.

The dog waited long enough to see they were following, before he trotted downstairs and went straight across to the cellar door. This time Adrian made no attempt to stop him but opened the door instead. Without waiting for any lights to be put on, the animal trotted down the stairs and made its way to a corner of the cellar. Here it stood, began to howl and started scratching on the flagstones on the floor.

'I knew you would find your way down here sooner or later,' Trevor's mocking voice came from behind them. 'The dog's right. There is a body buried down here, so Maggie dear, you'd better call in your troops.'

Adrian studied Trevor whilst he spoke. He said nothing preferring to be a witness and not a participant. His barrister's senses kicked in and once again he felt something was not right here.

Meanwhile Maggie was on her mobile phone to the local police. Although Trevor's house was well away from where she operated, her rank ensured she was taken seriously.

*   *   *

As what was left of the night wore on several police officers arrived accompanied by a Home Office pathologist and a team of forensic examiners, who started to dig through the floor, whilst a smirking Trevor sat on an old barrel calmly smoking cigars as he watched them.

A tired and very sceptical Detective Inspector John Logan scornfully addressed Maggie. 'With all due respect, ma'am, I accept you outrank me, but you've called this lot out after following a phantom dog who now seems to have vanished.' He waved his hand at the team digging up the floor. 'Who is going to pay for all this?'

Maggie said nothing. There was nothing she could say. The atmosphere in the cellar was electric, but Trevor still smirked with an air of wry amusement bordering on indifference. Suddenly the digging stopped.

'We've found something,' called one of the diggers. 'There are several bones here.'

The pathologist picked up his case, walked over to them and knelt by the side of the hole. Maggie bit her bottom lip and resisted the impulse to join him. Adrian looked at Trevor who was smirking all the more. After tonight there could be no going back: their friendship was irrevocably over,

Much to his surprise, Adrian felt relieved about it.

'Thank you for wasting my time!' snarled the pathologist as he stood up, brushing soil and cellar debris from his trousers. 'Yes, they're bones all right. Dog bones.'

Trevor burst out laughing.

'You said there was a body there,' retorted Maggie harshly.

'Quite right,' laughed Trevor. 'There was. But you didn't ask me whose body it was. Oh no. You preferred to believe a phantom dog. By the way, where is it? And for your information those are the bones of Anna's dog. He just pined away after she left. I buried him down here so the foxes wouldn't get him.'

Acting on John Logan's instructions, the forensics team began packing up their equipment whilst he stormed across to Maggie. 'Phantom dog! Phantom dog! How am I going to explain all this in my report? Nobody's seen it apart from you two…'

He broke off as a mournful howl filled the cellar coming from the still open grave. Everybody looked towards it and none of them would ever forget what they saw.

A large black dog was scrabbling away at the earth and howling all the time. Adrian noticed how Trevor was no longer smirking but had paled dramatically. Even John Logan had gone very quiet.

Maggie was the first to speak. 'Gentlemen, would you please dig down some more into that hole.'

They looked at John Logan who nodded his agreement.

After a few more minutes digging they stopped and called over the pathologist. He knelt on the soil and using a powerful torch examined the contents in the hole in more detail. Eventually he stood up and went across to Maggie and John.

'Please accept my apologies, superintendent,' he announced quietly. 'The other remains in this hole are definitely those of two human skeletons. One is certainly that of a male and the other a female. I would hazard a guess they have been here for a maximum of ten years but probably less.'

Seizing the opportunity when everyone was looking elsewhere, Trevor quietly stood up and made his way to the stairs only to be met by a burly policeman who shook his head at the fugitive as he put him in handcuffs.

'You are quite right,' said Trevor as John Logan cautioned him. 'I killed her and her damned dog.'

'And the other skeleton?' asked Logan, although he was not surprised at Trevor's answer.

'That's Ray Higgins. He was just too clever for his own good. He worked out I'd paid the two witnesses and killed Anna. I needed her money. I buried the dog on top of them to throw you lot off the scent. That's why I wanted you here to find the dog bones and stop all the rumours once and for all. And it would have worked if it hadn't been for that damned dog. Incidentally, where is it?'

But the dog had disappeared.

No Hands

'**Detective Superintendent Norton,**' said Lionel as he answered the telephone.

'Just to let you know, boss,' came the voice of Detective Sergeant Reg Mountford. 'We've had a report of a body being found…or to be more correct…a skeleton. I'm on my way there now.'

'Where?'

'Apparently there's some building work going on at Wolfe Manor School here in town, and that's where it has been found.'

'I'll see you there.'

Lionel put down the phone and sat back. Wolfe Manor School of all places.

It was where he had been educated some thirty-five years ago. How well he remembered the scandal when it broke in 1958. He wondered, fleetingly, if the skeleton was connected to it in any way. But he quickly dismissed the thought.

No, it was more likely to belong to yet another dead Roman legionary of which there were no shortages in the area, as he knew only too well, having lost count of the found ones he had attended. There had been a settlement nearby more than 2000 years ago and skeletons were uncovered fairly regularly, but each one had to be investigated first by the police. With any luck, he would be able to turn this one over to the archaeologists. Yet the thought still niggled especially as it was found at the school. What if it wasn't another Roman skeleton? What if…?

Either way he would soon find out.

Lionel was sent away to the boarding school in 1956 by his snobbish nouveau riche parents. They revelled in telling everyone who would listen, or who was a captive audience, how their son was at Wolfe Manor School. In fact, most people had never heard of Wolfe Manor, and were too disinterested to pursue the matter any further.

Unbeknown to them, Lionel was more than happy to be at school as it enabled him to escape from the stifling atmosphere at home. He loathed holiday times, especially in the summer when he had to accompany his parents, and their caravan, for the obligatory two weeks at Sidmouth. The end of the holidays and return to school could never come quickly enough for him.

Back at school the dining arrangements involved pupils sitting at various tables, each of which was overseen by a master. In 1958 Lionel's table was overseen by Basil Ferrers, who was always known just by his initials as BF. His parents had clearly not given any thought to that abbreviation when they chose his Christian name, making his initials short for *Bloody Fool*.

BF was an extrovert who always dressed in a flashy manner, complete with a bow tie, horn rimmed spectacles and straggly untidy hair. In many ways he resembled an eccentric professor, rather than the brilliant musician he really was. His passion was playing the organ which he did magnificently. Lionel owed his love of music to this man.

BF always carried a lucky charm which was a spent .303 calibre bullet case, complete with a silver top, which enclosed a pencil. The bullet had been accidentally fired at him by a fellow soldier during his army service. By some lucky chance it missed, but BF always kept the empty case as a reminder and a lucky charm. Whatever faults he may have had, and he had some, BF was a dedicated teacher highly regarded by his colleagues and respected by his pupils: unlike the fairly new headmaster.

At the time of the *Scandal* as it was always called, the headmaster, who also owned the school, was Major Quentin Davenport-Hallett. Wolfe Manor was one of the last privately-owned educational establishments in the area. Davenport-Hallett had no teaching qualifications, but the school had been owned by his parents-in-law. His wife, Angela, was their only child who inherited the school on their unexplained deaths in a gas filled room. The coroner brought in a verdict of *accidental death* caused by a leaking gas pipe in their bedroom. Effectively their deaths made Davenport-Hallett headmaster.

Angela was a gentle soul who often acted as a surrogate mother to the younger boys at the school. She was a complete contrast to her overbearing and bullying husband. It had not been a long marriage before she also died in strange circumstances, accompanied by rumours of taking her own life, but nothing ever came of them. The Davenport-Hallett's doctor was a long overdue for retirement wartime relic who was drunk most of the time. He signed the death certificate citing *natural causes* as the cause of her demise.

Davenport-Hallett was now in complete control as both the new owner and headmaster of the school.

Within a matter of days, the happy character of the school changed dramatically. To be fair, their exam results were extremely good. Members of the staff were too terrified not to put the maximum pressure onto the pupils. Their jobs depended on good results, and Major Davenport-Hallett accepted no excuses for failure. He insisted on retaining his former military rank of major.

At one stage he had been the military governor of a small island colonial state, which he ruled with an iron fist. He firmly believed in corporal punishment and used it regularly both as a governor and headmaster. His favourite punishment reputedly for dealing with theft, was to have the culprit's hands cut off. 'That'll stop 'em stealing again,' was his philosophy.

Whilst these tales might have been greatly exaggerated, it was known he had been suddenly removed from being governor under a very big cloud. The reasons were never disclosed but it was thought to be connected with an exceptionally hard punishment he had ordered. Fortunately for him, the war came along in 1939 and he re-joined the army. However, his old regiment refused to have him back and he served elsewhere.

It was against this background the *Scandal* happened.

On their return to school following the summer holidays, the pupils were informed of Angela's death. BF was particularly upset by the news. He had been teaching Angela to play the organ and considered her to be a very promising pupil.

The term was about half way through when a small crime wave hit the town one day where the school was sited. Items were stolen from various shops. Amongst them were a portable radio, expensive clothes from a gentlemen's outfitters and a series of music books.

On each occasion the offender was described as wearing a bow tie and horn-rimmed spectacles. And all the witnesses remembered his straggly unkempt hair. They added how he looked like the absent-minded professor from the school.

Two days after these thefts were reported, BF failed to appear at breakfast. Later that day Davenport-Hallett summoned the whole school into the assembly hall where he addressed them.

'It is my sad duty to inform you all that Mr Ferrers has been arrested by the police and charged with stealing goods from local shops.' He made no attempt to disguise the excitement and glee from his voice as he broke the news. His animosity to BF was well-known. BF had been at the school longer than Davenport-Hallett. Once he became headmaster, he tried every way he could to make him leave.

Until today, BF had always survived, but now it was a different matter.

'He will appear in court on Monday,' Davenport-Hallett continued remorselessly. 'In the meantime, he has been suspended from his school duties. As all of the stolen property was found in his room, you won't be seeing him again. If I had my way, I'd chop his hands off. He has really lived up to his nickname and been a real BF!'

He chortled merrily, and the rest of the staff joined in, albeit half-heartedly. They knew better than not to support the headmaster.

On the other hand, the boys were too shocked to react. Most of them, including Lionel, could not believe what they had been told.

BF's arrest was a big scandal which grew when he failed to appear in court. He was never seen again.

Soon after his disappearance, complaints were received about the school organ being played in the chapel at all hours of the day and night. But when people and the police arrived to investigate, they never found any signs of any organist.

In his younger days as a police constable walking the beat, Lionel often heard the organ. Sometimes he sat in the chapel and waited for the music to start, but when it did, he could never discover who was playing it.

Everyone who heard the organ agreed it was superbly played. Most people liked it, although if they had any criticism it was always solemn and never cheerful.

When Lionel found the police file on the BF affair some years later before it was shredded, he had taken a copy of it. From time to time he read through it again. He was appalled how nobody had paid any heed to BF's assertions about the stolen music books being much inferior to those editions he already owned, and which were far more valuable.

If that was true, Lionel reasoned, and assuming BF had stolen them, then questions should have been asked about his mental state. Even a basically qualified solicitor should have spotted such a weakness in the prosecution case. BF always denied the allegations.

BF maintained when the thefts happened, he was in the nearby woodlands having been sent there by Davenport-Hallett, to arrange a trail for some of the pupils to use later in the week. Davenport-Hallett always denied having given those instructions and nobody saw him in the woods.

Now in 1993, Lionel was back at Wolfe Manor School.

He parked his car by the other police vehicles, had his arrival logged and given directions to where the skeleton was in the headmaster's garden. Not that he needed the directions as this part of the school had not changed very much since he was a pupil here.

Lionel followed the marked route to where he saw a small tent. 'Anyone at home?' he called.

'Afternoon Lionel!' boomed the unmistakable voice of Charles Walton, the local Home Office pathologist. 'Come on in.'

'What have we got Charles?' Walton was only ever called Charles: never Charlie. Lionel joined him.

'At first glance I would say it's a male and been here about thirty to forty years.'

Lionel accepted it was not another dead Roman and immediately thought about the missing BF. Could this be him? 'Any ideas about the cause of death?'

'I would think probably of bleeding to death coupled with shock and trauma. Look!' Charles pointed to the skeleton and Lionel saw that both its hands were missing, and the remains of rotting clothing hung round it. 'Although it's possible they were removed after his death…'

'I don't think that's likely,' Lionel interrupted. 'If it's who I think he is, I would say their removal caused his death.'

'You know him?' Charles asked incredulously.

Lionel told him about the missing BF and Major Quentin Davenport-

Hallett.

'It's a good start,' replied Charles. 'But you'll need more than that to convince the coroner.'

The extra evidence came when the skeleton was moved.

Lying beneath it was a used bullet case, which was later confirmed as being .303 calibre and having a silver top.

When the bullet case was discovered, there suddenly came the sound of furiously playing organ music from the chapel.

Somehow Lionel was not surprised and after leaving Charles went across to the chapel and was not surprised to find there was no sign of the organist. Strangely the music was much lighter than he ever heard before, although it was still solemn.

'Where are your hands, BF?' he asked aloud.

'I'm sorry, sir?' queried a young constable who had just appeared.

'No, not you,' smiled Norton. 'Did you want me?'

'Yes, sir. There's an elderly gent here who wishes to speak to the officer in charge, and specially asked for you by name.'

Lionel followed him to another part of the chapel where an elderly man sat. Even after all these years, he had no difficulty in recognising Major Quentin Davenport-Hallett: the man who had once told him he would achieve nothing in his life and spend most of it on the dole.

'Well! Well! Well!' sneered Davenport-Hallett. 'Fancy seeing you here?' Although not as strong as it had once been, his voice still held some authority. 'I've followed your career with interest, not that I approved of any of my old boys going into the *police*.' There was a distinct sneer in his voice when he said *police*.

'What really happened to BF?' Lionel asked, adding the official police caution.

'You're much sharper than I remembered.'

Lionel was glad to see the young constable was still there and had now taken out his pen and notebook.

'It's a long story,' sighed Davenport-Hallett. 'And I don't have long to tell it, so here is the shortened version. Basically, he was having an affair with my wife. In fact, she was going to leave me for *him*.' Lionel noticed the sneer when he said *him*. 'I couldn't possibly allow that to happen, so she had to go.'

'But we all thought she had taken her own life.'

'She did,' laughed Davenport-Hallett, in between a coughing fit. 'But with quite a lot of help from me. It wasn't hard to convince the coroner and your bumbling predecessors how it had been an accident,' he paused. 'But I'm not sure I could have hoodwinked you so easily.'

In all the years Lionel had known Davenport-Hallett, this was the nearest the man had ever come to paying him a compliment.

Lionel sat back with his mind in a whirl and looked at the constable. The man was writing furiously. This confession of Davenport-Hallett to murdering his wife was the last thing he had expected. Suddenly a thought struck him. 'And her parents?'

'Such a tragic accident, wasn't it? A leaky gas pipe back in those days when gas was a killer. It was easy to loosen a joint in their bedroom having ensured the windows and door were tightly shut. That made sure Angela got the school and then it was mine after she went. She was destined not to live very long after them and her affair with BF was all the excuse I needed.' Davenport-Hallett looked at his watch as his breathing became faster.

'And BF?' asked Lionel.

'He was easy to impersonate with a wig and a bow tie whilst I stole those items and planted them in his room…then his arrest followed.' Davenport-Hallett was breathing evermore rapidly and sweat appeared on his forehead. Lionel thought it was all part of the stress the man was feeling.

'I wasn't sure the court would convict him…especially after the mistake I made with those…those…music books. So I instructed him to come to… to the house…where it was easy to drug him…and…and…cut…off…his hands…the ones he'd had on…my wife. How dare he!' Davenport-Hallett looked at his watch and his breath became more laboured.

Even before Lionel instructed him to do so, the constable was calling on his radio for an ambulance. It was obvious Davenport-Hallett was seriously ill.

Fighting now for breath, Davenport-Hallett looked at Lionel. 'Not long now,' he smirked. 'The poison…has…done…its job. And before…you ask. Yes…I watched him bleed…to death. I buried him…in…the garden.'

'Where are his hands?' asked Lionel.

Davenport-Hallett made no reply but with a last gasp fell forwards.

Both policemen did not have to be told he was dead.

A written confession was found in his jacket pocket, but it made no mention of where BF's hands were.

Later that evening after BF's skeleton and Davenport-Hallett's body had been removed, Lionel sat back in the chapel and waited. He had not been there long when the organ started playing *Toccata and Fugue* with a sense of triumph. Lionel went up into the organ loft and was not surprised to see BF sat on the stool playing the organ. However, he was at a loss to know how BF could do so without any hands.

'Where are they BF? Help me to re-unite them with you.'

BF turned and looked at him with the face Lionel remembered so well. He said nothing but started to play *Handel's Water Music*. After only a few bars, his image faded.

Disappointed, Lionel sat back and thought. Was there a clue in the last piece of music? Of course, there was! He suddenly remembered. There had always been a small water feature in the garden, and it was still in place. He would have it excavated tomorrow.

His hunch proved to be right and two skeletal hands were found by the old fountain. They were taken to the mortuary where Charles agreed they were from BF's skeleton. After all these years, BF was re-united with his hands.

Lionel went back to the chapel again in the evening and was not surprised to hear the organ playing. But unlike the other occasions it was rousing music and played magnificently. Going up into the organ loft, he saw BF playing there, but his hands were now visible on his arms.

BF turned to Lionel and smiled his thanks. Moments later he launched into *Zadok the Priest* and finished with the *Hallelujah Chorus*. As he finished there came a huge round of applause. Unbeknown to Lionel, a vast number of people had been drawn to the chapel by BF's superb music.

Turning to his audience, BF bowed to them. He followed this with a special bow to Lionel and disappeared.

BF never played the Wolfe Manor School organ again.

AUTHOR'S NOTE

A headmaster I had to endure acted rather like Davenport-Hallet, whose weekly assemblies resulted in publicly belittling any pupil who had not done well in the past few days. He would dish out his punishments then and there. These tended not to be physical, but if one did not improve, then a caning almost certainly followed. No members of staff dared to show any compassion in his presence. In my next school, there was a scandal when one of the teachers eloped with a deputy matron. There was no suggestion of foul play. We all wished them well and no mention was ever made in public about them. Combining one headmaster with such a scandal gave me the idea for this story.

Night at the Hare and Hounds

It had been a grand and glorious honeymoon for Gervaise and Emily Troughton, when they were finally able to enjoy it.

They were childhood sweethearts who became engaged in September 1914 prior to him being posted to France following the outbreak of war. They were married in 1916 whilst he was on a 48hours pass, which gave them no time for a honeymoon.

Gervaise had always been a farmer and in due course inherited his late father's estate. With his riding skills, it was only natural he became an officer in the local yeomanry, although they ultimately became dismounted and re-equipped with motor vehicles.

With the outbreak of war, his rapid departure on active service was a foregone conclusion. He was one of tens of thousands of young men in similar positions. Luckily, he had a reliable manager in John Bowman, a veteran of the Second Boer War, who was able to look after everything in his absence. John was in his late 40s and too old for military service in the immediate future. As an added bonus, Emily was a farmer's daughter and helped John manage the farm.

Soon after returning to duty following their wedding, Gervaise was seriously wounded and reported as *missing in action*. Emily never gave up hope and was relieved when the news finally arrived how he was a prisoner and effectively out of the war. Although she was glad to know he was away from front line service, Emily knew only too well not all prisoners were properly treated by the enemy. Even then news about him was scarce and his whereabouts were not known with any degree of certainty.

It was a long wait, following the Armistice in November 1918, before he was located, and proper news arrived about him.

But it was early summer in 1919 before he was well enough to be repatriated. Fortunately, he avoided the Spanish Flu, but the effects of his wounds and starvation rations in the prison camp took their toll on his health. Along with thousands of other prisoners, he would not have survived without the food parcels which had been sent from home.

Slowly Emily nursed her husband back to health, although he would never be as fit as he was in 1914. They both agreed with John that whenever possible, any vacancies on the farm should be offered first to de-mobilised servicemen. As 1919 ended and with no shortage of labour, they made plans to take their long-awaited honeymoon in the Spring.

Towards the middle of April 1920, they packed their luggage into Gervaise's car and drove away. Until the previous night, they had no clear idea of where they were going. After supper, they decided to head to Yorkshire.

Initially they spent a few days near Robin Hood Bay. Albeit slowly at first, Gervaise found some of the horrors of his recent years in France and later in Germany, began to subside. He never got rid of them completely and the worst ones stayed with him until he died. His wounds caused by an exploding shell left him with a permanent limp in his left leg. Emily was happy to find him relaxing at last and decided to extend their honeymoon by a few days.

Unbeknown to him, she had telephoned John Bowman who was more than happy to continue managing the farm in their absence for a few more days. Gervaise needed very little persuasion after Emily told him what she had arranged. But all too soon they knew the time was approaching when the honeymoon would have to end. On the way home, Emily arranged for them to stay with an old friend of hers, Dorothy Collard and her husband Frank, who lived in the Derbyshire Peak District.

They left the Yorkshire Coast late on a lovely sunny morning, but further inland, dark clouds appeared. On reaching Derbyshire, they were greeted by heavy rain which was rapidly turning to settling snow. Night fell early and driving conditions became increasingly difficult.

'It's no use, Em,' said Gervaise wearily. 'I can't drive in this for much longer. We're going to have to stop at the first available place.'

'I quite agree. Look! Over there!'

Even as she spoke, they saw the welcoming lights of a stone-built inn shining through the darkness. Gervaise needed no urging and pulled up alongside the inn, switched off the engine, sat back in the driving seat for a moment and sighed wearily. The last few miles had been very difficult driving.

They saw the inn was called the *Hare and Hounds*.

Emily led the way into a very *olde worlde* building, whose interior well matched its exterior. The general reception area consisted of oak panels which were covered in numerous framed sporting prints and sets of horse brasses. A huge blazing log fire roared out its warm welcome to the weather weary travellers. Its mantlepiece was home to a vast array of highly polished copper pots and pans.

There was no one to be seen, but Gervaise found a small bell on the counter, which he rang. 'I doubt anyone can hear it over all these noisy voices coming from the adjoining bar area.'

'It's certainly noisy,' she grinned in reply.

As if to prove him wrong, a small elderly man appeared.

'Good evening, madam, sir,' he announced in a pleasant voice. 'Welcome.'

'We're hoping you might have a room available for the night?' asked Gervaise hopefully and a little uncertainly.

'Of course,' smiled the landlord. 'I'm Jonas Makepeace and welcome to the *Hare and Hounds*. It's not a night to be out on the Peaks.'

He was a small wizened man with a face to match, which was framed by a pair of bushy sideburns. They matched his thin and greying hair. A small pair of spectacles rested on his nose.

It did not take Gervaise long to collect their luggage whilst Jonas disappeared, but he soon returned with a key and lit an oil lamp. 'Leave your luggage down here, I'll bring it up later.' he said leading the way to the stairs. 'I'm afraid there's no gas upstairs. That's why you'll need the oil lamp.'

Emily grinned mischievously which helped to re-assure her husband.

Gervaise had been used to oil lamps during the war and for a moment was frightened he was back in the trenches. His nostrils dilated, and he started to breath shallowly and quickly. Emily soon recognised the symptoms and her grin helped steer him away from those dark memories.

Once they were in their bedroom, Jonas set down the lamp and lit another three which were already there. Then he lit the fire before going downstairs for their luggage. He was only gone for a few minutes, but by the time he came back the fire was drawing well and already the room was feeling cosy.

'It's half past six now,' he said. 'I'll be serving food in half an hour. I'll reserve you a couple of places, but don't leave it too long. Today's market day and there's a lot of hungry farmers waiting to eat.'

They thanked him, and Jonas went back downstairs. Even in their bedroom, they heard the sound of their muted voices and laughter coming from underneath them. Emily quickly unpacked, and they went downstairs into the bar for a drink before they ate.

The bar was awash with jovial, red faced farmers, all of whom were enjoying their beers and an ever-growing volume of loud voices as the alcohol took effect. Jonas directed them to a single vast table in the middle of the room which was laid up for several places. 'It won't be a private meal,' he said. 'Sit anywhere you want. It'll soon fill up once the food arrives.'

About ten minutes later, Jonas and his staff appeared carrying several bowls of steaming stew and other dishes of vegetables. Their arrival caused a general rush to the unoccupied seats around the table. The snatches of conversation they heard, were mainly about farming and the weather. Gervaise was grateful not one of them mentioned the war. Undoubtedly, he thought, they had suffered their own personal sad experiences and did not want to discuss it.

They ate their supper and agreed it was excellent. Their fellow diners ignored them, not that the young couple minded. At one stage they remarked on how rough and ready the farmers looked. To call their clothes dated and very old fashioned was one way of describing them.

'They look like they've come from the last century,' Emily summed them up.

'I suppose they live in a backwater here and don't have any interest in fashion.'

'Whatever will Dorothy and her husband be wearing?' giggled Emily.

'Have you noticed how it seems as if they can't see us and are looking straight through us as if we're not here?' queried Gervaise. 'Don't you find that strange?'

Emily agreed.

Most of the farmers departed once they finished eating. The few who remained had another drink before departing with several noisy *good nights.* As if to prove Gervaise wrong for a second time, when he and Emily left, one of them called out. 'Sleep well…but don't miss the coach in the morning.'

'What a funny thing to say,' commented Emily.

Gervaise had no idea how long he had been asleep before he felt Emily shaking him.

'What's up?' he murmured sleepily.

'Listen!'

The sounds came from outside their bedroom window, and he climbed out of bed and went across to it with her. Looking out, they saw it had not snowed since their arrival and a bright moon now shone out of a cloudless sky onto the icy road below. By its light, Gervaise was surprised to see several people standing around, all well wrapped up against the cold. Their steaming breaths were clearly visible to him in the night air.

But that was not what really amazed him.

They were standing around an old-fashioned horse drawn stage coach which looked like a relic from the previous century.

'Em,' he called, uncertainly, not sure if his imagination was playing tricks. 'Do you see what I see?'

'Yes.'

As they watched, the four steaming horses were unhitched and led away to the rear of the inn, where warmth and food no doubt awaited them. They were quickly replaced by a fresh team. Once these were harnessed up to the coach, one of the passengers opened its door and climbed inside. The door was swiftly closed behind him. Four other passengers clamboured up onto its roof. No sooner were they on board than the driver cracked his whip and the horses moved off at a smart trot into the night, leaving their tracks and hoof prints in the snow. The other people quickly went back inside the inn, and peace and quiet returned.

'I didn't know they still used such coaches,' Gervaise shook his head in amazement.

'That must explain what the man said about not missing the coach. He must have thought we were waiting for it.'

When they dressed the following morning, the inn was strangely quiet. Emily packed their cases which Gervaise took out to the car. She joined him just as he came back inside.

'It's most strange,' she said. 'There's absolutely no one around. All the fires are out and that includes those in the kitchen. There's no breakfast I'm afraid,' Emily added shaking her head.

'I'm sure we'll survive,' he grinned. 'Let's go and settle up, then head over to Dorothy and Frank's for a late breakfast.'

They returned to the reception area where Gervaise rang the bell on the counter, but no one answered it. He rang it several times more, but still no one appeared.

Looking around they found an envelope and some paper. He put some money into it and wrote a short note to Jonas Makepeace explaining what had happened. Gervaise added their address in case the money was not enough.

Going back out to their car, Emily stopped and gripped her husband's arm. 'Look,' she said. 'Look at snow and tell me what you can see?'

But he had already seen what had attracted her attention.

'The same as you. Just the snowy road and our wheel tracks from last night and our footprints going in and out of the inn, but that's all. There's nothing else.'

'What about the tracks made by the coach?'

'Absolutely no trace whatsoever,' Gervaise was adamant. 'It's as if it had never been here. But we both saw it and those passengers didn't we? Tell me I didn't imagine it?' he added in a worried voice fearing it might be the return of one of his now faded wartime hallucinations.

'No, my love,' she reassured him gently, taking his hand. 'It wasn't your imagination running wild. We both saw it. And look at the way those farmers seemed look straight through us.'

'Another thing too,' he continued. 'When we looked out at the coach, did you see our car? It should have been where the coach was standing?'

She shook her head.

'Me neither.'

'All of a sudden I've got a bad feeling about this place and I think we ought to go.' Emily shivered, and it was not all due to the cold weather.

Gervaise needed no second urging.

It took them just over an hour to reach the large country house where

Dorothy and her much older husband Francis Collard lived. Both were at home enjoying a late breakfast and were pleasantly surprised to receive their visitors whom they had not expected until after lunch. Whilst Emily and Dorothy were talking, Francis, always called Frank, noticed Gervaise looking enviously at the remains of his breakfast.

'Would I be right in thinking you haven't had any breakfast yet today?' Frank asked him quizzically.

Gervaise nodded.

Several minutes later, he and Emily sat down to a much-appreciated breakfast. Their hosts waited patiently until they finished before speaking. 'Now can you put us out of our misery and tell us how you happened to arrive here this morning without having had any breakfast?' Frank asked.

He and Dorothy listened intently whilst the visitors related their story.

'I don't know where you stayed last night,' interrupted Frank, shaking his head when they mentioned the inn. 'But it certainly wasn't at the *Hare and Hounds.*'

'But we did stay there,' insisted Emily. 'The landlord was such a nice man. What was his name Gervaise?'

'Jonas Makepeace.'

Frank paused with his coffee cup half-way to his mouth. 'Jonas Makepeace you say? The Makepeaces did own the *Hare and Hounds* but that was way back in the last century and even earlier than that. It was an old coaching inn and survived despite the arrival of the railways.'

'We did see a coach and horses there early this morning,' added Emily. 'We both did, and it was waiting for passengers.'

'You can't have,' stressed Frank, shaking his head. 'The inn burnt down sometime in the 1860s and was never rebuilt. Over the years local farmers took away stones from the ruins and used them to build walls and outhouses. There's nothing left of it now.'

Gervaise and Emily were unable to convince their hosts about their experiences at the *Hare and Hounds*, and they suggested taking their hosts to show them the inn. Realising there was no other way of convincing their guests, Frank and Dorothy agreed.

After driving for just over an hour, Frank stopped the car by an open space, and they all got out. 'This is definitely where the inn stood. I well remember my grandfather bringing me here. But as you can see, there's no trace of it now. You didn't recognise it, did you? And look, how could you have stayed here?'

'Do you know where the main entrance was? asked Gervaise. 'I think this could be it, but it looks so different. What do you think Em?'

'I really don't know.'

'I'm not sure now, but yes...I think it could well be here. Let's go and look,' replied Frank confidently.

The wet ground around them was gently steaming as the snow melted in the sun.

Frank led the way to where he said the main entrance had once been situated. Gervaise and Emily refused to believe they had not stayed in the *Hare and Hounds* the previous night.

Suddenly Frank stopped and looked down at the ground. They all crowded round to see what he was studying, and then picked up.

It was a dry envelope lying on the soaking ground and addressed to Jonas Makepeace in Gervaise's handwriting. He opened it and found the letter and money Gervaise had placed there earlier that morning. Frank admitted to himself, there was no way Gervaise or Emily could have put the envelope there since they had just only arrived and not been out of his sight.

'I've lived here for several years and have never heard about the *Hare and Hounds*,' said Dorothy, breaking the silence following Frank's discovery. If that's the case, then how did Emily and Gervaise, who have never been here before, know about it unless they really were here last night?'

AUTHOR'S NOTE

Many returning servicemen in 1918-1919 had problems finding employment, regardless of the promises they had been given. Their pre-war jobs had been filled and employers were unwilling to dismiss their current staff, especially if they were good workers. In many cases, these positions had been given to women who also argued how they needed the money to feed and clothe their children, especially if they were widows, just as much as the returning servicemen did.

Gervaise's policy to only employ ex-servicemen was a generous offer, followed by some employers, but it was only a drop in the ocean.

Phantom coaches and horses at one time were popular ghostly appearances. I suspect today's volume and speed of travel has ended their ghostly journeys.

Obadiah

Although he liked to call himself the *Honourable Vernon Andrew Mainwaring*, he had no legitimate claim to such a title. Certainly, he had rarely done anything honest let alone honourable, in his life to date. Although Vernon had never known his father, Chester Mainwaring, he was grateful for his surname which was pronounced *Mannering*. He mistakenly believed it indicated he came from the upper classes of society.

His school mistress mother quickly realised her mistake soon after their marriage. She had fallen for Chester's drunken charms and delusions of grandeur when they first met. Unlike Vernon, her husband had done one honourable thing in his life. Once he knew she was carrying their unborn child, he married her. Fate then took a hand.

Chester never saw Vernon because he was killed just a few days after their marriage, in a drunken accident. His unexpected yet welcome death, freed his widow from a life of misery. The problem was he left her no money and she was forced to live on her wits and relying on whatever teaching positions arose.

Having a very young child to look after, made it difficult for her to find full time employment and she was forced to chase short term teaching posts wherever they appeared. One advantage of being a teacher meant Vernon was educated at the same schools where she worked. Thanks to his mother, he had been reasonably well educated. But no matter how hard he pressed, she told him next to nothing about his father.

All this moving around was good training for the young Vernon in his later life.

To be fair, he was a pleasant and plausible man who was now in his early forties. Vernon charmed his way through life and various members of the opposite sex, regardless of their marital status. Even more so if they had money, which was a commodity he always needed. Confrontations with irate husbands often followed, resulting in him leaving the area rather quickly. Going in such a fashion, meant bills were unpaid. As far as Vernon was concerned, these were unexpected bonuses.

From time to time, he indulged in small frauds usually by opening bank accounts without possessing any genuine security or funds for a deposit. Sadly, for him, this type of fraud became more difficult as banks tightened up their systems.

When he encountered cash flow problems, Vernon indulged in buying and selling on line. Perhaps buying was probably not the right word to use. Conning people and outright theft were more accurate.

But now Vernon was enjoying an entirely new experience.

Using the name of Vernon Thornbury, he had met and fallen in love with Maxine French. She enjoyed a similar way of life to himself and they soon moved in together.

Striving for some degree of stability in their lives, they concentrated on selling goods on e-bay. They both had sharp eyes, especially when it came to spotting a bargain, be it in shops, at car boot fairs, on the internet, reading through numerous adverts or downright theft if there was no alternative.

Vernon had a knack of finding empty properties either waiting to be sold, or better still awaiting demolition. Such buildings often housed all manner of treasures which had been missed when the houses were abandoned. Victorian and Edwardian houses were a treasure trove when they still had old tiles on the walls and floors. Sometimes there were exquisite china toilets and decorative wash basins complete with brass taps.

Vernon was very proficient at removing them.

He believed they had been abandoned, belonged to no one and would undoubtedly be destroyed when the property was demolished. As far as he was concerned, it was a case of *finders keepers*. It was the luck of the draw, and he never knew what he might find.

It was on one of these forays when he found Obadiah Turkman. Or to be more precise, Obadiah's skeleton.

Vernon quickly forced open the old boarded up house he had found tucked away at the end of a lane. It was a typical neglected relic from the mid-Victorian era and looked quite foreboding in the moonlight. He was pleased it was set back from the road in its own grounds, which made him less likely to be disturbed. A large notice informed everybody the house and grounds had been secured for redevelopment, which he knew was another term for a housing project.

Access to the house was not difficult using the old front drive. Granted it was overgrown with weeds and brambles, but he drove his car through them without any difficulty. But when he left his car, Vernon felt edgy, despite the large heavy-duty torch he carried. He suspected it was the general atmosphere surrounding this gloomy place and made a mental note never to come and live here. At one stage he even thought about giving up trying to find anything and going home. Then he recovered his nerve and soon found a way to get inside the house.

A quick look at the general rotten and dilapidated state of the ceilings, convinced him not to even think about looking upstairs, so he concentrated on the ground floor. Disappointed, he found nothing of any use to him. Vernon was just on the point of leaving when he discovered the cellar door. Moments later he had climbed down the steps and was in the cellar.

This was where he found Obadiah.

The first he saw of the skeleton was its grinning skull in his torchlight. Taken completely by surprise, and not a little frightened, he dropped his torch. Fortunately, it was a heavy-duty model and stayed alight. Vernon quickly picked it up and recovered his nerve. Shining the torch back at the skull, he saw it was attached to a skeleton.

The moment Vernon saw the skeleton he knew it would make an interesting item on e-bay.

Vernon looked closer and, as he suspected, it was a human skeleton whose bones had all been wired together. It was sitting on an old chair which looked to be in danger of collapsing. Judging by the amount of dust and accumulated grime, the skeleton had obviously not been touched for quite a while. As a bonus, he saw someone, possibly the skeleton's former owner had tied a label round its neck. Blowing the dust off it, he saw it was written in old copperplate black ink writing which was still visible and read:

My name is Obadiah Turkman
Touch me at your peril
because
I will bring you nothing but
Bad luck

Vernon snorted when he read the label and totally dismissed the warning. As far as he was concerned, this skeleton called Obadiah was a superb find, complete with a grinning skull. He had never come across anything like it before, which all added to the excitement. Never having sold a skeleton before, he had no idea of its potential value. With the minimum amount of luck, he hoped to make a tidy profit. As he had not paid any money for this Obadiah Turkman, whatever price he sold it for would represent a profit.

Hoisting Obadiah up onto his shoulder, Vernon carried him up the cellar steps and out of the house. For a moment he thought about belting him up in the passenger seat for a bit of fun. On second thoughts, he decided it might not be a good idea. He did not want to bring any attention to himself nor have any brush with the police.

Two hours later he was home.

Fortunately, Maxine was away for a few days visiting her mother who was in hospital as Vernon thought she might not appreciate sharing their house with Obadiah. Vernon sat the grinning Obadiah in a chair and took numerous photographs of him from all angles prior to putting the skeleton on e-bay. He even called him by his proper name.

As he did so, Vernon noticed Obadiah's right thumb was missing.

After breakfast the next morning, Vernon switched on his computer and logged on to e-bay to see how the sale of Obadiah was progressing. He was very disappointed to discover no bids had been made. Shrugging his shoulders resignedly, Vernon consoled himself in the knowledge no bids did not necessarily mean no one was interested. They would probably be playing a waiting game and it was early days yet.

Scrolling through his e-mails, he was on the point of sending one of them into spam when he looked again at the message title which read *Obadiah Turkman* and was from someone using the name of *Boneman.* Now thoroughly intrigued, he opened it and read the short message.

I suggest you look up Obadiah Turkman (1760-1790) before you
do anything else and be advised you are in very grave danger.

Vernon wasted no time in looking up Obadiah Turkman on his computer.
With any luck, it would give him some extra sales information.

Obadiah Turkman was born on 30th May 1760 to the Reverend Mathew
and Mrs Elizabeth Turkman in Warwick. Little is known about his younger
years except he ran away to London following a series of heated arguments
with his father concerning his numerous debaucheries. Whilst in London
he became involved in a Black Magic Cult who regularly held all manner
of orgies. In addition to gambling, Obadiah's main income came from
highway robberies, often using excessive force, not only in the London
area, but also elsewhere.

It was whilst robbing a traveller near Rugby in 1790 when he was
surprised by the arrival of three cavalry officers. During the ensuing
struggle, Obadiah's pistol exploded and blew off his right thumb. In due
course he was tried at Warwick Assizes and hanged. His body was sent
for dissection by surgeons.

Obadiah refused all ministrations and declined to receive any
visits from his family. Standing on the gallows he cursed the men
who had captured him, blaming them for the loss of his thumb. He
reserved other curses for the surgeons who would dissect him and
split up his body, sending its pieces to other places for research. His
final curse was reserved for the Assizes judge.

Nobody knows what happened to his body and skeleton after
his execution. Rumours abounded until it, supposedly, suddenly
appeared as an exhibit in a travelling circus during the late nineteenth
century. It was lost during a disastrous fire at the circus.

People who have made a study of Obadiah believe this skeleton
does belong to him and cite his missing right thumb as evidence.
They further believe Obadiah is cursed with having to search for all
eternity to find his missing thumb. Nobody else's will do. The belief is
Obadiah's skeleton changes places with his current owner and that is
how the curse works. Then that skeleton changes place with his new
owner and the search goes on. But the new body possessed by the

skeleton will not have a right thumb even if it had one before being possessed.

Until this happens, Obadiah's owner will have nothing but bad luck.

'What a load of rubbish,' snorted Vernon and he did not finish the article. 'Don't you agree, Obadiah?' He addressed these remarks to the skeleton, which was still sitting in the same chair where he had been placed the previous night.

Vernon knew the skeleton could not reply although it seemed his skull was grinning more than it had done the night before.

As the morning passed, Vernon kept checking e-bay but still no interest was being shown in Obadiah, or any other items he had for sale. Yet every time he looked at the skeleton, it seemed the skull was grinning more than ever. Vernon tried to pass it off as his imagination, but he began to feel the first gnawing worms of doubt.

What if there was some truth in the article, he had read earlier that morning? What if it was true and Obadiah wanted to take over his body in exchange for his skeleton? Perhaps he ought to get rid of Obadiah now whilst he could? He would not have lost any money. But then Vernon's mercenary side took over. No: he would wait for a while longer before making any firm decision.

The morning slowly dragged on. No matter how often he checked his computer, there was still no interest being shown in Obadiah or his other lots. After every check, Vernon looked at Obadiah and was convinced his grin was growing wider.

Suddenly he jumped when the phone rang.

It was Maxine and whilst he was pleased to hear from her, the news was not good. Her mother had now suffered a bad fall and was being kept in hospital where she was far from well. Maxine was going to stay with her for the time being because the next few hours would be critical as to whether or not she recovered.

Secretly Vernon was not sorry as it gave him more time to decide what to do with Obadiah, if he did not sell in the meantime. Putting the phone down, he looked at Obadiah once more.

This time he was convinced the skull was grinning even more. Surely it was his imagination playing tricks: wasn't it?

After enjoying a late lunch of cheese and biscuits, Vernon checked out his other e-bay lots. He was glad to see they were moving now, albeit slowly. The exception was Obadiah where no bids had been registered.

Slowly Vernon's head nodded, and he fell asleep.

The sound of a skidding car followed by a crash woke him.

Getting out of his chair, Vernon crossed to the window and looked out. He was just in time to see two youths, each wearing hoods, leap from their abandoned car and run away. Their car had destroyed most of his front garden wall. Even as he looked out at the scene, a police car arrived.

The last thing Vernon wanted was a visit from the police, but realised it was only a matter of time before they did so. In due course PC Laurie Cutler rang the doorbell and Vernon had no alternative but to let him inside.

Laurie had only recently moved to this force area to be nearer to his ageing parents. Too late Vernon remembered he had not hidden Obadiah. The skeleton was the first thing Laurie saw.

'Who's your friend?' he asked, more amused than suspicious.

Vernon explained how he liked unusual items and had added this one to his collection. He carefully avoided mentioning Obadiah by name and was glad the label had slipped round to the rear of the skeleton's skull.

'In my previous force,' continued Laurie. 'I once dealt with the theft of a skeleton from someone's collection. This skeleton had a name…What was it?…Oh yes I remember. He was called Obadiah Turkman. Apparently, he'd once been a highwayman who was hanged.'

Vernon never knew how he managed to keep a straight face. He took out a handkerchief and blew his nose to disguise any possible facial tremors.

'Actually, I think the collector was glad to get rid of him,' Laurie resumed his story. 'Obadiah brought him nothing but bad luck. There was a legend about the skeleton being cursed and would only bring bad luck to whoever owned him. Every time that happened, Obadiah's skull would grin all the more. Then when he was bored with doing that, and the skull's grin could not grow any wider, Obadiah would take over his owner's body and exchange his skeleton for his own. The new Obadiah then had to find someone else to take over. And so the curse goes on.'

'Did you ever find this Obadiah?' Vernon asked as casually as he could.

'No,' Laurie shook his head. 'And to be quite honest with you, that suited me. Whoever took Obadiah was welcome to him.'

Laurie gathered all the information he could from Vernon about the damaged wall and left. Vernon heaved a big sigh of relief as he watched the policeman drive away. Glancing back to Obadiah, he stopped. This time there was no doubt at all.

Obadiah's grin had definitely grown wider.

The day dragged on and still no bids had been made on Obadiah. Also bidding on Vernon's other lots had stopped well below their reserves. Looking at Obadiah yet again, he was certain the grin had grown.

Going back to the internet entry, Vernon read it completely.

It was almost a re-run of what the policeman had told him. He wondered if Obadiah's curse was working on him already. Was this why there were no bids on him, and the other bids had stopped? And what about his wall being demolished? What would be next?

As if on cue, the phone rang, and it was Maxine.

Her mother had taken a turn for the worse and was not expected to last through the night. Maxine felt very lonely and wanted him with her. Vernon readily agreed and quickly packed a few items. A quick look at Obadiah showed him the skull was grinning even more and it decided Vernon.

Never mind e-bay, Obadiah would have to go, and he had an idea.

Having put his case into the car, Vernon went back inside the house. Luckily there was an entrance from the house directly into the garage where his car was kept. He wrapped Obadiah in a blanket and carried him down to the car and laid him on the back seat.

Minutes later, they were driving away to join Maxine.

He drove at a steady rate and began to plan where he could drop Obadiah.

As it was now quite dark. Vernon drove off the main road and along a quiet lane which he knew from an earlier foray. It was now a building site but was very deserted at this time of night. He remembered there was a ditch somewhere along here which would be the ideal spot to dump the skeleton. There it was.

Vernon pulled on to the side of the lane close to a dense hedge which had the ditch running alongside it and stopped the car. Leaving the engine running, he started to undo his seat belt. Suddenly he felt someone tap him on the shoulder. Glancing in the driver's mirror he looked in horror at the ever-grinning skull of Obadiah Turkman looking back at him.

Several hours later, Maxine looked down at the now peaceful body of her mother. The past few hours had been very traumatic, and she was glad of Vernon's right arm around her shoulders. She reached up and clasped his hand and stopped in the surprise.

Although they had been lovers for many months, this was the first time she had ever noticed Vernon did not have a right thumb.

Wasps

The year 408 AD

The young shepherd boy named Arth heard the shouting and screaming coming from the settlement which he called home. It was where his widowed mother and sisters lived: and he was worried. Abandoning his sheep, he ran towards home to see what was happening. Clouds of dark smoke were rising, and he feared the worst.

It was common knowledge the Romans were abandoning the country, as they were recalled to defend other parts of their Empire. Society was breaking down and rumours abounded about a lawless group of Roman legionaries roaming the district who were leaving a trail of rape and pillaging behind them. Arth had a horrible feeling they were the cause of the screams and coming from his village.

His fears were soon realised when he saw many of the villagers running for their lives coming towards him. They all told him to run. Perhaps he might have done so, but nowhere could Arth see his mother and sisters and he feared for them.

Then he saw soldiers running towards him, pulling their struggling female captives along with them. Too late Arth realised they had seen him, and he ran towards the nearby forest, but they followed him. He saw there were perhaps twenty or so of them and he was disappointed his fellow villagers had not tried to stop them. But in reality, what chance would they have stood against heavily armed soldiers. Knowing he could not outrun them, Arth stopped, took out his sling and fitted a large stone into it, determined not to be killed or captured without a fight.

Running backwards he began to swing the sling, but just as he released it, Arth tripped over a fallen branch and the stone flew up into the trees. How the soldiers laughed! But their laughs soon turned to howls of pain.

Arth's slingshot went up into the trees, where it knocked a very big wasps' nest off a branch and onto his attackers. To say the wasps were furious was an understatement, and they turned their anger on the soldiers who tried to swat them away. But the more they swatted, the angrier the wasps became and many soon found their way through gaps in their antagonist's armour and stung them. Once they were in, the only way to dislodge them was for the soldiers to strip off their armour. By then it was too little and too late. One by one the soldiers succumbed to their stings.

Strangely, none of the captives, including his mother and sisters, was stung. Probably because they were too exhausted to do anything except lie still on the ground.

And so, the legend of the wasps began, and the village was now called *Waspdene*, meaning the *Valley of Wasps*.

The year 1920 AD

The Cotswolds village of *Waspdene*, had not changed much over the centuries. Its stone-built cottages nestled softly on the sides of the small valley, where their wood and mud predecessors had once stood. It was one of those places which time had passed by and the villagers enjoyed their seclusion which was greatly enhanced by its difficult access.

The only way in and out was via a small and narrow lane running off the main road. By some quirk in one of the council departments, there was no signpost advertising the village's location. To the unknowing eye, this lane was nothing more than a farm track. In other words, you had to know where *Waspdene* was located to be able to get there.

And for many hundreds of years it was a well-kept secret.

But with the growth of the tourist industry in the early twentieth century, the village became better known and accessible to ramblers and cyclists. The village's only pub, appropriately called *The Queen Wasp*, complete with a well painted inn sign to match, increased its trade and took in tourists on a bed and breakfast basis. Calling at *The Queen Wasp* was one of the reasons for visiting the village.

The pub was named after the legendary giant creature of the species whom the villagers had once worshipped as a goddess. It was rumoured many of them treated wasps as her children, and they were never harmed.

Being stung was considered a sign of good luck. In return, the wasps were reputed to protect the village in times of trouble, but only if they were asked to do so.

The locals knew it was only a legend, being adapted over the years from the story about Arth bringing the wasps nest down onto the marauding Romans. In reality no one knew what had really happened and even the modern-day villagers relied on stories from their parents and grandparents. Likewise, nobody could remember ever having asked for help from the wasps.

When the Cotswolds villages opened up for tourism, an unknown writer published a small booklet on Cotswolds Legends which included this one. It acted as a magnet and drew many tourists here. *The Queen Wasp* took advantage of the booklet to promote its own trade, which it did very successfully.

In common with just about every city, town, village and hamlet in England, *Waspdene* paid its own blood price during the Great War. When the war ended, life in the village began to get back to normal, but not for long.

Wars not only result in death and destruction, but they also pave the way to make some people very rich. Clement Tuck was such a person who had made a fortune manufacturing war materials. But in doing so became very unpopular in the Black Country town where he lived and worked. His short rotund figure was ample evidence to show how, unlike his workforce, he had not suffered from a lack of food or other essentials during the war. The fact his only son was killed on the 9th November 1918, just two days before the Armistice, and his wife dying soon afterwards, did nothing to reduce their animosity towards Tuck.

Following the Armistice, Tuck lost no time in re-marrying, but soon afterwards, he was assaulted in the street. This attack was quickly followed by all the windows in his house being broken, and his workers going on strike. He resolved the latter problem by dismissing the ringleaders and threatening similar treatment to the other strikers if they did not return to work. It might have put an end to the strike, but not to his problems.

Many of his customers, especially those who had lost family during the war moved to other suppliers. Realising he had no future in the *Black Country*, Tuck sold his company but not for the good price he wanted. Leaving there, he settled in the old manor house on the outskirts of *Waspdene*. Its location offered him somewhere to live in peace and seclusion. Within a few weeks, he quickly tired of such an unexciting existence, especially after his hectic and financially rewarding life in the Black Country.

Being a country squire was not for him. He missed his old business and began to look for ways to fill his time.

On his first arrival in the village, Tuck had been treated with a great deal of respect, but it was not scheduled to last.

Five of the villagers who went to war never returned. Those who did found it difficult to settle again into a normal life or even find work. Many of them had worked on the old manor estate before the war and hoped to be re-employed in their old jobs when they returned.

But Tuck had other ideas.

He decided to breed racehorses, which meant employing specialist workers from elsewhere. His decision meant no work for the returning soldiers and redundancy for most of the workers still employed on the estate. In only a matter of hours his popularity waned. Soon afterwards word was received about the vast profits he had made during the war, and Tuck became the most unpopular person in the district.

Not that he cared in the slightest.

Those workers on his estate lived in rented tied cottages for which they paid a peppercorn rent. Losing their jobs came the loss of their cottages as Tuck needed them for his specialist workers. He turned any surplus cottages into holiday homes.

And this gave him another idea.

His vision now was to take advantage of the growing tourist trade and turn *Waspdene* into an exclusive holiday complex. He bought up all the property in the village when it went on the market. Very much aware of his unpopularity, he used an agent to make these purchases to fool the locals, which delayed them discovering what he had done. Not that it made much difference as they did not have the money to compete with him, Tuck had already earmarked places for campsites and other venues for the new caravans which were beginning to appear.

In the meantime, the villagers struggled to survive. Many of them were out of work and others had no homes. Being a close-knit community, they cared for each other, but with autumn approaching, this was becoming increasingly more difficult. To make matters worse, when Tuck's racehorses and specialist staff arrived, they took most of the surviving jobs away from the locals.

The *invaders*, as the newcomers were called, soon discovered how unpopular they were as the villagers fought back in the only way they could.

The newcomers were shunned by the locals. The shop refused to serve them, and they were charged grossly inflated prices at *The Queen Wasp* for inferior and often watered-down drinks. This all changed after Tuck acquired the inn and the locals were actively discouraged from drinking there.

As it happened, the villagers were not the only people who were against Tuck's plans: so was his wife, Marian.

'They're only peasants,' he sneered, conveniently forgetting his own family's origins as an agricultural labourer, when she tried to reason with him about the villagers' plight, 'I don't give that for them,' he added snapping his right thumb and middle finger.

'Just be careful,' she said to him on more than one occasion. 'Just be careful you don't cause so much misery in the village, that it doesn't all bounce back on you.' Marian told him how she would not support him in any of his latest ventures.

'If you don't like it here, then go,' came his acid response. 'And if you do, I will change my will and leave you nothing.

Marian bit her lip and wondered, yet again, why she had married him. Part of the answer was she had no idea then, just how greedy and uncaring he really was.

She knew differently now.

His next target was *The Queen Wasp*. He purchased the business by simply making an offer, which was considerably more than the current value of the pub. It was an offer the landlord could not refuse. On the day the landlord left, Tuck set about planning how to modernise and extend it to make a classy country club and hotel.

Soon after Tuck bought the inn, the villagers met in the church hall.

'We've got to do something,' announced Abe Mablethorpe as he opened the meeting.

'That's all very well,' replied a villager. 'But what can we do?'

'Hear! Hear!' came a chorus of voices.

'I was thinking,' Abe said slowly. 'Perhaps it's time we called on the wasps for help.'

A stony silence greeted his suggestion.

'You believe in that tosh?' asked Ben Mason incredulously.

'Yes. I do,' Abe replied forcefully. 'What have we got to lose? If we don't find a way to stop Tuck, he'll end up owning the whole valley and we'll all be gone.'

'I think Abe is quite right about him owning the whole valley.' A quiet voice came from the rear of the church and a small hooded figure pushed through the villagers and approached Abe.

The villagers all gasped when the figure threw back her hood and they recognised Marion Tuck. 'You've got to do something to stop him or you'll lose everything,' she continued. 'I've tried to reason with him, but he's as good as thrown me out. What's this about wasps?'

'It's only an old legend,' started Abe and told her about the wasps and the Romans. Over the centuries whilst the story basically remained the same, many of the details were different. In his version, for instance, it was an entire legion which was destroyed by being pelted with wasps nests and not just one landing on twenty soldiers.

'Since then,' finished Abe. 'Wasps around here have been treated as godlike creatures. Hence that lovely inn sign at the pub which was put there to remind us to treat them with kindness and respect. Whatever you do, you must never offend the Queen Wasp. If you do, then you do so at your peril.'

'In return,' added another villager. 'They are pledged to help us if ever we should need them. But it has to be a real serious crisis, or they will turn on whoever summoned them.'

'Isn't it worth a try?' said Marion.

'The problem is it's autumn now,' said Abe. 'And they'll be hibernating.'

'If you won't do it,' said Marion. 'Then I will.'

The villagers shook their heads dubiously and tried to dissuade her. But it was to no avail. Marion was a strong-willed woman.

'I call upon the wasps to stop my husband's horse racing and the other detrimental plans he has for this village,' she intoned.

The church went eerily silent as people did not know what to expect. If any of them thought a vast swarm of wasps would suddenly appear, they were sadly disappointed. Much to the glee of the sceptics, nothing happened, and the meeting broke up.

A few days later, they all reconvened back in the church. The villagers were disappointed nothing had happened to Tuck who remained as obnoxious as ever. Luckily the church was one of the few buildings Tuck did not own, although he had tried. Unfortunately for him, the Church of England was not prepared to sell and exercised more influence than Tuck did in the matter.

It did not take long before the subject of the wasps arose.

'Nothing's happened,' said Ben. 'But then I knew it wouldn't. I told you so, didn't I? Anyway, where is that woman?'

As if awaiting her cue, the church door opened, and an obviously excited Marion came in. 'It worked!' she cried. 'It worked! The wasps did it!'

The others looked askance at her and waited.

'You see,' she explained. 'My husband had a very good horse, which was a born winner. The horse raced yesterday at a fixture where he was expected to win. So, my dearest Clement put a tremendous amount of money on the horse to win.' Marion paused, and they had all noticed the sneer in her voice when she said *my dearest Clement.* 'And he lost!' she laughed.

Her audience gazed at each other in amazement, not quite sure what make of the news and how it would affect them.

'His horse was leading for most of the race,' Marion continued. 'But it was just pipped at the post. And he got nothing back but has lost a tremendous amount of money and is on the point of bankruptcy.'

'I don't think you can credit the wasps with that,' derided Ben. 'That was just the luck of the draw.'

'Let me finish,' smiled Marion. 'The name of the winning horse is not important, but the jockey's colours were.' She paused for effect. 'They were black and yellow stripes…just like a wasp!'

Even the sceptics had no answer, and the stunned meeting broke up.

Tuck now had to sell his remaining horses to settle his more pressing creditors. With no horses, his specialist workers were quickly made redundant. Their houses went on the market, but still at a price most of the villagers could not afford. It was now he turned his attention to *The Queen Wasp* which he renamed *The Tuck Arms.*

Quite by chance, Abe and several villagers were walking by the inn when they saw the new sign waiting to be hung.

'You there!' called Tuck to Abe, holding a ladder. 'Do you want to earn half-a-crown?'

'Aye gaffer, I do.'

'Then take this ridiculous inn sign down and put the new one up instead.'

'No gaffer. I can't do that,' Abe replied. 'It'd bring bad luck on all of us: especially you. Wasps have to be respected in this village.'

'What absolute nonsense. I'll save the money and take it down myself.'

Ignoring all their protests, Tuck put his ladder up against the wall of the inn and climbed up it. Reaching out, he unhooked the existing sign and dropped it to the ground, where it bounced once, split and lay in two pieces.

After Tuck was back on the ground, he took the new sign and soon had it hanging in place. But as he climbed down the ladder, Tuck was aware of a buzzing sound in his ears. 'What's that buzzing sound?' he snapped.

The villagers shook their heads. They could not hear anything. Tuck rubbed his ears and the buzzing stopped.

He already had a bonfire burning and before the villagers realised what had happened, Tuck threw the two pieces of the old sign on to it. The fire took hold and the sign was soon burnt. Horrified by what had happened, the appalled villagers could only stand and watch it burn.

'Let that be an end to all this nonsense,' Tuck instructed and turned away and failed to see what the villagers had just seen.

The last piece of the sign to burn was the painted wasp's eyes, which now glared malevolently at Tuck.

'You shouldn't have done that,' Abe said very quietly. 'The wasps won't like that.'

'Enough of this superstitious rubbish,' Tuck hissed, shaking his head as the buzzing started again in his ears.

He strode off, climbed into his car and drove away.

Although he was not prepared to believe in tales of wasps and having to respect them, Tuck was beginning to worry about the buzzing sound in his ears. He thought there had to be a medical reason for them.

Instead of going straight home, he called on his doctor Marcus Welby. He examined his patient thoroughly but could not find anything wrong with him or offer any explanation for the buzzing. Even as he spoke, the buzzing stopped, and Tuck returned to his car.

But he had not travelled very far before it started again and was growing louder.

He was glad to arrive home and stopped outside his front door. Getting out of the car, he was aware the buzzing was still growing in intensity. Putting the key into the lock, Tuck looked behind himself and his blood froze.

Coming towards him was a large swarm of flying creatures which he now knew could only be wasps.

Opening the door quickly, he ran inside and slammed it shut behind him. It was not a moment too soon as he heard several of them crash into the door. Terrified he ran into every room calling for the servants and checked all the windows were closed. No servants appeared and later they would deny having heard him call. In the gathering gloom he saw the vast swarms of wasps flying around the house, trying to find a way in.

Finally, he ran into his own room, and collapsed on the bed.

Looking towards the window, all he could see was a swarm of wasps beating ineffectively against the old-fashioned leaded glass windows. How glad he was not to have agreed with Marion's plans to have them modernised.

Standing up, he crossed over to the window, took hold of the curtains and started to jerk them across the glass.

Suddenly, one of the small glass panes broke and the wasps started flying into the room. Tuck screamed as they landed all over him and he felt their stings.

Tuck's body was found soon afterwards by one of the servants who sent for Marcus Welby, but it was to no avail because his patient was already dead. At the subsequent post-mortem, the pathologist found no physical evidence to establish a cause of death. Secretly he believed Tuck had died of fright but had no way of proving it.

Being a sudden and unexplained death, the police were involved. However, the constable who searched Tuck's room paid no interest to the broken leaded light and the dead wasp lying near the body.

Although the coroner was unable to establish a cause of death, the villagers of *Waspdene* had their own theory about what had caused the death of Clement Tuck.

'I wish...'

'And what is your famous writer husband doing tonight?' Dr Patrick Travis asked sarcastically as he stretched languidly in bed alongside his lover Carole Arnold.

'Oh, dear Simon is delivering onc of his boring lectures on magic and superstitions,' she smiled in reply.

'Does anyone really believe in all that mumbo-jumbo rubbish?'

'You know they do, and you ask me that question every time we meet.' She punched him playfully on the shoulder. 'Be thankful he does as it gives us more time together.'

'What's his topic tonight?'

'Wishcraft.'

'Witchcraft?'

'No. cloth ears. Wishcraft...all about making wishes come true.'

'And can he?'

'He likes to think so. As he regularly tells us, he believes he has some special magical powers.' Carole smiled back and raised her eyes to the ceiling. 'Anyway, he's away for the night which gives us plenty of time.'

She rolled towards him.

Carole and Simon's marriage was a strange affair. It wasn't as if she did not love him: she did. But he was totally committed to writing horror and ghost stories for a living. To be fair, he was very good at it and had already sold some film rights. The problem was he believed what he wrote about, whilst Carole did not. She was a typical scientist who did not believe in anything unless it could be proved. Magic, ghosts and all that other *stuff,* as she called it, could not be proved, therefore they did not exist.

So, they agreed to disagree.

Simon was much in demand as a speaker both for small groups with different backgrounds to lecturing properly about ghosts, magic, superstitions etc to some university courses. Although she had no interest in the topic, Carole had tried going with him and offering her support, but the novelty quickly wore off. When Simon socialised after his talk, people tried talking to her, assuming she was just as knowledgeable as her husband. Once they realised this was not so, they moved on to other people. Carole quickly accepted he did not need her support at these functions and soon stopped going with him.

One night the laboratory where Carole worked had been invited to send some delegates to a symposium, and she was chosen as one of them. She had not really wanted to go, but Simon was away on a lecture tour, and with nothing else planned, she went. As she had anticipated, Carole knew nobody else there and was just on the point of leaving when she saw Patrick standing around on his own, clearly as bored as herself.

Both she and Simon attended the same medical practice where Patrick was based, and it seemed he was the one they saw the most often. He saw her at the same time and raised his glass in recognition and greeting. She had always found him good-looking and of a similar age to herself in his late forties. For reasons which she was never able to explain, Carole looked at his left hand for the first time. As she had hoped he was not wearing a wedding ring, accepting the fact it did not necessarily mean he was not married. He might just not like rings on his fingers. Not all men did.

'How come you're here on your own?' he asked.

'Nobody else was available from the laboratory and my dear husband is off giving another one of his *magic* lectures.' She hissed the word *magic*. 'And you?'

'A bit like you and won the short straw. All the practice nurses are married, and I had nobody else to ask.'

How her heart raced as he as good as told her he was not married. They spent a few more minutes at the reception before leaving and enjoying a meal together. It was something of a conversation stopper when he announced: 'I've got two tickets for the opera on Friday night in the City. I don't suppose you'd consider coming to it with me?'

Carole made a show of consulting her diary, although she knew Simon was away that night. 'Oh yes please. I'd love to.'

It was the beginning of a friendship which soon developed into something stronger and more meaningful.

The night at the opera was a great success, especially when followed by a quiet, unhurried but intimate supper. It was the first of several dates and quickly developed into a full-scale affair. There was the slight problem about her being married and one of his patients. They agreed she should quietly transfer to one of the other doctors in the practice. Otherwise, provided they were not discovered, there should be no problem. Consequently, they did most of their dating well outside the area except for the occasional coffees they had locally.

They reasoned if anybody saw them together in town, then their meeting would appear quite innocent. Would anybody really believe they were openly having an affair in such a small town where everyone knew them?

It worked.

Visiting a funfair one evening, they found themselves in a fortune teller's tent, where they had gone for a laugh. 'Tell me what you wish for,' said the old gypsy. 'But be careful. I can only grant one of them and the loser's wish will never happen.'

'I'll go first,' said Patrick. 'I wish to change places with your husband…' He broke off laughing.

Carole joined in the laughter. 'And I wish to get rid of my husband. Now which wish will come true?'

'I can't tell you that,' answered the gypsy. 'You'll have to wait and see.'

Laughing, they left the tent.

'Have you ever considered divorcing Simon?' Patrick asked later that night. 'If you did, then both our wishes would come true.'

'Many a time, but I've never raised it with him. And to be honest, I'm frightened about what he might do.'

'What could he do?'

'Summon up some of his evil spirits possibly and make life difficult for me.' She shrugged her shoulders. 'I really just don't know.'

'Surely you don't believe all that mumbo-jumbo drivel of his, do you? You're as bad as that gypsy fortune teller.' Patrick failed to keep the incredulity out of his voice.

'I really just don't know, but it frightens me sometimes. And deep down I don't think he'd agree to a divorce in any case.'

'Then we'll just have to kill him, and I know how to do it and make it look like natural causes.'

It was a bold statement and only half-uttered in jest. And so, the idea of murdering Simon was born.

Firstly, she arranged for Patrick to come and visit her on what appeared to be a house call when Simon was expected home. He arrived in the middle of Patrick treating her for chest pains. After Simon arrived, Patrick went through the motions of taking her blood pressure. Smiling, he pronounced her heart was fine and she had nothing to worry about. On the strength of this visit, Carole easily convinced Simon how they ought to invite Patrick round for a meal.   He agreed.

Unbeknown to him, Patrick had been creating a fake record about Simon's health and showing him as having a serious heart problem.

It was an enjoyable meal, but by the time they started on the port, Simon felt quite unwell. His head was spinning, and his heart began to beat at a furious rate. As a pain spread across his chest, Simon told Patrick about it.

'I know,' smiled Patrick mirthlessly. 'To the inexperienced and unknowing eye, you will have suffered a heart attack. My records now show you have had a heart problem for a while. As I have been treating you for this, no one will doubt that is what killed you.'

Simon looked askance at them

'Oh yes. We've just killed you.'

'Killed me? Who has just killed me?'

'Carole and me. You see We've been lovers for a while now. Since we first met, I've long since wished to take your place with her. And that's what I'm doing now. We'll marry after a decent interval and my wish will have come true.'

'Is…this…true…Carole?' gasped Simon in between bouts of pain.

'Yes. It's my wish to be rid of you.'

'Take my advice,' instructed Patrick. 'Let it happen. Don't fight it. Just let it happen as it'll be less painful that way.'

Summoning up his last breath, Simon glared at Patrick. 'Of course. Your visit to the gypsy fortune teller where she invited you to make a wish. Oh yes. I know all about that. Now, whose wish will come true? I'll be happy for you to take my place.' He grimaced with pain. Then, pointing to Carole, he gasped. 'But I won't grant your wish...You'll never be rid of me... I'll stay... and haunt you ...for...ever.'

Giving a final gasp, Simon fell forwards, slipped off his chair and landed on the floor. Patrick knelt beside him and felt for his pulse. There was none.

Simon was dead.

In the ensuing silence, they both realised what they had done. 'He took my replacing him very well,' said Patrick quietly. 'But how did he know about the gypsy. You didn't tell him, did you?'

'Of course not. Perhaps he really does these things. What did he mean about haunting me for ever?'

Patrick took her hands. 'Look my love,' he said softly. 'He's dead and there are no such things as ghosts, are there? You're a scientist. You know these things as well as I do. Trust me. If ghosts existed, we would have the proof by now.'

'I wish I could be sure of that.' Carole remained unconvinced.

The next two hours passed quickly as Patrick completed and signed the necessary paperwork. By doing so, coupled with his falsified medical records, there would not be any need for either a post-mortem examination or an inquest. There was a delay in finding some undertakers to come and remove Simon's body. At last two cadaverous and gaunt looking men arrived and explained how they were emergency locum undertakers and not local. This explained why Patrick did not know them.

He explained what had happened, which agreed with Carole's version of events. Once they had been given the necessary certificate, the men removed Simon's body.

Patrick had already arranged with Carole not to spend the night with her in case any of the neighbours noticed. He left just after the undertakers and arranged to phone her later next day. Surprisingly, she slept, but was awakened at about 5.00am by loud music coming from downstairs. Throwing on her dressing gown, she went to investigate.

She traced the music to Simon's I-pod which was switched on and playing his favourite music through a speaker system. Unable to understand what had happened, she remembered his curse about never being rid of him and haunting her for ever. Was this what was happening now? After switching the music system off, she took out her mobile phone and phoned Patrick.

There was no answer. Although she tried several more times, there was still no reply.

As soon as the surgery started, and the initial rush of early calls had ended, she phoned and asked to arrange an appointment with Dr Patrick Travis.

'I'm sorry,' replied the receptionist. 'But I'm not making any appointments for Dr Travis just at this moment. Can one of the other doctors help you?'

Carole hung up.

She called several more times during the day, but with the same result. Finally, she went to the surgery in the middle of the afternoon and demanded to see him. 'It's about my husband's death last night,' she explained. 'Dr Travis signed the death certificate, and I do need to talk to him about it.'

The receptionist asked to wait for a moment and disappeared. She returned several minutes later with the practice manager, who took Carole into a side room. 'Unfortunately, Mrs Arnold,' she explained. 'We don't know where he is. He hasn't turned up for duty or called in sick and isn't answering his phone.'

The practice manager logged onto a computer and made an entry. 'You say Dr Travis dealt with your husband's death last night?'

Carole nodded.

'That's strange. There's nothing recorded here.'

Totally bewildered Carole left the surgery. 'Where on earth was Patrick? Why hadn't he recorded Simon's death? What was he playing at?' she asked herself. Although they had agreed not to meet for a while, she went around to his flat.

His car was missing and there was no answer to her ringing the bell. 'Where are you?' she asked aloud. 'I need you.'

Carole only slept fitfully during most of the night until about 4.00am when she fell into a deep sleep. She was awoken just over an hour later by Simon's music playing loudly, with the lights flicking on and off and the electric kettle boiling away. Unable to even contemplate going back to bed, she phoned Patrick, but there was no answer. A later call to the surgery confirmed he had not made any contact with them.

Not wanting to stay another night in the house, she moved into a local hotel and was relieved not to have music playing in the early morning. Instead, every now and again, the bedclothes were pulled back off her. It really seemed Simon was haunting her. But where was Patrick and there was still no answer to her phone calls.

A few days later, she received a call from the undertakers giving her details of the funeral, which would just be a cremation. Back in the hotel bar, she idly watched the television before going to eat, when an item caught her attention.

It was a photograph of Patrick coupled with the information about him going missing and adding the police were concerned for his safety. 'Where are you, my love?' she muttered quietly.

Simon's funeral was much larger than she had anticipated, and it was standing room only in the crematorium. Carole was amazed at the turn-out especially as she had not advertised the fact. Granted she had told the university about his death and asked them to spread the word but had never expected this many people.

Knowing he was not very religious she had arranged for a non-denominational service. Taking her seat after following the coffin, Carole realised just how worn out she was with continually having disturbed nights. And she was still concerned about Patrick's disappearance.

The service was almost over when the main doors were thrust open and a man in a suit, accompanied by several uniformed police officers entered the chapel. **'Stop this service now!'** he instructed.

All heads, including Carole's turned towards him and a buzz of voices suddenly broke out, but not about his arrival, but at another man who stood beside him. Carole's hand went to her mouth as she gazed in horror at him. Like everyone else in the chapel, she had no difficulty in recognising Simon Arnold: her husband whose body they were supposed to be cremating here today.

To make matters worse, Simon was smiling at her. But, how could he be here? He was dead, wasn't he?

'Open that coffin!' the plain clothes policeman instructed his colleagues.

They quickly removed the coffin lid and stood back.

'Mrs Arnold!' said the plain clothes officer. 'Will you please take a look at the body in this coffin and tell me if it is your husband?'

'You know it's not. He's standing beside you.'

'Then who is it please. Do come and look.'

Knowing she had no alternative, Carole did so although she was certain who was in the coffin. 'It's Patrick Travis, Dr Travis,' she answered very quietly. Then she started screaming.

'Mrs Arnold,' said the plain clothes officer. 'I am arresting you for the murder of Dr Patrick Travis.'

As she was being led away, Carole looked at Simon. But all she saw was his malevolent grin.

Six months later, despite her plea of not guilty and the efforts of her defence team to have her declared unfit to plead, Carole was sentenced to life imprisonment with the recommendation she spent a minimum period of twenty years in prison.

She had stuck to her story about Simon dying of a heart attack and Patrick certifying his death. A post-mortem examination on Patrick's body revealed traces of a drug which imitated the symptoms of a heart attack which certainly caused his death. In any case, Simon had an unshakeable alibi proving him to be in Scotland at the time of his so-called death.

Carole collapsed in the dock when she was sentenced and had to be carried away. Once she had been checked by a doctor, Carole was the sole occupant of the security van taking her to prison. On the way, Simon appeared, or so she thought. 'I told you you'd never be rid of me,' he smiled. 'I'll remind you of that quite regularly. Make the most of your uninterrupted nights' sleep when you can. They will not last for ever. And Patrick got his wish to replace me. You really should have been more careful in making your wishes. I warned you only one of your wishes would come true and how the loser's wish would never happen.'

Simon faded and disappeared, leaving Carole to a very uncertain future.

The Face at the Window

It had been an acrimonious divorce, albeit for no reason on Hannah's part.

She and Wolfgang Meinz had met after leaving university, became friends and soon moved onto being lovers. He was tall, good looking with fair hair and blue eyes, which with his name, were all parts of his German ancestry. She was also tall, but with dark hair and deep brown eyes. Although Hannah studied history whilst he read science, the general feeling was they were made for each other. Their friends were not surprised when they married.

It was an ideal marriage, and all went well until Mia Stoneworth appeared on the scene.

Mia was a new and very attractive employee at the laboratory where Wolfgang worked and was attached to his team. Although she had only recently graduated, Mia was older than the usual students to be employed by Wolfgang's employers. Only when she had been taken on, did Mia set about finding some accommodation, but this was easier said than done. A large student influx from the local university caused a dire shortage of accommodation in the town, and Mia had to take up temporary residence at a local bed and breakfast guest house. She soon found this was a considerable drain on her finances and told everyone she would have to leave the laboratory.

Mia discussed the matter with Wolfgang who was her team leader. He was reluctant to lose her, knowing how capable she was, and suggested Mia moved in with Hannah and himself.

Mia jumped at the idea, although Hannah was not so keen.

She had met Mia on a couple of occasions and did not take to her. Hannah could not explain why, but she distrusted the other woman on sight. It had not taken her very long to realise how manipulative Mia was, especially with men. Her charms were much less effective where women were concerned. Despite her feelings, and against her better judgement, Hannah agreed to have Mia as a lodger, insisting that it was only for a short while. But that did not happen. Once she was in their house, Mia showed no signs of leaving and friction began between the two women.

As the days progressed into weeks, Mia made no attempts to find other lodgings. Whenever Hannah raised the topic, Mia's stock reply was: 'Wolfgang says it's fine and I can stay as long as I like.' Hannah also realised her husband was spending more time with Mia than with his wife.

They travelled backwards and forwards to work with each other, because Mia did not own a car. Sometimes they stopped for a drink on the way home. And Hannah began to resent always hearing Wolfgang continually talking about what Mia had done.

After only a few weeks, Mia began to mention casually how she had seen Hannah having lunch with a man. Gradually she made Wolfgang suspicious of Hannah with other tales about her, suggesting infidelity. He raised the issue with Hannah, who strenuously denied the allegation because it was completely untrue.

'Can't you see what she's doing?' Hannah exclaimed. 'She's after you at the expense of our marriage!'

'You're just jealous of her good looks and resent the working relationship we have. Grow up.'

It was the first of many more similar arguments.

Hannah tried speaking with some of the other women on Wolfgang's team about Mia. Their answers merely served to reinforce her views. They told her how Mia was universally disliked by the women and starting to be distrusted by the other men in the laboratory. But they could not add anything else.

Just as Hannah was leaving work one evening, a woman came up to her. 'I'm Sonia Kinnock and I work with Mia,' the woman said. 'And there's something you need to know, but we can't talk here. Let's meet at the *Plough and Partridge* on the Dales Road in a couple of hours. Do you know it?'

'I'll see you there.' Hannah thought Sonia looked a little out of place amongst so many youngsters at the laboratory, and her clothes looked so dated. She put her age at about forty-five.

*   *   *

It was a long two hours for Hannah. Just as she was wondering how much longer to wait, Sonia appeared. Having refilled her glass of merlot and bought a similar drink for Sonia, they moved to a table in a quiet corner of the bar.

'Wolfgang's making a big fool of himself,' Sonia said without any preamble. 'He can't see how Mia doesn't really want him. She wants everything you have. You. Your house. Your money. Your husband. His money. Everything. And she won't rest until she has it all and you have nothing. You're the one she's after.'

'But why? I've never met the woman before she came here?'

'Maybe,' continued Sonia. 'But she knows all about you. Your maiden name was Throckley, wasn't it.'

Hannah nodded.

'Does the name John Stoneworth mean anything to you?'

'John Stoneworth? John Stoneworth? Wasn't he one of the men killed in the factory explosion…?'

'You've got it. The explosion in your father's factory.'

'And because he was smoking amidst some highly combustible materials, he caused the explosion…'

'Because of that, his family never received any compensation.'

'I see,' nodded Hannah. 'My father and other innocent people were killed in the same explosion and she thinks she's going to get compensation from me, does she? Then she's got another think coming.'

Sonia nodded.

'Just a minute!' A thought struck Hannah. 'How do you know all this?'

'I lost family there too. Some of us formed a group afterwards. We thought about inviting you, but you had left the area. We talked about many things, such as who was to blame, revenge and so on.'

'I see that, but…'

'We knew about Mia and her not getting any compensation. Once she realised it would never happen, she swore to destroy your family in whatever way she could.'

Hannah had a sudden horrible thought. 'Is that why my mother and brother were killed in a car crash?'

Sonia nodded gravely.

'And Wolfgang? How does he fit into all this?'

'I'm sorry, but he only married you for your money. Mia put him up to it. You are intended to meet with a fatal accident soon, at which point all your money will go to him. I assume that's how your will reads?'

'Not after tomorrow. That's when I change my will and leave him.'

'Good on you. Let him go and go where fate directs you. It will all happen for a very good reason as you will discover. Mia will follow you but let her. It's important you don't stand in her way. And these will help you with a divorce.' Sonia handed her a large white envelope, which Hannah opened.

A cascade of photographs fell out. They all showed a naked Wolfgang and a naked Mia indulging in various sexual acts. Hannah now felt physically sick. Excusing herself from Sonia, she fled to the toilet. When she returned to the bar, Sonia had gone.

The following evening, Hannah told Wolfgang she was seeking a divorce.

'On what grounds?' he asked.

Hannah handed him some of the photographs. He looked at the first one or two, then his face fell. 'Oh,' was all he said.

'These are only a sample,' Hannah explained. 'The others are in a very safe place where you will never find them. I assume you will not be contesting the divorce, will you? And I have already changed my will from which you are excluded.'

He said nothing, just buried his face in his hands.

As Hannah had expected, Wolfgang did not contest the divorce. As the house was in her name, he was also excluded from there. Surprisingly Mia left with very little trouble, only a look of pure hatred. 'You haven't seen the last of me!' she hissed. 'I'll follow you wherever you go and won't rest until I've ruined you. I'll have the compensation that's due to me, one way or another.'

It was obvious to Hannah how she needed to move away. The town held too many bad memories for her. In some respects, she was sorry to leave the museum where she worked, but it held no long-term future: only waiting for dead men's shoes. Most of her work involved research which decided her. Once her house was on the market, Hannah resigned from the museum and set herself up as a self-employed researcher. The next problem was where to live? Hannah regularly scoured estate agents on line which was how she received details of a property known as the Old Mill. Although it had plenty of space and not in any danger of flooding, the property was not very expensive.

*   *   *

A few days later, Hannah waited at its entrance for the estate agent to arrive As she waited, Hannah had the time to take a good look at the outside of the building. It was clearly in need of some maintenance. Hannah was just on the point of turning away, when she saw a distinct movement at one of the upper windows. Looking closer, she was adamant a face was peering out at her.

It was a female's face of an indeterminate age with a 1940s type of hairstyle. Her hands were trying to push up the sash window. Whilst it was impossible to hear what she was saying, Hannah thought it was 'help me.' She was saved from making a decision by the arrival of Monica Barnard, the estate agent.

'Who's in the house?' Hannah demanded. 'I thought it came with vacant possession?'

'That's quite right,' replied Monica vaguely.

'Then who was that woman at that upstairs window?' Hannah demanded, pointing to the now empty window.

'There's nobody living there,' insisted Monica.

'I definitely saw a face at that window. So, if you want to stand any chance of selling this mill to me, I suggest you tell me who she is?'

'Let's go over to my car.'

'No! I want to see over the mill, and I want to know who that woman is and why won't you tell me about her?'

'OK,' replied Monica in a resigned voice. 'But you would be better hearing the story first before you go over the mill.' She led Hannah across to her car and they both got into it.

Monica told her the story.

The mill was built in the latter part of the eighteenth century and remained in the same family until 1868, when William Pendle died. He was the last of the family and a widower with no children. Nobody knew what had happened to his wife, Henrietta, other than she had apparently left to visit relatives in America several years earlier and had never returned. According to William, the ship had never arrived and Henrietta along with all the passengers and crew had been reported as being lost at sea. William never elaborated on what had happened and never discussed the affair with anyone.

'What's this got to do with the woman in the mill? The one I saw earlier?'

'Bear with me,' pleaded Monica.

She went on to explain how the mill remained empty for a while after William died, as the locals all said it was haunted. After several years, the mill was purchased, but the new owner quickly left, complaining about strange noises which frightened his wife, their children and even the family dogs would not enter it.

The next owner, who had lived in the village all his life and knew the story, was not deterred and moved in. He began a massive restoration programme, during which the workmen uncovered a boarded-up room. Inside it they found a mummified female body which one of the workmen believed was Henrietta Pendle, as he had seen her when he was younger.

'Everyone agreed it was Henrietta,' confirmed Monica. 'The police came and took her away. They were firmly convinced she had been murdered by William and her body bricked up. She was given a decent burial and that was thought to be the end of the matter.'

'Do I sense a *but* coming?'

'You do. Soon afterwards, Henrietta's ghost apparently appeared to the new owner. She told him she could never be free until another woman took her place. It had to be a single woman living on her own in the mill. When that happened, and only when that happened would she be free.'

'And would that be the end of it?'

'Hopefully, but nobody's put it to the test, although way back in the 1940s, during the war, the mill was taken over by some government department for hush-hush work which is still a secret. It was staffed by women, one of whom disappeared. But it was wartime, and nobody was too worried, That's the story of the mill. Am I right in thinking you would be living here on your own?'

'Yes.'

'I take it there's no point in showing it to you now?'

'On the contrary. I definitely want to have a look round.'

Hannah fell in love with the mill and agreed then and there to buy it. Monica tried, albeit very half-heartedly to talk her out of the idea, but Hannah would not change her mind. They agreed a sum, which was somewhat less than the asking price, shook hands on the deal and left the mill. Hannah said she would speak to Monica again in a few days, once she had arranged for a solicitor and for a surveyor.

Neither of them had been aware they were being watched, and had been since their arrival.

It took Hannah longer than she had intended before she could see Monica again. On arriving at her office, she was told Monica was out, but could anyone else help her?

'Yes. I'm buying the Old Mill and I need to arrange for my surveyor to gain access.'

'Certainly Ms Stoneworth…' replied the receptionist.

'That's not my name. I'm Hannah Throckley,' came her stiff reply. She had reverted to her maiden name after the divorce.

'Oh dear,' replied the receptionist. 'Monica really should have told you. Ms Stoneworth came into the office soon after Monica had returned from the Old Mill. I'm afraid she submitted a much higher offer than you did, which has been accepted by the vendor and she's also paid the deposit. Monica really…' But she was speaking to herself as Hannah had already left the agency.

Bloody Mia again!

Hannah now moved completely out of the area and it was five years later in early in 2017 when she was back in the locality. Quite by chance she bumped into Wolfgang and they went for a coffee together for old-times sake. There was no animosity between them. They were both re-married with children. Inevitably, the subject of Mia cropped up.

'I never saw her again after the divorce,' Wolfgang admitted. 'To be ever so honest, she made a fool of me and I don't even know where she is now; and I care less.'

She could see he spoke genuinely.

'Tell me,' he asked just as they were leaving. 'Where did you get those photographs of me from?'

'It was one of your team called Sonia Kinnock.'

'Sonia Kinnock? Sonia Kinnock? There was never anyone with that name working on my team or even in the laboratory.'

'That was the name she gave me.'

'Are you sure?'

'Positive.'

They left it there and went their separate ways.

*   *   *

Driving away, Hannah mulled over what Wolfgang had said about not knowing a Sonia Kinnock. It also made her think about Sonia and what she had said. What was it? Something about her being in a group and about letting fate take a hand and going where it led her, and not to worry about Mia. Acting on impulse, Hannah changed her plans, turned her car around and drove off towards the Old Mill.

She was not surprised to see a tired looking **FOR SALE** board outside the entrance to the property. Was it empty? Hannah asked herself as she drove down and parked once more outside the front of the building, confident she knew the answer. The building was just as rundown, if not more so than when she had seen it last. From its appearance, Hannah doubted if Mia had ever moved into it. Unable to resist, Hannah looked up at the window where she had seen the face on her first arrival and stopped in horror.

A woman stood there trying to open the window and mouthing 'save me!' just as it had all those years ago. Only now there was a big difference.

It was Mia's face which looked down pleadingly at her.

Hannah wasted no more time but drove away. Then, she stopped at the first lay-by and took out her laptop. Once it was up and running, she looked up the explosion at her father's factory. There were several sites, but the one she wanted was a list of the fatalities. She brought the site up and began scrolling down it. The fatalities were listed in alphabetical order and Hannah soon found the name she thought would be there.

It read…Sonia Kinnock, aged 43.

AUTHOR'S NOTE

There is a shop in Warwick (2019) which has a large face looking out through the window onto the pavement. It is actually a chair, and gave me the idea for this tale.

The Black Bear

'**Tell the men to mount up,**' Captain Will John Treen instructed his sergeant Cal Lootman.

His men did so quietly in a very sombre mood. They had all been affected by the devastation and sheer barbarity of the recent attack on this small settlement. Although the buildings still smouldered, they had arrived too late to be of any assistance to their pitifully few defenders. Even the older, hardened and more experienced men of his troop made no effort to wipe away the tears from their faces as they buried the pathetic butchered remains of the parents and their children.

It was their third such burial detail that day.

'What sort of creatures can do this?' A visibly shaken Lieutenant Gary Blackwell said to Will, summing up all the troopers' feelings. 'What the hell is the garrison at Fort Hunter doing? Does this mean the Rebs are using hostile Indians to further their cause?'

Will Treen was a professional soldier whose ambition had been to make his way to the top of his profession. Unfortunately, soon after graduating, America became embroiled in a bloody civil war between the States. This was not quite the glory Will had been seeking, but he stayed with the Union Army which represented the Northern States.

Being a West Point graduate Will had anticipated being posted to one of the new regiments and fighting in the expected major battles. But he was disappointed in being side-tracked to a training camp. Whilst this was a safe billet, it gave him no active service or battle experience, unlike most of his contemporaries.

Will accepted this because he had no option, but it did not stop him taking every opportunity to complain about his lot. It seemed to have done the trick in early 1863, when Will received a summons to his local headquarters for a meeting with a general he did not know. This man asked him if he would be prepared to undertake a special task, and without thinking for very long Will agreed to do it. He had forgotten the old soldier's advice about never volunteering for anything, especially without being given any details. It was only when his written orders arrived Will realised what he had volunteered to do.

He was to assemble a troop of cavalrymen and make his way Westwards to the furthest outpost of the Northern States, reinforce the small garrison based at Fort Hunter and keep the local Indians under control. There were rumours they were being encouraged by the Confederate Southern Government to join forces and wage war on the Northern supporters in that part of the country.

Will's heart sank when he realised there would be little chance of seeing much, if any action, out there. It was not what he had trained to do at West Point, but there was no use complaining. He was a soldier and had to obey his orders. However, a pleasant and unexpected surprise came with them.

To help give him some authority Will was promoted to the rank of captain, with immediate effect. Several weeks later, he was burying butchered families.

Yet again, it was not what he had expected to be doing when he left West Point. Waging war was one thing, but butchering civilians, especially women and children was something else.

If this is what hostile Indians were doing, then Will and his men would be glad to wage a similar war on them and their supporters.

Fort Hunter was just over an hour's ride from this ruined settlement and Will led his men at a gentle canter for the first ten minutes, slowing to a walk the closer they got to it. He had already posted scouts out in front and to his flanks.

Still taking no chances, Will called a halt approximately one mile away from the fort. Leaving Gary in charge, he, two other troopers and Sergeant Lootman moved cautiously towards the fort. Once they had it in sight, Will took out a pair of field glasses from one of his saddlebags and studied the immediate area. Only when satisfied there were no apparent Indians anywhere, he turned to the fort.

He was surprised, and not a little worried, to see the gates were wide open with no obvious signs of any military sentries. A closer inspection showed him what looked like civilians armed with rifles who were patrolling the walls. He handed the glasses to Cal and asked him what he thought.

Cal took the glasses and focussed on the fort.

'They sure don't look like soldiers to me,' he observed. 'But likewise, they don't look like hostiles either.'

'Are there any soldiers there?' Will voiced their joint concern. 'And if so, are they ours or rebs?'

'Let me go and take a closer look,' offered Cal. 'I'll take Trooper Hutton with me. If we're not out within ten minutes, then you can take it as read they are hostiles of some sort or another. Meanwhile I suggest we get the others up here, so we will all be together for whatever action is needed.'

Will agreed. Once Cal and the trooper left for the fort, he sent his other man back to Gary to bring the others up to re-join him. After which he settled down for a wait for his men to arrive and to see what was happening at the fort.

The wait was not long before Cal, Trooper Hutton and two other riders cantered back to Will. They arrived just as the remainder of his troop arrived.

'Cap'n,' Cal saluted as he arrived. 'You just won't believe what's happening in that fort. This is Dougal Fleming, the settlement spokesman and his brother Alistair. I'll let them explain.'

Cal indicated both men as he spoke. Dougal was a big brawny man with fiery red hair and a beard to match. Alistair was a younger version of Dougal and they were obviously related. Will saw they were genuinely very glad to see him and his men.

They explained how the fort and its occupants, both military and civilian, were under the control and protection of a small unit of Union soldiers commanded by Lieutenant Grant Marvin.

'And why is he not here with you?' Will interrupted.

'Almost certainly sleeping off his lunchtime drinking session,' replied Dougal scathingly.

'And his men?'

'The same.'

'I didn't see any soldiers,' confirmed Cal.

'That's why we have had to take over sentry duty on the walls,' added Alistair. 'The man just will not accept there is any danger here and both he and his men look upon this as an easy posting. They don't mount any guards or send out patrols.'

'Haven't they any idea of what's happening out here?' Will was furious. 'Look!' he instructed, pointing to the faint smudge of smoke clearly visible from the last homesteads they had visited. 'They could have helped there.'

The Fleming brothers nodded sadly in agreement.

'Perhaps if this Marvin had done his duty,' hissed Gary unable to help himself. 'Then we might have been spared all the burials we have had to do today on our way here.'

His words were accompanied by an angry murmur of approval from the nearby troopers who had heard him. They were quickly silenced by one of Cal's fierce glares.

'Do any of the soldiers in the fort know we are here?' asked Will.

'No sir,' answered Dougal. 'Your sergeant asked us not to tell any of them until he had spoken with you.'

'Good,' replied Will. 'Gather round men. This is what we are going to do.'

Thirty minutes later, Will and his men plus the Fleming brothers quietly entered Fort Hunter.

It did not take long for Cal to detail several of his men to patrol the walls. The Flemings showed Gary where the other soldiers were likely to be, and he moved in that direction.

Suddenly, an unshaven, partly dressed soldier appeared, reeking of whisky and was clearly drunk. He sobered up very quickly when two of Will's men took hold of him not very gently and held him tight. The man blinked at the captain who stood before him, pricking his neck with a sabre.

'And where can I find your commanding officer?' Will enquired in a quiet voice which belied the rage he felt inside.

'You heard the captain,' snarled one of the man's captors. 'Answer him!' The instruction was accompanied by a vicious twisting of the prisoner's arm.

An answer quickly followed.

Will discovered where Marvin was lying sound asleep in a drunken stupor. Once Will had a large bowl of cold water in his hands, he nodded to Cal, who signalled his bugler to stand by the sleeping officer and point his instrument at him. The man raised the bugle, licked his lips and blew the call for a general alarm. It was followed by the alarm bell in the outside compound being rung furiously. Moments later Will emptied the bowl of water over Lieutenant Grant Marvin as he struggled to wake.

The next few days were absolute hell for Marvin and his men. Cal and Sergeant Jock Murray drilled them unmercifully from dawn to dusk. They were denied any alcoholic liquor and spent much of their off-duty time making their uniforms presentable and repairing various defects in the fort's defences. Nobody, either military or civilian, had any sympathy for them.

Marvin protested he was an officer and demanded to see Will. Here he stated he would not carry out any drill or other fatigue duties.

Will was not entirely sure where he stood in such a situation. It was not one covered in his West Point training. 'Very well,' he said at last, noticing the sly smirk spreading over Marvin's face. 'You won't have to do drill or carry out any fatigue duties. Sergeant Lootman! Please place Mr Marvin in the cells and put him on half rations. He is to stay there until this immediate crisis is over, when he will face a court-martial on a charge of gross dereliction of duty. Take him away. His very presence here offends me.'

Will was satisfied to see Marvin was no longer smiling as he was led away.

Since taking over Fort Hunter Will ordered out regular patrols checking the local vicinity and for a while all was relatively peaceful. He also insisted local settlers came and took refuge in the fort with their families and livestock. It would be safer for them and give Will more guns and ammunition. The fort had its own water supply and could withstand a siege against just one tribe of hostile Indians. But it was rumoured several tribes were forming an alliance which would be something much different.

And he had no idea what the Confederacy planned to do in this part of the country.

He sent couriers back east with his concerns and requests for reinforcements. Even if they got through Will was realistic enough to know reinforcements would take time to arrive, even if they were sent. He was also very much aware his scouts were reporting Indians coming closer and closer to the fort.

In the meantime, Will knew he was well and truly on his own.

It soon became obvious an attack on the fort was not very far away and now was the time to plan his strategy.

Will held a council of war with Gary, the Flemings, Cal, Sergeant Jock Murray and several of the settlers. He was pleased to see none of them was in favour of surrendering the fort: they knew too well how the Indians could not be trusted. The outcome of the attack was by no means certain and they all knew their life expectancy was probably not very long.

One of Will's men had previously suggested the women and children should take shelter in the middle of the fort, but the idea was greeted with scorn. The soldiers were told in no uncertain terms how the frontier women could shoot as well, if not better than many of their menfolk. They would be very welcome in taking their places on the firing lines alongside their husbands, sons, brothers and lovers.

Secretly Will was glad as they would give him extra firepower. He was going to need it.

After the meeting, he, Gary and Jock Murray, sat drinking whisky with the Flemings when he noticed a set of bagpipes hanging on the wall.

'They belong to our family,' explained Dougal, pointing to the pipes. 'In fact, they were last blown here back in 1763, exactly one hundred years ago, during the wars against the French and the Indians.' Dougal refilled their glasses and related the story.

'Briefly, a large war party of Indians was chasing a group of fleeing settlers, men, women and children and picking them off one by one. If they caught anyone alive, then they tortured them in the hearing of the others, but well out of musket range. Quite unexpectedly they came across a company of redcoats, which included Piper Alistair Fleming, my ancestor. These redcoats could have left them to their fate and made their own escape, but instead they stayed here and held up the hostiles long enough for the settlers to escape. The soldiers were heavily outnumbered, and their deaths were inevitable. When the hostiles made their final attack, Alistair played his pipes throughout and then here comes the interesting part.'

Dougal took a large sip of whisky before continuing. The others waited expectantly.

'Although all of his comrades, including their officer, were killed, Alistair wasn't harmed. It seems the hostiles were scared of the bagpipes and thought he was some sort of god with strange magic and he was left alone. After the war when peace came, Alistair returned here and was instrumental in getting this settlement up and running. We survived the revolution and here we are today, back facing destruction again.'

He took another sip.

'Why have they risen up now?' queried Will.

'The Indians believed they had to wait for one hundred years to re-establish themselves here and defeat Alaistair's magic. If they fail to do so, then all their men will be destroyed.'

'So, it's nothing to do with the Rebs interfering?'

'No. As far as the Indians are concerned all white men are their enemies and must be destroyed.'

'Why haven't you left?'

'Because this is our home. And I suppose legend has it the redcoats will always protect this settlement, but only if it is a totally united community when you summon them. And they can only be summoned by Alistair's pipes hanging up there. They also want their revenge. That is if you believe such tales. What use will flintlock muskets be against modern rifles…' He left the sentence unfinished.

'Do you play them?' asked Jock.

'Fraid not. And I don't think anyone else can in the fort. Surely you don't believe in such tales?'

They were saved from answering as a messenger came in for Jock Murray, who was wanted elsewhere. As he left, Jock looked up at the bagpipes on the wall. 'Do they work?' he asked.

The Fleming brothers just shrugged their shoulders.

The first attack on the fort came the following morning.

Will was under no illusion it was just an exploratory attack to test the defenders and make them use up ammunition, so he only mounted a minimum number of defenders on the walls. As he had anticipated, it was not a serious attack.

Two more attacks followed during the rest of the day, each more serious than the previous one, so Will had to deploy more of his reserves. Clearly these hostiles knew what they were doing. Although they suffered numerous casualties, there was no shortage of replacements.

The defenders also received casualties, although the improvements Will had made to the fort helped to keep them low. All the same he knew it really was only a matter of time. He also decided to release Marvin and make him take his place on the walls.

As he had been advised, the attacking tactic was to charge the fort on horseback and then ride round it, shooting at the defenders. Granted their shooting was not very accurate, but it also made them more difficult to hit. What they had not anticipated was Will's men firing in volleys whenever possible, which resulted in causing many casualties.

It was a similar pattern the next day, but with one amazing difference.

As the second attack died away and the Indians retreated once more, Will watched them go through his field glasses.

'CAP'N!' shouted the lookout pointing. 'MORE RIDERS OVER TO THE LEFT! THEY LOOK LIKE CAVALRY!'

Will turned in that direction. The lookout was right.

A troop of about seventy cavalrymen was charging through the Indians with their sabres flashing and hacking. They were headed for the fort and were being hotly pursued by the Indians.

'OPEN THE GATES!' cried Will. 'BUT BEWARE OF TRICKS. Don't TAKE YOUR EYES OFF YOUR ALLOTTED SECTIONS.'

The cavalrymen galloped gratefully into the fort to a rousing cheer and reined to a halt. Their leader dismounted as Will arrived. He saluted Will and introduced himself in a Southern drawl: 'Lootenant Harvey Kendall, sir.'

As he did so, the cheers all died away and were replaced with a grim silence and a general shifting of weapons to cover the newcomers. Will realised their reinforcements all wore the light blue/grey uniforms of the Confederate States Army.

'We don't have any problems with those hostiles and are indifferent to them killing you. But,' Harvey waved his hand round the fort. 'It's a different matter where women and children are concerned. That being the case, me and my men are happy to put ourselves under your command.'

Will introduced himself adding. 'I don't know what you're doing here, but you're welcome to share what We've got.'

'We don't want no stinking rebs here,' snarled Marvin, raising his revolver.

But even as he did so, Marvin felt something cold press against his neck.

'You pull that trigger,' said Dougal. 'And it'll be the last thing you ever do.'

'Sergeant Murray!' instructed Will. 'Disarm Mr Marvin once more and return him to the guardhouse. Take one of Mr Kendall's men with you.'

With Marvin's removal, some of the tension eased, although both sets of soldiers kept to themselves. When food was served, Jock Murray shared his coffee with one of the newcomers and the tension eased further.

Even with these welcome reinforcements Will knew they remained heavily outnumbered, and he was not very hopeful on the outcome of the siege.

Two days later, he, Gary, Harvey and the Flemings held a council of war to make their final plans. It would all be over tomorrow. They were running short of ammunition and the walls had been attacked by fire arrows which were continuing to be fired all through the night. The wooden walls could not take much more. Once they were breached, it would be hand-to-hand fighting until the last man. Will ensured enough bullets had been reserved to shoot the women and children to prevent them being taken captive.

The men would have to take their chances.

By mid-morning the following day, the walls had nearly been breached and the Indians were preparing to make a final attack on the fort. The soldiers, regardless of the colour of their uniforms, the civilians and the women fought side by side, with their children reloading their weapons. But they all knew the end was approaching.

Marvin was amongst the earlier fatalities. Much to most people's surprise, he had been killed saving the life of a Confederate soldier.

Passing through the Flemings cabin, Jock Murray saw the bagpipes on the wall. Pausing for a moment, he took them down lovingly. He was a piper, but his pipes had long since been lost somewhere in transit. As far as he could see, despite their age, they were in good condition. If he was going to die this morning, then he would do it playing them. Wiping his lips, he blew and was gratified to find there were no leaks and the bag began to inflate.

Moments later he began to play *The Black Bear*, which seemed an appropriate epitaph. It was the fastest marching tune in the British Army and believed by some to owe its origin to the *Black Watch Regiment* who fought in America during the French and Indian Wars. The popular belief was its name was taken from the bearskin strip which members of the *Black Watch* fastened round their bonnets.

One hundred years later it was a popular and rousing tune for pipers and Jock had no hesitation in playing it. After all, with a name like his, he had Scottish ancestors, at least one of whom had been a piper in the *Black Watch* when it was stationed here in America.

Squaring his shoulders and leaving his carbine, he marched out of the cabin and up onto the walls.

As he mounted them, the sound of the pipes was heard over the noise of battle and he had to admit they were a wonderful set. At first, he was unaware of the sounds of battle dying away, and the fact the Indians had faltered in their attack.

'LOOK! LOOK OVER THERE!' shouted a trooper.

Those who heard him looked to where he was pointing and quickly called their comrades. The Indians had stopped shooting and were staring fixedly towards the same spot.

They all saw a thick greyish green coloured mist starting to rise from the ground. Almost as suddenly, the mist started to lift a little although some of it still swirled around just above ground level. As it cleared even more, the defenders gasped at what they saw.

Coming towards the fort was a marching column of infantry soldiers led by an officer riding a horse.

Will focussed his field glasses on them and shook his head in disbelief. He handed the glasses to Harvey. 'Tell me I'm dreaming.'

Harvey took the glasses and looked at the approaching soldiers. 'If you're dreaming, then so am I. They're redcoats, complete with bonnets, kilts and stockings. But we haven't had any of them here for fifty or more years. **LOOK!**'

Will and many others watched totally fascinated as more people appeared behind the redcoats, but these were not soldiers. These were a mixture of men, women and children all carrying firearms of sorts. Will's men had no difficulty in recognising many of them as the settlers who they had buried a few days earlier and had now risen from the dead.

But there were others.

The Indians just stood and stared at the approaching redcoats and risen dead without moving. Even as the defenders watched, the redcoats formed two lines and began firing volley after volley at the Indians, who continued standing still and making no attempt to move. The dead settlers also fired at their killers. Groups of Indians fell after each volley. They made no attempt to fight back or flee. It seemed to the watching defenders the Indians were rooted to the ground: too scared to move.

All the while Jock Murray continued playing the bagpipes.

Finally, no Indians were left standing.

The redcoats reformed, and with the dead settlers, began marching towards the fort.

'**EVERYONE OUTSIDE!**' cried Will. '**FORM A GUARD OF HONOUR FOR THEM!**' His instructions were repeated.

By the time the redcoats and the others, reached the fort, every available defender, including women and children had formed a guard of honour for them. Those who had weapons, presented them in a salute as their saviours passed. Their officer raised his sword to his lips and saluted Will as he passed. Will saluted him back.

Close to the redcoats it was seen that none of them had faces...only skulls. Likewise, their hands were only bones. Will had no doubt their uniforms hung on skeletons.

Just as suddenly as it had arisen and vanished, another grey green mist rose up. The redcoats and the dead settlers marched into it. Minutes later, it cleared, and there were no signs of their saviours.

'To think, we never believed in the legend,' said a chastened Dougal to Will.

'Didn't you say you had to be a united community?'

'Yes. And that's what we are today. Regardless of the rest of the country being at war, We've settled our differences and fought as one. Those men of 1763 and later victims have had their revenge. I doubt these Indians round here will cause us any trouble ever again.'

Several minutes later, the first of Will's scouts returned and reported. 'It's just unbelievable Cap'n. Out of all the hostiles We've looked at so far, they're all dead, but none of them are showing any wounds: they don't have a mark on them. Just a look of terror on their faces as if they have died of fright.'

'I have no doubt that's what happened to them.'

In the following hours, the Indian women appeared under a flag of truce and recovered their men's bodies, but only after all weapons had been removed.

It was time to tidy up inside the fort, which was where Will was met by a small deputation led by Cal Lootman and a Confederate sergeant.

'Sir,' said Cal. 'On behalf of all the men, we have a request to make.'

'I think I know what you are going to ask,' replied Will. 'And I agree. All our dead are to be buried together irrespective of the colour of their uniforms. They fought and died together fighting a common enemy and it is only right that they should lie together. That's how they will be remembered.'

'Thank you, sir!' Both sergeants saluted Will.

AUTHOR'S NOTE

There are a few suggestions as the origin of the Black Bear, but I have settled for the one as described in this tale. It dated back to the Seven Years War in America (1756-1763).

Light at the End of the Tunnel

The dreary late, cold November afternoon was dragging to an early close. It was one of those days which never really got light. Low clouds hung around all day, although their threat of rain never materialised. Len Chandler, which was the name he now used, pulled his jacket closer around himself whilst he tried to decide if he really wanted another beer with his fellow navvies, in the cosy warmth of the *Oak Inn*. The roaring fire in the bar was very inviting. Unlike most of his fellow work mates, he was not a great drinker.

Today had been a typical *randy*, which was the name navvies gave to their drinking excesses following being paid. Dressing in their finest and often colourful clothes, they headed to the nearest town for a spending and drinking spree. Being the year 1815, there were no police to stop them and the local parish constables played it very safe and kept out of their way. Whilst the local publicans did a roaring trade, other property owners were usually left with vast bills to pay for the damage the navvies caused. Those with any sense boarded up their windows before the navvies arrived.

Contrary to what was normally expected, Len's group was fairly restrained, and if anything, down-hearted. The effects of Napoleon's final defeat earlier in June, were now being felt. Suddenly the labour market was flooded with former soldiers and sailors; all of whom had been abandoned by their grateful government and left to fend for themselves in the labour market. Now there were more people looking for work than there were vacancies. Navvies were no exception and the new canal building owners had the upper hand with a vengeance.

Quite simply, you did what the owners said, or you were out of a job.

That was only part of the problem. Most canal companies supplied the tools, food and drink used by their workforce. In what originally seemed to be a generous move, they loaned money to their workers who regularly ran short nearing payday. Unfortunately, loans need to be repaid, and these interest rates were extortionate. Thus, at a stroke, the employers controlled most of their workers, who could do little or nothing about it.

But there were other reasons why Len's group was very dispirited. It concerned the next phase of their canal building project. They were moving up onto the Torregeman Moors, which was an area shunned by most people and animals.

The land was wild, windswept, cold and inhospitable. Two previous attempts had been made to cross it, by canal, but all to no avail. And now Len's employers wanted to try their luck again and have another go. To be fair, if completed, it would make this canal company a considerable amount of money by shortening the alternative route by several hours. In theory it was a straight forward enterprise, but there were various problems which had to be overcome.

Firstly, much of the ground was quite marshy and which required very strong shoring up within a matter of hours to prevent the sides from collapsing. The second difficulty was a hill which required tunnelling through and was a mixture of sand coupled with dense rock. As with the work on the moors, the sandy stretches needed instant shoring up with stonework faced with bricks. And there was a serious risk of flooding. It was anticipated the latest nineteenth century building skills could cope with these and other construction problems.

But were they up to combatting the ghostly protectors of Torregeman Moors, who had caused the previous attempts to fail?

Legend had it they had originally been home to a group of local families who fled there from the Roman invaders. Here they harassed the invaders for some time, using the marshy conditions to their advantage.

The area was a mass of tangled and wet paths with unexpected crevices appearing in the occasional rock formations. These led to a series of underground tunnels which were almost impossible to find by chance. You had to know they were there. The land then was much wetter and the locals used stilts for travelling through it. Encumbered by their armour, the Romans fell an easy prey to them.

The Romans left them alone for a while, whilst they learnt the arts of fighting on stilts. Then it was time for revenge.

A party of Romans managed to negotiate a truce with the defenders under the guise of ending the war and treating them as equals. It was a lengthy task, but the Romans were patient. Once the details were agreed, the Romans were taken into some of the places where their former enemies lived. Here they were treated as honoured guests for a day and night of feasting and other celebrations.

Most of their hosts, but not all of them, believed the Romans wanted peace and lowered their guard. During the night, the Romans murdered the sentries and lit a series of warning lights for the waiting legionaries who had followed them to attack the settlement. The surprise was almost complete, and very few men, women and children escaped.

Those who did were the ones who had distrusted their Roman guests, stayed away from the celebrations and remained in their secret hideaways.

The lucky ones were killed in the ensuing battle. Others were either very cruelly executed or taken as slaves. Roman justice spared nobody. Ever afterwards the site was shunned by humans, except for a few desperate men and women fleeing from justice. But even they were unable to hide out there for very long because of its unwelcoming and ghostly haunted atmosphere, especially when strange lights were seen from time to time. Their sleep was regularly disturbed by the screams of the tortured Roman victims.

As the years progressed, legends sprung up about the site being haunted and the strange lights were believed to be the ghosts of those people who had been massacred, by the treacherous Romans. It was said, although nobody could ever trace where the tale originated, how these ghosts had only one interest...revenge for their murder on anyone who foolishly trusted them. They effected it by using phantom lights to lure unwary travellers to their deaths. At least it was assumed to their deaths as most of them were never seen again.

Within some sixty years of the massacre happening, the area was believed to be inhabited by unearthly spirits and it was now known as Torregeman Moors after the local God of the Underworld. He was reputed to look most unfavourably on anyone entering his realm, both above and below ground. Anyone who needed to do so, for whatever reason, first had to ask his permission and, if requested, make a sacrifice to him. Normally such sacrifices were of animals although local folklore told of humans often being used. Torregeman's word was absolute, and you crossed or offended him at your peril.

It was a most unwelcoming place in a very hostile environment, shunned by humans and wildlife.

The two previous navvy attempts to build a canal had been driven off the site. There was some suggestion they had failed to appease or offended Torregeman in some way. Many navvies never went onto the site and those who did quickly left, complaining of hearing screams, seeing moving lights and feeling very frightened in what they described as *a terrible, hellish and unearthly atmosphere*. These men had been chosen originally for the site because they were the hardiest and most fearless of all the crews. If they had been frightened off so easily, what chance did the next crews stand?

This was the location where Len and his mates were destined for next.

Neither Len nor any of his fellow navvies had any wish or desire to go onto the site, but knew they had no option with all the unemployed men hanging around just waiting for their jobs. Faced with the inevitable, Len knew they had to go and remain there until the work was completed, the surveyors had left the site, or they were all dead.

Unlike the others, Len had been educated and kept mainly to himself which was accepted by the others. As a navvy you did not ask any questions about anyone's background or even their real name. Your fellow workers would tell you, if and when, they wanted to, and not before. Undoubtedly, many were fugitives from justice, as was Len.

His real name was Carver Leonard Maxstoke.

Until early 1809 he had been an infantry captain fighting against the French at Corunna. Although not being particularly wealthy, he was a practical and efficient soldier, which did not endear him to his superiors. Here he had the misfortune to be under the command of a major who had been promoted way beyond his level of competence. Len was able to cope with him, but the real problem was Sergeant Jasper Kent, who undermined Len's authority whenever it suited him. No matter what he was instructed to do, Kent only complied if it suited him, and rarely if ever obeyed any instruction he was given. Whenever Len tried to have the man disciplined, he was always thwarted by his major and other senior officers. Kent was considered to be a hero in his eyes, and he could do no wrong.

In reality, he had a considerable hold on the major, who was too scared to do anything about it.

At one stage during the Battle of Corunna, Len had been ordered to attack a French position. He passed the order on, but once the attack started, Kent overruled him and ordered the men to retreat. Len tried to stop them but was unable to do so. Unfortunately, he was seen running after his men trying to stop them, and it was considered he had joined in their flight. Kent agreed with this version and was believed over Len. A court-martial followed where Len was dishonourably discharged for cowardice in the face of the enemy and sentenced to transportation for life after returning to England.

Fortunately, some of his men were unhappy with what had happened but could not openly support him. But they arranged his escape and gave him some money and weapons and then he was on his own. Now he had a price on his head and faced being hanged if caught. Realistically he could only get his good name back by proving Kent to be a liar, but he knew that would never happen.

He had no other trade apart from being a soldier and re-enlisting in the ranks did not appeal to him. Len knew it would only be a matter of time before he was recognised. If that happened, then his chances of avoiding a death sentence were very unlikely. His only chance of survival was to disappear and adopt a new identity in an environment where that could happen.

Becoming one of many canal navigators or navvies as they were called, was one way of doing just that. Apart from the security it offered, he quite enjoyed the work. The years rolled on, and Napoleon was finally defeated earlier that year, but job security could no longer be guaranteed. Regardless of his feelings about starting work on Torregeman Moors, Len knew he would have to go up there.

All too soon, Monday morning arrived and in complete contrast to the weekend, it was a lovely sunny, clear but cold day. Len hoped it was a good sign as he joined the convoy of horses and carts which would take him, his mates and their equipment up to the moors. Their job was to dig out the tunnel, whilst other gangs worked on its approaches. Working on the tunnel was the more dangerous of the jobs. Like his mates, Len was wrapt in his own thoughts. Trying hard not to be superstitious, he wondered how many of them would return. Building canals was dangerous work with no shortages of injuries and deaths, without offending Torregeman.

Navvies had one big advantage over most other people, although it did not seem to have worked with the earlier ones up here.

They were very conscious of offending the spirits who inhabited the land they dug into. To offset this problem, when they were on site none of them ever used their real names, only nicknames. Len was known as the Moonraker because he came from Wiltshire.

'Is it true We've got a new foreman up here?' Len heard one of them ask.

'Yeah!' came a reply. 'Some soldier who's now out of a job.'

'I expect he knows nothing about canals,' commented another.

Much against his will, Len was interested but also concerned. An old soldier? What were the chances they would know one another? Negligible, he argued to himself. Len had been out of the army for nearly seven years and had changed considerably in that time. He had a much thicker body and his whiskers and beard, just like his hair, were a steely grey. No one would ever recognise him now. Or so he hoped.

All too soon the navvies arrived at the workings and climbed out of their carts where they were greeted by a large bald-headed man who was their new foreman. Even before the man spoke, Len's heart sank as he had no difficulty in recognising Jasper Kent.

'I'm your new foreman and you call me sergeant or Sergeant Kent. Now stow your gear and I want you ready to start digging within the hour. Understood?'

A muttering answered him.

'You call me sergeant! Now let's hear you!'

'Yes, sergeant!'

The men quickly set up their camp, gathered their tools and prepared to dig. Kent gave them their instructions. 'Any questions?'

'Yes,' replied one of them. 'When do we ask permission of Torregeman to enter his realm?'

'You can forget all that nonsense,' snarled Kent.

'But we need his permission and protection or he'll demand a sacrifice.

And it could be some of us. We have to get his permission first, or else his phantom lights will lure us to our deaths.'

'Another word from you or anybody else, and you'll be the sacrifice by going off the site. I don't give this for Torregeman.' Kent finished speaking, opened his breeches and urinated over the ground. He had already gathered some cronies who laughed loudly as they followed his example. 'Do your worst, Torregeman,' they cried.

There was a shocked silence, which was broken by Kent. 'Nothing's happened. Now get on with your work.'

Len stood at the rear of the group where he quietly begged Torregeman's forgiveness and permission to enter his realm. Several of the men nearby did the same. In the days which followed, Len kept out of Kent's way as best as he could, but he knew it could not last. He had seen Kent looking at him intently, clearly trying to remember where they had met. On one occasion he asked him outright, but Len shrugged his shoulders and assured Kent he was mistaken, but the sergeant was not convinced. Len knew Kent was asking the others about him and was grateful for having kept his past and true name a secret.

They started work on the tunnel after Kent and his cronies had performed their urinating ceremony. For several days all went well, but then the accidents started happening. It was soon realised the navvies who were being injured were the ones who had fallen foul of Kent. Whilst Len knew only too well how it was only a matter of time before Kent picked on him, he was surprised when it happened.

Kent suddenly called out to all the men to stop working. They laid their tools down or else leant on them. Marching over to Len, Kent pulled him out in front of the others. 'I know now who you are…Captain Carver Leonard Maxstoke, dismissed for cowardice in the face of the enemy. Sentenced to transportation but escaped. So now you have a price on your head, which I'm going to claim whilst you can look forward to being hanged…'

Before he had finished, there came a severe rumbling and the roof of the tunnel began collapsing, only held back temporarily by some of the stonework. Once the dust had settled, the men realised they were trapped.

But that was not all.

They were suddenly aware of numerous lights appearing all round them: far more than they had brought into the tunnel. Len was the first to see each lamp was held by a ragged looking person. These creatures surrounded the trapped navvies but then made a small path for the last arrival. Once again Len was the first to see him. He was taller than the others and his eyes seemed to burn like red hot coals. 'Lord Torregeman,' he said and bowed his head respectfully. Several of his closest workmates did the same.

'You have invaded my realm,' said Torregeman in a strange but recognisable English.

'We asked your permission,' replied Len, acting as spokesman.

'Some of you did, but others did not. You,' he signalled Kent. 'What is going on here?'

'This man here,' Kent pointed at Len. 'Is a coward and should be punished as such.'

Torregeman looked at Len. 'What have you got to say?'

'He knows as well as I do who the coward is. Him! He deliberately disobeyed the orders and ordered our men to run away. I followed and tried to stop them. At my trial, I was not believed and punished, whilst this man's treachery was not.'

As Len was speaking, he was aware how the lights were dimming.

'Obviously someone is lying and in here we do not approve of treachery.' A growl of support came from the other creatures. By now the lights had almost gone out with the exception of a single light at the end of the tunnel.

'Why should we believe you?' Torregeman asked Len. 'Prove it!'

Meanwhile, Kent threw caution to the winds and with his cronies ran off towards this remaining light. Len prevented his workmates from following. 'You fools!' he cried after Kent. 'Come back. Remember the legend!' But it was to no effect and they ran on.

'A wise decision,' said Torregeman. 'You clearly have concerns about the welfare even of your enemies and respect our customs. Wait for a proper light then go in peace.'

After only a few hours, Len and his men heard the welcome sounds of pickaxes which were soon accompanied by lights shining through the roof fall. He was quite surprised not to be arrested as he appeared in the open air. Instead he was asked numerous questions about what had happened and where was Sergeant Kent and the other men.

They had all agreed not to make any mention of Torregeman, fearing they would not be believed. Clearly something had happened to the missing men. All they said was a light had appeared at the end of the tunnel and Kent had led the race towards it.

The canal engineer shook his head. 'Didn't they know about the phantom lights around here which lure people to the deaths?'

'I tried to tell them,' replied Len. 'But they would not listen, but then Sergeant Kent would never take advice.'

The engineer looked at him strangely but said nothing.

Work on the canal ceased and was not resumed. Jasper Kent and his cronies were never seen again.

AUTHOR'S NOTE

Navvies were very superstitious when it came to digging into the ground, and disturbing the spirits there. They always asked for absolution before doing so, but still only used nicknames to be on the safe side.

The Battle of Corunna was fought on 16 January 1809 as part of the Peninsular War against Napoleon. Despite the harsh winter conditions, British troops had been chased across Spain by the French to Corunna. During the night, most of the British troops were evacuated but their commander Sir John Moore was killed. Both sides were able to claim a victory.

Wiltshire Moonrakers were supposedly the derogatory name given to some yokels during the 18th century, who were raking in a pond for smuggled goods when they were surprised by Excise men. The yokels explained they were trying to gather a great big cheese from the water, which in reality was the moon. It worked and the Excise Men left them to their *simple ways*.

As far as I am aware, there is no lord of the underworld called Torregeman.

The Inheritance

'Come here, Pascall!' instructed Prison Officer Fieldman. 'Get your gear together. You're leaving. Or do you like here so much you want to stay?'

Michael Carter smiled in acknowledgment and gritted his teeth. 'Coming, sir,' he replied. Throughout all the time he had been in this prison, Fieldman and the others only knew him as Mark Pascall, which was the name he had used on his arrest, although his proper name was Michael Carter.

The good news was he would be free in just a few minutes, after having served half of his sentence. Yet he would not be entirely free for a few more months, as per the terms of his licence. It would be silly now to overreact to Fieldman's goading and lose his remission for bad behaviour. Nevertheless, heaven help Fieldman if the man ever crossed him again.

It only took a few seconds to gather his pitifully few belongings and precede his tormenter off the wing. Several of his cellmates wished him luck and looked at him with envy as he passed. Michael quietly acknowledged their good wishes absently, taking care not to give Fieldman any excuse to cancel his release.

At last they were in reception where he exchanged his prison wear for his own clothes. They smelt musty and he would dispose of them as soon as he could. Then his electronic tag was fitted, the small door to the side of the main gate opened and he was free. At least he was as free as far as his tag would allow him. It was a pleasant summer morning and he decided to walk to the probation hostel which was to be his home for the next six months.

Nevertheless, a shortage of money was a pressing problem which needed to be addressed as soon as practical. So was having to work, at least until his licence had expired and the tag removed. He wondered what they had arranged for him.

*　　*　　*

Michael was a competent and capable fraudsman, who had only been caught by his own carelessness. He specialised in identity theft and emptying people's bank accounts before the victim knew the money had gone. As a general rule, he only used a fake character for a couple of days at the most, and preferably less if possible. He had no scruples whatsoever when it came to robbing people. If they suffered because of what he had done, then too bad. They should have been more careful.

He had been successful for quite a while and enjoyed an expensive lifestyle but was caught by the police, because he was careless and used several stolen cards at the same cashpoint. Unbeknown to him at the time, a fraud investigator was standing next in the queue. The detective became suspicious and followed Michael to another bank and watched him repeat the performance. Michael was arrested and found to be in possession of numerous bank cards, none of which was his. A prison sentence followed, but only regarding those cards, because he admitted nothing else.

This other money was still hidden, although he could not use the other cards as they were either out of date or had been stopped. All he had to do now was to keep out of trouble for the next six months.

At last, the time came for the tag to be removed. Somehow, he had managed to hold down a very boring cleaning job in a factory. Now he was free. The lease had long since expired on his lodgings whilst he was in prison, but the probation service helped him find somewhere else to live. The only thing in its favour was the rent was cheap. Given the state of the flat, the landlord could hardly charge him anymore.

Michael had only been there a few days, when he received a visitor.

Always suspicious of the unexpected, Michael was wary of this man, who introduced himself as Timothy Semple and produced a visiting card from a very upmarket firm of solicitors in London. The visiting card was a work of art in its own right. 'I believe you are Mr Mark Pascall and I've been tasked with giving you this letter,' smiled Semple.

Michael immediately stepped back making no attempt to take it.

'Don't worry,' Semple continued. 'It's not a summons. The complete opposite in fact. My senior partner needs to discuss a very substantial inheritance which is due to you. And I'm sure he would not want to come and see you here.' Semple pointed at the flat.

Michael had to agree, and his mind worked overtime. Who on earth had a substantial inheritance to pass on to him? He took another look at the letter and saw it was addressed to Mark Pascall, his prison name. And that was how Semple had addressed him. Having nothing to lose, he agreed to go with Semple to London straight away.

If first impressions counted, then Michael was staggered by the size and opulence of the offices where Semple worked. He was even more impressed by the way he was treated by the senior partner. Having stolen Mark Pascall's identity before his arrest, Michael had no problems answering questions about the man's background, helped by his being an only child. Once the questions had been answered to the solicitor's satisfaction, he sat back, smiled and explained what Michael was doing in his office.

Apparently, Mark Pascall was now the owner of a substantial fortune and large estate in South Warwickshire.

Michael wasted no time in going there and was impressed both by its size and isolation. It did not take him long to realise the house was far too big for his own use and his heart sank. One of the conditions imposed on him by the inheritance was he could never sell the house or the estate, although he could rent them out. He had been tempted to admit he was not Mark Pascall, but Michael did not relish the idea of giving away his true identity and meeting Prison Officer Fieldman again.

Land agent, David Hannay, met his new employer off the train, and showed him around the house and estate. He explained how several people worked on the estate lands and other domestic staff came in on a daily basis or when needed. After David had gone, Michael sat down to a light lunch of sandwiches and coffee. In between mouthfuls, he opened much of the accumulated post and read through it. There were many circulars and other junk mail along with some bills and other estimates. He would talk to Hannay about what to do with them.

It was then he saw the letter from the film company asking if they could use his premises for and land for location shots for a new production. The letter offered a very hefty daily fee for using the land and an even larger one for scenes shot inside the house. Even to Michael's limited architectural knowledge, he could see the potential for using it in films and television productions.

The house, known locally as Pascall Manor dated from the mid-late 18th century with later extensions at the back, leaving the front more or less in its original style. Its approach was along a wide avenue of trees with shrubs on either side, ending in a large circle for coach and horses to use. Michael found it easy to imagine what it would look like either surrounded by fog or with a full moon behind it.

Without waiting any longer, he telephoned the writer, but was too late. The letter had remained unanswered, and they had found somewhere else. It was a blow, but they promised to keep his details on their files.

During the next few days he spent much time with Hannay going over the estate accounts and discovering just what he owned. Hannay confirmed Michael was unable to sell or otherwise dispose of any of the property, although he could take whatever money it raised in rents and sale of produce.

'Why is there this embargo on my selling it?' he demanded one evening as he and Hannay sat in the library.

'It goes back a long time to before this house was built,' replied Hannay. 'Somehow the government of the day really had it in for you Pascalls. They took over the old house and the estate and rented it on a 1000 years lease with the proviso it could only be leased to the Pascall family. Thereby they ensured the Pascalls would be saddled with the property and unable to sell it before the year 2679. Since then it has become a money pit. All attempts to make money on the estate have failed.'

'Hasn't anyone tried?'

'Oh yes, but they usually end up upsetting Thomas Pascall's ghost and fail miserably.'

'Upsetting a ghost?' Michael demanded incredulously. 'A ghost? Surely you don't believe in such nonsense?'

Standing up, Hannay crossed over to the many books on the nearby shelves, selected one and opened it. After flicking through the pages, he handed it to Michael, pointing to a marked section. 'It's bit of light reading for you. I'll leave it with you for the night and we'll discuss it tomorrow.'

After he had gone, Michael poured himself another brandy and settled down to read.

In late 1722 the house then owned by Sir Lowery Pascall, known as Pascall Manor was built on the site of an earlier one which had been destroyed by fire in 1682, following the beheading of Thomas Pascall for treason in 1679. Local folklore maintained the fire had been caused by individuals who were loyal to the Crown and to cause more financial problems to the hated Pascall family. Regardless of whoever was responsible, the area was allowed to deteriorate with no money being spent on it and it was generally shunned by people. Many locals maintained the headless ghost of Thomas Pascall kept watch over the land, deterring anyone from settling there.

Sir Lowery was a wealthy rake and drunkard who in 1778 needed to leave London for a while, which denied him access to all the fleshpots and debauchery the Capital had to offer. Having once been a member of the now defunct Hell Fire Club of Francis Dashwood's fame, he set up his own version along those lines. Here he regularly arranged monthly meetings which lasted several days. In effect they were nothing more than orgies interspersed with satanic rituals and black masses. Admittance was strictly by invitation only. Having no shortage of money meant nobody could really challenge him on anything he chose to do. When he and his fellow revellers were performing, no woman regardless of her age and marital status was safe from their lechery.

If that was not enough, revellers rode roughshod over the land and nearby villages causing all manner of destruction. The local vicar was powerless to do anything and received no help whatsoever for his parishioners from the bishop. This was hardly surprising as he and Sir Lowery were distantly related. It was rumoured, but never proved, the bishop attended several of the meetings. The local inhabitants had no option but to accept these abuses, but not without great resentment.

By 1778 the War of American Independence was in full swing and used by some of the aristocracy to purchase commissions in the army and made their wayward sons go and fight. It certainly helped the locals. Within only a matter of weeks of starting up, Pascall's Club was well in decline, but the rancour was still rife in the area, inflamed by the way he continually raised their rents and evicted those who could not pay.

And now he had another pasttime with just a few of his older comrades.

Initially they found some women who were prepared to take part in his latest game. Even if they were unwilling, they had little option but to participate. They were given a head start and needed to get off his land before being caught. Dressing up in black hats and skull masks, they rode around the area at night time, holding blazing torches chasing these terrified women.

It was on the second of these forays when a strange rider, on a black horse and dressed all in black joined them. When they realised this rider did not have a head, they thought it was an excellent disguise. However, this rider took Sir Lowery on one side and instructed him to stop these games, advising him there would not be another warning. Once the game started, the riders spread out as they had not seen which direction the prey had taken. Whoever caught the prey had her for the night, so there was great rivalry.

Sir Lowery apparently ignored this warning and during the next time the game happened, one of the so called hunters, found himself with the headless horseman alongside him. Regarding him as a potential rival, he lashed out with his crop to deter the competition. The horseman said nothing, but merely steered his own massive horse into the other beast who stumbled, throwing his rider. The man hit the ground hard and broke his neck.

He was the first of several similar violent deaths and people soon gave Sir Lowery's club a wide berth.

FOOTENOTE

Nobody knows what happened to Sir Lowery. His headless body was found one morning close to a bloodstained thin rope which had been stretched across the road at neck height. It appeared he had been galloping along this track, as was his practice, and been beheaded. The head was never found. Neither was anyone charged with his murder. Most people thought Sir Thomas Pascall's headless ghost had been responsible.

His was the first of strange unexplained deaths, usually resulting in the headless body of the current tenant of Pascall Manor being found near a thin bloodstained cord stretched out across one of the many bridle paths on the estate.

'What absolute drivel,' Michael tossed the book to one side. 'A Headless Horseman indeed!' Then he stopped as an idea came to him. He would hold a pop concert here and market it as Headless Horseman Events. Michael had no doubts such an event would cause all manner of upset on the estate and elsewhere, but the locals were the least of his worries. A pop concert in such a venue would bring him in thousands. To hell with the locals.

*   *   *

As he expected, the first objections came from Hannay, who was quickly overruled. 'Were having it, and whether or not you like the idea, is of no importance to me. You can always go and look for another job.'

'All I am trying to do is warn you about not upsetting Sir Thomas's ghost.'

'Ghost! Ghost! Where are you living man? This is the twenty-first century…not the dark ages. Ghosts don't exist. End of story.' Michael gave a chopping motion with his right hand.

Hannay knew he was beaten. He was struggling to get his two daughters through university, and this was not the time to be out of a job. With a heavy heart he listened to Michael's plans for the pop festival. Despite himself, Hannay felt his employer seemed to know what he was doing.

People would start arriving on the Thursday with some smaller events happening. These would increase dramatically on the Friday and culminate on the Saturday night. It seemed Michael had picked a winner. The local residents and police felt differently and were far from happy, but there was nothing they could do about it.

Another person who was also far from happy made his views known personally to Michael on the Saturday night.

Michael had gone into part of the formal garden attached to the Manor when he was aware of a horse and rider standing there. As far as he could see, the rider was dressed in black and had no head. 'Who the hell are you?' Michael demanded. 'And don't give me all that crap about being the ghost of Sir Thomas bloody Pascall. There's no such thing as ghosts. Now get off my land!'

'As you obviously know who I am,' replied a dis-embodied voice. 'There is no point in having a conversation. Just be warned this noise must stop. There will be no other warning. If you persevere in spoiling my peace, you will regret it. Be warned.'

The rider disappeared before Michael could make any reply.

Michael had to admit the rider's outfit was impressive. Even down to how some of the horse's mane and tail seemed glow a phosphorous green colour, although some sort of synthesiser would explain the voice. 'I'll let you think you've won, matey, whoever you are,' he said aloud. 'Because there's nothing on tomorrow night. But just you wait till next month when I've got a big gathering of bikers coming on site with all their machines and pop music. They'll frighten your precious horse.'

On the Saturday of the bikers gathering, Michael waited in his garden for the horseman to appear and was not surprised when he did. Only this time Michael was sat astride his 1200cc motor bike, which he had adapted and removed his exhaust silencers. The noise it made was truly deafening. If this *phantom horseman* appeared again, he would run him off his land. How he sneered when he said the words *phantom horseman*.

Although he had only been half expecting the man to appear, Michael was surprised how quietly the horse had arrived. He was suddenly aware of horse and rider alongside him. They were as he remembered from their last meeting.

'I warned you last time we met...'

'And I told you to get off my land. Now go!' Even as he spoke, Michael revved up his motorbike. Surprisingly the horse was unaffected by its noise.

The Headless Horseman galloped away, and Michael followed just to make sure. He was both surprised and impressed by the speed of the horse and how unconcerned it was by the motorbike. Ever since having his first motorbike, Michael had enjoyed driving fast and noisily by horses and watching them scamper in fright. But this horse was different.

It remained totally unconcerned.

Michael's headless body was found during the following morning. Nearby was his motorbike with no obvious signs of damage except where it had slid along the ground. When he arrived at the scene, David Hannay looked knowingly at the bloodstained thin cord stretched across the path just where Michael's throat and neck would have been.   He was not surprised to see his head was missing.

Neither was he surprised to hear tales some time later about the ghost of a headless motorcyclist being seen and heard riding around the estate.

AUTHOR'S NOTE
The Hellfire Club was the name given to several exclusive clubs used by eighteenth century rakes, though the best known was operated by Sir Francis

Dashwood in and around High Wycombe between 1752 and 1762.

Headless horsemen are popular ghosts.

Harry Grant's Night

'**But you can't go into the *Green Dragon*, tonight,**' protested Police Constable Lee Savage. 'Not tonight of all nights!'

Newly promoted Sergeant Alan Marton paused, in his briefing of the Night Shift, and glared at the speaker. 'And just what do you mean by that remark?' A sudden silence followed in the parade room.

This was Alan's first Friday night duty as sergeant.

It was also the first of the town's two-day annual hiring fair, now called a *Mop Fair*. Today's event did not engage in the hiring of servants and labourers, but instead operated as a large fun fair in the town centre. Taking advantage of the many extra people coming into town for the evening, the pubs did a roaring trade and were permitted to stay open until 11.00pm. Visiting the pubs at closing time was an important part of police work especially on this night and tomorrow whilst the *Mop* was in town.

Alan Marton was an unimaginative man who had received a successful charisma by-pass operation. After being a constable for just over twenty-five years, he was suddenly promoted to sergeant and posted to the town earlier in the week and went straight on to night duty on Monday.

His promotion came as a complete surprise to everyone, including himself. The cynics, of which there is never a shortage in the police, all maintained it was a case of mistaken identity. They may have been right.

There was an Alan Merton elsewhere in the force, and it was believed he was the one who should have been promoted. But somewhere along the chain of command, it was rumoured Marton had been confused with Merton and an injustice had been done.

During the short time Marton was in post, he had seen his inspector once, and his chief inspector not at all. Being on nights meant he was virtually his own boss and could police the town as he wished, within certain parameters, and be fairly free from any interference from above.

When he was promoted, Marton was told by the chief constable how he still had ample opportunity of further promotion to inspector: and Sergeant Alan Marton was determined to make an impression.

With this very much in mind, he was not prepared to be told by a young constable just where he could and could not go.

'I'll ask you again. Just what do you mean by that remark, PC Savage?' Marton repeated.

Lee looked embarrassed and his ears started to go red. He was a young constable who had only been in post a few months. 'They say,' he swallowed. 'They say Harry Grant's ghost walks in there on the anniversary of his death. And that's tonight.'

The rest of the shift fidgeted uncomfortably and suddenly became interested at something in their pocket books.

Telling the story of Harry Grant was a regular wind-up for new members in this station and they saw no reason why their sergeant should be excluded. But if the truth was known, none of them ever went into the *Green Dragon* on a Harry Grant's Night.

And if they were honest, not one of them had any intention of ever doing so.

Marton took a deep breath and hissed. 'If I say that you or anybody else on this shift, will visit the *Green Dragon* tonight, then that is what we'll do. I will not have it said about this shift how the tail wags the dog. Is…that… clear?' He punctuated each word by wagging his right forefinger at Lee and the others.

The shift members nodded miserably.

Marton continued with his briefing before ordering them out onto their allotted duties. There were only four of them tonight plus himself. He watched them quietly collect their radios and leave the station but without any of their usual banter. The last one to leave was PC Jon Wallace, who was having a few final puffs on his pipe.

Jon was shortly due to retire after having served for more than thirty years in the police. He had spent most of his service here in the town. There was very little he did not know about policing and the town's inhabitants.

An unambitious man, Jon never wanted promotion and was quite content working the beat, where he was a father figure to the younger men and regularly fussed around them.

He was concerned tonight because Marton had upset them.

'What's wrong with young Savage, tonight, sarge?' he asked innocently, not having been at the briefing because he was dealing with an enquiry at the front of the station. Nevertheless, he was well aware of what had happened.

'I arranged with him to visit the *Green Dragon* tonight with me and he started rabbiting on about the anniversary of a ghost of someone called Grant. What a lot of rubbish.'

Jon took the pipe out of his mouth and looked directly at Marton. 'If you'll take my advice, don't go in the *Green Dragon* tonight. Go tomorrow after the *Mop* has finished or any other day but not tonight…It's Harry Grant's Night…and it's not safe.'

'Oh really,' sighed Marton. 'I credited you with more sense than to believe such utter rubbish. You mean to tell me you believe this nonsense about a ghost of someone who was killed in there?'

'I assure you it's true, but it didn't happen quite like that,' began Jon. 'It happened back in my great grandfather's time in 1879. That was Benjamin Wallace. There have always been Wallaces in the police, here in the town since 1840.'

'Get on with it,' Marton sighed in exasperation. 'I haven't got all night,' he added looking pointedly at his watch.

'It was the *Mop Night* of Friday October 24th in 1879 when Sergeant Fred Hervey went into the *Green Dragon* for some reason or other. It looked later as if he had been involved in a fight with Harry Grant, the landlord. The Grants had always been a bad lot and young Harry who runs the pub now is just as bad.' Jon paused and took a puff of his pipe.

'Nobody knows for sure what happened, but when great grandfather got there, the place was a shambles, caused by broken glass, spilt beer, blood, Upset chairs were everywhere. That's where he found Harry Grant kneeling over Fred Hervey's body with a blood covered axe in his hand.'

'What happened then?' asked Marton, clearly interested despite himself.

'Great grandfather knelt beside the dying Fred Hervey who struggled to say just three words…*Harry…Grant…did…* To cut a long story short, everyone thought it was a clear case of murder and Fred Hervey was blaming Harry Grant for it. The Assizes jury agreed, and Harry Grant was hanged.'

'Rightly so,' interjected Marton.

'Actually I'm not so sure,' replied Jon. 'Great grandfather always had his doubts and was adamant Fred Hervey was trying to say something else. In fact, he spoke up for Grant at his trial and nearly lost his job for doing so. Grant always maintained the pub was being robbed by two strangers when Fred had come to his aid and got murdered in the process. He stuck to his story about trying to help Fred when great grandfather arrived. Nobody else was ever found who might have burgled the place and the blame naturally fell on Grant. There had been a hiring fair in town that day and Grant always maintained two visitors or more likely fair men had committed the murder. He protested his innocence right up the very end on the scaffold just before Christmas.'

'And just where does this so-called ghost come in?' sneered Marton.

'As I said, Harry Grant always protested his innocence and since then, no bobby with any sense has gone into the *Green Dragon* on the anniversary nights of the murder. It is said Grant's ghost appears on *Mop nights* seeking revenge on the police for bringing about his execution for an offence he always denied. But tonight is special: it's the actual day and date of the murder.'

'Has anyone tried it?' asked Marton.

'They've got more sense,' replied Jon. 'Why do you think neither the inspector nor the chief inspector is on duty here tonight.'

'I've heard quite enough of this rubbish,' snarled Marton, as he walked towards the police station door. 'Ghost or no ghost, I'll be there tonight.'

'For God's sake, man,' called Jon after him. 'Don't say I didn't try to warn you. If you must go in there tonight, then take me instead of young Savage. At least the Grants tolerate me.'

Marton ignored him and moved out into the town.

'What a load of old rubbish. This is 1975 and there's no such things as ghosts,' Marton said to himself, as he went down the police station steps. 'These young bobbies today: they'll do anything rather than the job they're paid to do.'

Yet he was surprised at Jon Wallace believing in ghosts. The man was old enough to have more sense.

∗   ∗   ∗

Marton had every intention of checking the public houses in the town and no ghosts were going to stop him.

Despite it being a Friday night, the town was quiet, and the *Mop* had already closed, encouraged by some very heavy rain about an hour earlier which had sent the visitors home. In the distance he heard the church clock strike 10.30pm and knew he had half an hour in which to visit the *Green Dragon* in the Market Place, before it closed. He arrived there several minutes later to find an unhappy Lee Savage waiting for him. Marton nodded to him, opened the door and the two police officers entered the pub.

A wave of hot air, beer fumes and tobacco smoke greeted them. All conversation stopped when they approached the bar. But it was soon replaced by calls of: **'OINK! OINK!'** and **'I smell bacon,'** and other abusive comments. Lee followed Marton's example and ignored them, although he looked around nervously. He had never been in here before.

The pub looked like it might have been recently refurbished, but if so, it was a waste of money. Regardless of the fake beams and subdued lighting, the walls and ceiling were all smoke browned. Apart from the general air of hostility, Lee noted several local criminals huddled in a corner trying hard, but failing, to look inconspicuous. He made a mental note never to bring his girlfriend in here.

'Are you the landlord of these premises?' Marton asked a small middle-aged, balding man, with old fashioned sideburns running down each cheek of his sallow complexioned face. At the same time, he noticed a large sepia framed picture on the wall behind the bar, which looked like an older version of the man he was addressing. He looked closer and saw it was titled: *Harry Joseph Grant murdered by the police 1879.*

'Don't you know what night it is?' hissed the man oozing hostility at the policemen. He was clearly the landlord. 'You must be mad to come here tonight of all nights.'

Marton ignored the outburst, but Lee swallowed nervously and wished he had been on an early shift instead of nights. Roll on 6.00am when he could go home.

'I am not concerned about ghosts and curses,' replied Marton. 'But I am concerned about your obviously selling alcohol to persons who are clearly under age.' He indicated a group of youngsters sat to one side and instructed Lee to take their names and addresses. This did not take him long as he knew most of them.

'I'll ask you again. What is your name landlord?' demanded Marton.

'Henry Joseph Grant.'

After telling Grant he would be reported, Marton looked at his watch and warned him it was nearly closing time. He added he would be back again later to make sure the law was being obeyed.

'If you come back here again tonight,' warned Grant. 'It'll be the last thing you'll ever do.'

The ensuing ominous silence was suddenly broken when someone started whistling the Laurel and Hardy theme tune, which was taken up by all the other drinkers in the pub.

Lee was relieved to get out of the *Green Dragon* and into the relatively fresh air of the Market Place.

'Did you see any ghosts?' sneered Marton. 'Of course not. Now I want you to have a drunk driver before the night is out.'

At 2.30am next morning, Marton was back patrolling the town again after having finished his paperwork and sandwiches. Given the chance he always preferred to patrol on foot and on his own. Marton did not enjoy being isolated in a metal box known as a police car, although he accepted they had their uses from time to time. He restricted their use by his staff.

In his opinion, a policeman needed to be on foot which made him more approachable. It was how he learnt to police in the 1950s and 60s. Likewise he could not see the need for policewomen except in certain circumstances. Marton was very much in the minority and his blinkered approach to progress was not universally supported.

It had now become very foggy and the last of the late-night revellers had long since gone home. 'Probably all scared of Harry Grant's ghost,' he mused to himself. As he turned into the Market Place1787, he was aware of a sudden drop in the temperature and the fog becoming much thicker as it swirled around his feet.

Looking down the Market Place, he saw the skeletal arms of a piece of fairground equipment looking like the gigantic legs of some primeval monster coming at him through the fog.

Marton suddenly felt very much alone.

He quickly shrugged off the feeling. 'I'll be believing in Harry Grant's

Ghost next,' he muttered to himself. But at that very moment, he heard laughter coming from the *Green Dragon*. Walking determinedly towards the pub, he was amazed to see a light flickering through the windows.

'I don't believe it,' he said aloud. 'Grant's completely ignored my warning. This is too much. I'll have to teach him a lesson he'll never forget.'

Yet Marton was not completely stupid and he radioed for Lee to join him. Unfortunately, Lee had obeyed his instructions, and was engaged at the police station with a drunk driver and could not help him. Two of his other officers were not answering their radios. In the end the only constable who could help him was Jon Wallace, but he was the other side of town and would take some time to meet up with his sergeant. Marton had stopped him taking a car.

Having told control where he was, Marton thrust open the door and stepped into the *Green Dragon*, determined to lay the *Ghost of Harry Grant* once and for all. There would be no *no-go* areas in the town when he was on duty.

Somehow the pub was different to when he had last been in there only a few hours ago. The dull subdued lighting had gone and been replaced with hissing gas brackets. Even the walls looked as if they had never been scrubbed or painted. Damp sawdust littered the floor and several spittoons were visible. There was a faded picture hanging up behind the bar, not of Harry Grant as he seen earlier, but of Queen Victoria.

There were only three men in the bar who did not see him enter at first. One was Harry Grant, who Marton recognised from the picture he had seen on his earlier visit, and clearly an older version of the current landlord. He was being held, albeit struggling, by a big man, whilst another one threatened him with an axe, laughing as he did so. All three men had greasy unkempt hair and Grant's two assailants wore grubby and dirty clothes. What a motley crew, thought Marton, amazed he did not remember the place as being quite so grotty when he came in earlier, especially with a litter of broken glass and several bottles on the floor.

It was only then he realised what he was seeing.

The two men were obviously attacking Grant.

Only Grant saw Marton arrive and he called: 'For Christ's sake Fred, help me!'

Marton reached for his personal radio to summon help, but it was gone, and his uniform was different. His tunic now had a high-necked collar. The man with the axe was the first to react. Leaving Grant, he raised the axe and moved towards Marton. For all his faults, Marton was no coward and he stood his ground. 'Don't be silly, man. Put it down!' he instructed.

But the man ignored him and continued with his attack. Moments later, Marton was fighting for his life and losing the battle. It would never be known if the man intended to hit Marton with the axe, or just keep him at bay whilst his mate ran past the two men as he made his escape.

As he drew level with Marton, he pushed him to one side just as his mate lashed down heavily with the axe. If Marton had not been pushed, the axe would have missed him, but instead as he reeled to one side, the axe came down heavily onto his collar bone and ploughed deeply into his chest and lungs. Marton collapsed to his knees fighting a losing battle for breath and fell onto the floor, aware his assailants had gone.

Grant immediately ran across to him and believing he was helping, pulled the axe out of Marton's body. As he did so, the door opened, and Jon Wallace came in, but he only saw Marton lying on the floor and bleeding to death. Taking out his personal radio he called for an ambulance and urgent assistance.

As Marton died in Jon's arms, he was aware how the *Green Dragon* was now back in the twentieth century, not as it had been only a few moments ago. He was also aware his killer was not the landlord, and a great injustice had been done many years ago.

He tried to say Grant had not been the murderer, nor responsible for his own death just now. 'Harry…Grant…did…' was all he managed to say before he died.

In the following stillness, all Jon could hear was a deep mocking laugh which seemed to fill the whole of the *Green Dragon*.

Harry Grant had got his revenge.

The obvious suspect for this murder, especially after his earlier hostility, was the current landlord, Henry Joseph Grant. However, he had a watertight alibi.

At the time of Sergeant Marton's murder he was in custody at the police station, having been arrested by PC Lee Savage for being a drunk driver.

The Filtonbury Snuff Boxes

'And in here, ladies and gentlemen,' announced the guide at Filtonbury Park, which had once been a private estate. But now it was the property of some business consortium who kept it open for visitors, until they obtained planning permission to develop the site, which had not yet been granted. With the possibility of the house being closed in the near future, people flocked to view it. The attendance figures rose as they came specifically to see one legendary item.

'In here, we have the famous Filtonbury Snuffboxes, one of which was owned by the infamous Claude Filtonbury himself. In fact, this was what has given successive members of the family the desire to collect snuffboxes.'

Melanie Flitch, the guide, who was passionately fond of snuffboxes, led the way into the small turret chamber and stood to one side to let the visitors in. 'This is why we have to restrict the numbers of our groups because, as you can see, there is not very much room in here. Please come right inside.'

Strictly speaking, her remark was unnecessary as the size of the room spoke for itself.

The visitors shuffled into the room and gazed in wonder at the vast collection of snuff boxes situated in glass cases and shelves around the walls. Others were displayed on tables, some of which were covered by glass. The centrepiece was a magnificent gold snuff box on a table surrounded by other obviously valuable pieces.

'And here is Claude's fabulous snuff box!' Melanie proclaimed proudly and pointed to the table's magnificent centre piece. It was a solid gold table top snuff box, about the size of a large heavy horse's hoof

A hub-bub of conversation followed which quickly subsided into gasps of wonder and appreciation. Melanie gave them a few moments to settle down before starting on a brief history of snuffboxes starting in 1493 following the discovery of tobacco and snuff in the New World. 'By the time Charles II was back in England, snuff taking was extremely popular amongst the wealthy who had their personal snuff boxes and larger ones for putting on tables,' Melanie continued. 'Making snuff boxes out of gold, silver and other expensive commodities was a sure-fire way of impressing your friends and neighbours. It was also a good idea to have them specially made with identifying features as a good way of making them less easy to steal.'

'I would have thought these would all have been under glass. Surely you're asking to have them stolen?' queried an incredulous visitor.

'That's quite correct,' Melanie confirmed. 'But the infamous Claude put a curse on anyone who touched his box without permission. The curse was later updated by other family members to include all the other snuffboxes in the collection.'

As Melanie had anticipated, there was a suitable intake of breath from her audience.

'Surely people have tried?' came a scathing voice from her audience.

'Oh yes they certainly tried…but…they never succeeded,' Melanie replied in a serious voice. 'They were usually driven mad, or just simply disappeared. Let me tell you about him.' She pointed to an oil painting of a man with a very sharp almost rat like face and wearing seventeenth century clothing.

Claude Filtonbury was best described as a totally unscrupulous survivor. When the Civil War broke out in 1642, he neither supported Parliament nor the Crown and endeavoured to remain neutral. But as the war moved across the Midlands, he was unable to enjoy such a happy state for long. Parliamentarians sacked his estate when he was unable to convince them of his loyalty. Similar problems followed with the Royalists for the same reason.

Realising he was in a no-win contest Claude rallied his similar minded friends and employees and took to the roads as highwaymen. Unlike many of his counterparts at the time, he attacked supporters of both parties and anybody else his gang came across. During the period of the Commonwealth, he was paid by Parliament to cause all manner of problems and fear amongst the Royalists. And he had the ability to do so with no shortage of recruits.

Matters changed dramatically in 1660 when Charles II regained his throne. Whilst Charles was prepared to forgive many of the excesses committed during those times, there were two exceptions. He had no mercy for the regicides who had condemned his father. And he made it clear there would be no mercy for Claude, although he was not one of them.

Claude left a trail of devastation behind him. Rape, pillage and murder were only some of them. He also delved into the black arts, supposedly turning himself into a giant rat which was why Charles said publicly he would not pardon him.

During 1662, Charles was given a large table top snuff box made of pure gold. Claude heard about it as he was making plans to leave England for the New World. He reasoned it would be an extremely valuable asset in his new life. Also, it would be a final snub to this new monarch who continued to make life difficult for him.

When Claude stole the snuff box, he thought fleetingly how easy it had been. Surely there had to be a catch.

There was.

It had all been a carefully planned trap and Claude walked right into it. Although he put up a fierce struggle, he was finally subdued and taken before the king.

Much to Claude's surprise, the king was very affable and invited him to breakfast. Over the meal he questioned Claude about his activities. Claude told him, stressing how he had been neutral during the war and preyed on both sides, something of which the king was unaware. Another surprise awaited Claude at the end of the meal. The king offered him a full pardon, on one condition.

In return for his freedom, Claude was to work directly for Charles in whatever way he was needed. Although he suspected such work was probably illegal, Claude jumped at the idea. Much of his early work involved tracking down regicides who had fled England, thinking they were safe in exile abroad, and arranging their deaths, usually in what appeared to be a fatal accident. Other enemies of the king met similar fates. For the mot part the new host countries were aware of the real cause of these deaths, but happily played them down.

Normally he received his instructions through one the king's officers, although they occasionally met. At one such meeting, Charles presented him with a replica of the gold snuff box as a token of his appreciation.

On his death bed, Claude entrusted the snuff box to his family along with certain instructions. The main ones being the snuff box had to remain in the family and must never be held under lock and key.

Melanie finished her tale and watched the visitors' eyes as they all looked at Claude's portrait and then the snuff boxes. But they really only had eyes for the one from the king.

'What happens if it's stolen?' someone asked.

'It's cursed and all manner of misery and misfortune will befall the thief,' replied Melanie, in a hushed and fearful voice. 'It's protected by phantom rats. Great big green ones and they are joined by other nameless creatures.'

'Has it ever been stolen?' asked another.

'Not to my knowledge.'

'But you're asking for it to be stolen, leaving it loose on this table.'

'It's protected.'

'I don't see any alarms.'

'They're not needed,' Melanie continued, opening her eyes wide. 'No one is prepared to risk the curse. Does anybody want to give it a try? You'll only have to worry about the phantom rats!'

There were no takers.

Actually, that was not strictly quite true.

At the rear of the display room, Connor Barton and Mitchell Lockwood had secretly filmed the room, all the display items and recorded Melanie's patter. Now they sat in a pub some twenty miles away and talked over what they had seen and heard.

'What do you think?' asked Connor.

'Definitely got possibilities and with no alarm system I could see in that room, they're asking to be done…'

'It's too easy. Doesn't seem right. Why hasn't it been done before? Perhaps it really is cursed?'

'Sounds like you're not keen,' replied Mitchell.

'I think I'll give it a miss; and you?'

'I'm going for it,' Mitchell confirmed. 'And there's no time like tomorrow. I'll hide somewhere in the grounds until everybody's gone home. It'll be a piece of cake. Sure you won't join me?'

Connor shook his head.

*　　*　　*

Melanie was the last to leave Filtonbury Park the next evening and ensured the special protection system was operating before she locked up for the night. Hidden in the bushes, Mitchell watched her leave and waited until it was dark before making his move. An accomplished burglar, he had already seen a weakness in a poorly locked door which presented no problem to him entering the building. Quickly gathering his bearings, he went up into the snuffbox room and opened the door. As he had expected, it was not locked. He was only vaguely aware of the door closing behind him.

Mitchell shone his small Maglite torch onto the table and went to scoop up the main snuff box, but he had not appreciated how heavy it was and needed two hands. Putting down the torch he picked up the snuff box to put it into the sports bag he had brought with him. As he did so, the torch rolled off the table, fell onto the floor and went out. Swearing he put the snuffbox down and searched for his torch. Not that it made any difference when he found the Maglite. It had broken in the fall. Just then the moon came out which gave him enough light to fit the snuff box and some others into the bag and return to the door. Turning the handle, he pulled the door towards him.

It did not move, no matter which way he turned the handle. Effectively he was trapped in this room with a long night ahead of him.

He settled back and waited for the room to be opened when he hoped to take the guide unawares and make his escape. Taking these snuffboxes was not now going to happen this time. But there was always tomorrow and this time he would bring something to stop the door closing. Gradually he became aware of a scratching sound which grew louder and louder.

Looking in its direction, Mitchell saw a faint green light appear which grew bigger and brighter in time with the scratching. Finally, a large rat appeared which had the human face of Claude Filtonbury as he remembered it from the portrait. It was followed by others. The burglar screamed, drew his knees up to his chest and sobbed as they made their way towards him.

Mitchell was a gibbering wreck who had totally lost his mind when he was found in the morning.

After he had been taken away, Melanie had a brief meeting with her technicians. 'Well done. The system has proved its worth yet again.'

Rather than have the house spoiled by CCTV cameras and alarm systems, she had devised the idea of this scheme. She also created the legend of Claude Filtonbury.

Whilst he had worked as a special agent for Charles II and been given the golden snuffbox, everything else she told the visitors was pure make believe. As far as she knew, the portrait was fairly genuine having been painted in the seventeenth century, but there was no curse, and no evidence Claude had ever dabbled in black magic. Her stories were all about creating an atmosphere.

Would be thieves had tried on several occasions to steal the snuffbox, but without success. After entering the room, the door was programmed to lock any intruder inside. Here they were subjected to all manner of visual trickery imitating supernatural happenings. These thieves were usually rendered totally insane by their experience. She was not worried about the probable illegality of her scheme. As far as she was concerned, any would be thieves had been warned about Claude's curse and brought their misfortune on themselves.

Protecting the snuffboxes was all important.

A week later after the turret room had closed for the day, she was the last to leave as usual. But as she did so, her telephone rang. Normally Melanie would have answered it, but it was late, and she was going out and needed to get home and change. She ignored it, believing if it was important, they would call again in the morning.

Since the last attempted burglary, she had all the security locks changed and was fairly satisfied the chances of breaking in were all but now virtually impossible. Whilst Melanie was right, she had overlooked one important issue. What if the intruder was already inside when the building was locked?

It was some time after she had locked all the doors and left before Shaun Ellis moved out of his hiding place in an old cupboard. So far it had been ever so easy. He had spent several days checking out the entire building and was incredulous at the lack of any sophisticated alarm system, let alone any alarm system. Not for one moment did he believe in any curse. He had seen the unprotected snuffboxes and decided to steal them.

Shaun had brought a large bag with him. He knew the main box would be heavy, but he was not going to restrict his loot to just that one. No, he would take as many of the snuffboxes as he could. Hopefully this would be his last job and establish a nice pension for him. Making his way up to the turret room, Shaun savoured the moment: soon he would be rich beyond his wildest dreams.

As expected, the door swung open and he was quite happy for it to close behind him, but in his excitement, Shaun failed to hear it click softly as the locks moved into place. Now he put on a headband which held a torch, which left his hands free. It took him longer than expected to fill the bag. Putting it on the floor, he took another more flexible one out of his coat pocket. He placed the Filtonbury snuff box into this one. Picking up the other bag, he headed for the door and pulled its handle.

At first, he was not too worried when it failed to open but his nonchalance quickly turned to panic, especially when the sound of scratching started. Then a green light slowly started to glow, increasing in its intensity, and he was aware someone else was in the room.

He had no difficulty in recognising the rat like features of Claude Filtonbury.

'You were warned,' the figure said, pointing an accusing finger at him. 'Now you must take the consequences.' Even as he spoke, Claude turned into a huge rat, albeit still with his own face on its body.

Shaun cowered in a corner hardly daring to look but scared not to.

Other rats joined Claude and they scampered all around the hapless Shaun. Unable to take any more, Shaun crawled into a foetal position and whimpered.

That was how he was found in the morning, completely insane.

This time, Melanie had to answer some very searching questions from the police, who were becoming concerned at the number of mentally ill burglars being found in the turret room. After they had gone, she decided to have a normal burglar alarm installed. As soon as they had gone, she went to see her technicians and break the news about the future.

'I don't know what happened last night,' said their chief as she entered their office.

'I do. It did a good job as usual, but…'

'That's just it,' the man interrupted her. 'I tried phoning you last night, but you must have already gone. You see, there was a problem and the system wasn't working and it still isn't. So, I don't understand what happened last night, but it was certainly very effective.'

A Scent of Orange Blossom

Auctioneer Des Brewer studied the bidders in the hotel lounge with more than a passing interest. There was only one item for sale this evening and he was very interested in purchasing it for himself. His business partners had no problems with this: they had purchased their own houses in a similar fashion.

The only condition was Des had to ensure he conducted the sale properly and professionally.

Licking his dry lips and taking a deep breath, he began. 'Good evening ladies and gentlemen and welcome. As you know, I am here to sell the property on the outskirts of town, known as *The Old Priory*. I am sure you will have read all the details and been out to inspect it. As you will appreciate it is an interesting property, but in need of quite a bit of work doing on it.'

He added there was a preservation order on the house and its grounds, which effectively stopped any housing developers from purchasing the site. And it was not big enough to justify the expense needed to turn it into a care home or hotel.

If he had judged his audience correctly, and he was very experienced at doing just that, very few of them had registered their interest in buying and been given a bidding number, which meant most of them were here purely out of nosiness. It was what usually happened with old interesting properties, and he hoped tonight would be no different. If so, it increased the chances of purchasing what he considered was the house of his dreams.

It was more than thirty-five years ago when Des had come down from Scotland, looking for work here in Warwick. His first and still only job was with a local auctioneer and estate agent. He was employed here initially as a general assistant. Several years passed before he graduated to becoming a partner.

Des had only been employed by the estate agent for a few weeks before he sold *The Old Priory* to its recent late owner. Nevertheless, it was love at first sight for him, but only now did he have anything like the money he needed and the chance to buy the old house.

He had just started as a trainee auctioneer, when his first job was at *The Old Priory*, which was to be auctioned with all its contents. It was planned his duties would be sitting alongside the auctioneer and recording the lot numbers, their prices and who had purchased them. But during the night before the morning of the sale, the auctioneer had collapsed and been taken to hospital. There was no other auctioneer in the company, and Des suddenly found himself doing the job. Helped by a clerk from the office, he managed to sell the property and its contents.

Once he had overcome his initial nerves, Des thoroughly enjoyed the experience and it decided his future career.

He arrived long before the auction started and took the opportunity to wander round the house. It was partly out of curiosity, but it also gave him time to familiarise himself with it before the sale. The grounds were heavily overgrown and made it impractical to walk outside.

In a small back room, he found five framed watercolours. They were each of different scenes from the eighteenth century: a couple courting: the same woman marrying a different man: an apparent infidelity: a duel and a grave. Judging by the marks on the wall, there should have been three more, which were nowhere to be found. The pictures were in a very dirty condition making them difficult to see properly, but they fascinated him. He vividly remembered there was a faint smell of orange blossom in the room. It was a smell he knew well as it was an expensive scent his mother used regularly.

When the auction bidders arrived at the pictures, no one was really interested in them because of their dilapidated state, and Des bought them for £5. Not being sure what to do next, he wrapped them up carefully and put the bundle into his attic. Although they were never hung up anywhere, Des never forgot about them. And now there was a possibility he might be able to return them to *The Old Priory* after all these years.

He had been determined to buy the property next time it came on the market, but it was a long wait.

*   *   *

Back in the hotel lounge, Des handled the bidding in a professional manner. The bidding was slow, which could be a good sign, but he also knew, having seen it happen many times before, just as the hammer was about to fall, a fresh bidder could enter the sale and change everything.

He was now struggling to get any bids and decided it was time to make his play. But would it be enough?

Des had never been a gambling man as such with horses and cards, but he played the stock market. Over the years he had acquired a significant portfolio and a handsome return on his investments. Now he was about to make the biggest gamble of his life and hopefully purchase *The Old Priory*.

As similar old eighteenth century houses went, it was not particularly big. There were six bedrooms, kitchen, one bathroom and toilet, several living rooms, a good-sized cellar and several attic rooms. The grounds outside were still heavily overgrown, and in need of extensive clearing. Des looked forward to exploring them.

The Old Priory was part of a deceased's estate, and Des's company had been instructed to sell it on behalf of the family who all lived in New Zealand, and who had no intention of ever coming to England. A local solicitor acted for them, and she had instructed the auctioneers to get rid of it for *whatever money they could get for it: and no, they did not want any reserve price putting on it.*

As Des knew, the property needed quite a bit of money spending on it, which he hoped was to his advantage.

The bidding finally faltered, and Des now entered the contest. 'I have a fresh bidder on the books, and I can raise the price by £10,000. Do I have any advances on this?'

'Another £5,000,' said a bidder in the room.

'I am raising it by another £10,000,' said Des, mentally crossing his fingers.

There were no more bids and the hammer fell. Des was the new owner of *The Old Priory.*

Being a cash purchase, it did not take long to complete all the formalities and paperwork.

Meanwhile he put his own house on the market. Being in a much sought-after part of the town, it quickly sold.

Fortunately, his wife, Valerie, was completely in favour of the purchase. Their three married daughters thought they were mad, but secretly believed *The Old Priory* offered all manner of potential and encouraged them. One of the daughters was an interior designer, and she could not wait to be let loose to come up with some ideas for their parents' mad scheme.

Unfortunately, Valerie was unable to be with him when they moved houses because she was with their eldest daughter, who was in the throes of having her second child with complications.

The last of their furniture and other belongings were unloaded. Des paid the removal bill and watched the vans leave. Moments later, and at long last, he was in the house of his dreams. He mixed himself a large gin and tonic with loads of ice and lemon, and just sat in the kitchen enjoying his surroundings. Des had no real plans about where to start his unpacking and decided to leave it until the morning. His overnight necessities were in a separate suitcase It was then he caught the faint whiff of orange blossom scent, and his mind went back to when he had bought the pictures here all those years ago.

He realised with a start the said pictures were still in the boot of his car, where he had put them earlier that morning. Putting down his drink, Des went out to his car and brought them into the house. Carefully he unwrapped the yellow dusty newspapers he had used to wrap them in, and never changed over all those years. They had been covered in dust and grime then, but now were in an even worse state. He made a mental note to have them properly cleaned and restored in due course.

Des cleaned the frames and the glass as best as he could, but it took him far longer to do than expected. But it was worth the effort, and they looked much better for being cleaned. The next problem was where to hang them.

He quickly decided to put them back in their original place, which would become his study. Finding a hammer, some picture hooks and a tape measure, Des soon had them hanging on the wall where they had hung when he first saw them.

Standing back to admire them, he was reminded there were another three missing. And not for the first time, he wondered what was their story? Once again, he noticed the strong scent of orange blossom.

Before going to bed, Des took a last look at them. 'What is your story?' he asked aloud.

As if in reply, there was a renewed burst of orange blossom scent, and he felt it had something to do with the story of the pictures and possibly the remainder of the set.

Des was woken in the night by the sound of a low moaning coming from downstairs. It sounded like a long drawn out '**NO...o...o...o.**'

He quickly got out of bed and went to investigate but had not gone far before encountering a heavy scent of orange blossom on the stairs. Acting on impulse, he went straight to the study, realising he was following the scent in that direction.

In there, he found all five pictures were lying on the floor, but in a slightly different order, including spaces, to how he had originally hung them. He saw their strings and hooks were still in place, so they had been taken down and not fallen. Moving to rehang them in their original order, the orange blossom scent became almost overpowering, and he stopped.

'You don't like how I hung them, do you?' He addressed the room, as he placed the pictures on his desk, and decided to rehang them later in the morning. Almost at once the orange blossom scent faded.

Des returned to bed, and there were no more interruptions.

It was quite late the next day before Des was able to give the pictures his attention. He also realised he had never properly examined them. Granted he had seen them prior to their purchase, and when he wrapped them up, but that was all. They had lived all those years since then wrapped in newspaper.

He now gave them his full attention.

The first picture was of a young happy couple, dressed in mid-eighteenth-century clothes. They were clearly very much in love with each other. But, as he looked more closely, Des saw the faint shadow of another, larger man watching them through a window. His face and body oozed disapproval and aggression.

The second picture was of a couple in church being married. They stood facing the altar and their faces could not be seen. Whilst Des was certain the bride was the same woman as before, he doubted the groom was the same man as in the earlier picture. This figure was much larger and seemed to ooze the same aggression as the other man had. There was little doubt he had been the watcher in the first picture. Des was just about to put the picture down, when he saw a face looking through one of the church windows. It was the same young man, and he was clearly very unhappy.

The third scene reminded him of the same young couple from the first picture, in each other's arms. Somehow, he was not surprised to see the silhouette of the larger man watching them.

The fourth picture was of the young man, in shirtsleeves, lying on the ground clasping a pistol in his hand. Des saw the larger man standing over him clutching a smoking pistol. Clearly, they had been fighting a duel, almost certainly over the woman who was cradling the young man's head in her arms.

The fifth scene was of a gravestone, but Des was unable to read what it said. It made him determined to have the pictures professionally cleaned.

He decided not to rehang the pictures for the moment but left them leaning against the wall in what he now accepted as their correct order. Where were the others?

The more he thought about what was happening, the more Des felt it had something to do with the house and some previous occupants. Luckily his solicitor had found all the title deeds going back to the year 1746, when the house was first built. Its second owner, Charles Edward Plummerton, was the son of the first, and he kept it until 1788. The next owner was a Francis Musgrove Linton who remained there until 1845.

Clearly the pictures were painted around that time. Des saw little point concentrating after that date, as the style of the clothing was wrong for mid to late nineteenth century. What was their connection, if any, with *The Old Priory?* Yet, despite his doubts, Des was convinced they were connected somehow with the house and the orange blossom scent.

But what was the connection?

His next move was to try and find Charles Edward Plummerton on the internet. Disappointingly, there was next to nothing on anyone of that name. However, there was a small item which read: --- --- Summerton who was tried for murder at the local Assizes. There was no date, or any details given. Des was also very much aware the name was shown as Summerton and not Plummerton. As he knew only too well, the wrong names could be transcribed over time, and this case was not helped by a lack of Christian names or even initials.

Whilst it seemed to fit, Des kept an open mind, knowing he would have to investigate further. All the while, the scent of orange blossom was so overwhelming, he thought he had to be on the right track. Meanwhile he went to see his new grandson, and the Plummerton mystery would have to wait for a few days.

It was an ideal time whilst he was away to have the pictures cleaned properly and restored if possible. Fortunately, his company used a regular picture restorer, who happily agreed to do them quickly as a favour to Des.

Des remained with Valerie and his daughter's family for a week, then he had to return as there were some auctions coming up. Valerie stayed on for a few more days as it had been a difficult birth, and their daughter was glad of the extra help.

Having a free morning several days later, Des visited the local County Records Office, but did not discover any more than what he already knew. Unintentionally, Des thumped the table he was sitting at in frustration.

As luck had it, the duty archivist was Edwin Smart. He had been a senior archivist here for many years and although retired, still helped out from time to time in the search room. Well used to the frustrations of research, he was quick to recognise the signs in others and offered to help.

Des was only too happy to have some assistance and he explained his problems.

'In all the years I've worked here, you're the first to ask about them,' replied Edwin. He explained how the Plummertons were a very wealthy and influential family, with strong Jacobite sympathies. They had supported the *Young Pretender's* attempt to regain the Throne in 1745, and somehow survived its tragic aftermath. Nevertheless, they lost a vast amount of money which left them living in much smaller purpose-built premises called *The Old Priory*, taking its name from some old ruins in the grounds. This was the first Des had heard about any ruins, although he often wondered how his house had obtained its name. He assumed the ruins were somewhere in the overgrown gardens.

'Years later,' added Edwin. 'There was some sort of scandal and one of them was hanged for murder. But thanks to the family's continued influence the court records have disappeared.'

Indicating Des to remain where he was, Edwin moved across to a box of documents, which he opened and sifted through the contents. Picking one out, he brought it across to Des. 'This is the only record of the execution.' He showed it to Des, who read:

Charles Edward Plummerton.
Hanged for murder June 25 1788 at Warwick.

'Popular rumour,' he continued. 'Even today amongst the older members of this community, maintain it was something to do with a duel. This date makes it after his trial at the Assizes.'

'Would such an influential man really have been hanged for killing someone in a duel?'

'That's the rub. It had to be something more than that.'

Des enjoyed an uninterrupted night's sleep, which was just as well because a contractor was coming early to inspect the roof. Also, Valerie would be home later during the day. The contractor arrived soon after 8.0am and Des took him up into the attic after the man had been on the roof. On the way upstairs, especially close to the attic, they both noticed a strong scent of orange blossom, almost to the point of being overwhelming. Embarrassingly, Des was unaware there was no electricity in the attic, and he had to go and find a torch.

After the man had gone, Des returned to the attic, realising it was one place he had never really investigated. The other place was the overgrown garden. He wanted to find the ruins of the old priory which Edwin Smart had mentioned. But they would have to wait as he felt the attic was more pressing.

Just as it had been earlier that morning, there was no shortage of orange blossom scent.

The attic was quite large and consisted of several small rooms, which might have been where the servants had once slept, but that was pure speculation on Des's part. These rooms were full of old suitcases, trunks, boxes and pieces of furniture. How Valerie would love poking around up here. His wife was an antiques dealer and who knew what she might find.

He was about to leave the last room, when his torch picked out a flattish package leaning up against a wall behind a trunk. At the same time the orange blossom scent became very strong and seemed to be coming from there. He leant over the trunk and picked up the package. It was not very thick underneath the old newspapers and cloth which were wrapped around it. Des was certain it was a picture and he hoped it might be one of the missing ones.

Once downstairs, he was pleased to see it was a similar picture to the others but surprised to discover it was a picture of *The Old Priory*, possibly soon after it had been built. It was certainly before the gardens became overgrown. Just to the left-hand side, but in the distance, were the ruins of what looked like a church or some other religious building.

'Of course,' he said aloud. 'The old priory ruins.'

Taking a closer look at the picture, he saw there was a coach and horses in front of the house, and a man and a woman stood in front of it. The man was the same angry one who appeared in the other pictures and the woman was also from them, wearing her bridal gown. Obviously, they had just been married.

But instead of looking radiant and happy, the bride's face showed abject and total misery.

He reasoned if one of the missing pictures had been found in the attic, there was a very good chance the others might be also. Just then he was distracted because Valerie arrived home. The first thing she noticed was the scent of orange blossom.

'And just who have you been entertaining in my absence?' she teased, raising her eyebrows.

Luckily, he had already explained about the scent.

Several minutes later as they sat in the kitchen, cradling mugs of coffee, he brought her up to date over what had happened since they had last met. They agreed to do no more that night but would make a concentrated effort next day to find the missing pictures.

Des collected his torch after breakfast, and they went upstairs to the attic. Almost at once they were greeted by a scent of orange blossom, which led them into the far room, and hovered over an untidy heap of boxes and other items wrapped up in paper and cloth. Valerie held the torch whilst Des picked through them. Several minutes later he had found two packages which approximately matched the size of the other pictures. Once he had picked them up, the scent faded. Taking them back downstairs and into the kitchen, Valerie waited impatiently for him to unwrap them.

Just like the others when he had first examined them, they were very filthy. He saw the frames were on their last legs and grime was caked onto the glass. It took them sometime to clean them enough to be able to see what the pictures showed.

The first one showed a man clearly laying down the law to a young woman, who was upset. The silhouette of another large man stood alongside him smirking. And Des was not surprised to see another, albeit indistinct face, looking sadly through a window at them.

Looking closely at the second picture, they saw it was of a body hanging in a gibbet cage. Its title was mostly unreadable. They could just read:

...Hanged for murder June 25 1788.

'So, we still don't know who was murdered and who did it.' Des sighed with frustration.

'I wonder,' Valerie mused aloud. 'Who's the painter?' She pointed to the initials *FML*, which were clearly visible in the bottom righthand corner of the picture. Leaving the kitchen, she returned to the study, followed by her husband, and looked at the other pictures. Moving around the table, she picked up each one in turn and looked for the artist's initials.

They were all signed *FML*.

A car horn sounding outside in the drive stopped any further research. It was one of their other daughters and her family, who had come to look over the new house, and stay for a few days. Their grandchildren found it a wonderful house and gardens to explore

Whilst they were there, Des and Valerie were unable to spend any time on the mystery of the pictures. Strangely there was no orange blossom scent to be smelt whilst their visitors remained.

Early the first morning after they had gone, Valerie woke first, but only seconds before Des. It was still dark, and the scent of orange blossom was overpowering. That had not woken them, but the sound of voices coming from downstairs had. Stopping just long enough to put on their dressing gowns, Des picked up a heavy brass candlestick and led the way down to the ground floor with Valerie closely following.

The voices were coming from Des's study and they saw a flickering light showing under the door. Quietly they opened it, went inside and stopped in amazement. The study looked nothing like it had when they were last in there only a few hours ago. It was lit by several candles and furnished entirely in a mid-late 18th century style.

Sat on a sofa, holding hands and obviously very much in love, sat a young couple. Neither Des nor Valerie had any doubt they were the same couple from the first picture. Des took a quick glance towards the window and saw the shape of a man standing there, just as in the first picture.

The scene faded and was relit but in a different format. This time the young woman was obviously pleading with another man, who would not listen to her cries. 'No! You cannot marry Francis Linton,' he stressed. 'But you will marry Charles.' He pointed to the large man stood smirking alongside him.

And looking through a window was the shape of the young man from the first picture, now identified as Francis Linton. There was a facial similarity between the woman and the man she was pleading with.

'Father and daughter?' whispered Valerie.

'And marrying her off to the other man,' replied Des just as quietly. 'And with her unfortunate lover looking through the window.'

The scene faded again and became a marriage ceremony between the young woman and the big man. 'Do you Rebecca Jayne Foxton take Charles Edward Plummerton to be your lawful wedded husband?' intoned the vicar.

'No,' Rebecca whispered.

The vicar ignored her reply, as he had been paid to do, and continued with the ceremony.

'Now we know who they are,' whispered Des. 'Look at the window.'

Valerie did so and saw the unhappy face of Francis Linton looking through it.

As they expected, the next scene was very short and involved Rebecca's arrival at *The Old Priory*. Francis could be seen hiding and watching from behind a tree.

When the next scene started, Rebecca and Francis had obviously met in secret, or so they thought. But only seconds later, Plummerton appeared on the scene. He and Francis had words and Plummerton challenged him to a duel

'I think this is the crucial one,' whispered Des, as the scene changed to a small lawn close to the old priory ruins. Plummerton and Francis each held a pistol and stood back to back.

Des was horrified to see there were no seconds or anyone else watching, apart from Rebecca standing by a tree on what was obviously a cold winter's day.

'Remember,' snarled Plummerton. 'Turn after seven paces and fire then: not before.'

Francis muttered 'Yes.' And started walking.

When Plummerton counted six, he turned and fired at Francis, who collapsed to his knees and fell onto his front, having been shot in the back.

'That was murder,' cried a shocked Des.

Suddenly Valerie gripped his arm. 'Look!'

'**NO!** screamed Rebecca and ran towards Francis. Kneeling, she cradled his head in her arms.

No one was prepared for what happened next.

Plummerton walked over to them and took the unfired pistol from the other man's hand. Without saying anything, he pointed it at Rebecca and pulled the trigger. As the smoke cleared, they saw Rebecca lying on her back staring sightlessly at the sky. 'Let that be a lesson, whore,' he muttered. Tossing the pistol away, he bent down and picked up her body, hoisted it over his shoulders and walked off.

Des and Valerie heard him say: 'I'm going to bury you where you will never be found, and I will take that secret to my grave. You will never ever be re-united with your lover in this world or the next. I'll get rid of him later.'

When Plummerton returned to dispose of the other body, he was in for an unpleasant surprise.

Francis had gone, but waiting in his place were the local magistrate, several constables and his servants. One of them pointed to him and said. 'That's the man who shot the mistress.'

The next scene was very brief. It consisted of Plummerton standing on the scaffold waiting to be hanged. His last words were: 'I'll never tell you where she is.'

The final scene was of a grave, but it was too far away to read the name on the headstone.

As the early morning sunlight shone into the bedroom, Des opened his eyes and looked at Valerie. She opened hers at the same time.

'Did we imagine last night?' he asked.

'No, it was real.' Even as she spoke, the scent of orange blossom filled the room.

'What do you want us to do?' Des asked the scent. 'Give us some help.'

In answer to his question, they both saw a shadowy shape appear and hover whilst they dressed. Then it moved out of the bedroom, down the stairs and out into the garden. Here they slowly forced their way through the undergrowth as they followed it into the ruins of the old priory. Des thought the gardens were in an even worse state than when he had first been to the house. Everything in the ruins was also heavily overgrown, but the shadow stopped by an ivy-covered mound, where it faded only leaving behind a faint scent of orange blossom.

Des returned to the house and returned a few minutes later with two pairs of heavy-duty gloves and some sharp kitchen knives. He and Valerie began to cut back the ivy. Having been established for a long time, it took them quite a while to uncover a grave and later a headstone, which read:

FRANCIS MUSGROVE LINTON
1760–1845

'Of course,' said Valerie. 'The initials *FML* on the paintings: they're his. He's certainly not well known, and to be honest, whilst these pictures have a certain charm, they're not everyone's cup of tea.'

'So, he didn't die in the duel, but then bought *The Old Priory* after Plummerton's execution.'

'He must have spent the rest of his life trying to find Rebecca. The poor man. But how come she didn't appear to him, as she has done to us?'

'I don't know,' replied Des. 'I can only assume he was not as receptive as we are. What do we do now? Find Rebecca I think.'

Even as he spoke, the shadow reappeared and led them back to *The Old Priory* and into the cellar where it stopped in a corner.

'Be patient, Rebecca,' said Des, gently. 'We need to think carefully about this.'

Going back upstairs, they made some coffee and went into the study to discuss what to do.

'I suppose we ought to tell the police,' suggested Valerie half-heartedly.

'Do you really think they'll be interested in a two-hundred-year-old murder that's already been dealt with?'

'No. You're right…Look!' she broke off.

Whilst she had been speaking, Valerie was looking through the pictures, and pointed to one of the tombstones. Only now the name could be read easily, and it was identical to the one they had just uncovered. But that was not the only difference.

There was now another gravestone alongside the one for Francis Linton. This one read:

REBECCA JAYNE PLUMMERTON
Née FOXTON
1762–1788

'That's the answer,' grinned Des. 'This is what we'll do.'

They were busy for the next few days.

Acting on the assumption nobody knew about the grave in the old priory, Des carefully dug another one alongside it. Calling in another favour, he ordered a new headstone to look and read the same as the one in the picture. Whilst he was doing that, Valerie stitched together two blankets as a shroud for Rebecca's body, assuming she was still in the cellar. When everything was ready, they went into the cellar and began to carefully lift the stone slabs which made up the floor, in the corner the shadow had indicated.

This was where they found Rebecca.

She was dressed in eighteenth century clothes, although these crumbled to dust once they were in the fresh air. Her body was well preserved having been mummified, and she was still recognisable from her pictures.

They laid her gently in the shroud which Valerie had made and carefully tied it up. All the while there was a strong scent of orange blossom. There was no doubt now it was Rebecca's scent. They carried her out into the garden and across to the old priory. Here Des had already dug another grave beside the one belonging to her dead lover. Des gently removed the earth from the top of the first grave and the wall between the two of them. It was now a double grave.

'Rest in peace, now. Both of you,' they said after Rebecca had been laid into the grave alongside Francis, now with no diving wall, and began to fill it.

Suddenly a skeletal hand appeared from Francis's side. In a moment, Rebecca's hand appeared and held it.

When Des had finished filling in the grave, Valerie put some flowers on it, wiping away the tears that trickled down her cheeks as she did so. Finally, they set Rebecca's gravestone alongside her lover's.

All the while they had been working, there had been a strong scent of orange blossom, which now began to fade.

Hand in hand, Des and Valerie went back into the house and into the study, where he rehung all the pictures in their correct order. Valerie stopped as she handed him the last one. 'Look!'

Des looked.

The last picture had acquired a title which read:

TOGETHER AT LAST

Moments later there came a strong scent of orange blossom and two shadowy figures took shape. One was a male and immediately recognisable as Francis from his picture. He was holding Rebecca's hand. Neither Des nor Valerie had ever seen two people look so happy and so very much in love.

As they watched, Francis and Rebecca's figures slowly began to fade, but before they did so, the lovers turned to Des and Valerie and gave them two wonderful smiles. 'Thank you,' they both said. Moments later they and the orange blossom scent were gone. Des and Valerie never saw the lovers again.

But sometimes the faint smell of orange blossom was noticeable in the house.

Hand of Glory

'Prisoner at the bar, Tobias Ransome,' intoned the judge, at the Assize court, using his correct name. 'You have been found guilty of a multitude of felonies, and this is a verdict with which I fully agree.'

Tobias ignored him and stared out into space. Of course, he had been found guilty, because it was true.

Born the illegitimate son of a serving maid and her master, Tobias, or Toby as he was usually called, spent most of his life taking advantage of every opportunity which came his way. It was how he had survived this long. His father was already married and could not wait to get rid of his serving maid lover and her unborn bastard. She was dismissed instantly following Toby's birth.

To be fair to the man, he settled her in a cottage on a nearby estate and paid her rent. Unfortunately, soon after Toby was born, his father was killed in a shooting accident, and his widow quickly stopped paying rent on the cottage.

She then wasted no time in re-marrying, which made people enquire what had happened to her first husband. Was it really an accident? Only she and her new husband had been present when it happened.

With no money, Toby's mother had abandoned him at a nearby vicarage from where the boy went to an orphanage. Here he quickly became very streetwise. In no time at all, Toby could turn his hand to almost every type of crime. In his late teens, or so he thought, not knowing his exact age, Toby was a successful highwayman.

But three years ago, in 1802, Toby knew he was chancing his luck. He had been a highwayman for five years, which was good going when the average working life of such people was just over half of that period. His luck was due to run out soon, and robbing stagecoaches was becoming more difficult. They now travelled faster and were not so easy to stop.

It was time for a change.

Quite by chance he met up with Jack Anderson and they started talking. Through him Toby met Hal Smith and together they formed a gang under his leadership, and robbed isolated houses, whose owners employed few, if any residential staff. During the next few months they became very successful, adding Billy Curtis and his cousin Nathan Pope to their gang.

They built up a formidable reputation and soon had a large price on their heads. Not that this helped the forces of law and order, because no one knew their identities. Likewise, no one had any real idea of how many of them there were.

A well-known danger of working in any gang is the ever-present risk of betrayal. The authorities worked on this weakness and issued *wanted notices* for the gang. Their descriptions were so vague as to be virtually non-existent, but in a carefully planned strategy, they began increasing the price on the leader's head. Any informant, even if a member of the gang, would be allowed to *Turn King's Evidence* and claim the reward. In practice, *Turning King's Evidence* allowed the informant to testify against a wanted person, in return for being granted a pardon and immunity from any prosecution.

Once the reward reached £500, Billy decided it was time to act, and he quickly explained to Nathan what he had in mind. Quite simply, he would notify the authorities where to find Toby, having previously ensured some recognisable stolen property was found in his lodgings. This was to be Nathan's specific task. Nathan would also need to ensure the rest of the gang were well out of the way when the trial happened. Billy did not want them sharing any of the reward.

It all went according to plan.

The gang had been out celebrating and Billy had spiked Toby's drink. Not enough to make him lose consciousness, but enough to slow down his reactions. Using Toby's state of inebriation as an excuse, Billy told the others how he was going to take him home. Leading him by the arm, he took the swaying man back to his lodgings, unlocked the door and pushed him inside, where the waiting constables fell on him. Even as he struggled and called for help, Toby realised he had been betrayed, but had no idea then who had done it. He was aware Billy had gone, but then so would he have done in similar circumstances.

It was only when Billy appeared in court and testified against him, Toby realised what had happened, but was powerless to do anything about it now.

Toby came back to the present and watched impassively as the clerk of the court placed a piece of black cloth on the judge's head. He knew what was coming next. There was an air of expectant quiet in the court.

'Tobias Ransome,' intoned the judge. 'It is the sentence of this court that you shall be taken from here to whence you came. Then at the time and date appointed, you will be conveyed to a place of lawful execution, where you will be hanged by the neck until such time as you are dead. After which your body will be hanged in chains on a gibbet...'

Toby did not hear the last part of the judge's sentence, as he suddenly realised the full implication of his punishment.

His body would not be buried. Instead, it would be hung up in a cage until such times as it was stolen or fell apart. This was a fate worse than death.

At his execution, Toby stood on the scaffold as the rope was placed around his neck. On such occasions the condemned man was permitted to address the watching crowd. Toby was determined to have his say.

'I curse all those who have brought me to here, especially you Billy Curtis.' Toby paused for breath glaring at Billy, whom he had already seen in the crowd. Billy looked away, anywhere except at those hate filled eyes.

When he had finished, the hangman moved the cart off, and Toby was left swinging in the air.

Later that night, the gang stood beneath the gibbet where Toby's caged body swayed in the gentle breeze. Billy held a large knife in his hand.

'Are you sure this is a good idea?' asked a worried Nathan, speaking for all the gang.

'Yes. As I've already explained, a *Hand of Glory* will help our enterprises, and we can rob even more wealthier premises. And who better to give us his hand than the late Toby? It must be a right hand if we want to use all its magical powers. Then with a lit candle, made with fat from Toby's body, the *Hand of Glory* will send all the occupants, in any house we attack, into a deep charmed sleep. We won't have to worry about how many servants they have.

And with Toby's background, his hand will have even more magical powers. Anyway he's dead and can't hurt us.'

With Nathan's help, Billy climbed up the gibbet post and found Toby's right hand, which he started to remove using the knife he had brought with him. It took him much longer than he had anticipated, which all added to the rest of the gang's uneasiness.

At last the hand came away from Toby's wrist, and Billy distinctly heard the body cry out: 'I curse you, and may you never find any peace from me until my hand is reunited with my body.'

Billy tried to convince himself it was his imagination playing tricks, brought on by the ghostly atmosphere of the place. Yet, he was left with a slight lingering doubt. What if it hadn't been his imagination? What if he had really heard Toby? For a moment, he was tempted to run, but as none of the others appeared to have had heard the voice, Billy ignored it.

Putting the hand into a leather bag he had brought specially for it, Billy next cut off some of Toby's hair which would serve as wicks for the candles when they were made. These also went into the bag along with the flesh he next cut from Toby's buttocks and legs. After pulling the bag's drawstrings together, Billy quickly climbed down the gibbet post back onto the ground. 'Let's go,' he instructed.

His companions needed no further urging, and they gratefully fled from the gibbet back to their hide-out.

The next part was comparatively easy.

Billy put Toby's hand into a pot and pickled it for a month with a mixture of salt, animal and human urine. The next stage involved it being hung in the smoke made from numerous herbs and hay. Afterwards it was hung on an oak tree, and finally on a church door overnight. Whilst they waited, he boiled up Toby's flesh and made three small stubby candles and their wicks from the fat.

At last all was ready. A few nights later, the gang prepared to burgle their next house.

As usual, it was an isolated building on the outskirts of some woods with no other premises anywhere nearby. Billy spent some time studying the house until he was certain there were no dogs in it. Whilst he had every confidence in the magical properties of *The Hand of Glory,* when dealing with people, he was less certain of its effect on animals.

Waiting for a while after the last lights had gone out, Billy led them towards the rear of the house. Here he handed Toby's hand to Hal Smith and instructed him to hold it whilst he placed one of the candles in it.

'Why?' whined Hal. 'Why me? Why have I got to hold it?'

'So, I can light it,' sighed Billy.

'Wouldn't a lantern be better? Why's it got to be this 'and…Toby's 'and?'

'As I've already explained,' replied Billy through gritted teeth, 'This is known as a *Hand of Glory,* and it has magical powers. Once it has been lit, everyone inside this house will go into a deep sleep, and they won't hear a thing.'

Hal remained unconvinced, but he was more frightened of Billy than *The Hand of Glory.* They all knew Billy had betrayed Toby and realised he would do the same to them if it suited him. Having no other choice, Hal did as he was instructed. Billy lit the candle, reciting a magic spell as he did so. Moments later they gathered around the rear door of the house. Here Billy quickly retrieved a key from where he had previously seen servants hang it. The key worked smoothly: the door opened, and they were inside. Taking Toby's hand from Hal, Billy put it on the staircase where it spluttered, but remained alight.

'What happens if someone throws water over it?' queried Jack Anderson.

'Nothing,' replied Billy. 'Water can't put it out. They'll all be deeply asleep by now.'

Even as he spoke, Hal backed away from it and upset a pile of china which was on a nearby dresser. It landed and shattered with a loud crash and they all prepared to run.

'Wait!' hissed Billy. 'Wait and see.'

They waited, ready to run, but no one appeared.

'See! I told you so,' smiled Billy. 'Now to work.'

Confident now in the magical power of *The Hand of Glory,* they set to work and stole whatever could be carried. Billy was the last one to leave, waiting only long enough to pick up Toby's hand, and repeating the spell to extinguish it.

'Give me back my hand,' came a voice which Billy recognised as being Toby's. He dismissed it once again as being his imagination.

Their next burglary was just as successful. But once more, Billy thought he heard Toby saying: 'Give me back my hand. You have been warned.' Again, he put it down to his imagination, but the lingering doubts from when he had first cut off the hand returned.

But their next burglary was when things started to go wrong.

Just as they were leaving, a party of young men on horseback suddenly appeared. The riders quickly realised what was happening and rode straight at Billy's gang, who dropped what they had stolen and ran. Hal was the slowest to react and by the time he did so, it was too late. He stood for a long moment trying to decide which way to go, when the leading rider knocked him down and the others trampled over his body.

Hal died soon afterwards from his injuries.

Even as he fled, Billy thought he heard Toby's mocking laugh.

Their next venture was just as disastrous.

At first it had seemed a pushover. The house owners only employed staff in the daytime, relying on other plans to protect them during the hours of darkness. Plans which Billy knew nothing about.

Billy's gang broke into the house totally unaware of the booby traps which were set in various places every night. The gang was disappointed to find nothing of any real value downstairs, and Jack volunteered to look in the bedrooms. Stepping over *The Hand of Glory,* he climbed up the stairs whilst Billy and Nathan watched from below. The idea was for Jack to tell them when it was safe for them to join him.

But as Jack trod on the carpeted first floorboard on the landing, he gave a shriek and vanished, as it opened underneath him. Moments later they heard the sharp slapping thud as his body hit the solid stone floor of the cellar, at least two floors beneath him. They knew he was almost certainly dead after such a fall and agreed there was no point trying to find him. Not wanting to risk activating any other boobytraps, they fled.

Once again Billy heard Toby's laugh and his cry: 'Give me my hand back. You won't get many more warnings.' But as Nathan made no mention of having heard the voice, Billy wrote it off again to his imagination.

Badly shaken by what had happened, they decided to lie low for a while. It was a good idea in theory, but the money only lasted a few weeks before it was gone. They were left with no option but to rob another house.

The one Billy selected next, was another medium sized property situated in its own grounds, and less than a mile or so from the nearest village. In many respects it was not ideal, especially being comparatively close to the village, but Billy felt this disadvantage was far outweighed by what he knew about its occupants. They were two elderly sisters and reputed to be very wealthy and kept only a few elderly servants, most of whom were females.

Nathan agreed it should be well worth doing and several days later, he and Billy quietly went to the house.

At its rear, Billy took out Toby's hand and lit the candle. It was the work of only a few moments to force the door open. Once inside Billy put it on the stairs as usual and started searching in the dining room. Nathan was more cautious and waited a while longer for *The Hand of Glory* to take effect.

At first, neither of them realised there were several candles burning in the hallway, which probably meant at least one person was still awake downstairs. As Billy moved into the dining room, a door opened, and a maid appeared carrying a large bowl of milk.

She took one look at the burning hand, screamed and threw the milk over it. Nathan gazed in horror. The candle spluttered and went out.

Whilst Billy was correct in knowing water could not extinguish *The Hand of Glory*, he did not know milk could. And that had just happened.

His second mistake was in not checking this house out as thoroughly as he should have done, relying too much on *The Hand of Glory*. Had he been a little more thorough, Billy would have discovered the sisters had their nephew staying with them.

He was a major home on leave, from the army, with his servant. Having been a soldier for many years, he always slept with a pair of loaded pistols by his bedside.

The maid's scream woke him, and he was instantly awake. Leaping out of bed, he grabbed his pistols and moved to the bedroom door, calling for his servant. Once on the landing, the major saw Nathan's shadowy figure in the candlelight, and the flickering flames from the dying fire in the hall.

He fired both pistols at him. His first shot just nicked Nathan's ear, causing him to stumble, which ensured the second one missed him.

Billy had been in the dining-room, determined to find something to steal before leaving, when the major opened fire. This was something he had not expected and decided to stay in there for the time being, as there was now too much activity in the hall.

The major took charge and roused all the servants. He sent one them to find the local constable, whilst he instructed his servant to make sure the house was secure, and no one was left hiding inside. Hearing these instructions, Billy knew it was time for him to leave.

He tried first to open the window, but it had been screwed down. Billy needed to find another way to escape. There had to be one somewhere. Opening the door slowly, he peered into the hallway. Unable to believe his luck, he saw the rear door was still open and there was no one in the hall. Seizing this opportunity, Billy crept out of the dining room and made his way to the door.

On the way, he saw the forlorn looking *Hand of Glory* in a pool of milk and thought about going to retrieve it. But then he heard voices approaching, so he left it, fled through the open door and was soon running away.

Nathan wasted no time waiting for Billy after being shot, but quickly ran away from the house. He felt nothing but anger towards his greedy cousin. Everything had been going all right until he helped Billy in betraying Toby. Now there was only himself and Billy left. Perhaps it was time to have Billy arrested and *Turn King's Evidence* against him. Meanwhile he was in pain, still bleeding and did not know where Billy had gone. To make matters worse, Nathan was completely lost, and the moon had long since disappeared behind a cloud.

He stood for a few seconds wondering which way to go in the dark. Hearing the faint sound of running water, he headed towards it. With luck it would give him something to follow. At last he found the source of the water which came from a mill race. He stood there gazing at the rushing water as the moon reappeared and lit up the water mill with its turning wheel. He relaxed, relieved to see the whole area was deserted.

Suddenly a hand touched him on the shoulder.

Screaming with fear, Nathan spun round and saw Toby standing in front of him.

'Give me back my hand!' instructed Toby, waving his handless right arm.

'I haven't got it!' pleaded Nathan.

'Give me back my hand!' Toby instructed again, and he advanced towards Nathan, still waving his handless arm in front of him.

'I haven't got it!' screamed Nathan, stepping backwards into space.

The sound of his body hitting the water was not heard above the noise of the mill race. Nathan could not swim, and he soon drowned.

Unaware of what had happened to Nathan, Billy stayed in the woods. Having spent a little time in checking out the house, he had a rough idea of which way to go, and in due course found the water mill. Looking into the water, he saw a body floating on its back, gazing upwards with sightless eyes. Even in the shadowy moonlight, Billy had no difficulty in recognising Nathan.

Now all the members of his gang were dead, and he knew it was his fault.

Everything had been going so well until he had *Turned King's Evidence* on Toby, and then created *The Hand of Glory*. He cursed that magical charm for being the cause of his current situation. How Toby would be laughing.

As if on cue, he heard Toby's mocking laugh coming from somewhere behind him. But this time, unlike the others, Billy knew it was not his imagination. This time it was real. Turning around, he was not surprised to find Toby standing behind him.

'What do you want?' hissed Billy.

'You know full well. I want my hand back!' As he spoke, Toby waved his handless arm at Billy. 'You've got a week. And don't think you can escape me by running. I'll always find you wherever you try and hide.'

'If I get it back, will you leave me alone?'

But Toby had gone.

Billy remembered he had left the hand back at the house which left him with no alternative. He would have to return there and hopefully retrieve it. Giving a deep sigh, Billy went back into the woods and made his way towards the house.

As he had rightfully suspected, it was a hive of activity back at the house.

Many villagers and other people were gathered all around the property. Mostly they just stood in groups discussing what had happened. At any other time, Billy, would have been amused to listen to their versions of the recent burglary: but not now. All he wanted to do was to find the hand and get away.

Standing alongside one group, he was suddenly very interested in their exaggerated and fanciful conversation.

'They said it were a '*and of Glory*. You know one of them magical charms as what puts people to sleep.'

'Ah but the maid put it out. 'er threw some milk at it.'

'Where is it now?' asked Billy as innocently as he could. 'I've heard about them but never seen one and I'd like to.'

'You're too late, cocker,' replied the first speaker. 'The major threw it on the fire and it didn't half burn.'

'It were a big blue flame,' said another. 'I saw it all.'

A chorus of agreement from the others agreed with him.

Billy had to accept Toby's hand had gone forever and could never be re-united with him. He fully believed Toby would find him, wherever he went. Billy's future was not looking very bright. Knowing there was nothing else he could do at the house, he wandered off back into the woods, for the remainder of the night.

When the sun rose later next morning, Billy was cold, hungry and tired, but he also had the beginnings of a plan which might work, and if it didn't fool Toby, hopefully it might at least placate him.

All he had to do was find a fresh male body, remove its right hand and give it to Toby. The problem was finding a suitable corpse which was easier said than done.

It was another five days before Billy came across a funeral party standing in a local churchyard. He moved across to the mourners and stood at the rear, straining to catch any clue to identify the gender of the corpse. His patience paid off when he discovered the dead body was called John Archer.

Billy returned to the grave later that night, grateful it was very cloudy and there was little or no moon showing. He had already broken into the grave diggers hut and removed a spade. Lighting the lantern, he had brought with him, Billy began to dig. Not having dug into a grave before, it took him much longer than anticipated but at last he had uncovered the coffin. Wasting no more time, he forced open the lid and looked down at the waxen face of John Archer.

His next task was to remove John's right hand, which also took him longer than he expected. Finally, the hand came away from the arm. But as it did so, it seemed to him as if John's corpse moaned, and his eyes opened fleetingly. Billy put it down as a trick of the light, caused by the dying lantern candle, coupled with his own overwrought state.

Wrapping the severed hand in some rags, and not wasting time refilling the grave, Billy quickly left the churchyard. He could not wait to leave having felt someone was watching him the whole time.

The following night saw Billy back at the gibbet where Toby's body still hung.

He managed to climb up the post and found Toby's right arm. Using a needle which he had previously threaded, he stitched the hand onto Toby's stump. When he had finished, Billy was horrified to see the fingers moving and quickly climbed down the gibbet pole.

'It's not mine, is it?' came Toby's voice from the gibbet cage.

'No,' admitted Billy and explained what had happened.

'I suppose it will have to do.'

'Does this mean you'll stop haunting me?' pleaded Billy.

'Yes. I will stop haunting you,' replied Toby.

'But I won't,' came a new voice from behind Billy.

He spun around and stared in horror at the figure who stood behind him, nursing the stump of his right arm where his hand had recently been removed.

Billy had no difficulty in recognising John Archer, the man whose hand he had just given to Toby.

AUTHOR'S NOTE

A *Hand of Glory*, acquired and treated as described in this story, was a regular tool used by criminals in centuries past. It was supposed to put everyone in a house into a charmed sleep, so burglars would not be interrupted. As can be imagined, evidence as to its efficacy cannot really be produced. Legend maintains although it could not be extinguished by using water, milk would do the trick.

Adriana

Martin Davis was an uninteresting type of person: someone you could pass in the street and not really notice.

Already in his late 30s, he lived a confirmed bachelor's existence. Working as a clerk in a local government office, he could hardly be considered as a good catch for any hopeful female looking for a soulmate. Martin had tried numerous dating agencies, but all the women he met never suggested a second meeting.

Although educated at a minor public school, Martin was never given the opportunity to go to university, and consequently did not have any of the all-important letters after his name indicating which degree he had obtained. Now in the late 20th century, degrees were essential for anyone aspiring to have any hopes of obtaining reasonable employment. Whilst his self-made parents revelled in the snob value of having a son at public school, that was as far as they went.

Any form of further education was never going to be an option, either by his own efforts or with their assistance. Martin was expected to join his father's manufacturing company. When he indicated such a life was not what he wanted, the threats started.

'If that's what you think, then go and work on the assembly line at the local factory.'

Martin could have worked there or in a shop, but that was not what he wanted. Much to the chagrin of his parents, he settled for being a menial clerk with the local council. It wasn't much of a job but did pay his bills. Martin left home as soon as he could and never went back. The years rolled on and his humdrum life continued, albeit interspersed with the occasional introduction from one of the several dating agencies he used. Regardless of the agency, the results were always the same.

A single meeting with a female followed by nothing more.

It was all very frustrating to say the least, until one fateful Saturday morning.

Being the weekend, Martin was not working, and could find no valid reason to get out of bed just yet. Finally, an overwhelming need for a coffee spurred him into action. He was watching his coffee negotiate its way through the filter when the postman arrived and put several envelopes through the letter box. Martin went and collected his mail but waited until his coffee was ready before opening any of them.

For the most part they consisted of circulars or bills, but one had come from a new dating agency he had just started using. 'Who knows?' he asked himself. 'Could this be the one?'

Sitting at the kitchen table with his coffee alongside him, Martin opened the envelope and took out the smaller one he found inside. This was handwritten and addressed to *Martin SNBC 0007301*, which was the reference number he had been given by the site.

He put it to one side and drank some coffee. Then deciding not to waste any more time, he put his coffee to one side, opened the envelope and read the enclosed letter, which was accompanied by a photograph.

Briefly the sender was an Adriana Doward, who had seen his details on the dating site and decided to follow them up. The photograph was of a strikingly good-looking woman with olive coloured skin and complexion, framed by thick black hair. Martin found her most attractive and wondered why such a looker needed to use a dating agency. She ought to have been swamped with dates. What was wrong with her?

For a moment, but only for a moment, he thought about binning her details. Surely, he stood little or no chance of this ever developing into any lasting relationship? But there was something so appealing about her photograph and his doubts vanished. Picking up his mobile phone, he rang the number on the letter.

They met three days later in a nearby coffee bar.

Adriana was just as attractive as her photograph showed, and Martin was conscious of the envious looks he was getting from the other men, and some women, in the coffee bar. Surprisingly she had not been put off by his spiky ginger hair and old-fashioned spectacles. He had tried to wear contact lenses once but was unable to adapt to them.

One coffee led to another, although he failed to notice at the time how she never drank any of hers.

As they talked, Martin discovered Adriana also worked in a boring office, not unlike his own, but she never told him where. The next two hours quickly passed, and they agreed to meet one another again.

It was the first time one of these meetings had led to another. Could he dare hope this might lead to something?

During their second meeting, Martin discovered just how similar her past had been to his, and he found himself falling for her. As they parted company, he went to give her a kiss on the cheek, but she moved away. He thought it was because she was adjusting her scarf.

On their third meeting, she pressed him for details about where he lived, and which schools he had attended. By now Martin was totally smitten, and knew he was falling in love with her. He happily gave her his life story.

So, as can be imagined, he was more than a little disappointed when she cancelled their next meeting, with the flimsiest of excuses. It seemed she was just like all the others. After pumping him dry about his background, they quickly made an excuse not to see him anymore. He also realised just how little he knew about her, except she lived at 133 Hambledon Crescent on the far outskirts of the city.

It was several months before he saw her again, and then it was quite by chance.

Martin had been working late and was enjoying a gentle walk home on a warm summer's evening. Suddenly he saw Adriana crossing the road in front of him with another man. He thought about speaking to her but decided against it. Whilst he was wondering whether or not to speak to her, Martin saw the other man's face and he stopped short.

The man looked just like he did, complete with spiky ginger hair and old-fashioned spectacles. Martin knew what his own face looked like as he saw it most days in a mirror whenever he had a shave. It was an uncanny resemblance to himself. But that wasn't all.

He also knew the other man. His name was Charles Danby.

They had been at the same school together, where he was more senior and an insufferable bully. The boys had been so alike most of the staff, and other pupils, thought they were brothers. Along with all the younger boys and most of the staff, Martin had been glad to see him leave school.

Even as he watched, they turned off the main pavement and went on to the Common. Martin shrugged his shoulders and walked away.

They were welcome to each other. Charles Danby for being the bully at school and Adriana for the way she had treated him.

*　　*　　*

It was sometime after Christmas when Martin was summoned for his annual appraisal with Bill Harris, his departmental head.

Once he was in the office and sat down, Bill spoke: 'I'll come straight to the point, Martin. You're wasting your time here.' He held up his hand and smiled. 'Don't get me wrong. I'm not sacking you, but I think you are worthy of better things.' Bill handed him an internal memo. 'Read this. I think it's got your name on it and has a hefty salary increase as well.'

Martin did so and agreed with Bill. It was a job in the planning department which required him to check out development sites, interview people in affected areas, and investigate any complaints. It meant being regularly out of the office and meeting other people. For once Martin was glad of his public school background, which meant he never had any problems in talking to people.

After a successful interview, Martin was awarded the position, which was a vast improvement from just being a clerk.

It also had an unexpected bonus.

One house he visited was owned by an elderly couple, and it just so happened their unmarried daughter, Janice Warburton, was visiting them. She and Martin were immediately attracted to each other, and it was a genuine case of love at first sight.

Prior to their marriage, and keen to make a fresh start, Martin shredded all the correspondence to and from his various dating agencies. He would tell Janice about them one day, but not just yet. For some strange unknown reason, he kept Adriana's picture.

One Saturday morning, several months after their return from honeymoon, they were enjoying a leisurely breakfast. Martin was doing a crossword puzzle in one of the week-end supplements, whilst Janice read the local newspaper. Suddenly she gave a horrified gasp.

'What's wrong my love?' queried Martin putting down his crossword, and shocked to see how white her face had become.

'You never told me you had a twin,' she replied, only half in jest, and handed him the newspaper. She pointed to an article and photograph, not that he needed to be shown.

The article concerned the skeleton of a male which had been found on the nearby Common. His face had been forensically reconstructed in the hope of someone recognising it. Martin went cold as he saw what had shocked Janice and now himself.

It was a face very similar to his own: one which he had last seen going on to the Common with Adriana Doward.

There could be no doubt in his mind it was Charles Danby.

'Are you all right, my love?' asked a worried Janice. 'You look like you've seen a ghost. Do you know him?'

Martin nodded.

She waited as he refilled their coffee mugs. 'It's a long story,' he said at last.

Martin held nothing back and told her about how he knew Charles. She smiled and called: 'SNAP!' when he spoke about using dating agencies. Their subsequent laugher eased the tension. He talked about Adriana, and seeing Charles go onto the Common with her, that night about two years earlier.

When he had finished his tale, Janice said nothing but looked thoughtful for a moment. 'I think you ought to have a word with Herbo when we go around to mum and dad tomorrow night.'

Janice's brother, Herbert Warburton, always known as Herbo, was a detective sergeant in the City Police. Much to Martin's surprise, he was most interested in his story.

'I don't suppose you can remember where she lived?' he asked when Martin had finished.

'That's one of the embarrassing things about it,' replied Martin, chewing his bottom lip. 'Not long after I started my new job, I had to visit someone in the same crescent, and thought to look her up. That's when I discovered her house didn't exist. She'd played me for a fool the whole time.'

'I don't suppose you can remember the name of the dating agency?'

'That's another embarrassment, I've used so many over the years, they've all just merged into one another.'

Herbo said nothing for a moment, then mentioned a name which Martin recognised.

'Yes. That's it. I remember it now. How did you know that?'

'Can I answer that tomorrow,' he replied mysteriously.

The next day, Herbo took him to the police station handling the skeleton case and introduced him to Detective Chief Inspector Lucy Hargreaves. Martin repeated his story, whilst Lucy made several notes.

'What I am going to tell you now, must remain strictly between ourselves. Are you agreed?' Lucy said when he had finished his tale.

Martin nodded.

'As you so rightly suspect, the skeleton we believe is almost certainly Charles Danby, but we need confirmation, especially as it is only his skeleton. The pathologist puts his death at about the time you saw him go onto the Common, especially as that was where he was found. We also had him reported as missing from home by his parents, at about the same time. Unfortunately, they have both since died, and we don't know of any other relatives, so DNA isn't going to help us. We're waiting for confirmation from his dental records, but there are none held locally, and we are having to go further afield.'

'Forgive me if I'm telling you how to do your job, and I appreciate we are talking about a skeleton, but can you confirm if his right arm has ever been broken at any stage?' Martin asked.

Lucy consulted her notes, nodded and then looked up at Martin. 'It was. Why do you ask?'

Martin told her about going to school with Charles Danby, and how they were often mistaken for brothers, adding how Charles had broken his right arm playing rugger. He went on to name the school.

'I think we can take it as read if our skeleton has such an injury, then it has to be the late Charles Danby,' Herbo said.

'It certainly looks like it,' replied Lucy as she consulted her notes again, cursed under her breath and frowned. Picking up her phone, she pressed some numbers and asked the incident room where Charles Danby went to school. 'Then find out please and check with the other forces who have similar enquiries on the go.' She put down the phone and sighed in exasperation. 'Would you believe it. We haven't got them. You see,' she explained. 'Charles Danby is one of six similar cases various police forces are investigating at the moment.'

Several minutes later, her phone rang. She answered it and a slow smile spread across her face. 'You are quite right, Mr Davis. You both went to the same school. And Warwick police have confirmed so did their victim.'

During the next hour, confirmation was received how all six victims had been to the same school, were single, and had used the same dating agency. Martin did not recognise these other names but being older, they had probably left school before he started. He only knew Danby from his first year at school, which had been the bully's last.

Lucy explained they had all used the same dating agency as Martin had. Herbo gave a sly grin when Martin looked at him. 'Hence how I knew the name, when you mentioned it last night,' he explained.

'And he's the sixth case the police are looking at involving finding the bodies, or skeletons, of other men who used this same agency. We have no doubt there is a serial killer about, but We've no idea why these men have been targeted. It seems for some reason, you've been very lucky,' Lucy added.

'Surely,' queried Martin. 'If you know the dating agency site, why don't you just go and arrest them?'

'Don't you think we haven't thought about that? If only it were that simple. Nobody knows where they operated from and it might not even be in this country. How did they contact you?'

'By e-mail or forwarded letters from possible dates.'

'Exactly. No one has an address for them, and the site no longer exists. Now, how do you and Herbo fancy going back to your old school tomorrow?'

Martin had mixed feelings about returning to his old school.

Whilst not being unhappy there, he was not sorry to leave. Once gone, he had never wanted to go back, nor subscribe to the *old boys' newsletter*. His fears subsided when they arrived, albeit for an unexpected reason.

Neither he, nor Herbo, were aware the school had been sold some years earlier, and was now an upmarket hotel, country and golf club.

Luckily the old school lists were preserved in the local County Records office, which is where they went next. They decided to take details of all the pupils, who had left in the four years prior to Martin's arrival, in case there were any other connections they might have missed.

There were no immediate connections between the six victims, except they all had a reputation for being unruly: and their parents had been advised if their sons continued in such a manner, they faced a very serious risk of being expelled.

Other than confirming the school connection between the victims, they were no further forward.

Just as Martin was closing his file, he noticed an envelope tucked away at the very back. It had no immediately obvious connection to the school, but he decided to look, more out of curiosity than anything else. He opened it and found it contained two newspaper clippings.

The article related to a fatal car crash in 1983, eighteen years earlier, which involved six old boys from the school.

They had been at an old school reunion week-end.

On the Saturday, they all crammed into Charles Danby's car and driven off for the evening, having a few drinks on the way. At some stage, and for reasons which were never fully explained, Danby lost control of the car, which skidded and collided with an oncoming vehicle.

In this car, the father was killed outright, but his wife survived, thanks to the efforts of the ambulance crew. There was no mention of any other passengers.

Danby was only charged with careless driving, because he had not been over the legal drink/drive limit. The magistrates and prosecuting solicitor had gone out of their way to be helpful towards him. Consequently, he only received a nominal fine. Martin recognised the old school tie network when he saw it.

Before she left court after the hearing, the widow cursed all the occupants of Danby's car. The gist of her curse was none of the people in the car would ever marry, and they would all meet a violent end. As would everybody else who helped them, in any way over the outcome of the crash. These would die first. If they were married, their wives would die violently within five years of their marriage. Finally, she called on other members of her family to help fulfil the curse, if she was unable to carry them out.

A list of the boys' names was given and it tallied with all the murder victims. The name of the family in the other car was shown at the end of the press cutting. Somehow Martin was not surprised when he saw their names.

It was Stevo and Kezia Doward and gave their address as 133 Hambledon Crescent, in the same city where Martin lived.

The other newspaper clipping was titled: **DYING GYPSY'S CURSE COMES TRUE?** It was dated exactly five years to the day of the fatal crash and was Kezia's obituary.

Reading down he found it referred to the fatal crash and Kezia's curse, emphasising how she and Stevo were from the gypsy fraternity. It detailed how the prosecuting solicitor, the magistrates, and the headmaster of the school had died in a violent manner: all within five years of the crash. There was a postscript at the end which reminded the readers of the curse made by the seriously injured Kezia Doward, though no mention was made of Danby and his fellow passengers.

If Adriana was their killer, it would explain the delay between the first killings, and their re-starting. Perhaps they had to wait for Adriana to become old enough to fulfil the family's curse?

Martin and Herbo agreed there seemed little doubt that Adriana Doward, who was clearly of the same family, was the killer.

All the police had to do now was to find her.

Armed with copies of Adriana's photograph, thanks to Martin, a team of Lucy's detectives descended on Hambledon Crescent to try and find her.

Martin waited anxiously in his office for their return. At last Lucy phoned him, but she was obviously not in the best of moods.

'Did you find her?' he asked excitedly.

'No, although she and her family did once live at number 133. However, Kezia did not stay there for long after the crash. They were domiciled gypsies, and it was rented accommodation, which she gave back to the council. However, no other subsequent tenants would stay there for long. They all said it was haunted.' Lucy paused. 'So, the council knocked it down and never rebuilt on the site. It had such a bad reputation.'

'But what about Adriana? Didn't you discover where she is now? Surely someone must have seen her? I gave you her photograph.'

'Oh yes! We had her photograph and one set of neighbours agreed it could have been her in later life…But…the problem is unless you believe in ghosts, I don't know how we'll find her. You see, it was never reported anywhere but Adriana Doward was also killed in that crash all those years ago.'

Miss Smith's House

Nobody knew how old Miss Smith really was when she died. The very few people who knew about her, rather than actually knew her, always maintained she was born old and had never changed. In any case, her death and subsequent funeral were very low-key affairs. She was one of those people who is known by everybody, who really knew nothing at all about her. And if you pushed them, they had never seen her, and had no idea what she looked like.

Her obituary notice in the Warwick newspaper merely stated Miss Agnes Barbara Smith, late of *Canal House*, had died. The notice added her private funeral had already taken place but gave no further details. If any interested party bothered to read the public notice which followed, they would have seen all claims on her estate were being handled by a London based solicitor.

And that was all.

As far as anyone could remember, or so it was said, Agnes Smith lived at *Canal House* all her life, inheriting the property from her parents on their deaths. She reputedly shared the house with two very large and unfriendly black cats. When these died, always assuming they had, they were replaced with identical coloured and temperamental beasts.

They helped fuel the rumours about her being a witch.

Over the years, most local children were threatened by their parents: *'If you do not behave, then Aggie Smith and her cats will come and get you'*. It was not surprising how she quickly obtained the reputation of being a witch, with the cats as her familiars.

Children drew pictures of her riding a broomstick and wearing a pointed hat, with only the cats for company sitting behind her. Some children, either braver or more foolhardy than their friends, and usually for a dare, ran around her house. Popular belief said if you ran around it seven times, then Aggie and the cats would appear on her broomstick. Regardless of their boasting tales, no child ever ran around the house more than six times, and only then as an initiation rite when joining a local gang.

She was only believed to have three visitors, who always came on a Thursday night.

One was Peter Lapslie, a retired balding grey-haired policeman. Another was Evan Cartwright, a clerical gentleman with sad dark eyes who lived in a nearby village. The third man was another stranger who was always dressed in black, regardless of the weather. He had a long mournful face, and no one could ever remember seeing him smile, neither did they ever discover his name. The watching children gave them all nicknames. Miss Smith was *the Witch*: Peter Lapslie was *the Jailer*: The cleric became *Dr Death* and the man in black became known as *the Hangman*.

They all played classical musical instruments, which to the appreciative ear, produced good music. Children and non-classical music lovers described their music as more like cats arguing and fighting. Somebody once likened them to the gang in the film *The Lady Killers*, who went through the motion of playing music as part of their cover for something more sinister.

Despite being called *Canal House,* it was nowhere near the canal. It had been so named by its first owner, who built canals and his profits paid for the house. But it was not the best of sites for such a building.

Before any work started on the site, he was advised by the locals not to build there because it was on an old pagan burial ground. They went on to warn him how the site was haunted, and bad luck would follow whoever lived there. The man totally dismissed these tales and had the house built, although he never lived there.

He was killed in an accident whilst moving into it.

The house quickly acquired a reputation for being haunted and no one would buy the property or even live in it. After a while, it became a lunatic asylum complete with its own tales of moving furniture and wailing people. It was too much for the inmates and staff who quickly left. The house and grounds were abandoned for several years until Miss Smith's parents acquired it in the late 1940s. Following their deaths, she lived there for another sixty years and the ghosts never seemed to bother her. Perhaps she really was a witch!

At one time, an elderly couple helped look after *Canal House* and its grounds in a desultory fashion, but they had not been seen for many years. Nobody ever knew anything about them or where they originated. As the years progressed, now left unattended, the gardens slowly but irrevocably lost their battle against weeds and the ever-encroaching undergrowth. Consequently, obtaining access to the house became very difficult, which all added to its mystery, especially as no one knew what was inside.

Little mail was ever delivered, and then it was always left in a special box by the gates. Following an arrangement with the post office, her outgoing mail was also collected from there. Her financial business was handled by the London based solicitors.

Over the years, several serious-minded criminals had tried their luck at burgling the premises. Many of them had fled empty handed and gibbering wrecks, who would not or could not talk about what they had seen. They were the lucky ones: others had reputedly never been seen again. The house contents still remained a mystery, although rumours abounded about it being full of valuable antiques.

But as the days progressed following her funeral, notices appeared advertising the forthcoming sale of *Canal House* and its contents. If the house was pulled down, it would provide a wonderful opportunity for builders who wanted to develop the land. Estate agents and developers had been circling around the property for years, just like predatory sharks waiting to make an attack.

One such developer was Timothy David Cadkington.

A divorced, childless and not very big man, he had always lived in Warwick, and his long-term ambition was to own the *Canal House,* and its extensive grounds. His long-term plans were to develop some of the site and keep the rest for himself. *Canal House* would have to go and be replaced by a *state-of-the-art* modern building. It was the location Timothy wanted: not the old building. This was the easy part. The next was more difficult, because it involved him acquiring the necessary funds.

Fortunately, his divorce was very amicable, and suited all parties. His former wife married a multi-millionaire and made no financial demands on him. Taking advantage of her generosity, he had made several risky investments over the years, and their returns went a long way towards funding his *project*, as he liked to call his long-term plans. But he still needed more money, and Timothy had no intention of sharing his *project* with any other developer. Looking on the positive side, he had two very great advantages over his competitors.

Having once been inside *Canal House,* and as far as he believed, the only person who knew what was to be found inside it. At present, but not for very much longer, according to his informant, he knew the auctioneers had not yet catalogued any of the items in the house.

In other words, they had no idea what the house held.

His other advantage included knowing about Miss Smith's visitors. Whilst he could not be certain they were all dead, there was every chance they had to be. They had been elderly, older than she was when he was a young boy. And nobody reported hearing any music coming from there for several years. If they were still alive, they would all be well into their hundreds, which was unlikely. So, with Agnes Smith having died, there should be little or no chance of anyone else being inside the house when he planned his next visit.

This one would be different from the last time as he planned to steal only small but very valuable items.

Time was now of the essence, and Timothy planned the burglary for this night, provided he could still get inside. Thinking positively, he reasoned if the state of the garden maintenance was anything to go on, getting into the house should not be a problem.

Luckily it was a moonless night as he climbed over the garden wall and into the grounds. It took him much longer than expected to get through the undergrowth before he reached the house. He wondered, fleetingly, how prospective buyers would manage to get into the house for the auction. A pathway would have to be cut for them. Anyway, it wasn't his problem.

Forcing his way through the last of the undergrowth, Timothy reached the house, where he followed the wall around and came to the old entrance into the coal cellar. This was the way he and Ossie Garton had used all those years ago.

For a moment his courage failed him as he recalled his last visit, which must have been in the region of forty or more years earlier.

He and Ossie planned this *great adventure*, as they called it, between themselves. They had no idea what might be discovered in the house but finding out was their aim. assuming they could get inside it. Nobody knew, or if they did, it was a well-kept secret. Nevertheless, they were determined to find out for themselves.

It was gone midnight when they crept out of their homes and went up the road to *Canal House*.

They only saw a patrolling policeman who did not see them. By the time they reached the house, the moon was shining brightly, which was just as well because they had forgotten to bring a torch with them. All was still and quiet, which was spooky enough. Suddenly a wedge of geese flew across the moon in a **V** shaped formation honking raucously. For a moment they thought about running and going back home, but in the end, thanks to Timothy's urging, agreed to carry on and find a way into the house.

On reflection, it was a bad mistake and one which haunted him for the rest of his life.

It was much easier to break into the house than they expected. At the rear and a bit to one side of the kitchen, were two wooden trapdoors where coal was delivered. They were not locked, and it was a simple matter to open them and slide down the chute into the cellar. It was not very steep and could be climbed easily enough, when they left the house. Granted the coal was dirty, where previous deliveries had left a trail of debris in the chute, but the boys did not notice how dirty they had become.

Neither did they see the two pairs of malevolent green eyes watching their every movement.

In the distance, coming from another part of the house, and echoing all round, came the strains of classical music being played. They had completely forgotten it was music night at *Canal House.*

But what stuck in Timothy's memory, and would do so for all time, was the state of the hall. He could not believe what he was seeing. Everywhere he looked, countless expensive looking pictures adorned the walls. similar looking furniture was all around the hallway, littered with jewel encrusted small boxes. Later he discovered these were called snuff boxes and quite valuable. Gentle subdued lighting highlighted some of the pictures and furniture.

Even to Timothy and Ossie's young eyes, they knew this was wealth, and a standard of living they had never experienced before, or even knew existed. Whilst they had not known what to expect, it had not been all this wealth. The hall was an absolute treasure trove. What was the rest of the house like? They stood there open-mouthed.

Suddenly the music stopped playing, and they heard voices coming their way.

Timothy ran back towards the kitchen with Ossie hard on his heels. Wrenching open the door, they were no longer concerned about being seen…just not being caught.

Neither needed any reminding about the stories of children going into Aggie Smith's house and never being seen again. From time to time, children went missing and she was always blamed for taking them.

But as Timothy opened the kitchen door, he was met on the other side by two ferocious coal black cats, with their hackles raised, tails flicking and accompanied by much hissing. Only their white fangs and green eyes broke up their blackness. Clearly there was no escape this way.

Ossie had already moved back into the hall just as the musicians appeared, and he was the first person they saw. As they moved towards him, Timothy climbed into the large grandfather clock standing alongside the stairs. He never knew how long he hid inside it but waited until all was quiet before daring to move.

Only when Timothy felt it was safe to do so, did he leave the clock. Going back into the kitchen, he heaved a great sigh of relief as there was no sign of the cats and he quickly climbed out of the coal cellar and ran home. Fortunately, the dirt on his clothes was more dust than anything else and he managed to brush most of it off on the way home.

His last view of Ossie was seeing his friend being led away by the musicians and he was never seen again. Timothy never told anyone where they had been that night.

As Timothy hovered by the entrance to the coal cellar, he knew there were two main reasons for going back into the house. Firstly, to see if the antiques were still there, and if so, he would help himself to as many as he could carry.

After all, Agnes Smith was dead and none of the items inside the house had been catalogued yet, so it would not be noticed if any of them went missing.

Secondly, he had a hope, albeit a forlorn one, he might discover what happened to Ossie. Timothy felt he owed his friend that, even if he had done nothing about it before. Had he really been too frightened to tell anyone? Had that really been the case?

Surprisingly he found the old entrance to the coal cellar was still unlocked. He opened it up and paused for a moment. 'Is this really a good idea?' he asked himself. As if to echo his thoughts, a wedge of geese flew over the house, honking raucously, just as they had done so all those years ago. 'Of course, it is,' he answered himself. There was no real alternative if he wanted to realise his dream of owning the *Canal House* and its lands. He needed more money, and this was where he planned to get it.

Anyway, he argued, what better use for some of these antiques than help him acquire *Canal House*?

Plucking up his courage, Timothy dropped down onto the chute and moments later was in the coal cellar. This time he brought a torch with him, and there was no blundering around in the dark. Even so, he failed to see two pairs of malevolent green eyes watching him, just as they had on his last visit.

Cautiously he opened the kitchen door into the hall, stopped and sighed with relief.

It was just as he had remembered it.

The walls were still covered in oil paintings and the rich furniture didn't look a day older. He was glad to see the numerous jewelled snuff boxes still littered the tables and dressers. If this was what the hall looked like, he wondered what was in the other rooms: the ones he had never been in before.

Suddenly he realised it was not his torch which was lighting the hall. No, it was just as it had been on his last visit. Then his heart missed a beat.

The sound of classical music came from one of the rooms. He had forgotten it was Thursday night. 'Who the hell is playing that?' he asked himself. 'It can't be Aggie Smith and her lot. They're all dead.' Even as he asked himself the question, the music stopped. Taking his courage in both hands, he wrenched open the door into the room.

Just like the hall, it was well lit and full of more antiques, including an old wind up gramophone which looked to be in perfect condition. Even as he looked at its large brass horn, Timothy saw there was an old black record still spinning on the turntable.

'Hello Tim,' said a young voice which he remembered very well. Only in his younger days had he been called Tim. Now he always insisted on Timothy.

Turning he was not surprised to see Ossie Garton standing there looking at him accusingly. His childhood friend was still the same and had not aged a day since they last met.

'What could I do?' he pleaded in answer to Ossie's unspoken question. 'Nobody believed me.'

Ossie shook his head sadly. 'No, Tim. That's not true. Is it?'

'No,' he replied in a small voice, shaking his head. 'I was too scared.'

'That's also not completely true, is it? You really wanted to keep all these treasures a secret until you could come back and steal them. That's more the truth, isn't it?'

There was nothing Timothy could say, knowing Ossie was right. Originally, it was true: he was too frightened to tell where they had been. But in the following hours he began to think of the future, and kept quiet hoping Ossie would re-appear, although he never did.

For some reason, Timothy was never interviewed by the police. Had that happened, he would have admitted where they had been. And the longer Ossie's disappearance went on, the easier it became to say nothing. And as he now recalled, during his younger years, other children had gone missing and Agnes Smith was always blamed for their disappearance. Perhaps there was some truth in those old folktales?

'You've got to be punished for coming in here twice and abandoning me. You know that don't you?' Ossie broke in on his thoughts.

Timothy was suddenly aware other people were in the room. People who he had no difficulty in recognising. People whom he believed…no…whom he knew were dead. Or were they?

Peter Lapslie took him by the arm and led the way into another room, which resembled a court. He escorted Timothy into the dock and followed him into it. Sitting in front of them, all dressed in black and wearing a white wig, was the judge, Reverend Evan Cartwright. On either side of him sat a large and malevolent looking black cat with hard green eyes. Their tails continually twitched as they hissed at Timothy. Meanwhile Ossie had climbed into the witness box and related what had happened, when he had broken into the house where Timothy had left him to his fate.

Timothy watched as if he was in a trance, unable to believe what he was seeing and partly hearing. Somehow their voices sounded distant, and he was reminded of hearing in a similar muted fashion sometimes when flying, and his ears were suffering from the cabin air pressure. He was conscious of a small sparrow like woman, standing by the door. She was dressed in black and could only be Miss Smith.

The judge droned on, but then Timothy was horrified to see the other man, the one they all called *The Hangman* was standing by him and living up to his nickname. The man was making a hangman's noose and looking at Timothy all the while. The implication was obvious.

The noose was intended for him.

Timothy's hearing suddenly returned, and he heard the judge say: 'Does the prisoner wish to say anything before sentence of death is passed?' As he spoke, the judge placed a square of black cloth on his head. Everybody now looked at the judge, waiting for him to sentence Timothy to be hanged.

Seizing the opportunity, Timothy leapt out of the dock and ran to the door, closely followed by the cats. He was momentarily surprised to find a smiling Agnes standing in front of it. But she merely opened the door for him. Moments later he was through it, faintly aware she had closed the door behind him.

Timothy doubted he would be able to escape them in the dark and decided to hide and wait for daylight. Anyway, he thought, weren't they all ghosts? And with any luck, they would think he had escaped and not be able to follow him in daylight, which could not be too far away. The ideal place to hide was where he had hidden before: in the old grandfather clock. Luckily it was a large clock. Timothy quickly opened the door and clambered inside. He was not a moment too soon as he heard the others running past him. For once in his life, Timothy was grateful for being small.

Suppressing the urge to heave a big sigh of relief, Timothy knew he was safe: at least for the moment.

It was nearly six weeks later when the auction was held.

Viewing of the items was the day before the auction sale started. As the auctioneers had anticipated, there was a vast amount of interest being shown, at least on the viewing day. Many visitors were locals, only too well aware of the mysteries and tales surrounding *Canal House* and its late owner. Now they wanted to see inside for themselves. People queued long before the house opened.

The house had not been open very long, and the genuine dealers struggled to compete with the inquisitive locals. One female dealer who specialised in clocks elbowed her way to the staircase. Here she stopped at the grandfather clock. It bore the lot number **732** and looked fine from the outside, but it was not working, and she needed to know why. Was something missing? Was it broken? Or did it just need winding up? The only way to find out was to open the door, but here she met a problem. The door was locked.

She needed a porter to unlock it for her.

There was one standing by the kitchen door. The fact he was answering a question to do with another item in the catalogue made no difference to her. 'My man!' her sharp upper-class, cut glass voice called out imperiously, making sure everybody heard her. 'My man! Over here!'

He ambled slowly across to her. 'Yes madam. Can I help you?'

'Why do you think I called you? I wouldn't have spoken to you otherwise. The door to this grandfather clock appears to be locked and I want to see inside it.'

'Certainly madam. Bear me with me please whilst I find the key.' He produced a bunch of keys and selected one with a tag bearing the number **732**. He put it in the keyhole and unlocked the door.

Just then he was needed elsewhere in another part of the hall, and leaving the door unlocked, went to assist another viewer. He had not gone very far when a piercing scream brought the room to a standstill. It came from the woman at the grandfather clock, who had just opened the door. The porter fought his way over to her.

What happened next seemed to be in slow motion.

The woman slowly sank to her knees and fainted on the floor. In falling, she released her hold on the clock's door, which swung fully open. Everybody stared in horror as Timothy's body fell out of it and joined the unconscious woman on the floor.

Any hopes the police had of recording this as an accidental death were dismissed by the post-mortem examination of Timothy's body. Being in the clock had nothing to do with his death.

Prior to being placed there, he had been hanged.

Old Cavendish

'And last, but by no means least,' intoned Police Sergeant Hugh Mansell, as he briefed the night shift for duty. 'We've got to give the Crags Road some attention. I know it's only Monday night, but the info is there will be a *Run* here sometime this week, probably on Saturday, so we will be expected to put the *Plan* into operation.'

A communal groan greeted his words. Nobody enjoyed patrolling the Crags Road, especially on a summer's evening with a *Run* in the offing, but as they all knew only too well, this was the time of year for such events.

Starting on the lower heathland, the narrow Crags Road snaked up through the forest before climbing steeply to the top of the Dales, to the area known as The Crags. It was a popular venue during the summer months for motorists, hikers and even some intrepid cyclists. Everybody's aim was to reach the large carpark on the Crags. From here, before the last government boundary review and provided the weather was fine, it had once been possible to see eleven counties. Now, nobody knew how many there were.

The final approach to the Crags was steep, and not always accessible if the weather was bad. There was a sense of achievement for those who succeeded in getting to the top. It was worth the effort as the local inn, *The Red Flash*, sold its own well brewed ale and good food.

A popular venue with locals and tourists, *The Red Flash* was originally built in the 1880s as a private house, becoming an inn during the early 1930s. The inn sign was a portrait of a man wearing a large cap, goggles and leather gauntlets. It was modelled after the last owner of the house, Walter Pultney Cavendish, sitting inside his Morris Oxford Red Flash 1925 racing car and offering a lift to a young lady in a fur coat with a long cigarette holder.

This was a lonely and sometimes creepy part of the country after dark, when all the visitors had gone. During the tourist season, the car park was a honey pot for thieves with many cars being broken into, and their contents stolen.

Few people knew there was a carefully camouflaged radio aerial nearby, which ensured the police had good communications in this part of the county. To all outward appearances, Nick Foley, landlord of *The Red Flash* was anti-police, but he was the absolute opposite, being a retired policeman and one of Hugh's many cousins.

With the arrival of better weather, the annual policing problems started, especially when the *Crags Run* season began. Usually just referred to as the *Run*, it started in 1926, thanks to the very wealthy Walter Cavendish, who was as fanatical about racing cars as he was about women.

Like many of his contemporaries, Walter had been unable to settle down after the war, when he left the army in 1919. Totally unconcerned about upsetting his neighbours, he started the *Run,* which was another name for a motor car race which started on the *Crags* and went down the road where it ended. Young women regularly gathered here and always accompanied Cavendish and most of the other drivers.

As the first *Runs* only lasted for a few weeks, people thought it would be a short-lived affair, forgetting it was late in the summer. They soon discovered their mistake the following year. In a very short space of time, the *Crags Run* was happening on most nights of the week.

Numerous complaints followed, but the police only made half-hearted attempts to stop it. The law seemed unable or unwilling to stop Cavendish and his racing friends. It was believed, but never proved, Cavendish had the chief constable, Lonsdale Martinson, in his pocket and encouraged him to look the other way.

Their suspicions were well founded.

Martinson had been Cavendish's commanding officer during the war and owed him several favours.

Fed up with the police lack of action, in late summer 1927, four of Cavendish's frustrated neighbours decided to teach him a lesson and slow him down. Tragically their booby trap of placing a large rock across the road backfired. As sometimes happened, a thick swirling fog suddenly came down and Cavendish did not see the rock until it was too late to brake and swerved round it. In doing so, he collided with a tree, where he and his never identified female companion were thrown out of the car and killed instantly. She was wearing a fur coat and her long cigarette holder was found nearby. Ever afterwards the tree, which still stood, was known as *Cavendish's Tree*. It was marked accordingly with a plaque and regularly maintained.

Luckily for his neighbours, or so it seemed at the time, his death was thought to have been an accident, caused by his reckless driving. This view suited the chief constable who stopped any further enquiries being made, although he suspected what had happened.

Cavendish was useful to him during the war and had once saved both his life and career. Whilst the chief constable was very grateful, Cavendish never let him forget the incident, and quickly became an embarrassment. He regularly demanded numerous favours in return for keeping quiet, about what had happened when they were in the army. Revealing such information would have been highly damaging to Martinson's reputation and his current position of chief constable. His untimely death stopped all that and Martinson was glad and relieved to see him go.

A few years later, Walter's house became *The Red Flash*.

Denied natural justice surrounding his death, Cavendish's restless ghost haunted the Crags Road, but nowhere else, still driving his 1925 Morris Oxford Red Flash. In only a few short weeks, two of the four neighbours died in motor car crashes on the Crags Road, and always at the same spot and tree where Cavendish had met his end. The surviving two neighbours blamed Cavendish, left the area and survived.

And so, the legend grew. *Old Cavendish,* as he was now called, could only take his revenge on Martinson, his neighbours, their families and descendants.

Not prepared to take any chances, the chief constable kept well away from the Crags Road and lived until he was eighty-three.

Since the resurrection of the *Crags Run*, reports of *Old Cavendish* being seen, were rare. But he was frequently heard as he held his own *Crags Run*. According to local folklore, he only appeared when any of his potential victims were on the Crags, otherwise he was just heard.

*   *   *

'As you will recall,' said Hugh at his Saturday night briefing. 'We've practised our version of the *Plan* many, many times, and we know it will work.' His staff chuckled wryly.

The *Plan* had been devised as a blueprint for the best method of dealing with the *Run* being promoted as the official strategy for policing such events. But it had been drawn up by the *shineys,* a derogatory name for the desk driving experts at headquarters. These people had little idea and even less experience of real policing. For the most part they were civilians, under the control of a high-flying superintendent and the finance manager.

Fortunately, Hugh's superintendent was more practically minded and allowed his staff to adapt the *Plan* to suit the circumstances, based on their own experience and local knowledge.

Whilst the *Run* was a problem and a drain on resources, Hugh would have no hesitation in calling his officers away from it if circumstances changed and they were needed elsewhere.

'Do you think *Old Cavendish* will be around tonight, sarge?' asked PC Ivan Hubbard, the youngest, newest and most impressionable member of Hugh's shift.

'Who knows? It depends if you believe in ghosts,' replied Hugh. 'I do. Anyway, you come with me tonight.'

Up in *The Red Flash*, Nick Foley and his staff were rushed off their feet as drivers and hordes of spectators gathered. Conscious of the need to be seen as a responsible publican, he also sold gallons of soft drinks plus tea and coffee along, with hot dogs and various burgers.

Seizing a moment on the excuse of needing the toilet, he quickly texted Hugh to let him know the *Run* would be starting in about an hour.

Once he received the text, Hugh called his Shift together, which was easier said than done. Two of them were dealing with a serious collision on the by-pass, and another constable was back in the station processing a burglar he had caught. Including himself, Hugh had just five officers to deal with the *Run.* His inspector was a newly promoted high flier, who happily found an excuse to visit the other end of the county, and left Hugh in charge.

The event always started at *The Red Flash*, went down the hill to the bottom, where it ended. From a policing point of view, the narrow approach road up to the Crags was the only way up and the same one down. It made closing the road much easier.

Hugh's first car away was unmarked and driven by Constable Gillian Poole. Her job was to mingle with the other vehicles up on the Crags. When she was given the signal, Gillian would park her car across the road and effectively stop the *Run* from starting. Her chosen place had large rocks on either side, so for contestants trying to drive off the road to circumnavigate the block, it was not an option.

The *Run* took place between here and the bottom of the road. There were only a few places where overtaking was possible, and they were fiercely contested. But before any racers might have got there, Hugh placed another car as a road block to stop any late vehicles trying to get up the hill and being caught in between.

Once the blocks were in place, Hugh drove to the top of the road and radioed Gillian. She drove her unmarked car across the road and activated her previously hidden blue lights. Hugh appeared at the same time with his blue lights flashing.

The *Run* was stopped.

A loud booing and hissing started up from the spectators and contestants, as they realised their fun was stopped for the evening.

'That's it, folks!' Hugh called good naturedly over his public-address system. 'The fun's over and it's time to go home.'

At first nobody moved, so Hugh left Ivan in the car and walked purposefully across to the *The Red Flash*.

'Morning Nick!' he called cheerfully. 'Time to pack up please.'

Nick glowered in reply and gave an impressive performance to anyone watching that they did not like each other. In fact, Nick was glad to do so, and not just because he had helped stop the *Run*, but *the Red Flash* had almost run out of most drinks and food. He would have closed within the next half-an-hour, but now the police could be blamed.

'I just hope you haven't disturbed *Old Cavendish*,' cautioned Hugh.

Nick nodded wisely as they both believed in the legend. Once he had been disturbed, *Old Cavendish* would be heard driving furiously all over the Crags until dawn, reliving his final fatal ride all those years ago. Many people heard, and a few maintained they had seen him: but none of them enjoyed the experience.

The only consolation was it was summer time and dawn was not too far away.

Caroline Huxtall was far from happy and not just because the *Run* had been stopped by the police. As if the *Runs* did any harm?

She accepted they were noisy, damaged verges and smashed fences, but that was all part of the fun. And if a few sheep were run over, then too bad. She considered such trivialities to be unimportant. In any case, those wealthy pariahs of landowners could afford it.

She thought, fleetingly, about complaining to daddy when she got home, but knew it would be a waste of time. He was the local Police and Crime Commissioner and keen to stop such unlawful events. Despite her socialist principles, Caroline had no intention of abandoning her comfortable way of life, living at home plus eating and dressing well.

There was also another reason for her not complaining to him. He had specifically banned her from coming to these events, although he never explained why. Not that it would have made any difference if he had. Caroline would do and go wherever she wanted, with or without his permission. Meanwhile she had a more pressing problem.

Somehow in the general melee, following the arrival of the police, she had lost contact with her friends and been left behind. As the last of the stragglers moved away, she realised it would be a long walk home. Needing to answer a call of nature, she moved behind a tree.

When she finished, Caroline pulled up her jeans, and saw a car's headlights approaching. The car stopped beside her.

'Is everything all right, miss?' Hugh called out cheerfully through the open car window. He sat in the front passenger seat, being driven by Gillian Poole. Ivan Hubbard had taken his car to another incident.

Caroline recognised the car as the one which had blocked the road and stopped the *Run* from happening. She turned her face away from Hugh not wanting to be recognised.

'Do you want a lift down the hill?' he asked. 'Everybody else has gone.'

Caroline paused for a moment, but not for long. 'No!' she spat vehemently. 'I couldn't possibly accept any help from you fascist pigs, especially after you stopped all the fun.'

'Please yourself,' replied Hugh. 'But I wouldn't want my daughter to be out here on her own at night.'

'Just sod off,' she hissed. 'I'm not frightened of *Old Cavendish.*'

'Perhaps you ought to be. Good night miss.'

'I'm sure I've seen her somewhere before,' puzzled Gillian as she drove off.

'So have I, but I can't remember where.'

As the car drove away, Caroline realised she was now very much on her own and frightened. To make matters worse, a sudden fog started descending on the Crags, as sometimes happened. Quickly changing her mind, she ran after the police car shouting and waving her arms. But it was too late: the car had vanished out of sight.

In a move totally alien to her, she sat down on a fallen tree trunk and burst into tears. She had had forgotten to charge her mobile phone and it had gone flat.

She well remembered the stories about the bogeyman *Old Cavendish* seeking his revenge. So what? It didn't concern her, and anyway, such tales were just to frighten children. Weren't they? Caroline was so absorbed in her misery, she failed to see a car's headlights coming towards her. The car stopped beside her, but the first time she noticed it was when a posh voice drawled. 'I say old girl, are you in some sort of trouble? What?'

She looked up and saw the speaker was a man who looked to be in his thirties, and his clothes were old fashioned. They were topped by a large cap with goggles perched on its peak, and a pair of leather gauntlets adorned his hands.

Then she saw his car for the first time. Thanks to the inn sign on Nick Foley's pub, she had no trouble in identifying it as a 1925 Morris Oxford Red Flash, and the man looked just like the picture of *Old Cavendish.* Surely it couldn't be him? Could it? No, he doesn't exist, or does he? Nevertheless, it was the most beautiful car she had ever seen.

Although Caroline was not religious, she would have sold her soul to the Devil, at that moment, for a ride in such a motor, even if it was being driven by *Old Cavendish.* As if reading her thoughts, he smiled: 'I gather old girl that you've missed your lift. What?'

'It was the police,' she replied miserably, and with her fingers crossed behind her back, hoping he would offer her a lift. 'They ruined everything.'

'They always do,' he replied bitterly after a moment's silence. 'Come on, I'll give you a lift up to *The Red Flash,* and you can get a cab from there.'

She needed no urging and gratefully climbed into his car, which he confirmed was a 1925 Morris Oxford Red Flash. What a tale she would have to tell her friends.

At first, she was thrilled and excited by the way he handled the car. But it became frightening as he accelerated, regardless of the twisting road and the ever-increasing fog. The car's throaty roar echoed off the nearby rocks, accompanied by his maniacal laughter.

'Please stop!' she pleaded, suddenly remembering all the tales about *Old Cavendish.* Hadn't he met his end on a night such as this? And now she was very, very scared.

Ignoring her pleas, he burst into even louder and more maniacal laughter, and drove faster.

Caroline screamed as she saw what looked like a large rock lying in the road. Still laughing, he swerved to miss it, but losing control of the car, it skidded and smashed head on into a tree, with a deafening crash.

She was thrown out of the car onto the road, amidst all manner of debris from the wrecked car.

Back in the police station, Hugh and his staff waited for the kettle to boil, and a welcome mug of tea, when the phone rang. He answered it and was surprised to hear Nick Foley.

'*Old Cavendish* has really been upset this time. You'd better come quickly. I've already sent for an ambulance.'

Hugh and Gillian drove up to *The Red Flash,* where Nick flagged them down with a torch. The fog had now cleared, and an ambulance was there already. He led them over to where a female lay in a pool of blood on the road.

'Do you see who she is?' asked Gillian.

Hugh nodded, as he too recognised the young woman they had spoken to not that long ago. It seemed as if she had been thrown from a car.

One of the ambulance crew walked over to Hugh, shaking his head. 'Sorry but there was nothing we could do. Her neck's broken and other serious injuries suggest she was thrown out of a car.' He handed a small purse and mobile phone to Hugh. 'This was the only property she had.'

Hugh and Gillian agreed about the car, as there was no way she could have walked up to *The Red Flash* in the time since they had last seen her. She must have had a lift from someone, but who? That was the question.

'There was this hell of a noise soon after you'd all gone. It was the definite sound of a car crashing…but…We've had a look round and found nothing. But then you know what this spot is,' Nick pointed to what was locally known as *Old Cavendish's Tree*.

'Yes,' replied Hugh absently, as he stared at the dead woman's driving licence. 'Yes, it's where *Old Cavendish* was killed. And this unfortunate woman is Caroline Huxtall, and she is the Police Commissioner's daughter.'

'That's not all,' added Nick sombrely. 'Her late mother was Juliana Martinson, and a direct descendant of the chief constable who covered up Cavendish's death.'

'But if she's been thrown from a car after a collision, which by your report, which I don't doubt, would have rendered it undriveable, then where is it?' queried Hugh. '*Old Cavendish's Tree* would have been the only point of contact, but there are no marks on it. Nor are there any on the road or any other debris to be seen.'

The silence which followed was broken by *Old Cavendish's* mocking laughter echoing all over the Crags.

Bonn and Warwick…
June and July 1908

Although Heinrich Muller was well pleased with his day, he had no inkling of how it would end.

He had completed a very good deal and earned £5,000 in the process. Although he was a German citizen living in his own country, he preferred to be paid in sterling and kept his money in England. He did this for two very good reasons.

The first was to avoid paying any income or other tax on it: and the second was just as important.

All of his money came from the proceeds of crime: and banking in England made it more difficult to trace. Whilst Heinrich gathered a fortune from his criminal enterprises, he also made some dangerous enemies along the way. But he prided himself in always keeping one step ahead of them, and found regularly changing his name, address and appearance usually worked.

At present, he went by the name of Oskar Dietrich.

As he sat swirling his *courvoisier* round in its glass, Heinrich chuckled at how easy it had been to trick the gullible American. The man believed he was purchasing one of *Marcel Slade's* genuine oil paintings, which was known to have been stolen. But such knowledge made it a prize exhibit for wealthy and unscrupulous collector Hiram C. Buckrose. Such men, and the occasional women, were easy prey for Heinrich, especially where members of the fairer sex were involved.

If the time ever came when Buckrose realised he had purchased a forgery, albeit a very good one, specially created by Heinrich's partner in crime, Anton Jaeger, Oskar Dietrich would have disappeared. The joy of the whole scheme was his victims could hardly report him to the police, for fraudulently being sold a very valuable painting, which they knew had been stolen. In any case when Heinrich re-appeared, it would be as someone completely different.

Heinrich smiled and putting his nose close to the rim of his Bohemian cut glass crystal brandy goblet, inhaled deeply. The *courvoisier* was an excellent way to end the dinner, but there was more enjoyment to come. As if on cue, Petra Dutkanova returned to the room. Ever the gentleman, Heinrich emptied his glass, stood up and took her arm. Together they left the room and made their way upstairs.

Yes, thought Heinrich: this is a good night which can only get better.

He would not have been so happy had he realised his true identity was known, and his current address was being watched as they moved up to bed. One of his numerous victims wanted revenge, and had long savoured the moment, which was due to happen tonight.

Heinrich was in his late forties with a sturdy but well-kept body. At five feet ten inches tall, his strong face with dark-brown curly hair and sideburns, framed an intense pair of hypnotic and magnetic greenish blue coloured eyes. These had a dramatic effect on women. Having once looked into his eyes they would, if he wished, come completely under his control, and be unable to resist him and do whatever he asked of them. It was an art Heinrich regularly used to his advantage, and he only slept alone from personal choice.

Petra had been his constant companion for the past few months, and seemed quite content to be with him, especially as he kept her well fed, dressed and supplied with jewels. Money to him was no object. However, Heinrich was tiring of her, and had already planned how to make the most of what little time they had left together.

From very humble beginnings, as his mother had been in service with a local count and countess, Heinrich had clawed his way up the social ladder, mainly by living on his wits. He had no other alternative, after his mother died when he was only ten years old.

He had always believed his father was dead, having died soon after Heinrich was born. Following his mother's death, her former employers had no intention of caring for the orphan and wasted no time in casting him loose into the world.

If they believed that was the end of him, they were sadly mistaken.

Although only aged ten, Heinrich could read and write without any difficulty and had done so from an early age, thanks to his mother. One afternoon, and quite by chance, he had been wandering around the castle, when the count, his family and most of the servants, had gone to Bonn for the season. Being inquisitive, Heinrich found himself in the count's study and discovered the man's desk was unlocked. Here he spent a pleasant afternoon reading through some of the documents he found in it. Suddenly he stopped and read a letter again, which referred to himself in some detail.

The letter confirmed he was the illegitimate son of the count via his mother. At his age, Heinrich did not understand what being illegitimate meant. That knowledge would come later.

Almost immediately after his mother died, Heinrich was cast out of the castle, with only the clothes he was wearing. Luckily for him, or so it seemed at the time, an old woman in the nearby village took pity on the bewildered boy. Taking the orphan into her cottage, she gave him some food and shelter. She knew who he was and during the next few days asked him about the count's castle, especially where the valuables were kept.

Several days later, she introduced him to a young thickset man called Lukas. He also questioned Heinrich about the castle. Finally, Lukas asked if Heinrich would show him around the castle, one night when the count was away. Heinrich was happy to agree.

Nothing happened for several weeks then Lukas, and some other young men, came to the old woman's cottage and asked if Heinrich would take them around the castle later that night. He readily agreed, excited at the prospect. He was under no illusions fully understanding what they planned was wrong, but it just added to the excitement and sense of adventure.

Lukas had taken great pains to fill in some of the gaps about his birth. Thanks to him, Heinrich learned why he was the only child belonging to a servant permitted to live in the castle. Whilst his mother lived, his father felt some responsibility for him, but after she died, he was cast out. It also explained the countess's hostility towards him. And he felt very bitter about the way he had been treated by his real father.

This burglary would be a fitting revenge.

It was Heinrich's first taste of burglary, which he enjoyed and so began his life of crime.

As he grew older, he left Lukas's gang and started operating on his own. Heinrich specialised in only burgling wealthy houses and taking quality items. He quickly developed an eye for these and knew where to sell them for a good profit. As a rule, it was safer this way with less chance of being betrayed. From here he specialised in art theft and forgery, having met up with an expert forger, Anton Jaeger.

They quickly formed a strong working relationship.

Anton's work was second to none, and its quality fooled most experts. Heinrich happily paid him to copy stolen paintings, which he then sold, but kept the originals in his own private collection. In this fashion, he became exceedingly rich, was a popular guest at dinner parties and a great favourite with the ladies. Whilst he was there, Heinrich used the time to locate the next paintings and other valuables to be stolen and copied.

He could not go wrong at first, but after a while not everyone appreciated the way he cheated them. Which was why Bruno Geston, a professional killer, now waited in Heinrich's garden. Bruno was unaware he was not the only watcher in the garden that night. There were other men who also had an interest in both him and Heinrich.

Bruno was a patient man who knew careful planning, combined with not rushing a job, was how he kept alive. He waited for all the lights to go out in the house, and then gave it another hour. Only when he was completely satisfied all was quiet, did he move towards the small side door of the house.

It did not take long to locate the key, which had been specially left out for him. Petra had done well, and he thought it was a pity she would also have to die.

Bruno was not a man for taking chances: Petra could identify him.

He unlocked the door and slipped inside the house. As Heinrich did not like dogs, he knew there would not be any in there or around the grounds. Whilst he did not expect anything to go wrong, Bruno left the door unlocked, and on the jar, just in case he had to make a quick escape.

Thanks to Petra he knew where Heinrich's bedroom was, and the thick carpet deadened any sound his feet might have made. His small electric torch gave him all the light he needed.

It also gave the other men, whom he did not know were behind him, a light to follow.

Always a light sleeper, Heinrich was suddenly aware of the bedroom light being switched on. Screwing his eyelids up against the glare, he saw Bruno standing by his bedside and pointing a revolver at him. Heinrich carefully slid his right hand under the pillow, but his revolver had gone. Only Petra could have taken it, and he was aware she had already slipped out of bed.

The treacherous bitch, he thought.

'What do you want?' he croaked through a mouth and lips, which had suddenly gone very dry. 'I've got money!'

'I know you have and quite a bit of it belongs to my employer, a certain Mr Yang Fu, for the picture you sold him of a certain horse...Need I say more?'

'I'll happily give him the money back, but I bought the picture in all good faith...'

'My employer could not care less about the money, nor your protestations about good faith, but you have made him look very stupid amongst his fellow collectors, and that can only be put right by your death. You're lucky it'll be quick. He's not normally so generous.' As he spoke, Bruno screwed a strange device onto his revolver. 'It's new,' he explained. 'It reduces the sound of gunshots and won't disturb the servants. Say your prayers!'

Heinrich felt very cold and knew he was in serious trouble. Unless some sort of miracle happened in the next few seconds, he would be dead. He was only too aware the hypnotic effect of his eyes only worked on women: not men.

The miracle happened.

'DROP THE GUN!' The new voice came from behind Bruno.

Forgetting about Heinrich, Bruno spun around still clutching his revolver, and saw three men standing in the doorway behind him. One of them pointed a large revolver at him which was also fitted with a silencer. It was the last thing Bruno saw before a heavy bullet hit him in the chest. He collapsed to the floor and died soon afterwards.

'Get dressed!' the man who had fired instructed Heinrich.

'Who are you?' Heinrich demanded, slowly realising he was still alive, but not yet out of trouble.

'Get dressed!' The man's voice was cold and authoritative. 'I shan't tell you again. You can come with us in your night clothes for all I care.'

Heinrich knew he was beaten, climbed out of bed and pulled off his night shirt. As he dropped it on the bed, one of the other men took it. At the same time, he saw two other men entering the room carrying the body of another man between them. This body was completely naked, and had recently been shot in the face. Even as he dressed and unable to take his eyes off the second dead man, Heinrich watched as they pulled his night shirt over the body which they laid near the bed.

'I think he could be mistaken for you, don't you agree?' The leader said to Heinrich. 'Take him away.' He watched as two of the men led him away.

'A good job, Petra. You did well. And the servants?'

'Sleeping well after the sleeping potions I put in their food.'

'Good. I take it you'll help yourself to his money and anything else that's untraceable?' He grinned. 'I'll be in touch.'

Heinrich was aware of being bundled down the stairs, out into the chilly night air of the back garden, through the small gate in the wall and unceremoniously bundled into a motor car. Here he was forced onto the floor as it drove away. He quickly lost all sense of direction and time, as fear and nausea took over.

'You dirty bastard!' hissed one of the men as Heinrich vomited over his shoes and trousers. The man kicked him in revenge, but it was only a gesture, as the cramped conditions in the back of the car did not give him room for a more powerful kick.

After what seemed an eternity, the car finally stopped and one of his captors got out. There were muffled voices in the distance, and Heinrich heard some gates being opened. The car started up again and drove into what felt like a cobbled courtyard. Here the car stopped, its doors opened, and Heinrich was pulled out.

In the time it took for him to be hauled to his feet, and frog marched through a large door, Heinrich knew he was in real trouble. He realised this was the dreaded prison, nicknamed *Das Vergessen* or *The Forgotten*, which was what usually happened to the special and political prisoners housed here. Very few ever left it or were allowed visitors except for official ones.

Once in here, as its name suggested, you were forgotten.

Obviously, he was expected, and Heinrich was taken to a cell, pushed inside and the door locked behind him. Surprisingly, and contrary to what he had expected, the cell was fairly comfortably equipped, yet it was still a cell. But why was he here? And why had the police, or whoever they were, left a body wearing his nightshirt behind? The inference was they wanted people to think it was him and he was dead. But why?

With nothing else to do, Heinrich lay on the bed for a while, but what was left of the night was cold and he soon climbed into it.

How could a day which had started so well, end so badly? He suspected worse was to come.

Surprisingly, he slept and was woken only by a guard bringing him some breakfast, which was not unappetising. The man made no reply to Heinrich's questions. It was the same when other meals arrived throughout the day.

When his breakfast arrived the next morning, it was accompanied by a page torn from the local newspaper.

The page read:

DOUBLE SHOOTING FATALITY MYSTERY

Police were summoned yesterday morning to the house of wealthy art dealer Oskar Dietrich, by his worried servants. They had found their master dead in his bedroom with the body of another man lying nearby. Both men had received fatal gunshot wounds.

The second man has been identified as Bruno Geston, a professional criminal and murderer, and who was wanted by the police in several countries. It would seem Geston broke into the house, obviously intent on stealing, but was surprised by Herr Dietrich. Both men were armed and apparently shot each other dead. Herr Dietrich's funeral will take place this afternoon.

The police are not looking for any other suspects in this matter.

Heinrich quickly realised if everyone now thought he was dead, then in effect he was. The only person who might have reported him missing was Petra, but she had obviously played some part in what had happened.

During the late afternoon, two guards arrived and escorted him to another part of the prison. Like the other guards he had seen, none of his questions were answered. They finally stopped before a wooden door and one of them knocked on it.

'Enter!' came the reply.

Heinrich was led into a well-furnished room and taken to a chair, in front of a highly polished leather topped wooden desk. A large portrait of Kaiser Wilhelm II hung over the desk, but Heinrich was more interested in the man sitting underneath it. This was the same man who had taken him prisoner.

'Good afternoon, Herr Dietrich, or perhaps I should say Herr Muller,' the man spoke. 'I must say that you had a most impressive funeral this afternoon.'

'What is going on?' demanded Heinrich. 'I have a right to know!'

'Actually that's not true. In here, I decide what rights you have or do not have. Do you understand?' The speaker glared at Heinrich with a pair of cold steely blue eyes, and there was an aura of menace about him, despite the monocle which hung around his neck.

Heinrich studied the other man whilst he was speaking. It was the same man who had shot Geston, and the fact he was still alive gave Heinrich some cause for hope, albeit not too great.

Even though he was not in uniform, the man had a military appearance, complete with duelling scars on his cheeks. His close cropped and one-time black hair now sported many grey ones. Heinrich judged him to be in his mid-50s, and he was not very far wrong. When he stood, the man's military bearing became obvious standing at nearly six feet tall and well-built.

'I am Colonel Reinhard von Achim,' the man introduced himself. 'I work directly for the Kaiser, and you have been chosen for a very special and sensitive mission.'

'But why me? What have I done to deserve this?'

'Shall we say we have had an eye on your various activities for some time now, and we believe you are the man for us. We are most impressed by your activities going back to your childhood. As you will have read in the paper, you no longer exist, but should you not do as we want, then quite simply you will be miraculously resurrected, and suddenly appear outside the house of a certain Oriental gentleman, who will enjoy inflicting much pain on you before you die...' Von Achim left the threat unfinished. 'It's your choice. Work for me or...!'

'I don't really have any choice, do I?'

Von Achim shook his head.

'What do I have to do?'

'Quite simply, you will now work for the State. You will move your various criminal and other dubious operations to England, and work from there as normal, until we summon you. It won't be for a year or two or even longer, so in effect you will become a sleeping agent for me. When you arrive in England, you will be met and introduced to other members of the group we have already established there.'

'What will you want me to do?'

'All in good time.'

'And money? What will I do for money?'

'I'm glad you asked that question. All your assets here now belong to the State. Likewise, so does your money in England since you are officially dead. We are negotiating with your banks for that money to be returned here. We will let you have some of it to set up the operation, but the rest will belong to the State, so you will have to make your own money.' He paused. 'And by that, I mean just that as I will explain in a minute. You will continue with your forgery and other criminal activities and…'

'I don't know what you're talking about,' protested Heinrich. But it was a weak protest and completely ignored by von Achim.

'As I was saying before you so rudely interrupted me, you will need to build up some degree of respectability in England, because you will need access to the right ears for when you are really called upon. The money we will give you will not last for very long: just long enough for you to find suitable premises, to enable other parts of the operation to be set up, but after that you will need to fund the operation yourself. Even as we speak work over there has already been started.'

Heinrich leaned forwards, snorting with anger, and put his hands on von Achim's desk. His captor ignored the gesture and continued.

'Having defrauded your country of a considerable amount of revenue, it is only right you should repay it…and with interest. If you don't agree with my proposals or try to run away, then we shall find you and the Oriental gentleman will be informed of your whereabouts. Do you understand?'

Heinrich nodded his head miserably, and sat back, knowing there was no alternative but to agree with von Achim's plans.

'Provided the operation is successful, you can keep any profits you make. Meanwhile you will stay here, be fully briefed and trained for what is required of you. Then we will get you across to England, and we know you speak their language well. Firstly you'll go to London and meet up with our main agent for this special enterprise. From there you will go to a place called Warwick, where you will be based. However, most of the money will have been spent by then, and money- making schemes will be a priority for your work. You will need it for all your special activities, as well as getting yourself established locally. You will need a lot of money.'

'What do I have to do?' Heinrich asked resignedly.

'That's better. Your group will be based in isolated premises, but you will need a more suitable place to live and entertain people. In due course, but only after being instructed to do so, you will contact a certain high-class forger who we know. His instructions are to help you create a printing press that will print fake British currency. This will be released and circulated when instructed, with the aim of undermining their economy. Be warned! These fake banknotes must not be circulated until you are ordered to do so. There will be other specific tasks for you to perform which will be revealed later.'

'It will take a lot of money...'

'Exactly, so you will have to put your criminal mind to work and come up with some good ideas, won't you? But be warned yet again: failure is not an option. Just remember! It will not be difficult for me to advise Mr Yang Fu where to find you.'

Von Achim rang a small bell on his desk and the two guards re-appeared. As Heinrich stood up with his brain whirling, von Achim gave him a large packet. 'Details of your new identity are all in here. Learn them well as your life may well depend on it. The man who had it before you, is dead and he no longer needs it.' He smiled cruelly. 'But it will be useful to you. Further instructions will follow later. And, who knows? You might even come to enjoy the work.'

Heinrich said nothing, but just nodded in mute acceptance and went to the door with his guards.

'Remember,' called von Achim. 'Failure is not an option if you want to keep away from Mr Yang Fu.'

These last words were said in such a cold tone that Heinrich shivered knowing von Achim meant every word he said. He was taken to a different and less harsh part of the prison.

Once Heinrich had left, von Achim lifted a telephone on his desk. 'Extension seven,' he instructed the operator when the man answered.

'Seven!' came a tinny sounding voice in his ear.

'Von Achim here. The last of the sleepers has been recruited and will soon be in place. When the time is right, Britain will cease to be a stumbling block to our Royal Master's plans, and the Warwick police will regret their earlier meddling in his affairs. They will be ready when ordered to awaken.'

On the same day Heinrich was arrested, Arthur Hayward of *Hayward's Estate Agency*, situated in High Street, Warwick, looked up as his front door bell rang.

'Good morning, sir,' he spoke to the well-dressed, fair haired tall man in his mid-40s, complete with a pair of blue eyes which peered at him through thick rimmed spectacles.

The man had something of a stoop, which made him look like a professor who had spent his life poring over books and manuscripts. He was in complete contrast to Arthur's scruffy appearance.

'I'm looking for a farmhouse which has several outbuildings, and is situated somewhere near here,' replied the visitor. 'I do not wish to farm, but I need some outbuildings for my research work. Some place where I am not overlooked and can work without interruption.'

Much to Arthur's chagrin, the man did not elaborate on the nature of his work. And there was something about his stance and general bearing which deterred him from asking.

Arthur made a show of looking through the large leather-bound ledger which he kept on his desk, but he already knew which property to offer. It had been on his books for several months, and he would be glad to see it move, even if only for a few months. Leaving the ledger open, he moved to another part of the office and opened a filing cabinet. Moments later he took out a folder and returned with it to his visitor. Opening the folder, he took out a typewritten sheet of paper which he handed to the man.

'I think this could be what you are after. This is all about *Jackdaw Farm*,' he explained. 'The farm is part of a deceased's estate. The elderly new owners live in Canada and have no intention of ever coming here. It is well set back from the Hampton Road and on the very edge of town. There are several outbuildings and a large cellar. I should warn you however, that the property is not in the best of condition.'

As the new tenant would soon discover, this was something of an understatement.

'That's not important. It sounds just right for what I want. I'll pay you a year's rent in advance, although I will probably stay longer.'

Arthur could not believe his good luck. It did not take him long to complete the transaction, accept the advanced rent and hand over the keys to *Jackdaw Farm* to Franz Koenig, who went by the name of Frank Castle now he was in England. The other members of his unit would also only be known by their English names.

Frank Castle took the keys and listened to the instructions he was given, returned to his car and drove off into Friars Street, Hampton Street and finally Hampton Road. The Racecourse on the opposite side of the road was an extra bonus as it reduced the risks of being overlooked. As Arthur had warned him, the farm was not easy to find which made it more secure and secluded.

Arthur might have thought his visitor was a professor of sorts, but academia was not his scene.

Frank was a dedicated German agent, who spoke very good English, and was a master of disguises. Whilst serving in the *1st (Emperor Francis) Guards Grenadiers* in Berlin, he had been spotted by one of von Achim's agents as having certain talents, which could be useful. In addition to his linguistic ability, Frank was a ruthless killer who obeyed his orders without question, regardless of what they were.

Although he had no great hatred of the British, Frank loved his work and was totally devoted to the Kaiser, who did not know the man existed. Frank was the strongarm member of the group who never hesitated to use violence when instructed, even if innocent people were hurt in the process.

The rest of Frank's group arrived during the next few days with their temporary and main leaders coming later.

The Kaiser had expansionist ambitions, which included the future annexing of Morocco and Serbia, but only when he was ready to do so. There was much planning to do first. Part of which involved flooding England with forged banknotes, intended to destabilise the British economy. On its own, this might not stop them supporting Morocco and Serbia, but he had devised two additional schemes which should ensure England remained neutral. He was assisted in this planning by Colonel Reinhard von Achim, head of the German Secret Service.

In May 1902, a plan to assassinate King Edward VII had been foiled at Warwick, with the destruction of several German agents. It had taken some time to re-establish German agents in England, and Frank was one of the first. Whilst von Achim had been promoted following that failure, he had deliberately chosen Warwick as the venue for the Kaiser's latest plans.

It would be a fitting revenge.

Several days later, Frank waited on Warwick Railway Station for the arrival of his temporary leader who went by the name of Stephen Lomax. His real name was Stefan Liebert: another of von Achim's agents from Germany.

In accordance with von Achim's instructions, this was all Frank needed to know about him

As the engine's smoke and steam cleared from the platform, Frank saw several passengers disembark from the train and move to the exit. One of them, a tall, smartly dressed well-built man in his mid-40s, and sporting a thick black beard, detached himself from the others and approached him.

'Are you Uncle Gregory's man?' The stranger asked, using the agreed code.

'I am. Welcome to Warwick, sir. My car awaits you.'

Having summoned a porter to carry the luggage, Frank led the way to his parked car after first handing over their tickets on leaving the platform. Having settled the new arrival in the passenger seat, Frank supervised the loading of the luggage, tipped the porter, climbed into the car and drove away.

Stephen Lomax alias Stefan Liebert had arrived in Warwick, and he had several tasks.

The first was to oversee the arrival of the other agents. His second was more involved. It was necessary for him to get to know Warwickshire and the surrounding counties, to discover suitable isolated houses which could be robbed. It would then be his next task to sell off these stolen goods. Stephen had been in England almost as long as Frank. He was aware his time in overall command would only be for a few weeks.

Lastly, Stephen knew their money was disappearing quickly, and needed replacing fairly urgently. He was very much aware how von Achim did not trust Heinrich with vast sums of money. Once the initial outlay had been spent, they would have to budget very carefully, and raise their own funds. Large scale burglaries were one such option.

Von Achim had employed Stephen for several years, rating him as one of his best and most effective agents. He was not a violent man, and his real talent lay in persuading people to comply with his wishes. This was achieved by gentle persuasion, reinforced with blackmail if necessary: he was an expert in exploiting people's weaknesses. His speciality was creating honey traps, usually of a sexual nature, but not always. Having been in England now for some years, he had his own network of people who were on standby to help him when needed, either willingly or unwillingly.

Frank drove him to *Jackdaw Farm* and introduced him to the others.

Hans Sturman, now called Ian Stoughton, was a tall, dark, brooding, impatient muscular man, and a jack-of-all-trades, but his real passion was explosives. He enjoyed creating all manner of explosive devices for different purposes. If he could not get access to ready-made explosives, he made his own. Having been apprenticed to a clock maker before joining the army, Ian was an expert in making timing devices. The only time he deployed any patience was when he was making and setting bombs. At other times he often acted impulsively and without thinking.

If there was anything Ian could not do, the others had yet to find it. He had a reasonable command of English and was an accomplished thief. But it did not take Stephen long to notice there was a vicious streak to his nature, and he enjoyed hurting people. Whilst Stephen appreciated Ian had some useful abilities, he also realised his impatience and sadism made him a liability.

Next was Ernst Weber, whose name translated very easily into Ernest Webb. In his mid-40s, he had a burning hatred of the British, having lost his left foot in South Africa during the recent war in that country. He had gone to fight with the Boers, supposedly as a German volunteer, but his instructions were to see how the British fought and report back accordingly. An exploding shell at the *Battle of Colenso* had given him that experience and put paid to a budding military career. Now he was an expert armourer, who also enjoyed coding and decoding messages.

Passionately devoted to Germany, he was reduced to begging after being discharged from the army. Whilst begging on the streets, he had been recruited into von Achim's service, and happily let himself be further indoctrinated in his hatred of the British. On the way he conveniently forgot how it was a British doctor, who had saved his life and taught him to walk again. His time in hospital honed his expertise in English, although he still had an accent, which made most people believe he was a South African.

The last member was Ernest's wife, Helga Weber or Helga Webb which was her English name. She was a similar age to Ernest and was responsible for acquiring and cooking most of their food. Enjoying a photographic memory, she used her trips into Warwick to further their growing knowledge of the town. In the following weeks she created a whole series of maps for the others to learn. However, Helga's main skill was being a seamstress, and she regularly made up general clothes or disguises for her *boys*, as she liked to call her fellow unit members.

She was also a very competent driver.

A few weeks later, Stephen collected Heinrich and another man, Anton Jaeger, from Warwick railway station.

Von Achim's unit of sleeping agents was now complete and awaiting their orders to awake.